W9-AEM-058

NEW AMERICAN SHORT STORIES 2

While the stories in the introductory volume of *New American Short Stories* reflects the wide diversity of American life, the fiction selected by the authors in this second collection reflects one theme more than any other—the private worlds of love. Many of the stories deal with the delicately balanced emotions of men and women, from Tobias Wolff's haunting tale "Smorgasbord," which explores an adolescent boy's first sexual desires, to Mark Helprin's rich, lyrical tale of separated lovers during World War II, "The Pacific." Other stories examine the troubled relationships between parents and children, including Mona Simpson's shocking story of incest, "Lawns," and Judith Rossner's tale of another kind of parent/ child betrayal in "The Unfaithful Father." This exciting volume of short fiction, concerned with feelings and the inner life, echoes the way we live our lives today.

GLORIA NORRIS is a short story writer whose works have appeared in *O. Henry Prize Stories* collections and in *New Stories from the South: The Year's Best in 1986. Her novel, *Looking for Bobby*, was published in 1985. She edited the highly acclaimed first volume of *New American Short Stories*, also available in a Plume edition.

NEW AMERICAN
SHORT STORIES 2

THE WRITERS SELECT THEIR OWN FAVORITES

EDITED BY GLORIA NORRIS

A PLUME BOOK

PUBLISHER'S NOTE

These stories are works of fiction. Names, characters, places, and incidents either are the product of the authors' imagination or are used fictitiously, and any resemblance to actual persons, living or dead, events, or locales is entirely coincidental.

BOOKS ARE AVAILABLE AT QUANTITY DISCOUNTS WHEN USED
TO PROMOTE PRODUCTS OR SERVICES. FOR INFORMATION PLEASE
WRITE TO PREMIUM MARKETING DIVISION, PENGUIN BOOKS USA INC.,
375 HUDSON STREET, NEW YORK, NEW YORK 10014.

Copyright © 1989 by Gloria Norris

All rights reserved. Published simultaneously in Canada by Penguin Books Canada Limited.

A hardcover edition of *New American Short Stories 2* has been published simultaneously by New American Library and, in Canada, Penguin Books Canada Limited.

ACKNOWLEDGMENTS

"The Pacific" by Mark Helprin. This story first appeared in *The Atlantic*. Copyright © 1986 by Mark Helprin. Reprinted by permission of the Wendy Weil Agency, Inc.

"Squirrelly's Grouper" by Bob Shacochis. The story first appeared in a slightly different form in *Playboy* magazine; from the collection *Burstin in Air*, Crown Publishers Inc. Copyright © 1988 by Bob Shacochis. Reprinted by permission of Brandt & Brandt Literary Agents.

"The Unfaithful Father" by Judith Rossner. This story first appeared in *Mademoiselle* magazine. Copyright © 1986 by Judith Rossner. Reprinted by permission of the Wendy Weil Agency, Inc.

"Smorgasbord" by Tobias Wolff. This story first appeared in *Esquire* magazine. Copyright © 1987 by Tobias Wolff. Reprinted by permission of the author.

"The Wars of Heaven" by Richard Currey. This story first appeared in *High Plains Literary Review*. Copyright © 1986 by Richard Currey. Reprinted by permission of the author.

"Temporary Shelter" by Mary Gordon. From *Temporary Shelter*. Copyright © 1987 by Mary Gordon. Reprinted by permission of Sterling Lord Literistic, Inc.

"Research" by Max Apple. This story first appeared in *Harper's* magazine. Copyright © 1987 by Max Apple. Reprinted by permission of International Creative Management.

"Lawns" by Mona Simpson. This story first appeared in *The Iowa Review*. Copyright © 1984 by Mona Simpson. Reprinted by permission of International Creative Management.

"Facing the Music" by Larry Brown. This story first appeared in *The Mississippi Review*. Reprinted from *Facing the Music: Stories by Larry Brown*. Copyright © 1986 by Larry Brown. Reprinted by permission of Algonquin Books.

"Cooker" by Frederick Barthelme. This story first appeared in *The New Yorker*. Copyright © 1987 by Frederick Barthelme. Reprinted by permission of the author.

"A Lot in Common" by Veronica Geng. From *Love Trouble Is My Business*. Copyright © 1988 by Veronica Geng. Reprinted by permission of Harper & Row.

"Orpha Knitting" by Isabel Huggan. This story first appeared in *Western Living*. Copyright © 1987 by Isabel Huggan. Reprinted by permission of the author and the Colbert Agency.

The following page constitutes an extension of this copyright page.

"The Phantom of the Movie Palace" by Robert Coover. From *A Night at the Movies*. Copyright © 1986 by Robert Coover. Reprinted by permission of Linden Press.

"Travel" by Sue Miller. From *Inventing the Abbotts and Other Stories*. Copyright © 1987 by Sue Miller. Reprinted by permission of Harper & Row.

"The Curse" by Andre Dubus. This story first appeared in *Playboy*. Copyright © 1988 by Andre Dubus. Reprinted by permission of the author.

"The Gift of the Prodigal" by Peter Taylor. This story first appeared in *The New Yorker*. Copyright © 1981 by Peter Taylor. Reprinted by permission of Russel & Volkening, Inc.

"Be-Bop, Re-Bop & All Those Obligatos" by Xam Wilson Cartiér. From *Be-Bop, Re-Bop*. Copyright © 1987 by Xam Wilson Cartiér. Reprinted by permission of Ballantine Books.

"Wejumpka" by Rick Bass. Copyright © 1988 by Rick Bass. Reprinted by permission of the Schaffner Agency.

"Memphis" by Bobbie Ann Mason. This story first appeared in *The New Yorker*. Copyright © 1988 by Bobbie Ann Mason. Reprinted by permission of International Creative Management.

"Queen of the Day" by Russell Banks. From *Success Stories*. Copyright © 1986 by Russell Banks. Reprinted by permission of Harper & Row.

 REGISTERED TRADEMARK—MARCA REGISTRADA

Library of Congress Cataloging-in-Publication Data
(Revised for vol. 2)

New American short stories.

1. Shortstories, American. 2. American fiction—20th century. I. Norris, Gloria.
PS648.S5N36   1987   813'.01'08   86-23447
ISBN 0-453-00656-6
ISBN 0-452-26217-8 (pbk.)

First Printing, May, 1989

2   3   4   5   6   7   8   9

PRINTED IN THE UNITED STATES OF AMERICA

CONTENTS

INTRODUCTION

Why does one particular story remain a favorite with its author? The reasons vary as much as the authors' experiences in writing them. Andre Dubus's "The Curse" remains special for him because it was the first story he was able to complete after a serious accident that subjected him to eleven operations. Veronica Geng chose a story that is uncharacteristic of her work because she was lucky enough to write it "in a state of joyfully controlled abandon. This is my ideal of what every writing experience should be."

Russell Banks's "Queen for a Day" remains special for him because it ended an obsession with a certain theme and opened the way for Banks to write about new experiences. Whatever the reasons, the stories in this 1989 edition of *NEW AMERICAN SHORT STORIES* reveal twenty of today's most accomplished short-story writers in fine form.

The collection also represents a sequel to a successful book. Two years ago the first *NEW AMERICAN SHORT STORIES* brought such strong response from readers and aspiring writers that a second seemed called for, showcasing a different gallery of writers. Again, I selected authors who wrote in a variety of styles and asked them to pick one or several stories of their own, published in the last three years, that had remained a favorite.

As the new stories came in, I was surprised by one unexpected pattern. The first volume had been filled with stories on many themes. This time three-fourths of the stories selected deal with two themes that might be called the private worlds of love. The first is the relation between women and men, and the writers deal with all the points on that spectrum, from first love to painful parting—bringing to life for us the emotions of love gained, love lost, corrupted, or reaffirmed, and even those of that uncomfortable state so many find themselves in—divorced but not yet really parted. The second theme that dominates the volume is one that is also much on people's minds: the sometimes painful, sometimes joyous, but always risky relations between parent and child. These stories deal, to an extraordinary degree, with how we live now.

That said, I rush to add that the vision, language, technique, and character of each of the writers make each story unique.

Mark Helprin's "The Pacific" is told in lyrical language that returns again and again to the light that surrounds his characters, from the pure light of the West Coast to the blue-white light of welders' fire in the World War II airplane-instruments factory where a young wife works. Pauline bravely believes in the return of her Marine husband fighting in the Pacific. They share a love so strong that Pauline feels it capable of reaching across the ocean and keeping him alive. And how much these two make of their short time together! Riding by train from their Southern home to the West Coast where he'll be shipped out, they are entranced by the beauty of the passing country, intent on sharing these intense hours "because they knew that should things not turn out the way they wanted this would have to have been enough." Seldom is such strong, enduring, and moving love written about.

Tobias Wolff's haunting "Smorgasbord" evokes the powerful awakening of sexual desire among boys in an Eastern prep school. Adolescent ignorance and rivalry can stunt the tender expression of love in such times. The young hero still dreams of idealistic love and sex with his girl, but that dream is cruelly tested in Wolff's story.

In "Research," Max Apple takes us among Los Alamos scientists in the story of a researcher who lovingly uses a sample of his wife's blood in his experiments, dangerously tying up both his work and his love in the same woman.

In Larry Brown's "Facing the Music," a fireman and his wife uneasily watch Ray Milland in *The Lost Weekend* on their bedroom TV. As Milland's life falls to pieces, their own marriage is approaching a crisis over the husband's reluctance to make love to his wife after her illness. At the movie's end, as Milland tries to reconstruct his life, the man must also decide if he can face the music—if he, like Milland, "has responsibilities to people who love him and need him."

Frederick Barthelme's wry "Cooker" shows a man so disaffected with the world's hypocrisy that he complains to his wife that he's even tired of complaining: "about my job, about the people I work with, about the kids and the way the kids don't seem to be coming along, about the country, the things the politicians say on television on 'Nightline' and on 'Crossfire' . . . tired of complaining about everybody lying all the time or skirting the truth. . . ." His sense of distance extends to his wife and children during a long family evening as he threatens to become undone.

Isabel Huggan's "Orpha Knitting" describes a woman's experience of being wife and mother. In hopes of disguising her impatience with her husband and children, and her lack of constant love for them, she takes up knitting and tries to look placid. But the space between perfectly contented wife and mother and reality is large. Fortunately Orpha discovers why she doesn't have to go on knitting.

In "Travel," Sue Miller's vulnerable young woman, Olympia, is persuaded to join her former lover, a photographer, in Peru for lovemaking and exotic sightseeing. Olympia escapes for a time, as we can in travel, but she must decide, as we all do, how to return to herself.

In Bobbie Ann Mason's "Memphis," a divorced Kentucky mother ponders why she and her husband Joe can't let go of each other. When he's transferred to another city—upsetting their delicate arrangement with each other—she's confronted with the problem of whether to join him again or to hold out for other unknown options.

The betrayal of a child by a parent is the subject of three powerful stories. In Judith Rossner's "The Unfaithful Father," a girl becomes close to her father as they face her mother's lingering death. Over time, as he is inevitably drawn toward a new woman, the girl desperately tries to deny his betrayal.

In Mary Gordon's "Temporary Shelter," the son of a bitter Catholic housekeeper finds a new more desirable family in his mother's cultivated and kindly Jewish employer and his daughter, who becomes the boy's best friend. But without the ties of blood, can such adoptions be more than temporary shelters?

In "Lawns," Mona Simpson writes about a college girl who steals. With mounting tension we learn about the brutal facts in the girl's family that lie behind her crime.

In Peter Taylor's "The Gift of the Prodigal," an elderly, successful Virginia lawyer is visited by his "bad son," who has gotten into one more scrape, and the father slowly and unconsciously reveals how he's aided and abetted the boy in his repeated troubles with women and with the law. Taylor masterfully uses his unreliable narrator to expose the complicated truth about father and son.

"Be-Bop, Re-Bob & All Those Obliggatos" is Xam Wilson Cartiér's high-spirited tribute to her father, who loved jazz and left the heritage of its joy to her. Her heroine uses it to give a surprising upbeat turn to a funeral.

In "Wejumpka," Rick Bass's poignant story, a man worries about his troubled godson, who, anticipating the breakup of his parents, becomes a nervous clinger who embarrassingly hugs everyone in sight, even the school janitor. Yet the boy learns to last through the losses—and gives promise that he'll do better than his father and mother.

Russell Banks's powerful "Queen for a Day" shows another kind of strength in a boy whose alcoholic father abandons his family, leaving the boy to take charge of his mother and siblings. This story of family loss is both shatteringly real and finally affirmative through the sheer force of the truth it reveals—as difficult a trick to bring off in art as in life.

Five other stories take us to five distinctive worlds. Bob Shacochis's "Squirrelly's Grouper" begins, "A fish story is like any other, never about a fish but always about a man and a place." The place is the Outer Banks of North Carolina, where fishermen ply their trade in an enclosed world. The man is an odd, unpopular fisherman who brings back a record-breaking fish—a huge, finned, scaled leviathan whose aura of primal force brings crowds of sightseers and television cameras to the little town. And as Shacochis tells us, the story is only tangentially about the fish.

Richard Currey's "The Wars of Heaven" is set in a different time—1913 in West Virginia. The story is a poetic evocation of a doomed man surrounded by snow in a small church, where he confronts his crime and seeks redemption. It hypnotizes us with the forceful voice of this anonymous voyager in life, lost "in the frozen waste of time."

Robert Coover's "The Phantom of the Movie Palace" is a tour with a movie projectionist through a zany collage of images and characters from our Hollywood culture. Abandoned by audiences in an old movie house, the projectionist is driven mad as he's assaulted by the madly mixed images of cowboys, Indians, war heroes, ingenues, and jungle explorers on the old reels. Their incoherence tells us much about the dislocations of American culture.

Veronica Geng's "A Lot in Common" playfully constructs the ties between two friends who meet in New York. Though the woman grew up in St. Louis and the man in New Jersey, their lives share a series of strange coincidences. Geng amusingly shows us the mysterious correspondences that lie behind good friendships.

In "The Curse," Andre Dubus's powerful story of violence in a bar outside Boston, a decent bartender is forced to witness a crime by a gang of motorcyclists who invade the bar late at night. Though no one blames him, the man must confront his own guilt. The story is told in the crystalline prose that is a Dubus trademark.

The authors' words about their stories reveal not only why they were chosen but also something about the mysteries of the creative process. When a short story is good, its characters coming effortlessly to life, we often think: Ah, this is so good it must have sprung full-blown from the writer's head. Or we suspect that it came directly from an author's experience. But the authors describe their writing as more a cut-and-paste affair involving all kinds of stimuli. Rick Bass describes the writing of "Wejumpka" as "a typical scavenger hunt type of story using bits and pieces of whatever was going on at the time." He drew on the divorce of one friend, the birth of a child to another, an odd photograph of an old car someone sent him, as well as his own childhood memory of a water-skiing mishap.

Sue Miller says her creation of "Travel" was "a fictional stew that simmered for a long time in my subconscious or preconscious mind—or wherever it is that ideas for stories take shape." The name was borrowed from one of her writing students, and the scene sprang from Miller's own trip to Peru and a seedy professor she met there.

And Mona Simpson's "Lawns" had an even more unusual evolution. It began as a nonfiction article on abused women before Simpson slowly and painfully transmuted it into fiction.

A few practical notes are in order. Three of the authors in this collection have names that are often mispronounced: Frederick Barthelme [BAR-thel-me], Andre Dubus [dew-BEWS] and Bob Shacochis [sha-KO-chis]. One of the stories here, "The Gift of the Prodigal" by Peter Taylor, was published in 1981 rather than during the past three years.

I wish to express appreciation to Arnold Dolin, Vice President and Editor-in-Chief of New American Library, for his continued support and enthusiasm for these collections. I also thank the writers who underwent the sometimes difficult task of writing about their own stories.

Here, then, are twenty contemporary stories that span a variety of views on how we live. Happily for us as readers, the authors have undergone all the pain and work of translating the raw materials of experience into the refined shapes of art. It only remains for us to read them with "joyfully controlled abandon." In the process, you are bound to recognize yourself and those you know and love.

Gloria Norris
New York City

MARK HELPRIN

THE PACIFIC

This was probably the last place in the world for a factory. There were pine-covered hills and windy bluffs stopped still in a wavelike roll down to the Pacific, groves of fragrant trees with clay-red trunks and soft greenery that made a white sound in the wind, and a chain of boiling, fuming coves and bays in which the water—when it was not rocketing foam—was a miracle of glassy curves in cold blue or opalescent turquoise, depending upon the season, and depending upon the light.

A dirt road went through the town and followed the sea from point to point as if it had been made for the naturalists who had come before the war to watch the seals, sea otters, and fleets of whales passing offshore. It took three or four opportunities to travel into the hills and run through long valleys onto a series of flat mesas as large as battlefields, which for a hundred years had been a perfect place for raising horses. And horses still pressed up against the fences or stood in family groupings in golden pastures as if there were no such thing as time, and as if many of the boys who had ridden them had never grown up and had never left. At least a dozen fishing boats had once bobbed at the pier and ridden the horizon, but they had been turned into minesweepers and sent to Pearl Harbor, San Diego, and the Aleutians.

The factory itself, a long low building in which more than five hundred women and several hundred men made aircraft instruments, had been built in two months, along with a forty-mile railroad spur that had been laid down to connect it to the Union Pacific main line. In this part of the state the railroad had been used heavily only during the harvests and was usually rusty for the rest of the year. Now even the spur was gleaming and weedless, and small steam engines pulling several freight cars shuttled back and forth, their hammerlike exhalations silencing the cicadas, breaking up perfect afternoons, and shattering perfect nights.

The main halls and outbuildings were only a mile from the sea but were placed in such a way, taking up almost all of the level ground on the floor of a wide ravine, that they were out of the line of fire of naval guns. And because they were situated in a narrow trench between hills, they were protected from bombing.

"But what about landings?" a woman had asked an Army officer who had been brought very early one morning to urge the night shift to maintain the blackout and keep silent about their work. Just after dawn the entire shift had finished up and gathered on the railroad siding.

"Who's speaking, please?" the officer had asked, unable to see in the dim light who was putting the question.

"Do you want my name?" she asked back in surprise. She had not intended to say anything, and now everyone was listening to her.

Nor had the officer intended to ask her name. "Sure," he answered. "You're from the South."

"That's right," she said. "South Carolina. My name is Paulette Ferry."

"What do you do?"

"I'm a precision welder."

That she should have the word *precision* in her title seemed just. She was neat, handsome, and delicate. Every gesture seemed well considered. Her hands were small—hardly welder's hands, even those of a precision welder.

"You don't have to worry about troop landings," the officer said. "It's too far for the Japanese to come in a ship small enough to slip through our seaward defenses, and it's too far for airplanes, too."

He put his hands up to shield his eyes. The sun was rising, and as its rays found bright paths between the firs, he was blinded. "The only danger here is sabotage. Three or four men could hike in with a few satchels of explosive and do a lot of damage. But the sea is clear. Japanese submarines just don't have the range, and the Navy's out there, though you seldom see it. If you lived in San Francisco or San Diego, believe me, you'd see it. The harbors are choked with warships."

Then the meeting dissolved, because the officer was eager to move on. He had to drive to Bakersfield and speak at two more factories, both of which were more vulnerable and more important than this one. And this place was so out of the way and so beautiful that it seemed to have nothing to do with the war.

Before her husband left for the South Pacific, he and Paulette had found a place for her to live, a small house above the ocean, on a cliff, looking out, where it seemed that nothing would be between them but the air over the water.

Though warships were not visible off the coast, she could see from her windows the freighters that moved silently within the naval cordon. Sometimes one of these ships would defy the blackout and become a castle of lights that glided on the horizon like a skater with a torch.

"Paulette," he had said, when he was still in training at Parris Island, "after the war's over, everything's going to be different. When I get back—if I get back," he added, because he knew that not all Marine lieutenants were going to make it home—"I want to go to California. The light there is supposed to be extraordinary. I've heard that because of the light, living there is like living in a dream. I want to be in a place like that—not so much as a reward for seeing it through, but because we will already have been so disconnected from everything we know. Do you understand?"

She had understood, and she had come quickly to a passionate agreement about California, swept into it not only by the logic and the hope but by the way he had looked at her when he had said—"if I get back." For he thought truly nothing was as beautiful as Paulette in a storm, riding above it smoothly, just about to break, quivering, but never breaking.

When he was shifted from South Carolina to the Marine base at Twentynine Palms, they had their chance to go to California, and she rode out with him on the train. Rather than have them suffer the whole trip in a Pullman with stiff green curtains, her parents had paid for a compartment. Ever since Lee had been inducted, both sets of parents had fallen into a steady devotion. It seemed as if they would not be satisfied until they had given all their attention and everything they had to their children. Packages arrived almost daily for Paulette. War bonds accumulated for the baby that did not yet exist. Paulette's father, a schoolteacher, was a good carpenter, and he had vowed that when Lee got back, if they wanted him to, he would come out to California to help with his own hands in building them a house. Their parents were getting old. They moved and talked slowly now, but they were ferociously determined to protect their children, and though they could do little more than book railway compartments and buy war bonds, they did whatever they could, hoping that it would somehow keep Lee alive and prevent Paulette from becoming a widow at the age of twenty-six.

For three nearly speechless days in early September, the Marine lieutenant and his young wife stared out the open window of their compartment as they crossed the country in perfect weather and north light. Magnificent thunderstorms would close on the train like Indian riders and then withdraw in favor of the clear. Oceans of wheat, the deserts, and the sky were gold, white, and infinitely blue, blue. And at night, as the train charged across the empty prairie, its spotlight flashing against the tracks that lay far ahead of it straight and true, the stars hung close and bright. Stunned by the beauty of all this, Paulette and Lee were intent upon remembering, because they wanted what they saw to give them strength, and because they knew that should things not turn out the way they wanted, this would have to have been enough.

Distant whirlwinds and dust storms, mountain rivers leaping coolly against the sides of their courses, four-hundred-mile straightaways, fifty-mile bends, massive canyons and defiles, still forests, and glowing lakes calmed them and set them up for their first view of the Pacific's easy waves rolling onto the deserted beaches south of Los Angeles.

Paulette lived in a small white cottage that was next to an orange grove, and worked for six months on instrumentation for P-38s. The factory was a mile away, and to get to it, she had to go through the ranks of trees. Lee thought that this might be dangerous, until one morning he accompanied her and was amazed to see several thousand women walking silently through the orange grove on their way to and from factories that worked around the clock.

Though Lee had more leave than he would have had as an enlisted man, he didn't have much, and the occasional weekends, odd days, and one or two weeks when he came home during the half year at Twentynine Palms were as tightly packed as stage plays. At the beginning of each furlough the many hours ahead (they always broke the time into hours) seemed like great riches. But as the hours passed and only a few remained, Lee no less than Paulette would feel that they would soon be parting as if never to be reunited. He was stationed only a few hours away and they knew that he would try to be back in two weeks, but they knew as well that someday he would leave for the Pacific.

When his orders finally came, he had ten days before he went overseas, and when Paulette came home from work the evening of the first day and saw him sitting on the porch, she was able to tell just by looking at him that he was going. She cried for half an hour, but then he was able to comfort her by saying that though it did not seem right or natural that they should be put to this kind of test in their middle twenties, everyone in the world had to face death and separation sometime, and it was finally what they would have to endure anyway.

On his last leave they took the train north and then hitch-hiked forty miles to the coast to look at a town and a new factory to which Lockheed was shifting employees from its plants in Los Angeles. At first Paulette had refused to move there, despite an offer of more money and a housing allowance, because it was too far from Twentynine Palms. But now that Lee was on his way overseas, it seemed perfect. Here she would wait, she would dream of his return, and she would work so hard that, indirectly, she might help to bring him back.

This town, isolated at the foot of hills that fronted the sea, this out-of-the-way group of houses with its factory that would vanish when the war was over, seemed like the proper place for her to hold her ground in full view of the abyss. After he had been gone for two or three weeks, she packed her belongings and moved up there, and though she was sad to give up her twice-daily walks through the orange groves with the thousands of other women, who appeared among the trees as if by magic, she wanted to be in the little house that overlooked the Pacific, so that nothing would be between them but the air over the water.

To withstand gravitational forces as fighter planes rose, banked, and dived, and to remain intact over the vibrations of two-thousand horsepower engines, buffeting crosswinds, rapid-fire cannon, and rough landings, aircraft instruments had spot welds wherever possible rather than screw or rivets. Each instrument might require as many as several hundred welds, and the factory was in full production of a dozen different mechanisms: altimeters, air-speed indicators, fuel gauges, attitude indicators, counters, timers, compasses, gyroscopes—all those things that would measure and confine objective forces and put them, like weapons, in the hands of the fighter pilots who attacked fortified islands and fought high over empty seas.

On fifteen production lines, depending upon the instrument in manufacture, the course of construction was interspersed with anywhere from twenty to forty welders. Amidst the welders were machine-tool operators, inspectors, assemblers, and supervisors. Because each man or woman had to have a lot of room in which to keep parts, tools, and the work itself as it came down the line, and because the ravine and, therefore, the building were narrow, the lines stretched for a quarter of a mile.

Welders' light is almost pure. Despite the spectral differences between the various techniques, the flash of any one of them gives rise to illusions of depth and dimension. No gaudy showers of dancing sparks fall as with a cutting torch, and no beams break through the darkness to carry the eye on a wave of blue. One sees only points of light so faithful and pure that they seem to race into themselves. The silvery whiteness is like the imagined birth of stars or souls. Though each flash is beautiful and stretches out time, it seldom lasts long. For despite the magnetizing brightness, or perhaps because of it, the flash is born to fade. Still, the sharp burst of light is a brave and wonderful thing that makes observers count the seconds and cheer it on.

From her station on the altimeter line, Paulette could see over gray steel tables down the length of the shed. Of the four hundred electric-arc or gas-welding torches in operation, the number lighted varied at any one time from twenty or thirty to almost all of them. As each welder pulled down her mask, bent over as if in a dive, and squeezed the lever on her torch, the pattern of the lights emerged, and it was never the same twice. Through the dark glass of the face plate the flames in the distance were like a spectacular convocation of fireflies on a hot, moonless night. With the mask up, the plane of the work tables looked like the floor of the universe, the smoky place where stars were born. All the lights, even those that were distant, commanded attention and assaulted the senses—by the score, by the hundreds.

Directly across from Paulette was a woman whose job was to make oxyacetylene welds on the outer cases of the altimeters. The cases were finished, and then carried by trolley to the end of the line, where they would be hooded over the instruments themselves. Paulette, who worked with an electric arc, never tired of watching this woman adjust her torch. When she lit it, the flame was white inside but surrounded by a yellow envelope that sent up twisting columns of smoke. Then she changed the mixture and a plug of intense white appeared at the end of the torch, in the center of a small orange flare. When finally she got her neutral flame—with a tighter white plug, a colorless core, and a sapphire-blue casing—she lowered her mask and bent over the work.

Paulette had many things to do on one altimeter. She had to attach all the brass, copper, and aluminum alloy parts to the steel superstructure of the instrument. She had to use several kinds of flux; she had to assemble and brace the components; and she had to jump from one operation to the other in just the right order, because if she did not, pieces due for insertion would be blocked or bent.

She had such a complicated routine only because she was doing the work of two. The woman who had been next to her got sick one day, and Paulette had taken on her tasks. Everyone assumed that the line would slow down. But Paulette doubled her speed and kept up the pace.

"I don't know how you do it, Paulette," her supervisor had said, as she worked with seemingly effortless intensity.

"I'm going twice as fast, Mr. Hannon," she replied.

"Can you keep it up?"

"I sure can," she answered. "In fact, when Lindy comes back, you can put her down the line and give her work to me." Whereas Lindy always talked about clothes and shoes, Paulette preferred to concentrate on the instrument that she was fashioning. She was granted her wish. Among other things, Hannon and just about everyone else on the line wanted to see how long she could continue the pace before she broke. But she knew this, and she didn't break. She got better, and she got faster.

When Paulette got home in the morning, the sea was illuminated as the sun came up behind her. The open and fluid light of the Pacific was as entrancing as the light of the Carolinas in springtime. At times the sea looked just like the wind-blue mottled waters of the Albemarle, and the enormous clouds that rose in huge columns far out over the ocean were like the aromatic pine smoke that ascended undisturbed from a farmer's clearing fire toward a flawless blue sky.

She was elated in the morning. Joy and relief came not only from the light on the waves but also from having passed the great test of the day, which was to open the mailbox and check the area near the front door. The mailman, who served as the telegraph messenger, thought that he was obliged to wedge telegrams tightly in the doorway. One of the women, a lathe operator who had had to go back to her family in Chicago, had found her telegram actually nailed down. The mailman had feared that it might blow into the sea, and that then she would find out in some shocking, incidental manner that her husband had been killed. At the factory were fifty women whose husbands, like Lee, had passed through Twentynine Palms into the Second Marine Division. They had been deeply distressed when their men were thrown into the fighting on Guadalcanal, but, miraculously, of the fifty Marines whose wives were gathered in this one place only a few had been wounded and none had been killed.

When her work was done, knowing that she had made the best part of thirty altimeters that would go into thirty fighters, and that each of these fighters would do a great deal to protect the ships on which the Marines sailed, and pummel the beaches on which they had to fight, Paulette felt deserving of sleep. She would change into a nightgown, turn down the covers, and then sit in a chair next to the bed, staring at the Pacific as the light got stronger, trying to master the fatigue and stay awake. Sometimes she would listen to the wind for an hour, nod asleep, and force herself to open her eyes, until she fell into bed and slept until two in the afternoon.

Lee had returned from his training at Parris Island with little respect for what he once had thought were human limitations. His company had marched for three days, day and night, without stopping. Some recruits, young men, had died of heart attacks.

"How can you walk for three whole days without stopping?" she had asked. "It seems impossible."

"We had forty-pound packs, rifles, and ammunition," he answered. "We had to carry mortars, bazookas, stretchers, and other equipment, some of it very heavy, that was passed from shoulder to shoulder."

"For three days?"

"For three days. And when we finally stopped, I was picked as a sentinel. I had to stand guard for two hours while everyone else slept. And you know what happens if you fall asleep, God help you, on sentry duty?"

She shook her head, but did know.

"Article eighty-six of the Articles of War: 'Misbehavior of a sentinel.'" He recited it from memory. '"Any sentinel who is found drunk or sleeping upon his post, or leaves it before he is regularly relieved, shall, if the offense is committed in time of war, suffer death or such other punishment as a court-martial may direct.'

"I was so tired . . . My eyelids weighed ten thousand pounds apiece. But I stayed up, even though the only enemies we had were officers and mosquitoes. They were always coming around to check."

"Who?" she asked. "Mosquitoes?"

"Yeah," Lee replied. "And as you know, officers are hatched in stagnant pools."

So when Paulette returned from her ten-hour shifts, she sat in a chair and tried not to sleep, staring over the Pacific like a sentinel.

She had the privilege of awakening at two in the afternoon, when the day was strongest, and not having to be ashamed of having slept through the morning. In the six hours before the shift began, she would rise, bathe, eat lunch, and gather her garden tools. Then she walked a few miles down the winding coast road—the rake, hoe, and shovel resting painfully upon her shoulders—to her garden. No shed was anywhere near it, and had one been there she probably would have carried the tools anyway.

Because she shared the garden with an old man who came in the morning and two factory women who were on the second day shift, she was almost always alone there. Usually she worked in the strong sun until five-thirty. To allow herself this much hard labor she did her shopping and eating at a brisk pace. The hours in the garden made her strong and fit. She was perpetually sunburned, and her hair became lighter. She had never been so beautiful, and when people looked at her, they kept on looking. Seeing her speed through the various and difficult chores of cultivation, no one would ever have guessed that she might shoulder her tools, walk home as fast as she could, and then set off for ten hours on a production line.

"Don't write about the garden anymore," he had written from a place undisclosed. "Don't write about the goddamned altimeters. Don't write about what we're going to do when the war is over. Just tell me about you. They have altimeters here, they even have gardens. Tell me what you're thinking. Describe yourself as if we had never met. Tell me in detail how you take your bath. Do you sing to yourself? What do the sheets on the bed look like—I mean do they have a pattern or are they a color? I never saw them. Take pictures, and send them. Send me your barrette. (I don't want to wear it myself, I want to keep it in my pocket.) I care so much about you, Paulette. I love you. And I'm doing my best to stay alive. You should see me when it gets tight. I don't throw myself up front, but I don't hold my breath either. I run around like hell, alert and listening every second. My aim is sure and I don't let off shots when I don't have to. You'd never know me, Paulette, and I don't know if there's anything left of me. But I'm going to come home."

Although she didn't write about the garden anymore, she tilled it deep. The rows were straight, and not a single weed was to be seen, and when she walked home with the tools on her shoulders, she welcomed their weight.

They exchanged postscripts for two months in letters that were late in coming and always crossed. "P.S. What do you eat?" he wrote.

"P.S. What do you mean, what do I eat? Why do you want to know? What do you eat?"

"P.S. I want to know because I'm hungry. I eat crud. It all comes from a can, it's very salty, and it has a lot of what seems to be pork fat. Some local vegetables haven't been bombed, or crushed by heavy vehicles, but if you eat them you can wave good-bye to your intestines. Sometimes we have cakes that are baked in pans four feet by five feet. The bottom is cinder and the top is raw dough. What happened to steak? No one has it here, and I haven't seen one in a year. Where are they keeping it? Is there going to be a big barbecue after the war?"

"P.S. You're right, we have no beef around here and practically no sugar or butter, either. I thought maybe you were getting it. I eat a lot of fresh vegetables, rice, fish that I get in exchange for the stuff in my garden, and chicken now and then. I've lost some weight, but I look real good. I drink my tea black, and I mean black, because at the plant they have a huge samovar thing where it boils for hours. What with your pay mounting up in one account, and my pay mounting up in another, and what the parents have been sending us lately, when the war is over we're going to have a lot of money. We have almost four thousand dollars now. We'll have the biggest barbecue you've ever seen."

As long as she did her work and as long as he stayed alive, she sensed some sort of justice and equilibrium. She enjoyed the feminine triumph in the factory, where the women, doing men's work, sometimes broke into song that was as tentative and beautiful as only women's voices can be. They did not sing often. The beauty and the power embarrassed them, for they had their independence only because their men were at risk and the world was at war. But sometimes they couldn't help it, and a song would rise above the production lines, lighter than the ascending smoke, more luminous than the blue and white arcs.

The Pacific and California's golden hills caught the clear sunshine but made it seem like a dream in which sight was confused and the dreamer giddy. The sea, with its cold colors and foaming cauldrons in which seals were cradle-rocked, was the northern part of the same ocean that held ten thousand tropical islands. All these things, these reversals, paradoxes, and contradictions, were burned in day by day until they seemed to make sense, until it appeared as if some great thing were being accomplished, greater than perhaps they knew. For they felt tremendous velocity in the way they worked, the way they lived, and even in the way they sang.

On the twentieth of November, 1943, five thousand men of the Second Marine Division landed on the beaches of Tarawa. The action of war, the noise, smoke, and intense labor of battle, seemed frozen when it reached home, especially for those whose husbands or sons were engaged in the fighting. A battle from afar is only a thing of silence, of souls ascending as if drawn up in slow motion by malevolent angels floating above the fray. Tarawa, a battle afar, seemed no more real than a painting. Paulette and the others had no chance to act. They were forced to listen fitfully to the silence and stare faithfully into the dark.

Now, when the line broke into song, the women did not sing the energetic popular music that could stoke production until it glowed. Nor did they sing the graceful ballads that had kept them on the line when they would otherwise have faltered.

Now the songs were from the hymnal, and they were sung not in a spirit of patriotism or of production but in prayer.

As the battle was fought on Tarawa, two women fell from the line. One had been called from her position and summoned to what they knew as the office, which was a maze of wavy-glass partitions beyond which other people did the paperwork, and she, like the lathe operator from Chicago, simply dropped away. Another had been given a telegram as she worked; no one really knew how to tell anyone such a thing. But with so many women working, the absence of two did not slow their industry. Two had been beaten. Five hundred were not, and the lights still flickered down the line.

Paulette had known from the first that Lee was on the beach. She wondered which was more difficult, being aware that he might be in any battle, or knowing for sure that he was in one. The first thing she did when she got the newspaper was to scan the casualty lists, dropping immediately to the *F*s. It did not matter that they sent telegrams; telegrams sometimes blew into the sea. Next she raced through reports of the fighting, tracing if she could the progress of his unit and looking for any mention of him. Only then would she read the narrative so as to judge the progress of the offensive and the chances of victory, though she cared not so much for victory as for what it meant to the men in the field who were still alive.

The line was hypnotic and it swallowed up time. If she wanted to do good work, she couldn't think about anything except what was directly in front of her, especially since she was doing the work of two. But when she was free she now dreamed almost continually of her young husband, as if the landings in Tarawa, across the Pacific, had been designed to make her imagine him.

During these days the garden needed little attention, so she did whatever she could and then went down to a sheltered cove by the sea, where she lay on the sand, in the sun, half asleep. For as long as her eyes were closed and the sea seemed to pound everything but dreams into meaningless foam and air, she lay with him, tightly, a slight smile on her face, listening to him breathe. She would awake from this half sleep to find that she was holding her hands and arms in such a way that had he been there she would have been embracing him.

She often spoke to him under her breath, informing him, as if he could hear her, of everything she thought and did—of the fact that she was turning off the flame under the kettle, of the sunrise and its golden-red light flooding against the pines, of how the ocean looked when it was joyously misbehaving.

These were the things she could do, the powers to which she was limited, in the town on the Pacific that was probably the last place in the world for a factory or the working of transcendent miracles too difficult to explain or name. But she felt that somehow her devotion and her sharp attention would have repercussions, that, just as in a concert hall, where music could only truly rise within the hearts of its listeners, she could forge a connection over the thin air. When a good wave rolled against the rocks of the cove, it sent up rockets of foam that hung in the sun, motionlessly and—if one could look at them hard enough to make them stand still—forever. To make them a target, to sight them with concentration as absolute as a burning weld, to draw a bead, to hold them in place with the eye, was to change the world.

The factory was her place for this, for precision, devotion, and concentration. Here the repercussions might begin. Here, in the darkness, the light that was so white it was almost blue—sapphire-colored—flashed continually, like muzzle bursts, and steel was set to steel as if swords were being made. Here she could push herself, drive herself, and work until she could hardly stand—all for him.

As the battle of Tarawa became more and more difficult, and men fell, Paulette doubled and redoubled her efforts. Every weld was true. She built the instruments with the disciplined ferocity that comes only from love. For the rhythm of the work seemed to signify something far greater than the work itself. The timing of her welds, the blinking of the arc, the light touch that held two parts together and was then withdrawn, the patience and the quickness, the generation of blinding flares and small pencil-shots of smoke: these acts, qualities, and their progress, like the repetitions in the hymns that the women sang on the line, made a kind of quiet thunder that rolled through all things, and that, in Paulette's deepest wishes, shot across the Pacific in performance of a miracle she dared not even name—though that miracle was not to be hers.

―――――――――――

"I believe that in war the strongest emotions and the most powerful effects are not those of the front itself, but those that follow the well-traveled lines from the front to the home front, and back again. As an undergraduate, I was appalled when audiences at the Brattle Theater in Cambridge, attempting to conform to a fashionable political ethos, hissed and ridiculed scenes of soldiers taking leave of their loved ones. The very things that elicited their contempt moved me a great deal, and eventually it even came to be my turn, and I found myself saying good-bye to my wife, at the bus station, with the rifle slung across my back obscenely included in our embrace. So, in this story, I was working from memory as well as from belief. I think that it is my favorite not just because of the way that it is written, or because of the strong presence of a wonderful landscape, but because I feel for Paulette, the protagonist, the kind of overwhelming love and admiration that she most certainly deserves."

Mark Helprin is the author of A Dove of the East, & Other Stories; Ellis Island, & Other Stories; *and two novels:* Refiner's Fire *and* Winter's Tale. *He has been publishing short stories in* The New Yorker *for two decades, and his work has appeared as well in* The Atlantic, Esquire, The New Criterion, The New York Times, The Wall Street Journal *and in many other publications and anthologies both here and abroad.*

Published in The Atlantic

BOB SHACOCHIS

SQUIRRELLY'S GROUPER

A fish story is like any other, never about a fish but always about a man and a place. I wouldn't even mention it if I thought everybody knew. When you cut down to the bone of the matter, a fish is just Pleasure with a capital P. Rule of thumb—the bigger the fish, the bigger the pleasure. That's one side of the coin of fishing, the personal best and finest, but this is Hatteras, and there's that other side. On the Outer Banks of North Carolina, you can't pitch a rock in the air in the morning without rock-throwing becoming widespread ruthless competition by the time the sun goes down over Pamlico Sound, and that is because we go to sea for our living, and because commercial fishermen think they are God's own image of male perfection. I've seen it go on all my life here on the coast, each generation afflicted with the same desire to lord, bully and triumph, doesn't even matter where they come from once they're here, north or south or bumbled in from Ohio and beyond like Willie Striker. So that's the other side where size counts, wakes the sleepyheads right up, subdues the swollen-head gang and becomes everybody's business.

We saw the boats off that morning like we always do, and near an hour later Mrs. Mitty Terbill came in the marina store to post a sign she had made, a little gray cardboard square she had scissored from the back of a cereal box. It said:

Lost Dog. Yorkshire Terrier. Name—Prince Ed, My Sole Companion. Reward, and then a number to reach her at.

"What's the reward, Mitty?" I asked. It was five dollars, which is about right for a Yorkie, measured by appeal per pound. Mitty Terbill is not an upright-standing woman but then considerable woe has befallen her and keeps her squashed into her pumpkin self, allowing for only brief religious ascension. She spent that much plus tax on a twelve-pack and trudged back out the door, foot-heavy in her fishwife's boots, going back to her empty house on the beach to sit by the phone. Well, this story's not about the widow Terbill, though plenty of stories are since she lost her old man and her dope-pirate offspring two Januarys ago when they ran into weather off Cape May, up there flounder fishing I believe it was. That's just how I remember the day settling down after the dawn rush, with Mitty coming in, some of the fellows cracking jokes about how one of the boys must have mistook Prince Ed for bait and gone out for shark, and although Mitty likes her opinions to be known and gets the last word in on most events, let me please go on.

Life is slack at a marina between the time the boats go out early and vacationers get burnt off the beach about noon and come round to browse, then in the afternoons all hell breaks when the boats return. Anyway, after Mitty stopped in, Junior left to pull crab pots; Buddy said he's driving out to Cape Point to see if the red drum are in on the shoals with the tide change; Vickilee took a biscuit breakfast over to her cousins at the firehouse; Albert went down to the Coast Guard station to ingratiate himself to uniformed men; Brainless was out at the pumps refueling his uncle's trawler so he could get back to the shrimp wars, which left just me, my manager Emory Plum, and my two sacked-out bay retrievers in the place when I hear what might be an emergency broadcast on the citizen's band, because it's old grouch Striker calling J.B. on channel seventeen. Willie Striker has been one to spurn the advancement of radio and the charity of fellow captains, not like the other jackers out there bounced wave to wave on the ocean. They yammer the livelong day, going on like a team of evangelical auctioneers about where the fish aren't to be found, lying about how they barely filled a hundred-pound box, complaining how there's too many boats these days on the Banks and too many yankees on land, in a rage because the boys up in Manteo are fetching a nickel more for yellowfin, and who messed with who, and who's been reborn in Christ, and who knows that college girl's name from Rodanthe, and who's going to get theirs if they don't watch it. Willie Striker has something to say himself but you wouldn't find him reaching out. He kept to himself and preferred to talk that way, to himself, unless he had a word for his wife, Issabell. Keeping to himself was no accident, and I'll tell you why if you just hold on.

J.B.J.B. . . . come in, Tarbaby, I hear, and even though an individual's voice coming through the squawkbox fizzes like buggy tires on a flooded road, you know it's Willie Striker transmitting because he left words of no consequence out of a sentence and had the added weight of an accent, nothing much, just a low spin or bite on some words. Like mullet, Willie Striker would say, *maul*-it.

Tarbaby Tarbaby . . . come in. That was the name of J.B.'s workboat.

I was restocking baits, ballyhoo and chum, my head bent into the freezer locker, and Emory he was back behind the counter studying delinquent accounts. "Turn her up a bit there, Emory," I told him, "if you please."

He didn't need to look to do it he'd done it so many times, he just reached behind and spun the dial to volume nine, put a hailstorm and fifty-knot blow between us and the boats. "Well who's that we're listening to?" Emory yelled out. "That's not our Mr. Squirrel, is it?"

Some twenty-five years it's been I guess that Willie Striker had lived among us, married Issabell Preddy, one of our own, came south it was said sick and tired of Dayton and a factory job, and from the day he showed his jumpy self at Old Christmas in Salvo, folks called Striker Squirrelly. If you've seen his picture in the paper you might think you know why. Squirrelly's got a small shrewd but skittish face with darting then locking eyes, a chin that never grew, some skinny teeth right out in the front of his mouth and his upper lip was short, tight, some called it a sneer. The top of his head was ball-round and bald up to the crown, then silver hair spread smooth like fur-Ben. Like any good made-up name that fits and stays, there was more to it than manner of appearance.

Way-of-life on Hatteras Island has long been settled, that's just the way it is. A couple dozen families like mine, we lived together close back to Indian times, wreckers and victims of wrecks, freebooters and lifesavers, outcasts and hermits, beachcombers and pound netters and cargo ferrymen, scoundrels and tired saintly women, until they put the bridge across Oregon Inlet not long after Willie moved down. Outsiders meant complications to us one way or another; the truth is we don't take to them very well—which used to have significance but doesn't anymore, not since the herd stampeded in the last ten years to buy up the dunes and then bulldoze the aquifer. That's the island mascot these days, the yellow bulldozer, and the Park Service rules the beach like communists. That's one thing, but the fact is, Willie Striker wouldn't care and never did if a Midgett or a Burrus or a Foster ever said "Fine day, iddn't skipper" to him or not. He wasn't that type of man, and we weren't that type of community to look twice at anything unless it had our blood and our history, but Issabell Preddy was the type of woman inwardly endeared to signs of acceptance, which you could say was the result of having a drunkard father and a drunkard mother. Issabell and her brothers went to live with their Aunt Betty in Salvo until they finished school, but Betty had seven children of her own, a husband who wouldn't get off the water and no time to love them all. I went to school with Issabell and have always known her to be sweet in a motionless way, and not the first on anybody's list. She had one eye floating and purblind from when her daddy socked her when she was small, wore hand-down boy's clothes or sack dresses on Sundays, her fuzzy red hair always had a chewed-on aspect about it, and her skin was such thin milk you never saw her outside all summer unless she was swaddled like an Arab. Back then something inside Issabell made her afraid of a good time, which made her the only Preddy in existence with a docile nature, and the truth is a quiet girl who is no beauty is like a ghost ship or a desert isle to the eyes of young and active men, no matter how curious you are you don't want to be stuck on it.

One by one Issabell's brothers quit school and took off, joined the Navy and the Merchant Marines, and Issabell herself moved back down the road to Hatteras, rented the apartment above the fishhouse and got employed packing trout, prospered modestly on the modest fringe, didn't hide herself exactly but wouldn't so much as sneeze in company without written invitation. The charter fleet was something new back then; there were not unfriendly rumors that Issabell upon occasion would entertain a first mate or two during the season. These rumors were not so bad for her reputation as you might expect in a Christian village except none of us really believed them, and it would have come as no surprise if sooner or later one of our crowd got around to marrying Issabell Preddy but the island had temporarily run out of eligible men by the time Terry Newman met Willie Striker in a Norfolk juke joint and brought him back with him for Old Christmas in Salvo. Old Christmas all the long-time families come together to feast by day, to game and make music and catch up with the facts of the year; by night we loudly take issue with one another and drink like only folks in a dry county can, and of course we fistfight— brother and cousin and father and godfather and grandfather and in-law; the whole bunch—and kid about it for three hundred sixty-five days until we can do it again. A few years back a lady from a city magazine came to write about our Old Christmas, called it culture, and I told her call it what the hell you want but it's still just a bust-loose party, gal, and when night fell and the fur started to fly she jumped up on a table above the ruckus, took flashbulb pictures and asked me afterward why Hatterasmen liked to brawl. I told her there's nothing to explain, we all think we're twelve years old, and if it was real fighting somebody'd be dead. Anyway, Terry Newman showed up that January with his twenty-four-hour buddy Willie Striker, and it was the year that Terry's brother Bull Newman decided Terry was a good-for-nothing and needed to be taught a lesson. One minute Bull had his arm across Terry's shoulder laughing, and the next he had knocked him down and out cold, continued through the room rapping heads of all he perceived to have exercised bad influence on his younger brother, including the skull of his own daddy, until he arrived at Willie nursing a bottle of beer off by himself at a table in the corner. Bull was a huge man but dim; Willie Striker was no young buck but was given to juvenile movements the eye couldn't properly follow— twitches and shoulder jerks and sudden frightening turns, so even as he sat there holding his beer he seemed capable of attack. Bull towered over him with an unsure expression, a doglike concern, trying to anticipate in which direction Willie was going to uncoil, attempting also to determine who this person was and if he was someone he held an unidentifiable grudge against or someone he was going to hit on principle alone, and when he swung Willie dodged and lunged, laid Bull's nose flat with his beer bottle without breaking the glass, threw open the window at his back and scrambled out.

"That'll teach you to go messin' with squirrels," someone said to Bull.

No one saw Will Striker again until a week later, raking scallops in the Sound with Issabell Preddy. The way I heard it was, Willie got to the road that night about the same time Issabell was headed back to Hatteras from her visit with her Aunt Betty, driving a fifty-dollar Ford truck she had bought off Albert James, her Christmas present to herself, and even though Willie was hitching back north, she stopped and he got in anyway and went with her south, neither of them, the story goes, exchanging a word until they passed the lighthouse and got to the village, everything shut down dark and locked up, not a soul in sight of course, and Issabell said to him, so the story goes, that he could sleep in the truck if he wanted, or if he was going to be around for the week he could come upstairs and have the couch for thirty cents a night, or if he had plans to stay longer he could give her bed a try. Willie went the whole route: truck, couch, Issabell Preddy's lonely single bed.

In those days scalloping was women's work, so it was hard to raise any sort of positive opinion about Willie. He was a mainlander and worse, some brand of foreigner; out there wading in the Sound it appeared he had come to work, but not work seriously, not do man's work; he had moved into Issabell's apartment above the fishhouse and burdened her social load with scandal; and he had clobbered Bull Newman, which was all right by itself, but he hadn't held his ground to take licks in kind. He had run away.

The following Old Christmas Willie wedded Issabell Preddy in her Aunt Betty's kitchen, though for her sake I'm ashamed to say the ceremony was not well attended. She wanted kids, I heard, but there was talk among the wives that Willie Striker had been made unfit for planting seed due to unspecified wounds. For a few years there he went from one boat to another, close-mouthed and sore-fingered, every captain and crew's backup boy, and Issabell scalloped and packed fish and picked crabs until they together had saved enough for a downpayment on the *Sea Eagle*. Since that day he had bottom-fished by himself, on the reefs and sunken wrecks, at the edge of the Stream or off the shoals, got himself electric reels a couple years ago, wouldn't drop a line until the fleet was out of sight, wouldn't share loran numbers, hoarded whatever fell into his hands so he wouldn't have to borrow when the fish weren't there, growled to himself and was all-around gumptious, a squirrel-hearted stand-alone, forever on guard against inva-sion of self, and in that sense he ended up where he belonged, maybe, because nobody interfered with Willie Striker, we let him be, and as far as I know no one had the gall to look him straight in his gun-barrel eyes and call him Squirrelly, though he knew that's what he was called behind his back. Whatever world Willie had fallen from at midlife, he wound up in the right place with the right woman to bury it. Maybe he had fallen from a great height, and if the plunge made him a loon, it also made him a man of uncommon independence, and so in our minds he was not fully without virtue.

Squirrelly finally connected with J.B., who bottom-fished as well, not possessing the craft or the personal etiquette—that is to say, willingness to baby the drunken or fish-crazed rich—to charter out for sport. Likewise, he was a mainlander, a West Virginian with a fancy for the rough peace of the sea, and for these reasons Willie, I suspect, was not loathe to chance his debt. They switched radio channels to twenty-two in order to gain privacy and I asked Emory to follow them over. Up at their trailer in Trent, Issabell had been listening in too; hers was the first voice we found when we transferred. She ques-tioned Willie about what was wrong; he asked her to pipe down.

"What you need there, *Sea Eagle?*" J.B. squawked. After a

moment Willie came back on, hard to tell through the greasy sizzle but he sounded apologetic.

"*Tarbaby,*" he said, "(something . . . something) . . . require assistance. Can you. . . ?"

"What's he say was the trouble?" Emory bellowed. "I couldn't tell, could you?"

"Roger, *Sea Eagle,*" J.B. answered. "Broke down, are you, captain?" Willie failed to respond, though J.B. assumed he did. "I didn't get that, Willie," he said. "Where the hell are you, gimme your numbers and I'll come rescue your sorry ass."

"Negative," he heard Willie say. "Report your numbers and I come to you."

So that's how it went, Striker ignoring his Issabell's pleas to divulge the nature of his trouble, J.B. staying at location while the *Sea Eagle* slowly motored through three-foot seas to find him while we sat around the marina, trying to figure out what it meant. Squirrelly had a problem but it didn't seem to be with his boat; he needed help, but he would come to it rather than have it go to him. J.B. was about twenty miles out southeast of the shoals, tile fishing; likely Willie was farther east, sitting over one of his secret spots, a hundred fathoms at the brink of the continental shelf. We heard no further radio contact except once, more than an hour later, when Striker advised J.B. he had the *Tarbaby* in sight and would come up on his starboard side. Back at the marina the Parcel Service man lugged in eighteen cartons of merchandise and we were fairly occupied. Then past twelve J.B. called into us, jigging the news.

"Diamond Shoals Marina," J.B. crowed, "y'all come in. Dillon," he said to me, "better clean up things around there and get ready for a fuss. Squirrelly caught himself a fat bejesus."

I picked up the transmitter and asked for more information but J.B. declined, claiming he would not be responsible for spoiling the suspense. I slid over to channel twenty-two, waited for Issabell to stop badgering Willie and asked him what was up.

"*Up?*" he spit into the microphone. "I tell you *up!* Up come victory, by God. Up come justice . . . going to seventeen," he muttered, and I flipped channels to hear him advertise his fortune to a wider audience. "Ya-ha-ha," we all heard him cackle. "Cover your goddamn eyes, sons of bitches. Hang your heads. Age of Squirrelly has come . . ."

We had never heard him express himself at such provocative length.

The island's like one small room of gossip-fed biddies when something like this happens. People commenced telephoning the marina, took no more than five minutes for the noise to travel sixty miles, south to north to Nags Head, then jump Albemarle Sound to Manteo and the mainland. "Don't know a thing more than you," Emory told each and every caller, "best get down here to see for yourself when he comes in around three." I took a handcart to the stockroom and loaded the coolers with Coca-Cola and beer.

Now, there are three types of beast brought in to the dock, first kind are useless except as a sight to see, tourists gather round and take snapshots, Miss Luelle brings her day-care kids down to pee their pants, old stories of similar beasts caught or seen are told once more, then when the beast gets rank somebody kicks it back into the water and that's that. I'm talking sharks or anything big, bony, red-meated and weird. Second style of beast is your sport beast: marlins, tuna, wahoo, barracuda, et cetera, but primarily billfish, the stallions of wide-open blue water. This class of beast prompts tourists to sign up for the Stream, but Miss Luelle and her children stay home as do the rest of the locals unless a record's shattered, because these are regular beasts on the Outer Banks, at least for a few more years until they are gone forever, and after the captain and the angler quit swaggering around thinking they're movie stars, I send Brainless out to cut down that poor dead and stinking hero-fish and tow it into the Sound for the crabs and eels, and that's that too. The third style of beast is kidnapped from the bottom of the world and is worth a ransom, and that's what Striker would have. He wouldn't bring anything in for its freak value, he was the last man on earth to recognize sport— all he did day in day out was labor for a living, like most but not all of us out here, so I figured he hooked himself a windfall beast destined for finer restaurants, he'd weigh it and set it on ice for brief display, then haul it to the fishhouse, exchange beast for cash and steer home to Issabell for supper and his bottle of beer, go to bed and rise before dawn and be down here at his slip getting rigged, then on the water before the sun was up.

First in was J.B. on the *Tarbaby*, which is a Wanchese boat and faster than most; J.B. likes to steam up a wake anyway, put spray in the air. Already the multitudes converged in the parking lot and out on the porch, elbowing in to the store. Vickilee came back across the street with her cousins from the firehouse to start her second shift; Buddy led a caravan of four-wheelers down the beach from Cape Point. Packers and pickers and shuckers shuffled drag-ass from inside the fishhouse, gas station geniuses sauntered over from the garage. Coast Guard swabs drove up in a van, the girls from Bubba's Barbeque, Barris from Scales and Tales, Deedee from the video rental, Cornbread from the surf shop, Sheriff Spine, Sam and Maggie from over at the deli, the tellers from the bank, Daddy Wiss leading a pack of elders and tourists galore drawn by the scent of photo opportunity and fish history. Before three all Hatteras had closed and come down, appetites inflamed, wondering what the devil Willie Striker was bringing in from the ocean floor that was so humongous he had to defy his own personal code and ask for help.

J.B.'s mate tossed a bowline to Brainless; took him in the face as usual because the poor boy can't catch. J.B. stepped ashore in his yellow oilskins and scale-smeared boots, saying, "I can't take credit for anything, but damn if I can't tell my grandkids I was there to lend a hand." Without further elaboration he walked directly up the steps to the store, went to the glass cooler and purchased one of the bottles of French champagne we stock for high rollers and unequaled luck. Paid twenty-eight dollars, the first time I recall J.B. daring to go first class. He bought a case of ice-colds too for his crew, went back out to the *Tarbaby* with it under his arm, going to clean tile fish.

"Well come on, J.B.," the crowd begged, making way for him, "tell us what old Squirrelly yanked from the deep"—but J.B. knew the game, he knew fishing by now and what it was about when it wasn't about paying rent, and kept his mouth glued shut, grinning up at the throng from the deck, all hill-billy charm, as he flung guts to the pelicans.

Someone shouted, *He just come through the inlet!* The crowd buzzed. Someone else said, *I heard tell it's only a mako shark.* Another shouted, *I heard it was a tiger!* Then, *No sir, a great white's what I hear. Hell it is,* said another boy, *it's a dang big tuttie. Them's illegal,* says his friend, *take your butt right to jail.* One of our more God-fearing citizens maneuvered to take advantage of the gathering. I wasn't going to have that, I stepped back off the porch and switched on the public address system. *Jerry Bomfield,* I announced in the lot, *this ain't Sunday and this property you're on ain't church. I don't want to see nobody speaking in tongues and rolling on the asphalt out there,* I said. *This is a nonreligious, nondenominational event.* You have to take things in hand before they twist out of control, and I run the business on a family standard.

Here he comes now, someone hollered. We all craned our necks to look as the *Sea Eagle* rounded the buoy into harbor waters and a rebel cheer was given. Cars parked in the street, fouling traffic. The rescue squad came with lights flashing for a fainted woman. I went and got my binoculars from under the counter and muscled back out among the porch rats to the rail, focused in as Willie throttled down at the bend in the cut. I could see through the glasses that this old man without kind-ness or neighborly acts who neither gave nor received had the look of newfound leverage to the set of his jaw. You just can't tell what a prize fish is going to do to the insides of a man, the way it will turn on the bulb over his head and shape how he wants himself seen.

I went back inside to help Emory at the register. Issabell Striker was in there, arguing politely with Vickilee, who threw up her hands. Emory shot me a dirty look. Issabell was being very serious—not upset, exactly, just serious. "Mister Aldie," she declared, "you must make everyone go away."

"No problem, Mizz Striker," I said, and grabbed the micro-phone to the P.A. *Y'all go home now, get,* I said. I shrugged my shoulders and looked at this awkward lonesome woman, her floppy straw hat wrapped with a lime green scarf to shade her delicate face, swoops of frosty strawberry hair poking out, her skin unpainted and pinkish, that loose eye drifting, and Issabell just not familiar enough with people to be used to making sense. "Didn't work."

Her expression was firm in innocence; she had her mind set on results but little idea how to influence an outcome. "Issabell," I said to her, "what's wrong, hon?" The thought that she might have to assert herself against the many made her weak, but finally it came out. She had spent the last hours calling television stations. When she came down to the water and saw the traffic tie-up and gobs of people, her worry was that the reporter men and camera men wouldn't get through, and she wanted them to get through with all her sheltered heart, for Willie's sake, so he could get the recognition he deserved which he couldn't get any other way on earth, given the nature of Hatteras and the nature of her husband.

Issabell had changed some but not much in all the years she had been paired with Squirrelly in a plain but honest life. She still held herself apart, but not as far. Not because she believed herself better; it never crossed our minds to think so. Her brothers had all turned out bad, and I believe she felt the pull of a family deficiency that would sweep her away were she not on guard.

Her hands had curled up from working at the fishhouse. Striker bought her a set of Jack Russell terriers and she began to breed them for sale, and on weekends during the season she'd have a little roadside flea market out in front of their place, and then of course there was being wife to a waterman, but what I'm saying is she had spare time and she used it for the quiet good of others, baking for the church, attending environmental meetings even though she sat in the back of the school auditorium and never spoke a word, baby-sitting for kids when someone died. Once I even saw her dance when Buddy's daughter got married, but it wasn't with Willie she danced because Willie went to sea or Willie stayed home, and that was that. I don't think she ever pushed him; she knew how things were. The only difference between the two of them was that she had an ever-strengthening ray of faith that convinced her someday life would change and she'd fit in right; Willie had faith that the life he'd found in Hatteras was set in concrete. The man was providing, you know, just providing, bending his spine and risking his neck to pay bills the way he knew how, and all he asked in return was for folks to let him be. All right, I say, but if he didn't want excitement he should've reconsidered before he chose the life of a waterman and flirted with the beauty of the unknown, as we have it here.

"Mizz Striker, don't worry," I comforted the woman. A big fish is about the best advertisement a marina can have besides. "Any TV people come round here, I'll make it my business they get what they want."

"Every man needs a little attention now and then," she said, but her own opinion made her shy. She lowered her eyes and blushed, tender soul. "Is that not right, Dillon," she questioned, "if he's done something to make us all proud?"

Out the bayside window we could watch the *Sea Eagle* angling to dock, come alongside the block and tackle hoist, the mob pressing forward to gape in the stern, children riding high on their daddies' shoulders. Willie stood in the wheelhouse easing her in, his face enclosed by the bill of his cap and sunglasses, and when he shut down the engines I saw his head jerk around, a smile of satisfaction form and vanish, he pinched his nose with his left hand and batted the air with the other, surveying the army of folks, then he looked up toward me and his wife. You could read his lips saying, *Phooey*.

"What in tarnation did he catch anyway?" I said, nudging Issabell.

"All he told me was 'a big one,' " she admitted.

One of the porch layabouts had clambered down dockside and back, bursting through the screen door with a report. "I only got close enough to see its tail," he hooted. "Looked near the size of a brush you'd need to paint a battleship."

"*What in the devil is it?*" Emory said. "I'm tired of waitin' to find out."

"Warsaw grouper," said the porch rat. "Size of an Oldsmobile, I'm told."

"Record buster, is she?"

"Does a whale have tits?" said the rat. "'Scuse me, Mizz Striker."

You can't buy publicity like that for an outfit or even an entire state, and taking the record on a grouper is enough to make the angler a famous and well-thought-of man. I looked back out the bayside window. Squirrelly was up above the congregation on the lid of his fishbox, J.B. next to him. Squirrelly had his arms outstretched like Preacher exhorting his flock. J.B. had whisked off the old man's cap. Willie's tongue was hanging out, lapping at a baptism of foamy champagne.

"Old Squirrel come out of his nest," Emory remarked. I fixed him with a sour look for speaking that way in front of Issabell. "Old Squirrel's on top of the world."

Issabell's pale eyes glistened. "Squirrelly," she repeated, strangely pleased. "That's what y'all call Willie, isn't it?" She took for herself a deep and surprising breath of gratitude. "I just think it's so nice of y'all to give him a pet name like that."

The crowd multiplied; a state trooper came to try to clear a lane on Highway 12. At intervals boats from the charter fleet arrived back from the Gulf Stream, captains and crew saluting Squirrelly from the bridge. Issabell went down to be with her champion. Emory and I and Vickilee had all we could do to handle customers, sold out of camera film in nothing flat, moved thirty-eight cases of beer mostly by the can. I figured it was time I walked down and congratulated Willie, verify if he had made himself newsworthy or was just being a stinker. First thing though, I placed a call to Fort Lauderdale and got educated on the state, national and world records for said variety of beast so at least there'd be one of us on the dock knew what he was talking about.

Being in large crowds is tough on my nerves so I untied my outboard runabout over at the top of the slips and puttered across the harbor, tied up on the stern of *Sea Eagle* and J.B. gave me a hand aboard. For the first time I saw that awesome fish, had to hike over it in fact. Let me just say this: you live on the Outer Banks all your life and you're destined to have your run-ins with leviathans, you're bound to see things and be called on to believe things that others elsewhere wouldn't, wonders that are in a class by themselves, gruesome creatures, underwater shocks and marvels, fearsome life forms, finned shapes vicious as jaguars, quick and pretty as racehorses, sleek as guided missles and exploding with power, and the more damn sights you see the more you never know what to expect next. Only a dead man would take what's below the surface for granted, and so when I looked upon Squirrelly's grouper I confess my legs lost strength and my eyes bugged, it was as though Preacher had taken grip on my thoughts, and I said to myself, *Monster and miracle greater than me, darkness which may be felt*.

J.B. revered the beast. "Fattest damn unprecedented jumbo specimen of Mongolian sea pig known to man," he said, he could be an eloquent fool. "St. Gompus, king of terrors, immortal 'til this day." He leaned into me, whispering, fairly snockered by now, which was proper for the occasion. "Dillon," he confided, "don't think I'm queer." He wanted to crawl down the beast's throat and see what it felt like inside, have his picture taken with his tootsies sticking out the maw.

"Stay out of the fish," I warned J.B. "I don't have insurance for that sort of prank."

A big fish is naturally a source of crude and pagan inspirations. I knew what J.B. had in mind: get my marina photographer to snap his picture being swallowed and make a bundle selling copies, print the image on T-shirts and posters too. He could snuggle in there, no doubt, take his wife and three kids with him, there was room. The fish had a mouth wide as a bicycle tire, with lips as black and hard, and you could look past the rigid shovel of tongue in as far as the puckered folds of the gullet, the red spiky scythes of gills, and shudder at the notion of being sucked through that portal, wolfed down in one screaming piece into the dungeon of its gut. Don't for a minute think it hasn't happened before.

Willie wasn't in sight, I noticed. I asked J.B. where the old man had put himself, it being high time to hang the beast and weigh it, see where we stood on the record, have the photographer take pictures, let tourists view the creature so we could move traffic and the other fishermen would have space to go about their daily business, lay the beast on ice while Willie planned what he wanted to do.

"He's up there in the cuddy cabin with Issabell," J.B. said, nodding sideways. "Something's gotten into him, don't ask me what." Vacationers shouted inquiries our way; J.B. squared his shoulders to respond to an imprudent gal in a string bikini. "Well, ma'am," he bragged, "this kind of fish is a hippocampus grumpus. Round here we call 'em *wads*. This one's a damn big wad, iddn't it." As I walked forward I heard her ask if she could step aboard and touch it, and there was beast worship in her voice.

I opened the door to the wheelhouse; ahead past the step-down there was Willie Striker, his scrawny behind on a five-gallon bucket, the salty bill of his cap tugged down to the radish of his pug nose, hunched elbows on threadbare knees with a pint of mint schnapps clutched in his hands. If you've seen a man who's been skunked seven days running and towed back to port by his worst enemy, you know how Willie looked when I found him in there. Issabell was schooched on the galley bench, her hands in front of her on the chart. She was baffled and cheerless, casting glances at Willie but maybe afraid to confront him, at least in front of me, and she played nervously with her hair where it stuck out under her hat, twisting it back and forth with her crooked fingers.

I tried to lighten the atmosphere of domestic strife. "You Strikers're going to have to hold down the celebration," I teased. "People been calling up about you two disturbing the peace."

"He don't want credit, Dillon," Issabell said in guilty exasperation. "A cloud's passed over the man's golden moment in the sun."

Here was a change of heart for which I was not prepared. "Willie," I began, but stopped. You have to allow a man's differences and I was about to tell him he was acting backwards. He cocked his chin to look up at me from under his cap, had his sunglasses off and the skin around his eyes was branded with a raccoon's mask of whiteness and I'm telling you there was such a blast of ardent if not furious pride in his expression right then, and the chill of so much bitterness trapped in his mouth, it was something new and profound for me, to be in the presence of a fellow so deeply filled with hate for his life, and I saw there was no truth guiding his nature, I saw there was only will.

His face contorted and hardened with pitiless humor; he understood my revelation and mocked my concern, made an ogreish laugh in his throat and nodded like, All right, my friend, so now you know my secret, but since you're dumb as a jar of dirt what does it matter, and he passed his bottle of bohunk lightning to me. Say I was confused. Then he mooned over at Issabell and eased off, he took back the pint and rinsed the taste of undeserved years of hardship from his mouth with peppermint and jerked his thumb aft.

"Where I come from," Willie said, rubbing the silvery stubble on his cheek, "we let them go when they are like that one." His face cracked into a net of shallow lines; he let a smile rise just so far and then refused it. "Too small." (*Smull*, is how he said it.) "Not worth so much troubles."

I thought what the hell, let him be what he is, reached over and clapped him on the back, feeling the spareness of his frame underneath my palm. "Step on out of here now, captain," I said. "Time for that beast to be strung up and made official."

"Willie," coaxed Issabell with a surge of hope, "folks want to shake your hand." He was unmoved by this thought. "It might mean nothing to you," she said, "but it makes a difference to me."

Striker didn't budge except to relight his meerschaum pipe and bite down stubbornly on its stem between front teeth. On the insides of his hands were welts and fresh slices where nylon line had cut, scars and streaks of old burns, calluses like globs of old varnish, boillike infections from slime poison.

"What's the matter, honey?" Issabell persisted. "Tell me, Willie, because it hurts to know you can't look your own happiness in the face. We've both been like that far too long." She tried to smile too but only made herself look desperate. "I wish," she said, "I wish . . ." Issabell faltered but then went on. "You know what I wish, Willie, I wish I knew you when you were young."

Issabell jumped up, brushing by me and out back into the sunshine and the crowd. Willie just said he was staying put for a while, that he had a cramp in his leg and an old man's backache. He had let the fish exhilarate and transform him out alone on the water, and for that one brief moment when J.B.

poured the victor's juice on his head, but the pleasure was gone, killed, in my opinion, by distaste for civilization, such as we were.

"Now she will despise me," Willie said suddenly, and I turned to leave.

J.B., me and Brainless rigged the block and tackle and hoisted the beast to the scales. The crowd saw first the mouth rising over the gunnel like upturned jaws on a steam shovel, fixed to sink into sky. People roared when they saw the grisly bulging eyeball, dead as glass but still gleaming with black wild mysteries. Its gill plates, the size of trash-can lids, were gashed with white scars, its pectoral fins like elephant ears, its back protected by a hedge of wicked spikes, and it smelled to me in my imagination like the inside of a castle in a cold and rainy land. You could hear all the camera shutters clicking, like a bushel of live crabs. When I started fidgeting with the counterweights the whole place hushed, and out of the corner of my eye I could see Striker come to stand in his wheelhouse window looking on, the lines in his face all turned to the clenched pipe. He was in there percolating with vinegar and stubbornness and desire, you know, and I thought what is it, you old bastard, have you decided Issabell is worth the gamble? The grouper balanced. I wiped sweat from my brow and doublechecked the numbers. Squirrelly had it all right, broke the state mark by more than two hundred pounds, the world by twenty-six pounds seven ounces. I looked over at him there in the wheelhouse and brother he knew.

I made the announcement, people covered their ears while the fleet blasted air horns. A group of college boys mistook J.B. for the angler and attempted to raise him to their shoulders. A tape recorder was poked in his face; I saw Issabell push it away. Willie stepped out of the wheelhouse then and came ashore to assume command.

You might reasonably suspect that it was a matter of honor, that Willie was obliged to make us acknowledge that after twenty-five years on the Outer Banks his dues were paid, and furthermore obliged to let his wife Issabell share the blessing of public affections so the poor woman might for once experience the joy of popularity just as she was quick to jump at the misery of leading a hidden life, so ready to identify with the isolation of the unwanted that night of Old Christmas all those years ago. Willie knew who he was but maybe he didn't know Issabell so well after all, didn't see she was still not at home in her life the way he was, and now she was asking him to take a step forward into the light, then one step over so she could squeeze next to him. You just can't figure bottom-dwellers.

Anyway I swear no man I am familiar with has ever been more vain about achievement, or so mishandled the trickier rewards of success than Willie after he climbed off *Sea Eagle*. The crowd and the sun and the glamour went straight to his head and resulted in a boom of self-importance until we were all fed up with him. He came without a word to stand beside the fish as if it were a private place. At first he was wary and grave, then humble as more and more glory fell his way, then a bit coy I'd say and then Bull Newman plowed through the crowd, stooped down as if to tackle Willie but instead wrapped his arms around Willie's knees and lifted him up above our heads so that together like that they matched the length of the fish. The applause rallied from dockside to highway.

"I make all you no-goodniks famous today," Willie proclaimed, crooking his wiry arms like a body builder, showing off. Bull lowered him back down.

"Looks like you ran into some luck there, Squirrelly," Bull conceded.

"You will call me Mister Squirrel."

"Purty fish, Mister Squirrel."

"You are jealous."

"Naw," Bull drawled, "I've had my share of the big ones."

"So tell me, how many world records you have."

Bull's nostrils flared. "Records are made to be broken, *Mister* Squirrel," he said, grinding molars.

"Yah, yah"—Willie's accent became heavier and clipped as he spoke—"und so is noses."

Bull's wife pulled him out of there by the back of his pants. Willie strutted on bow legs and posed for picture takers. His old adversaries came forward to offer praise—Ootsie Pickering,

Dave Jonson, Milford Lee, all the old alcoholic captains who in years gone by had worked Willie like a slave. They proposed to buy him a beer, to haul him aboard their vessels for a toast of whiskey or come round the house for a game of cards, and Willie had his most fun yet acting like he couldn't quite recall their names, asking if they were from around here or Johnny-come-latelies, and I changed my mind about Willie hating himself so much since it was clear it was us he hated more. Leonard Purse, the owner of the fishhouse, was unable to approach closer than three-deep to Willie; he waved and yessirred until he caught Squirrelly's eye and an impossible negotiation ensued. Both spoke merrily enough but with an icy twinkle in their eyes.

"Purty fish, Willie. How much that monster weigh?"

"Eight dollars," Willie said, a forthright suggestion of an outrageous price per pound.

"Money like that would ruin your white-trash life. Give you a dollar ten as she hangs."

"Nine dollars," Willie said, crazy, elated.

"Dollar fifteen."

"You are a swine."

"Meat's likely to be veined with gristle on a beast that size."

"I will kill you in your schleep."

"Heh-heh-heh. Must have made you sick to ask J.B. for help."

"Ha-ha! Too bad you are chicken of der wadder, or maybe I could ask you."

Vickilee fought her way out of the store to inform me that the phone had been ringing off the hook. TV people from New Bern and Raleigh, Greenville and Norfolk were scheduled by her one after the other for the morning; newspaper people had already arrived from up the coast, she and Emory had talked to them and they were waiting for the crowd to loosen up before they tried to push through to us, and one of them had phoned a syndicate so the news had gone out on the wire, which meant big-city coverage from up north, and of course all the sport magazines said they'd try to send somebody down, and make sure the fish stayed intact. Also, scientists were coming from the marine research center in Wilmington, and professors from

Duke hoped they could drive out tomorrow if we would promise to keep the fish in one piece until they got here. The beer trucks were going to make special deliveries in the morning, the snack man too. Charters were filling up for weeks in advance.

So you see Squirrelly and his grouper were instant industry, the event took on a dimension of its own and Willie embraced his role, knew he was at last scot-free to say what he pleased without penalty and play the admiral without making us complain. He sponged up energy off the crowd and let it make him boastful and abrupt, a real nautical character, and the folks from around here loved his arrogance and thought we were all little squirrelly devils. Issabell seemed anxious too, this was not quite how she had envisioned Willie behaving, him telling reporters he was the only man on Hatteras who knew where the big fish were, but she beamed naïvely and chattered with the other wives and seemed to enjoy herself, even her goofed eye shined with excitement. It was a thrill and maybe her first one of magnitude and she wasn't going to darken it for herself by being embarrassed.

Willie left the fish suspended until after the sun went down, when I finally got him to agree to put it back on the boat and layer it with ice. Its scales had stiffened and dried, its brown and brownish-green marbled colors turned flat and chalky. Both he and Issabell remained on the boat that night, receiving a stream of visitors until well past midnight, whooping it up and having a grand time, playing country music on the radio so loud I could hear it word for word in my apartment above the store. I looked out the window once and saw Willie waltzing his wife under one of the security lightpoles, a dog and some kids standing there watching as they carefully spun in circles. I said to myself, That's the ticket, old Squirrel.

Life in Hatteras is generally calm but Tuesday was carnival day from start to finish. Willie was up at his customary time before dawn, fiddling around the *Sea Eagle* as if it were his intention to go to work. When the fleet started out the harbor, though, he and Issabell promenaded across the road for breakfast at the café, and when he got back I helped him winch the fish into the air and like magic we had ourselves a crowd again,

families driving down from Nags Head, families who took the
ferry from Ocracoke, Willie signing autographs for children,
full of coastal authority and lore for the adults, cocky as hell to
any fisherman who wandered over. A camera crew pulled up in
a van around ten, the rest arrived soon after. What's it feel like
to catch a fish so big? they asked. For a second he was hostile,
glaring at the microphone, the camera lens, the interviewer
with his necktie loosened in the heat. Then he grinned imp-
ishly and said, I won't tell you. You broke the world's record, is
that right? Maybe, he allowed indifferently and winked over
the TV person's shoulder at me and Issabell. When the next
crew set up he more or less hinted he was God Almighty and
predicted his record would never be broken. After two more
crews finished with him the sun was high; I made him take the
fish down, throw a blanket of ice on it. Every few minutes
Emory was on the P.A., informing Squirrelly he had a phone
call. Vickilee came out and handed Willie a telegram from the
governor, commending him for "the catch of the century." I
guess the biggest treat for most of us was when the seaplane
landed outside the cut, though nobody around here particularly cared for the fellows crammed in there, Fish and Game
boys over to authenticate the grouper, so we pulled the fish
back out of the boat and secured it to the scales. Hour later
Willie took it down again to stick in ice, but not ten minutes
after that a truck came by with a load of National Park Rangers
wanting to have individual pictures taken with Squirrelly and
the grouper, so he hung it back up, then a new wave of
sightseers came by at midafternoon, another wave when the
fleet came in at five, so he just let it dangle there on the arm of
the hoist, beginning to sag from the amount of euphoric han-
dling and heat, until it was too dark for cameras and that's
when he relented to lower it down and we muscled it back to
the boat, he took her down past the slips to the fishhouse, I
thought to finally sell the beast to Leonard, but no, he collected a fresh half ton of ice. Willie wanted to play with the
grouper for still another day.

That's almost all there is to tell if it wasn't for Squirrelly's
unsolved past, the youth that Issabell regretted she had missed.
On Wednesday he strung the fish up and dropped it down I'd

say about a dozen times, the flow of onlookers and congratula-
tors and hangarounds had decreased, Issabell was animated as
a real estate agent and girlish as we'd ever seen, but by midday
the glow was off. She had been accidentally bumped into the
harbor by a fan, was pulled out muddy and slicked with diesel
oil, yet still she had discovered the uninhibiting powers of fame
and had vowed not to miss out on the fun the rest of her life,
and swore that she had been endowed by the presence of the
fish with clearer social vision.

By the time Squirrely did get his grouper over to the fishhouse
and they knifed it open, it was all mush inside, not worth a
penny. He shipped the skin, the head and the fins away to a
taxidermist in Florida, and I suppose the pieces are all still
there, sitting in a box like junk.

Now, if you don't already know, this story winds up with a
punch from so far out in left field there's just no way you could
see it coming, but I can't apologize for that, no more than I
could take responsibility for a hurricane. About a week after
everything got back to normal down here, and Squirrelly seemed
content with memories and retreated back to his habits of
seclusion, Brainless came crashing through the screen door,
arms and legs flapping, his tongue too twisted with what he
was dying to say for us to make sense of his message.

Emory looked up from his books, I was on the phone to a
man wanting a half-day charter to the Stream, arguing with him
that there was no such thing as a half-day charter that went out
that far. "When's that boy going grow up," Emory clucked. He
told Brainless to slow down and concentrate on speaking right.

"They's takin' Squirrelly away," Brainless said. He pointed
back out the door.

I told the fellow on the line I might call him back if I had
something and hung up, went around the counter and outside
on the porch, Emory too, everybody came in fact, Vickilee and
Buddy and Junior and Albert and two customers in the store. It
was a foggy drizzly morning, the security lamps casting soupy
columns of light down to the dock, most of the boats hadn't left
but their engines were warming up. I don't think the sun had
come up yet but you couldn't be sure. The boy was right, a
group of men in mackintoshes were putting handcuffs on Squir-

relly and taking him off the *Sea Eagle*. The other captains and
crews stood around in the mist, watching it happen. The men
had on street shoes and looked official, you know, as you'd
expect, and they led Willie to a dark sedan with government
license plates. One of them opened the rear door for Willie,
who kept his head bowed, and sort of helped him, pushed him,
into the car. None of us tried to stop it, not one of us spoke up
and said, Hey, what's going on? He was still an outsider to us
and his life was none of our business. None of us said or even
thought of saying, Willie, good-bye. We all just thought: There
goes Willie, not in high style. The sedan pulled out of the lot
and turned north.

"He's a goddamn Natsy!" squealed Brainless, shaking us out
of our spell.

"I told you not to cuss around here," Emory said. That was
all anybody said.

Squirrelly's true name, the papers told us, was Wilhelm
Strechenberger, and they took him back somewhere to Europe
or Russia, I believe it was, to stand trial for things he supposedly did during the war. The TV said Squirrelly had been a
young guard for the Germans in one of their camps. He had
been "long sought" by "authorities," who thought he was living
in Ohio. One of his victims who survived said something like
Squirrelly was the cruelest individual he had ever met in his
entire life.

Boy oh boy—that's all we could say. Did we believe it? Hell
no. Then, little by little, yes, though it seemed far beyond our
abilities to know and to understand.

Issabell says it's a case of mistaken identity although she
won't mention Willie when she comes out in public, and if you
ask me I'd say she blames us for her loss of him, as if what he
had been all those years ago as well as what he became when
he caught the fish, as if that behavior were somehow our fault.

Mitty Terbill was convinced it was Willie who grabbed her
Prince Ed for some unspeakable purpose. She's entitled to her
opinion, of course, but she shouldn't have expressed it in front
of Issabell, who forfeited her reputation as the last and only
docile Preddy by stamping the widow Terbill on her foot and
breaking one of the old lady's toes. She filed assault charges

against Issabell, saying Issabell and Willie were two of a kind. Like Mitty, you might think that Willie Striker being a war criminal explains a lot, you might even think it explains everything, but I have to tell you I don't.

Now that we know the story, or at least think we do, of Willie's past, we still differ about why Willie came off the boat that day to expose himself, to be electronically reproduced all over the land: was it for Issabell or the fish, and I say I don't know if Willie actually liked fishing, I expect he didn't unless he craved punishing work, and I don't know what he felt about Issabell besides safe, but I do know this. Like many people around here, Willie liked being envied. The Willie we knew was a lot like us, that's why he lasted here when others from the outside didn't, and that's what we saw for ourselves from the time he conked Bull Newman on the nose, to the way he abused what he gained when he brought in that beast from the deep and hung it up for all to admire. He was, in his manner, much like us.

We still talk about the grouper all right, but when we do we automatically disconnect that prize fish from Willie—whether that's right or wrong is not for me to say—and we talk about it hanging in the air off the scale reeking a powerful smell of creation, Day One, so to speak, and it sounds like it appeared among us like . . . well, like an immaculate moment in sport. We've been outside things for a long time here on the very edge of the continent, so what I'm saying, maybe, is that we, like Issabell, we're only just discovering what it's like to be part of the world.

"The first line of my affection for 'Squirrelly's Grouper' runs innocently to the characters' names: the widow Mitty Terbill, Dillon Aldie, Issabell Preddy and of course Willie Striker a.k.a. Squirrelly. These names are the flesh-and-blood language, or music, of a place; names with no pretense of fortune or high taste, no hint of the audacity of ideals. Such names, though

imaginary, have a quality that integrates with the folklore of the rural South; they breathe a tangible spirit into a hard-to-know part of the country like the Outer Banks of North Carolina. They weave the ethos of community, preservation, and circumscribed ambitions.

"My second line of affection runs to the monster, the beast—not Willie Striker but the fish, the primal element suddenly visible and animated. Last year while I was living in Hatteras, someone caught a fish near the size of the grouper in the story. The sensation of the creature, the unreality of it, drew an enormous crowd. Clearly, the fish was nature's perfect representative for all the overwhelming mysterious forces that spin below the surface of our lives and, suspended in the midst of its admirers, the perfect image of the magnetic horror of evil. To marry a character like Willie Striker with a sinister marvel of the natural universe, and to have Willie's experience as an outsider with a wicked past express the actual transition of a place from a sheltered world to one exposed to the vicissitude of contemporary affairs—that was the challenge of the story, its logistical agony and ultimately its pleasure. After all, when we have cause to abandon the faith we have granted to the past of a person or place, we're confronted with one of life's most stinging betrayals."

Bob Shacochis's short stories have been collected in Celebrations of a New World *and* Easy in the Islands, *which won the* American Book Award for First Fiction. *His stories have appeared in* Esquire, Missouri Review, The Paris Review *and many other publications, and have also been selected for the* Pushcart Prize *anthology and* New Stories from the South—The Year's Best.

Published in Playboy.

JUDITH ROSSNER

THE UNFAITHFUL FATHER

There are events in one's life so powerful that they become a filter through which subsequent events must pass to find their color, or meaning. When I was seven years old my mother died of a brain tumor diagnosed too late to be operable. One year and one week later my father married her younger sister Lilah. It is doubtful that this marriage surprised anyone in our family but me. If we were a family without religion, we were not without that strong secular Judaism that has been the island many Jews remained on when the vessel that was the idea of God sank in the modern night. In Jewish tradition it is more than desirable to marry the sibling of a dead wife or husband.

My mother and Lilah were so extraordinarily different in looks and temperament that people often found it difficult to believe they were sisters. How much more difficult it must have been, even for family members less concerned than I, to believe that the same man might love both of them. The adults were constrained to conceal any negative reaction to my father's rapid realignment of feeling. But I was under no such constraint.

We lived in a two-bedroom apartment near the Brooklyn Museum on Eastern Parkway. Lilah lived with my grandmother and a younger sister, Estelle, in a six-room apartment two buildings down on the parkway. My grandfather had lived there with them until his death a few years earlier.

My mother was a direct and powerful human being, large and warm with a full head of (prematurely) gray and very curly hair. I remember a wonderful laugh, very nearly booming and tinkly at the same time; a large bosom in the kind of embroidered Rumanian peasant blouse one saw on later generations and might have seen on earlier ones but seldom found on her own; the smell of certain foods that no one else made the same way (cabbage soup with ham, potato pancakes with cheese, a chocolate cake with bits of candied orange peel). Her voice had an extraordinary range and she read stories aloud better than any mother in the neighborhood. I cannot remember the specific changes during the months of her illness. I remember a darkened room; the smell of Nivea that was applied to her bedsores (for years the smell of Nivea made me ill); my father stroking my head and telling me that I was a wonderful, grown-up girl.

Lilah, the second of the three sisters, was four years younger than my mother, a couple of inches shorter, and slender yet voluptuous (even now I resist this description) in the manner of an unmarried woman. Often I heard her called pretty but the notion that she was any such thing was and is foreign to me. My mother had always said that personally, she preferred Estelle's "sweet, quiet" looks. To this day, when I look at pictures of Lilah, trying to force my adult eyes to appreciate what the child's could not, I find too-small eyes, too-large lips emphasized with too-dark lipstick, and hair bleached then curled in that gruesome fashion that would later identify the cheap home permanent. She wore red a lot of the time as though she were afraid you wouldn't notice her, and was addicted to chunky costume jewelry in an era when other women in the neighborhood put on a locket or a string of pearls for special occasions.

Furthermore, Lilah was a businesswoman, a title that had a certain vague but negative connotation to it.

Not from my own parents but from other adults I'd caught intimations that my aunt, who was the office manager of a button company in Manhattan, dressed the way she did because she was an unmarried businesswoman. Or perhaps it was vice versa. In any event, there was something a little fishy about being who Lilah was.

Estelle taught kindergarten. She was very soft and a little shy with adults but giggly and girlish-easy with me.

My father was an accountant for Abraham & Strauss, the

Brooklyn department store. During the months after the hospital sent my mother home to die, my grandmother took care of her during the week so that my father could go to his office. Estelle relieved my grandmother between three-thirty and four o'clock in the afternoon and remained with us until my father returned to reheat the dinner my grandmother had prepared in the morning. It was understood that Lilah could not be with us during the week because of the long hours she maintained at her job.

I found life more reasonable during those months than anyone knowing my situation would have expected. My father was competent in the kitchen and I was beginning to develop the elementary skills. On the weekends we shopped when someone could stay with my mother, cleaned the house together and did our laundry at the big, old wringer-style washing machine in the kitchen. Small shopping errands—a container of milk, a prescription to be filled—I did at neighborhood stores with notes from my father. We tended to resist the sympathies of the well-meaning. On the other hand, it was clear to me, without thinking much about it, that our lives would become easier once the unrecognizable creature in the master bedroom whom people called my mother no longer required attention.

In the morning, once he had tended to *her* needs, my father made our breakfast. In the afternoon, I used my key to enter the apartment, said hello to my grandmother or Estelle and got my afternoon snack. Some days I went to a friend's; other days I occupied myself or played cards or games with Estelle until my father returned. Then he and I would have dinner, do the dishes, go over my homework.

How pleasant a routine this would become when there was no almost-recognizable human lump lying in my father's bed, half of its hair shaved away, half of its volume gone, muttering words I couldn't make out and moaning as it moved to a more comfortable position! How much more easily I would breathe when no one was urging me to give It a kiss because that was what Its mutterings were about—It wanted a kiss from me! My mother had disappeared and I was being urged to show affection for this ghastly creature who also, it was clear, would not be with us for long. The shorter a time the better, as far as I could see.

I am told that during this period I consistently referred to my mother as though she were elsewhere and spoke of the creature in the bed not at all.

I have always disdained the euphemism "passed away" and yet it comes quite naturally now to write that having died to me some time earlier, my mother passed away on a cold, gray day in November, one year and two months after the day we had learned that she was gravely ill. At the funeral I sat between my father and my grandmother; Lilah sat on my father's other side. (I have never given the matter of where we sat a moment's thought yet I wrote that sentence as readily as though our seating had been uppermost in my mind for the past thirty years.) We rode to and from the cemetery in a limosine, my grandmother between my father and me in the back, my aunts on the two jump seats in front of us, and came to my grandmother's to sit *shiva*, the next step in the mourning-healing process. My father and I remained in that apartment all week, going home to sleep and to change our clothes. Friends and relatives came and went, bringing food so no one had to cook. At one point Lilah said something and my father laughed.

There it is again, waiting for me when I hadn't suspected it was there. My most distinct memory of the entire week. We spent most of our time sitting around the kitchen table. I usually had a book with me . . . I seem to recall going back to *Little Women* with even greater pleasure than I'd found in it earlier . . . and read while paying just enough attention to the conversation so that I could put aside the book if something interesting arose.

Lilah was telling a story about her office. As usual, it involved the wife of one of her two bosses, a woman who held the mistaken belief that she was important in running the company. She and Lilah crossed whenever both were in the office. On this particular occasion, Lilah had frostily rejected some suggestion that could not possibly have helped in her work. In a rage, the woman had flounced out of Lilah's office, only to trip at the threshold and go "flying so far down the hallway you'd have thought she had wings!"

There was laughter. Hearty laughter. *Belly laughs*.

I looked up. My father was among the laughers. I stared at him, openmouthed. He felt me watching him and looked away. The laughter subsided. Someone told another, less humorous story about office life.

Time passed. Life returned to normal, except that it was better, or so I felt, because we no longer had that dual sense of dread and obligation hanging over us. My father was sad, sometimes even sadder than he'd seemed when my mother was alive, which I couldn't understand. Once or twice I came upon him weeping and he denied that this was what he was doing. Unwilling to understand the enormity of my loss, I refused to understand the reality of his, and kept trying to make matters perfectly all right, as surely they had once been. One day I surprised him with cookies made from *The Joy of Cooking* because I was convinced that the homemade cookies that had once filled our ceramic jar were the only item missing from our lives.

In the spring, my father's mood lightened somewhat. I was happy, too. At school I had more friends than ever, my natural qualities, such as they were, being enhanced in my classmates' eyes by the unimaginably sad fact of my having lost my mother, and an additional nobility I had gained from never wanting to talk about my loss.

In the months following my mother's death it had been virtually impossible to pry me from my father's side once he returned from his office. But now we fell into a routine in which each Friday night I had a sleepover with my aunt Estelle, who had a pull-out daybed in her room. The sleepovers were a particular pleasure because Lilah, who had begun to irritate me for reasons I couldn't identify, was invariably out on a date.

On Saturday, if there was a movie playing that was accept-able for kids, my father might take me. Occasionally, Lilah joined us and then we walked her back to her apartment before retiring to ours. On Sunday we had dinner at my grandmoth-

er's. During the week we stayed home, except that as the
weather grew warmer, my father often was seized by the urge
to take a walk. If the urge seized him while I was still awake,
and if I didn't have too much homework, I might join him.
Otherwise he would give me a kiss and murmur, "Back in half
an hour."

Once when I was already in bed and half asleep, he whispered from the doorway that he'd be back soon. I lay in bed,
suddenly awake, wishing I'd dressed and gone with him. Finally I got out of bed and went to sit at my window, looking
down at the lighted parkway. Leaning on the hood of a car
parked in front of our building, looking more like a couple of
kids than like the grown-ups they were supposed to be, were
my father and Lilah, she unmistakable in a fluffy lavender
sweater that was exactly the sort of garment that made women
whisper about her. I went back to bed, making a mental note
to ask my father where he had run into her, but fell asleep
before he came in and did not, as far as I can recall, remember
to raise the subject in the morning.

May, June. School ended. I had resisted the notion of sleep-
away camp but my father had convinced me that it was the
only sensible choice for July. In August we would have a cabin
on Lake Buell, near Stockbridge. My grandmother, Aunt Estelle and I would remain at the cabin during the week. My
father and Lilah would drive up to join us for the first two
weekends, then remain with us during the second half of the
month.

My good times both at camp and in Stockbridge were punc-
tuated by concern over my father's being alone in the apartment at night. I called him more often than other kids called
home. Once Lilah picked up the phone and I was briefly
confused, thinking I'd given the operator the wrong number.
But my father got on and explained that Lilah had brought him
some dinner and was providing him with company in my
absence.

I was uneasy and little incidents reinforced my unease. I
would be looking for my father and neither Estelle nor my
grandmother would know where he was and Lilah was never
around to be asked. Then there was the matter of the looks that

passed between them that they couldn't explain when I asked what was funny, or what was going on. Aside from this uneasiness, though, it was a wonderful, busy summer, and for a while after our return to the city I thought a great deal about how much we might improve on it the next year. My father would have a longer vacation (my mother's illness the previous year had cost him some of his days) and perhaps we would have a cottage of our own, close to, instead of right in with, the others.

In the time of my mother's illness I had made over to my father perhaps more thoroughly than does a child not enduring such a loss. If I loved Estelle and my grandmother, it was with my father only that I discussed important questions, decisions that had to be made. As time passed and I became willing to, say, make a last-minute date to play after school at a friend's, I didn't call my grandmother's house, but phoned my father at work. I had been to his office on an occasional school holiday and during those phone conversations, as well as at other times of the day when there was no particular reason to do so, I would picture him working at his desk; or opening the sandwich he'd prepared for himself while making my lunch; or having a conversation with one of the men in his office.

Of the people he saw daily at work, he spoke ill of one, well of two and little of the others. I didn't question his judgment of these people any more than I questioned, say, his looks; he was the standard for what men were supposed to look like, and for the way they were supposed to be. Always slender to the point where the family teased him, he had gained a substantial amount of weight in the months following my mother's death. But I knew this not from observation—I was much too close to see him—but from his complaints about not being able to fit into his clothes, and the comments people made on his new ones. If I could tell that the ties he was bringing home were livelier than the ones he'd had for a while, I doubt that I would have noticed if he hadn't joked about them himself.

My father was kind but one did not see him seeking out friends or speaking casually to people on the street, as my mother often had. During the period of her illness and for some time after her death, I'd been aware as we walked together that my father looked at me or at the sidewalk when he wasn't checking out store windows. And then one day during that autumn, a group of giggly young women passed us and I was looking up at him and I saw that he was watching them and smiling.

"What's funny?" I asked, squeezing his hand, happy because he was happy.

"Oh, nothing, really," he replied, squeezing back. "I'm just feeling . . . It's nice to see happy young girls on the street. It makes me happy to see them happy."

I remember that a distinct if not lasting sense of anxiety swept over me; it was the first sign I was willing to receive that he was returning to a world that was about more than just him and me.

In the ensuing weeks I watched him more closely than I had before. I remember noting, on open-school night, that my teacher, Miss Margolin, who was rather stern and magisterial in class, smiled a great deal when she talked to him. And once or twice I became irritated with casual friends or with shop girls I thought were asking for more time or greater interest than their business required. It was during this period that Lilah's appearance, for some time a source of negative interest, became the object of my serious disapproval. As the months wore on and she spent more and more time at our apartment, I found myself cataloging in a way that was new to me unsavory details of her looks and behavior.

One Saturday morning I awakened early in Estelle's room and thought about the errands my father and I had to do that day. Estelle was sleeping soundly. After lying quietly for a few minutes, I decided to surprise my father at our apartment. I dressed and went into the kitchen, where my grandmother sat at the table over her morning tea. She stood up when she saw me (that generation of women never remained seated when someone entered the kitchen) and went to the refrigerator. I ran to her, hugged her around the middle and told her not to get anything for me. I was going to surprise my father and have breakfast with him.

"Wait a minute," she said.

Time might have exaggerated the panic in her voice but I remember the words as clearly as I remember anything in the first ten years of my life.

"Wait a minute. You don't have to go, yet. It's too early."

"I have my key," I said, still the conspirator. "I want to surprise him."

She was silent. If she'd ordered me to stay, I might have. In any event, she must have called them the moment I left her apartment, for by the time I arrived at ours, my father was dressed and making coffee in the kitchen. Down the hall, the toilet flushed.

"Is someone here?" I asked.

"Your aunt Lilah dropped by," my father said, setting two cups and three plates on the kitchen table. "I invited her to go shopping with us."

"Why?" I asked. "We don't need any help with the shopping."

"It's good," he said after a moment, "to have another point of view."

About what? V-8 or Sacramento? Chicken of the Sea or some new brand of tuna? The idea was so idiotic that there could be no argument with it.

My father put some Danish pastries on a plate on the table. This was even more peculiar; we never had cake for breakfast except on Sundays. Seeing my expression, my father said he had picked them up the night before. An explanation that explained nothing.

I got the orange juice from the refrigerator, poured it into a glass—a tricky act I often let him perform for me—and sat with it at the table, trying to understand why the world felt both unpleasant and odd. A short while later Lilah entered the kitchen, fully dressed and made up, and in her usual ridiculously high heels. Instead of saying hello I demanded to know how she could possibly walk with us in those heels.

Lilah smiled cheerfully, bent over to kiss my cheek.

"Silly, I always wear heels like this. I can't walk in anything *else*."

I wiped the lipstick from my burning cheek and remained silent. Lilah went to the refrigerator and got the juice, then poured herself a glass, an act she might have performed in some variation hundreds of times, at my house as well as her own, but that struck me for the first time as being nervy beyond belief.

Where did she think she was?

She sat down.

I watched her, *examined* her, this outsider in my home, trying to find out what was making me so angry and being unable to locate any source except Lilah. I saw the mascara on her eyes, the rouge on her cheeks, the purple lipstick my mother and Estelle had giggled over. She was wearing one of her fluffy sweaters, a white one, and a black skirt. She looked—I had heard it said of the girls who went to parochial school and dashed home to change from their uniforms into something more attractive—she looked *cheap*.

Then there were the peculiar things she *did*. Lilah was the only person I knew who used saccharin, and when she took her little pillbox from her skirt pocket and carefully extracted one tiny tablet, which she dropped into her coffee, I watched as though I had never previously understood the sinister nature of the act.

She looked up and saw me watching her and smiled.

Had her mouth always opened so wide and showed so much of her teeth? Why did her smile not look truly friendly to me? What was really on her mind? Did she want to get rid of me just as much as I wanted to get rid of her?

A short while later we went to do our Saturday shopping. Except, of course, it wasn't ours anymore. A very noticeable person with ridiculously high heels that clicked threateningly on the pavement walked with us, on the other side of my father, attracting somewhat more notice than he and I alone ever did, keeping up a stream of chatter that turned our lovely ritual expedition into a low-key nightmare.

On the following Friday morning I announced at breakfast that I didn't want to go to my grandmother's that night.

My father set down his coffee cup.

"Oh?"

As I describe the moment thirty years later I cannot find it in myself to be amused at the black cloud that settled over him, the dreadful silence that ensued. Finally, in a voice I'd heard him use very rarely, and then always in imitation of one of the bad guys at his office, he asked, "Why's that?"

I didn't know the answer, or at least I didn't have the specifics. I felt as though I'd been away from the house an awful lot. Perhaps too much. If my father hadn't been lonely, why would he have been letting Lilah hang around all the time? It had seemed to me, as I thought about the matter during the week, that Lilah had been at our place even more than I'd realized until now. What had happened to her precious job in Manhattan that had always kept her late a couple of evenings a week, and much too busy to help with family chores? Not to speak of her always being too busy to be at my grandmother's on Friday nights.

I shrugged.

"I don't know. I'm not feeling so good."

It wasn't really a lie.

"But you're feeling good enough to go to school?"

I was silent. Truthful by habit . . . not because I wanted to be but because I'd always believed grown-ups could tell the difference . . . I knew that the truth, what I could grasp of it, was unacceptable, and I hadn't prepared a lie. I tried to push Lilah out of my mind, telling myself this really had nothing to do with her, but I couldn't manage to believe it.

I nodded and looked down at the table.

"Well," my father said after a while, "we could certainly stay home together tonight. But then I would ask you to go to Grandma's tomorrow night."

"Why?" I burst out. I was close to tears. "Why do I have to go if I don't feel like it?"

For a moment he watched me, gauging the force of my feeling, trying to figure out what he could reasonably tell me. Then he put down his coffee cup, rubbed his eyes and reached across the table to take my hands in his.

"Because I love to be with you, Nell," he said, patting one of my hands as he spoke. "But sometimes I need to be with just a grown-up."

Grown-up. Did he mean Lilah? What was so grown up about Lilah? She didn't even cook or clean the house!

"All day you're with grown-ups," I pointed out.

"That's true," he said slowly. "But it's different because it's work. I'm not having a particularly good time." Mildly flustered by some implication he heard in his words, he quickly elaborated. "That is, I enjoy my work, but it's not the same as, say, having a nice dinner someplace. Going to a movie."

"I love movies," I pointed out.

"Sure you do." He squeezed my hands. "And I take you to the ones that are right for your age, don't I."

It wasn't a question asked but a point scored.

"But there are movies that are just for adults. And there are other activities adults enjoy." A pause. "Like dancing."

"Dancing!" I stared at him in disbelief. I'd never seen either of my parents dance but, on the contrary, had heard lots of jokes about how they'd come together because neither knew how. "You don't know how to dance!"

"Well . . ." He released my hands, rubbed his eyes again, smiled at me. "That's the funny thing. We . . . I never did know how. That's true. But it turns out . . . Your aunt Lilah's a very good dancer, as you may know. And she's been teaching me."

"No!" Rage piled upon disbelief and left me trembling and on the verge of tears. "I don't believe you!"

He sighed and released my hands, but I couldn't stop.

"You're lying!"

He stood up. He had been so careful with me, and the thanks he got was to be called a liar.

"That's enough, Nell." He looked at the clock. "I think you'd better go to school now. You'll be late."

"I don't care!" I was in no condition to back off. I needed a resolution, even if it was the spanking I'd occasionally been threatened with but never received. "I don't care if I'm late. I don't care if I never go to school again!"

I burst into tears and ran from the kitchen, through the long hallway, back to my bedroom, where I slammed the door and tried to lock it, an impossibility since our last paint job four years earlier. As I would have known if I had ever tried to lock it before.

I threw myself on the bed and wept bitterly for what seemed to be hours before my father came into the room, sat down on the bed, patted my back.

"Listen to me, love. You're upset. We're both upset. Tonight we'll stay home together and have a real talk."

Slowly the tears abated.

"This is something a little new for us, isn't it, sweetheart."

"What is it?" I asked. "What is it that's new?"

"We have to talk," he repeated. "Tonight we'll have a good talk."

I don't know what I thought I heard him say. I think I might have turned his words into a promise that if having Lilah around remained a problem for me, he wouldn't have her around except with the others. In any event, I pulled myself together, washed my face and set off for school.

He must have believed that I would grow accustomed to her. All I hoped was that someday he would realize she was dumb and dull and make her retreat to her proper position in the family. He must have hoped that she would win me over with the charm that was so visible to him, and perhaps if I had been a boy she would have made a more serious attempt to woo me. I think if he had known how intractable we would turn out to be he would have lain awake nights in fearful anticipation. But of course he would have married her anyway.

I can acknowledge, now, though without pleasure or humor, that Lilah was hot stuff, probably my father's first encounter with the genre. It is probably unnecessary to say that I did not then comprehend her allure. Even now when I speak of her I notice how reluctantly I grant her any quality worthy of his interest. Not to speak of mine. She had ruined my life, or what I had thought was going to be my life. If my adult self knows it was unlikely that my father and I would have remained together alone and happy until the day *I* was ready to leave *him*, Lilah was the instrument through which this reality was made known to me. I could never forgive her.

That night my father and I worked out a sort of agreement. If I did not understand his occasional need for adult companionship (he said he might choose to play cards with some of the men from work, or have dinner with a friend), I would have to grant that he felt this need. Two nights a week I would stay at my grandmother's or have a sleepover at a friend's. Three nights a week he and I would be alone for sure. On the remaining two we would be together, perhaps with friends or family members, perhaps alone.

It was part of the package that I was to be civil to Lilah; he hoped that eventually I would become much more than civil, that I would come to appreciate her as much as he did. (Fat chance, I thought.) He said that as I grew up I would discover problems in life that were best discussed with another female, and when that time came, I would be particularly happy to have Lilah around. (How could that be, when Lilah was my only problem?) In the meantime . . .

I kept my end of the bargain, as he did his. Lilah and I were civil, if not friendly. Well-bred strangers on a too-long train ride. My father was careful that I not learn more about their lives than I could bear to know. Then, just a few days after we had marked the year since my mother's death by setting in place her tombstone, he informed me that he and Lilah were going to be married.

It would be impossible to exaggerate the sense of betrayal I felt. I had kept our agreement, done my schoolwork, spent a lot of time with my friends and in general adjusted to my unpleasant new circumstances. I had been, in short, extremely virtuous—only to find that my virtue had paved the way for those unpleasant circumstances to grow a thousand times worse!

"Married?" I stared at him uncomprehendingly. We were sitting on the living-room couch, having set up the board on the coffee table for our ritual Sunday night checker "tournament." Sunday night was sacred. No dates. No family. Just the two of us. Together. Forever. "Married? *What for? Where?*"

He smiled, if a trifle grimly. He had long since relinquished the hope that this might be an easy conversation.

"That's what people do when they love each other, Nellie.

And as far as Where goes, it will be in your grandmother's apartment."

But I hadn't meant, Where will the wedding be? I had meant something that could better be phrased as, Where will you keep her? It was clear to me without even having to think about it that there was no room for Lilah in our apartment.

My father had grown more self-protective. Canny, if you will.

"I think," he said after a moment, "we'll be more comfortable once we're all really settled here together." He smiled. "The two of you will sort of have to get used to each other, instead of always wondering how . . . how much . . ."

He trailed off but I barely noticed. Settled together? What was he talking about? In this apartment there were only two bedrooms, my parents' and mine. For a long time I had thought of that room as my father's but now, suddenly and without my even noticing the change, it was my parents' again. *What was he talking about?* Surely he didn't mean, he couldn't mean, that Lilah was going to move into the bedroom that had once been my mother's! My mother came to me now with a clarity and intensity that I'd refused to allow her from the time I'd known she was mortally ill.

Mama! Where are you? Help me!

I stood up so suddenly that I knocked into the board on the table and sent the checkers flying.

My father watched me, waited, made no move to calm me or to pick up the checkers.

"There's no room for her here!" I shouted. "There's just enough room for the two of us or for . . . Where will she go? *Why doesn't she just stay at her office?*"

At that last line he gave way and smiled a little, with whatever mixture of feelings. And seeing him smile, I grew even angrier. At the top of my lungs I invoked my mother's name and memory as a reason that Lilah should not only not marry my father, but should not be his friend. My mother hadn't even *liked* Lilah! My mother had made jokes about Lilah's makeup and the way she did her hair!

My father grew stern. He was willing to talk to me. I was upset and he wanted to help me feel better. But there was no

rule that allowed me to say bad things about Lilah, whom he
loved.

I calmed down slightly. Or at least a layer of calm fell over
the volcanic feelings. *Loved? What did he mean, loved?*

"I thought you loved Mommy."

"Of course I loved your mother. And one of the reasons I
love Lilah is that she reminds me of your mother."

I stared at him. What was he talking about? Lilah looked
more like Betty Grable or some other cheap tart (my grandmother's phrase) out of the movies than like the soft, round,
gray-haired woman who happened to have been her sister.

I remained silent. It was quite clear that there were thoughts
I was not allowed to voice, less clear precisely which of all my
hostile thoughts those might be. I sat on the arm of a chair
facing the sofa and waited. After a while he began to speak.

There would be a small wedding at my grandmother's house
the following week. *The following week!* I froze. Little by little,
Lilah would be moving her clothing and other possessions into
the closets and drawers. *Closets and drawers? Which closets
and drawers? Was it possible they'd been throwing away my
mother's clothes without telling me?* Later one of two pieces of
Lilah's furniture might be brought over. *His* room would, of
course, become *their* room. *Their room. Their room. If I said
it to myself a million times I still wouldn't believe it.* Aside from
that, they planned no major changes for now. Later on some
redecorating might be done. *Redecorating? What did that
mean? There was nothing wrong with our apartment. I would
kill her if she tried to change anything in my room!* Lilah
would remain at her job for a while. *Why only for a while? Did
she think she was going to hang around the apartment all day
and boss me around?* The routine of our lives would change
very little. He had learned in these past months what he had
failed to understand before, that it was difficult for me to
accept the idea of a new woman in my mother's place. He
hoped . . . and he *believed* . . . or he would be much more
upset . . . that my feelings toward Lilah would gradually change.
That as I grew accustomed to the idea of sharing him with her I
would also come to see what a wonderful, loving, intelli—

But I had stopped listening with the phrase *your mother's*

place, and now I could sit still no longer. I jumped out of my chair, wanting to run out of the room but sensing that I must not do this, then using the sound of a siren on the parkway as an excuse to run to the window, instead.

My mother's place, indeed. If anyone had been able to take my mother's place it would have been me, her daughter, but of course no one could, certainly not the bleached blonde . . . I looked down. There was the ambulance, speeding along, orange and white with a flashing red light on top. Maybe Lilah had been hit by a car and lay dying on the street!

I turned to my father, frightened that he might have been able to guess my thoughts. Seeing the look on my face, he held out his arms. I ran to the sofa and collapsed against him, weeping as his arms enfolded me.

"Mommy! I want my mommy!"

Weeping over the unfairness of the world, its unpredictability, its utter failure to make sense. But more than that, weeping bitterly over the loss of my mother, whom I hadn't known I missed until now. Memories that I'd shut out from the time I knew she was going to die flooded my brain and made my body weak.

My mother giggling as she showed us a sprig of mistletoe she'd bought one Christmas; I'd wanted a tree so badly and they'd worked at explaining why Jews simply didn't have trees. Besides, mistletoe was better because she'd get to kiss me a hundred times a day.

My mother hiding under a sofa pillow the argyle sweater she was knitting for my birthday that I wasn't supposed to know about.

My mother making a game out of cleaning up my room with me when games, toys and books were scattered all over the place.

I'd had my holiday, my time alone with my adored father. We'd managed well, made believe everything was all right. Now it was time for life to return to normal. I remembered how sometimes when we'd been kidding around, having a pillow fight, say, or a tickling session on the living-room rug, my mother would suddenly say, "Whoops, time to be serious."

Well, it was time to be serious now. It was time for the three rightful occupants of that apartment to resume our lives.

I couldn't stop crying but finally I drifted to sleep in my father's arms, waking up once or twice before I really let go, thinking the last of those times that it was my mother's arms that were holding me.

My father must have carried me to bed. I remember that I awakened fully dressed the next day, Saturday, and that it took me much longer than usual to reach a fully conscious state. When I did, I realized that I had turned my pillow so that it was in a vertical position instead of the usual horizontal one, and my arms were wrapped around it as though it were a large, soft, female person.

Judith Rossner grew up in the Bronx and has lived in New York for most of her life, with the exception of brief stints in Croton-on-Hudson and in New Hampshire when her children were young.

Between 1966 and 1983 she published seven novels, of which her own favorites are Attachments *and* Emmeline. *This story is one of the few pieces of short fiction she has written.*

Published in Mademoiselle.

TOBIAS WOLFF

SMORGASBORD

"**A** prep school in March is like a ship in the dol-drums." Our history master said this, as if to himself, while we were waiting for the bell to ring after class. He stood by the window and tapped the glass with his ring in a dreamy, abstracted way meant to make us think he'd forgotten we were there. We were supposed to get the impression that when we weren't around he turned into someone interesting, someone witty and profound, who uttered impromptu bons mots and had a poetic vision of life.

The bell rang.

I went to lunch. The dining hall was almost empty, because it was a free weekend and most of the boys in school had gone to New York, or home, or to their friends' homes, as soon as their last class let out. About the only ones left were foreigners and scholarship students like me and a few other untouchables of various stripes. The school had laid on a nice lunch for us, cheese soufflé, but the portions were small and I went back to my room still hungry. I was always hungry.

Snow and rain fell past my window. The snow on the quad looked grimy; it had melted above the underground heating pipes, exposing long brown lines of mud.

I couldn't get to work. On the next floor down someone kept playing "Mack the Knife." That one song incessantly repeating itself made the dorm seem not just empty but abandoned, as if those who had left were never coming back. I cleaned my room. I tried to read. I looked out the window. I sat down at my desk and studied the new picture my girlfriend had sent me, unable to imagine her from it; I had to close my eyes to do that, and then I could see her, see her solemn eyes and the heavy white breasts she would gravely let me hold sometimes, but not kiss . . . not yet, anyway. But I had a promise. That summer, as soon as I got home, we were going to become lovers. "Become lovers." That was how she'd said it, very deliberately, listening to the words as she spoke them. All year I had repeated them to myself to take the edge off my loneliness and the fits of lust that made me want to scream and drive my fists through walls. We were going to become lovers that summer, and we were going to be lovers all through college, true to each other even if we ended up thousands of miles apart again, and after college we were going to marry and join the Peace Corps and then do something together that would help people. This was our plan. Back in September, the night before I left for school, we wrote it all down along with a lot of other specifics concerning our future: number of children (six), their names, the kinds of dogs we would own, a sketch of our perfect house. We sealed the paper in a bottle and buried it in her backyard. On our golden anniversary we were going to dig it up again and show it to our children and grandchildren to prove that dreams can come true.

I was writing her a letter when Crosley came to my room. Crosley was a science whiz. He won the science prize every year and spent his summers working as an intern in different laboratories. He was also a fanatical weight lifter. His arms were so knotty that he had to hold them out from his sides as he walked, as if he were carrying buckets. Even his features seemed muscular. His face was red. Crosley lived down the hall by himself in one of the only singles in the school. He was said to be a thief; that supposedly was the reason he'd ended up without a roommate. I didn't know if it was true, and I tried to avoid forming an opinion on the matter, but whenever we passed each other I felt embarrassed and dropped my eyes.

Crosley leaned in the door and asked me how things were.

I said okay.

He stepped inside and looked around the room, tilting his head to read my roommate's pennants and the titles of our books. I was uneasy. I said, "So what can I do for you," not meaning to sound as cold as I did but not exactly regretting it either.

He caught my tone and smiled. It was the kind of smile you put on when you pass a group of people you suspect are talking about you. It was his usual expression.

He said, "You know Garcia, right?"

"Garcia? Sure. I think so."

"You know him," Crosley said. "He runs around with Hidalgo and those guys. He's the tall one."

"Sure," I said. "I know who Garcia is."

"Well, his stepmother is in New York for a fashion show or something, and she's going to drive up and take him out to dinner tonight. She told him to bring along some friends. You want to come?"

"What about Hidalgo and the rest of them?"

"They're at some kind of polo deal in Maryland. Buying horses. Or ponies, I guess it would be."

The notion of someone my age buying ponies to play a game with was so unexpected that I couldn't quite take it in. "Jesus," I said.

Crosley said, "How about it. You want to come?"

I'd never even spoken to Garcia. He was the nephew of a famous dictator, and all his friends were nephews and cousins of other dictators. They lived as they pleased here. Most of them kept cars a few blocks from the campus, though that was completely against the rules, and I'd heard that some of them kept women as well. They were cocky and prankish and charming. They moved everywhere in a body with sunglasses pushed up on their heads and jackets slung over their shoulders, twittering all at once like birds, *chinga* this and *chinga* that. The headmaster was completely buffaloed. After Christmas vacation a bunch of them came down with gonorrhea, and all he did was call them in and advise them that they should not be in too great a hurry to lose their innocence. It became a school joke. All you had to do was say the word *innocence* and everyone would crack up.

"I don't know," I said.

"Come on," Crosley said.

"But I don't even know the guy."

"So what? I don't either."

"Then why did he ask you?"

"I was sitting next to him at lunch."

"Terrific," I said. "That explains you. What about me? How come he asked me?"

"He didn't. He told me to bring someone else."

"What, just anybody? Just whoever happened to present himself to your attention?"

Crosely shrugged.

I laughed. Crosley gave me a look to make sure I wasn't laughing at him, then he laughed, too. "Sounds great," I said. "Sounds like a recipe for a really memorable evening."

"You got something better to do?" Crosley asked.

"No," I said.

The limousine picked us up under the awning of the head-master's house. The driver, an old man, got out slowly and then slowly adjusted his cap before opening the door for us. Garcia slid in beside the woman in back. Crosley and I sat across from them on seats that pulled down. I caught her scent immediately. For some years afterward I bought perfume for women, and I was never able to find that one.

Garcia erupted into Spanish as soon as the driver closed the door behind me. He sounded angry, spitting words at the woman and gesticulating violently. She rocked back a little, then let loose a burst of her own. I stared openly at her. Her skin was very white. She wore a black cape over a black dress cut just low enough to show her pale throat and the bones at the base of her throat. Her mouth was red. There was a spot of rouge high on each cheek, not rubbed in to look like real color but left there carelessly, or carefully, to make you think again how white her skin was. Her teeth were small and sharp-looking, and she bared them in concert with certain gestures and inflections. As she talked, her little pointed tongue flicked in and out.

She wasn't a lot older than we were. Twenty-five at the most. Maybe younger.

She said something definitive and cut her hand through the air. Garcia began to answer her, but she said "No!" and chopped the air again. Then she turned and smiled at Crosley and me. It was a completely false smile. She said, "Where would you fellows like to eat?" Her voice sounded lower in English, even a little harsh, though the harshness could have come from her accent. She called us *fallows*.

"Anywhere is fine with me," I said.

"Anywhere," she repeated. She narrowed her big black eyes and pushed her lips together. I could see that my answer disappointed her. She looked at Crosley.

"There's supposed to be a good French restaurant in Newbury," Crosley said. "Also an Italian place. It depends on what you want."

"No," she said. "It depends on what you want. I am not so hungry."

If Garcia had a preference, he kept it to himself. He sulked in the corner, his round shoulders slumped and his hands between his knees. He seemed to be trying to make a point of some kind.

"There's also a smorgasbord," Crosley said. "If you like smorgasbords."

"Smorgasbord," she said. She repeated the word to Garcia. He frowned, then answered her in a sullen monotone.

I couldn't believe Crosley had suggested the smorgasbord. It was an egregiously uncouth suggestion. The smorgasbord was where the local fatties went to binge. Football coaches brought whole teams there to bulk up. The food was good enough, and God knows there was plenty of it, all you could eat, actually, but the atmosphere was brutally matter-of-fact. The food was good, though. Big platters of shrimp on crushed ice. Barons of beef. Smoked turkey. No end of food, really.

She was smiling. Obviously the concept was new to her. "You—do you like smorgasbords?" she asked Crosley.

"Yes," he said.

"And you?" she said to me.

I nodded. Then, not to seem wishy-washy, I said, "You bet."

"Smorgasbord," she said. She laughed and clapped her hands. "Smorgasbord!"

Crosley gave directions to the driver, and we drove slowly away from the school. She said something to Garcia. He nodded at each of us in turn and gave our names, then looked away again, out the window, where the snowy fields were turning dark. His face was long, his eyes sorrowful as a hound's. He had barely talked to us while we were waiting for the limousine. I didn't know why he was mad at his stepmother, or why he wouldn't talk to us, or why he'd even asked us along, but by now I didn't really care. By now my sentiments were, basically, Fuck him.

She studied us and repeated our names skeptically. "No," she said. She pointed at Crosley and said, "El Blanco." She pointed at me and said, "El Negro." Then she pointed at herself and said, "I am Linda."

"Leen-da," Crosley said. He really overdid it, but she showed her sharp little teeth and said, *"Exactamente."*

Then she settled back against the seat and pulled her cape close around her shoulders. It soon fell open again. She was restless. She sat forward and leaned back, crossed and recrossed her legs, swung her feet impatiently. She had on black high heels fastened by a thin strap; I could see almost her entire foot. I heard the silky rub of her stockings against each other, and breathed in a fresh breath of her perfume every time she moved. That perfume had a certain effect on me. It didn't reach me as just a smell; it was personal, it seemed to issue from her very privacy. It made the hair bristle on my arms. It entered my veins like fine, tingling wires, widening my eyes, tightening my spine, sending faint chills across my shoulders and the backs of my knees. Every time she moved I felt a little tug, and followed her motion with some slight motion of my own.

When we arrived at the smorgasbord—Swenson's, I believe it was, or maybe Hansen's, some such honest Swede of a name—Garcia refused to get out of the limousine. Linda tried to persuade him, but he shrank back into his corner and would not answer or even look at her. She threw up her hands. "Ah!" she said, and turned away. Crosley and I followed her across the parking lot toward the big red barn. Her dress rustled as she walked. Her heels clicked on the cement.

You could say one thing for the smorgasbord; it wasn't pretentious. It was in a real barn, not some quaint fantasy of a barn with butter-churn lamps and little brass ornaments nailed to the walls on strips of leather. At one end of the barn was the kitchen. The rest of it had been left open and filled with picnic tables. Blazing light bulbs hung from the rafters. In the middle of the barn stood what my English master would have called the groaning board—a great table heaped with food, every kind of food you could think of, and more. I had been there several times, and it always gave me a small, pleasant shock to see how much food there was.

Girls wearing dirndls hustled around the barn, cleaning up messes, changing tablecloths, bringing fresh platters of food from the kitchen.

We stood blinking in the sudden light. Linda paid up, then we followed one of the waitresses across the floor. Linda walked slowly, gazing around like a tourist. Several men looked up from their food as she passed. I was behind her, and I looked forbiddingly back at them so they would think she was my wife.

We were lucky; we got a table to ourselves. On crowded nights they usually doubled you up with another party, and that could be an extremely unromantic experience. Linda shrugged off her cape and waved us toward the food. "Go on," she said. She sat down and opened her purse. When I looked back she was lighting a cigarette.

"You're pretty quiet tonight," Crosley said as we filled our plates. "You pissed off about something?"

I shook my head. "Maybe I'm just quiet, Crosley, you know?"

He speared a slice of meat and said, "When she called you El Negro, that didn't mean she thought you were a Negro. She just said that because your hair is dark. Mine is light, that's how come she called me El Blanco."

"I know that, Crosley. Jesus. You think I couldn't figure that out? Give me some credit, okay?" Then, as we moved around the table, I said, "You speak Spanish?"

"*Un poco*. Actually more like *un poquito*."

"What's Garcia mad about?"

"Money. Something about money."

"Like what?"

He shook his head. "That's all I could get. But it's definitely about money."

I'd meant to start off slow but by the time I reached the end of the table my plate was full. Potato salad, ham, jumbo shrimp, toast, barbecued beef, Eggs Benny. Crosley's was full, too. We walked back toward Linda, who was leaning forward on her elbows and looking around the barn. She took a long drag off her cigarette, lifted her chin, and blew a stream of smoke up toward the rafters. I sat down across from her. "Scoot down," Crosley said, and settled in beside me.

She watched us eat for a while.

"So," she said, "El Blanco. Are you from New York?"

Crosley looked up in surprise. "No, ma'am," he said. "I'm from Virginia."

Linda stabbed out her cigarette. She had long fingernails painted the same deep red as the lipstick smears on her cigarette butt. She said, "I just came from New York, and I can tell you that is one crazy place. Just incredible. Listen to this. I am in a taxicab, you know, and we are stopping in this traffic jam for a long time and there is a taxicab next to us with this fellow in it who stares at me. Like this, you know." She made her eyes go round. "Of course I ignore him. So guess what, my door opens and he gets into my cab. 'Excuse me,' he says, 'I want to marry you.' 'That's nice,' I say. 'Ask my husband.' 'I don't care about your husband,' he says. 'Your husband is history. So is my wife.' Of course I had to laugh. 'Okay,' he says. 'You think that's funny? How about this.' Then he says—" Linda looked sharply at each of us. She sniffed and made a face. "He says things you would never believe. Never. He wants to do this and he wants to do that. Well, I act like I am about to scream. I open my mouth like this. 'Hey,' he says, 'okay, okay. Relax.' Then he gets out and goes back to his taxicab. We are still sitting there for a long time again, and you know what he is doing? He is reading the newspaper. With his hat on. Go ahead, eat," she said to us, and nodded toward the food.

A tall, blond girl was carving slices of roast beef onto a platter. She smiled at us. She was hale and bosomy—I could see the laces on her bodice straining. Her cheeks glowed. Her bare arms and shoulders were ruddy with exertion. Crosley raised his eyebrows at me. I raised mine back but my heart wasn't in it. She was a Viking dream, pure gemütlichkeit, but I was drunk on Garcia's stepmother, and in that condition you don't want a glass of milk, you want more of what's making you stumble and fall.

Crosley and I filled our plates again and headed back.

"I'm always hungry," he said.

"I know what you mean," I told him.

Linda smoked another cigarette while we ate. She watched the other tables as if she were at a movie. I tried to eat with a little finesse and so did Crosley, dabbing his lips with a napkin between every bulging mouthful, but some of the people around us had completely slipped their moorings. They ducked their heads low to receive their food, and while they chewed it up they looked around suspiciously and kept their forearms close to their plates. A big family to our left was the worst. There was something competitive and desperate about them; they seemed to be eating their way toward a condition where they would never have to eat again. You would have thought that they were refugees from a great hunger, that outside these walls the land was afflicted with drought and barrenness. I felt a kind of desperation myself; I felt as if I were growing emptier with every bite I took.

There was a din in the air, a steady roar like that of a waterfall.

Linda looked around her with a pleased expression. She bore no likeness to anyone here, but she seemed completely at home. She sent us back for another plate, then dessert and coffee, and while we were finishing up she asked El Blanco if he had a girlfriend.

"No, ma'am," Crosley said. "We broke up," he added, and his red face turned purple. It was clear that he was lying.

"You. How about you?"

I nodded.

"Ha!" she said. "El Negro is the one! So. What's her name?"

"Jane."

"Jaaane," Linda drawled. "Okay, let's hear about Jaaane."

"Jane," I said again.

Linda smiled.

I told her everything. I told her how my girlfriend and I had met and what she looked like and what our plans were. I told her more than everything, because I gave certain coy but definite suggestions about the extremes to which our passion had already driven us. I meant to impress her with my potency, to inflame her, to wipe that smile off her face, but the more I told her the more wolfishly she smiled and the more her eyes laughed at me.

Laughing eyes—now there's a cliché my English master would have eaten me alive for. "How exactly did these eyes laugh?" he would have asked, looking up from my paper while my classmates snorted around me. "Did they titter, or did they merely chortle? Did they give a great guffaw? Did they, perhaps, *scream* with laughter?"

I am here to tell you that eyes can scream with laughter. Linda's did. As I played big hombre for her I could see exactly how complete my failure was, I could hear her saying, *Okay, El Negro, go on, talk about your little gorlfren, how pretty she is and so on, but we know what you want, don't we?—you want to suck on my tongue and slobber on my titties and lick my belly and bury your face in me. That's what you want.*

Crosley interrupted me. "Ma'am . . ." he said, and nodded toward the door. Garcia was leaning there with his arms crossed and an expression of fury on his face. When she looked at him he turned and walked out the door.

Her eyes went flat. She sat there for a moment. She began to take a cigarette from her case, then put it back and stood up. "Let's go," she said.

Garcia was waiting in the car, rigid and silent. He said nothing on the drive back. Linda swung her foot and stared out the window at the passing houses and bright, moonlit fields. Just before we reached the school, Garcia leaned forward and began speaking to her in a low voice. She listened impassively and did not answer. He was still talking when the limousine stopped in front of the headmaster's house. The driver opened the door. Garcia fixed his eyes on her. Still impassive, she took her pocketbook out of her purse. She opened it and looked inside. She meditated over the contents, then withdrew a bill and offered it to Garcia. It was a one-hundred-dollar bill. "Boolshit!" he said, and sat back angrily. With no change of expression she turned and held the bill out to me. I didn't know what else to do but take it. She got another one from her pocketbook and presented it to Crosley, who hesitated even less than I did. Then she gave us the same false smile she had greeted us with, and said, "Goodnight, it was a pleasure to meet you. Goodnight, goodnight," she said to Garcia.

The three of us got out of the limousine. I went a few steps and then slowed down, and began to look back.

"Keep walking!" Crosley hissed.

Garcia let off a string of words as the driver closed the door. I faced around again and walked with Crosley across the quad. As we approached our dorm he quickened his pace. "I don't believe it," he whispered. "A hundred bucks." When we were inside the door he stopped and shouted, "A hundred bucks! A hundred fucking dollars!"

"Pipe down," someone called.

"All right, all right. Fuck you!" he added.

We went up the stairs to our floor, laughing and banging into each other. "Do you fucking believe it?" he said.

I shook my head. We were standing outside my door.

"No, really now, listen." He put his hands on my shoulders and looked into my eyes. He said, "Do you fucking *believe* it?"

I told him I didn't.

"Well, neither do I. I don't fucking believe it."

There didn't seem to be much to say after that. I would have invited Crosley in, but to tell the truth I still thought of him as a thief. We laughed a few more times and said goodnight.

My room was cold. I took the bill out of my pocket and looked at it. It was new and stiff, the kind of bill you associate with kidnappings. The picture of Franklin was surprisingly lifelike. I looked at it for a while. A hundred dollars was a lot of money then. I had never had a hundred dollars before, not in one chunk like this. To be on the safe side I taped it to a page in *Profiles in Courage*—page 100, so I wouldn't forget where it was.

I had trouble getting to sleep. The food I had eaten sat like a stone in me, and I was miserable about the things I had said. I understood that I had been a liar and a fool. I kept shifting under the covers, then I sat up and turned on my reading lamp. I picked up the new picture my girlfriend had sent me, and closed my eyes, and when I had some peace of mind I renewed my promises to her.

We broke up a month after I got home. Her parents were away one night, and we seized the opportunity to make love in their canopied bed. This was the fifth time that we had made love. She got up immediately afterward and started putting her clothes on. When I asked her what the problem was, she wouldn't answer me. I thought, *Oh Christ, what now.* "Come on," I said. "What's the problem?"

She was tying her shoes. She looked up and said, "You don't love me."

It surprised me to hear this, not because she said it but because it was true. Before this moment I hadn't known it was true, but it was—I didn't love her.

For a long time afterward I told myself that I had never really loved her, but this was a lie.

We're supposed to smile at the passions of the young, and at what we recall of our own passions, as if they were no more than a series of sweet frauds we had fooled ourselves with and then wised up to. Not only the passion of boys and girls for each other but the others, too—passion for justice, for doing right, for turning the world around—all these come in their time under our wintry smiles. But there was nothing foolish about what we felt. Nothing merely young. I just wasn't up to it. I let the light go out.

Sometime later I heard a soft knock at my door. I was still wide awake. "Yeah," I said.

Crosley stepped inside. He was wearing a blue dressing gown of some silky material that shimmered in the dim light of the hallway. He said, "Have you got any Tums or anything?"

"No. I wish I did."

"You too, huh?" He closed the door and sat on my roommate's bunk. "Do you feel as bad as I do?"

"How bad do you feel?"

"Like I'm dying. I think there was something wrong with the shrimp."

"Come on, Crosley. You ate everything but the barn."

"So did you."

"That's right. That's why I'm not complaining."

He moaned and rocked back and forth on the bed. I could hear real pain in his voice. I sat up. "Crosley, are you okay?"

"I guess," he said.

"You want me to call the nurse?"

"God," he said. "No. That's all right." He kept rocking. Then, in a carefully offhand way, he said, "Look, is it okay if I just stay here for a while?"

I almost said no, then I caught myself. "Sure," I told him. "Make yourself at home."

He must have heard my hesitation. "Forget it," he said bitterly. "Sorry I asked." But he made no move to go.

I felt confused, tender toward Crosley because he was in pain, repelled because of what I had heard about him. But maybe what I had heard about him wasn't true. I wanted to be fair, so I said, "Hey, Crosley, do you mind if I ask you a question?"

"That depends."

I sat up. Crosley was watching me. In the moonlight his dressing gown was iridescent as oil. He had his arms crossed over his stomach. "Is it true that you got caught stealing?"

"You fucker," he said. He looked down at the floor.

I waited.

He said, "You want to hear about it, just ask someone. Everybody knows all about it, right?"

"I don't."

"That's right, you don't." He raised his head. "You don't know shit about it and neither does anyone else." He tried to smile. His teeth appeared almost luminous in the cold silver light. "The really hilarious part is, I didn't actually get caught stealing it, I got caught putting it back. Not to make excuses. I stole the fucker, all right."

"Stole what?"

"The coat," he said. "Robinson's overcoat. Don't tell me you didn't know that."

I shook my head.

"Then you must have been living in a cave or something. You know Robinson, right? Robinson was my roommate. He had this camel's hair overcoat, this really just beautiful overcoat. I kind of got obsessed with it. I thought about it all the time. Whenever he went somewhere without it I would put it on and stand in front of the mirror. Then one day I just took the fucker. I stuck it in my locker over at the gym. Robinson was really upset. He'd go to his closet ten, twenty times a day, like he thought the coat had just gone for a walk or something. So anyway, I brought it back. He came into the room while I was hanging it up." Crosley bent forward suddenly, then leaned back.

"You're lucky they didn't kick you out."

"I wish they had," he said. "The dean wanted to play Jesus. He got all choked up over the fact that I had brought it back." Crosley rubbed his arms. "Man, did I want that coat. It was ridiculous how much I wanted that coat. You know?" He looked right at me. "Do you know what I'm talking about?"

I nodded.

"Really?"

"Yes."

"Good." Crosley lay back against the pillow, then lifted his feet onto the bed. "Say," he said, "I think I figured out how come Garcia invited me."

"Yeah? How come?"

"He was mad at his stepmother, right? He wanted to punish her."

"So?"

"So I'm the punishment. He probably heard I was the biggest asshole in the school, and figured whoever came with me would have to be an asshole, too. That's my theory, anyway."

I started laughing. It hurt my stomach, but I couldn't stop. Crosley said, "Come on, man, don't make me laugh," then he started laughing and moaning at the same time.

We lay without talking for a time. Crosley said, "El Negro."

"Yeah."

"What are you going to do with your C-note?"

"I don't know. What are you going to do?"

"Buy a woman."

"Buy a woman?"

"I haven't gotten laid in a really long time. In fact," he said, "I've never gotten laid."

"Me either."

I thought about his words. *Buy a woman*. He could actually do it. I could do it myself. I didn't have to wait, I didn't have to burn like this for month after month until Jane decided she was ready to give me relief. Three months was a long time to wait. It was an unreasonable time to wait for anything if you had no good reason to wait, if you could just buy what you needed. And to think that you could buy this—buy a mouth for your mouth, and arms and legs to wrap you tight. I had never considered this before. I thought of the money in my book. I could almost feel it there. Pure possibility.

Jane would never know. It wouldn't hurt her at all, and in a certain way it might help, because it was going to be very awkward at first if neither of us had any experience. As a man, I should know what I was doing. It would be a lot better that way.

I told Crosley that I liked his idea. "The time has come to lose our innocence," I said.

"*Exactamente*," he said.

And so we sat up and took counsel, leaning toward each other from the beds, holding our swollen bellies, whispering back and forth about how this thing might be done, and where, and when.

"I have been wanting to write this story for several years. It wasn't so much the events themselves—which memory and invention have eclipsed anyway—that wanted to be recorded as it was a certain pitch of longing, appetite, that I remember from those years. I am not through with desire, but I can't imagine feeling it the way I did then, so piercingly and continuously. It was a harsh governor. And yet how can we be young without it, without wanting to devour the world whole?

"And I was drawn also to the sense of possibility that lies over my memory of that time. The sense that anything can happen, the corruption of love, the making of a friend, almost in the same

instant and from the same impulse, with lasting effects. This is not an innocent, carefree time: it is a thrillingly dangerous time in which the hungry soul is setting forth to find or lose its way."

Tobias Wolff grew up in Utah and Washington State, where his recent memoir, This Boy's Life, *is set. He is the author of two collections of short stories,* In the Garden of North American Martyrs *and* Back in the World, *and also of the short novel* The Barracks Thief, *which received the PEN/Faulkner Award for fiction in 1985. He is the editor of* Matters of Life and Death, *an anthology of contemporary short stories, and also recently edited a selection of Chekhov's stories entitled* A Doctor's Visit. *He lives in upstate New York and teaches at Syracuse University.*

Published in Esquire.

RICHARD CURREY

THE WARS OF HEAVEN

L isten. Hear me talking to you. Rockwell Lee Junior remembering the glow in your kitchen, Momma, the light
that was a mix of gold and blue on a winter's night and the
way our talk drifted around like big slow birds in the warm air
and Oh what I wouldn't give for one more day in the sweetness of
what I didn't know back when, the days before, when I was just
a grinning boy in a dirty white shirt, an innocent yes indeed. Or
the afternoons sitting at your kitchen table when you'd make
me a mug of your coffee, Momma, and sweeten it with clover
honey and color it with goat's milk. Always liked your coffee,
you know that I did, even when I was a kid I'd ask you for a
taste and you'd let me sip from your cup and Daddy grinning at
me from across the table. I remember the little circle of heat
that would come up from your cup, touch my lips, and what I
wouldn't have given for a cup of your coffee, trapped as I was
in that icehouse of a sky full of snow where any direction I
looked and as far as I could see it was white, whiteness in the
trees, humped up against the mountains, whiteness. At least
the wind had died down, that was the morning of St. Valentine's Day, at least I could say that because that's what kills
you, that's what steals the air out of your lungs, steals the light
straight out of your eyes, if anything can do that it's the wind in
winter across a field of snow bearing down on you like a ghost
train out of nowhere. Early that morning the wind passed off to
the north, I could nearly see it go, so God was merciful and I
thanked God for that. I dropped to my knees taking care to
keep my rifle butt-down and upright leaning against my left
shoulder, and I prayed. Thank you Jesus. No wind today. No
wind to freeze what life I got left, to steal the light out of my

93

eyes. Thank you Jesus. One more day of life. And Momma you might ask how it was the condemned man still prayed to his God in the wilderness, you'll say, What could I have to say to God and Jesus out there on the run. Where could I be going that was any salvation at all after what I done. Maybe this is all I really wanted, a chance at rectitude, restitution by myself and alone and in a place of my own choosing. A simple place where what dreams I might still have harbored could die a tranquil death, lonely as time itself and peaceful as light. And you know the Sheriff's posse caught up to me here at Judson Church so there may be a justice in this, an understanding. You know you always said that dreams were made of water and human desire, that dreams went no mortal place at all, they were only man's way to confuse himself and convince himself that a fire was lit at the heart of things. You always said it was nothing but cinder and ashes and now I don't know, the way I walked out there in that whole world of snow with that posse surely on my trail, I don't know, I swear I can't be sure. When I shot that girl you know I saw her fall down right there on her daddy's porch, fall down like a puppet whose strings got cut and I swear I saw the life drawing out of her like light coming out of a window at night. And I was not the man you knew. In that instant I was not the man you ever knew. I was that skeleton engineer on the phantom locomotive in that scare-story you told when I was a kid, I was just one headlong scream into oblivion, I swear. At the moment she fell down like an empty sack and I knew what I had done I was lost as I am right now up here in the hills in the snow. Now that it's all too late I think you were wrong, Momma, I think that there is a light down somewhere in the center of things and that if a man knew that for a solid fact he could go down to that place and warm his hands on a cold night. Because how could I be so desperate and finished and on the run and see everything so beautiful and transfixing and everlasting, everywhere I turned was like looking forever, like a picture up on somebody's wall so I had to stop and stand and look into the world for the first and last time, wondering why I never saw it before.

When I got to Judson Church there was enough wood to light a fire and I hung my coat and warmed myself over that stove

and thanked the Lord there was no moon that night, no moonlight to let any sheriff's posse see my smoke. No moonlight to
show my footprints walking across the snowfield and right up to
the church steps. I'd been on the move at night, hiding in
tumbledown houses all day with my rifle up and ready and
afraid to sleep, and I had my time to think, reflect on things,
see where it had all gone bad and Momma, you know I think it
was losing Daddy that did it to us, both of us. It was losing
Daddy that took the life out of you, took your own life away
from you, that made you so hard and tired and unforgiving. That
let your own bitterness rail against you inside like a snow-wind
of the very heart and soul I swear, that made you turn away in
your loss and violent mind. Momma, I think you died on that
old covered bridge with Daddy, I swear I think you did.
Daddy was the true anchor, he was the root our lives were
growing from when he died only we didn't know it, we were
innocents, the two of us. So you claim you know Daddy's
killer, that you'd know the face of the devil if you looked
straight into that face, and maybe so. But I don't know. All we
know is Daddy's body was found on that bridge with his watch
and money gone, that's all we really know, and it could have
been anybody, it could have been a neighbor or a stranger and
we'll never know and that's a fact.

So it's a terrible strange thing that I came to be the very one
that killed Daddy for a pittance in the cover of darkness. For
we are all of one bad wind, you know that Momma, all of us
robbers and murderers are one evil man split down into a
hundred wild boys, all doing the cruel bidding of some kind of
master within. I had heard that before and now I know it to be
true but I never once thought about it, what was happening to
me, I never once saw it all coming as I should. I could have
turned back a hundred times but I didn't, I was like a man on a
spooked horse, riding straight into the eyes of a fire and just
hanging on for dear life.

You could say it was friends or circumstance or some of both
but I can feel now it was simply Daddy going out the way he
did, lost the way he was in some terrible whirlpool of time and
I swear I was nothing but a useless boy hanging on a spike
thrown this way and that, born under a bad sign, condemned

to howl at the moon, to preach to the wind, and I drifted like a rotting boat cut loose on floodwaters after a hard rain, breathing from one tree to another until I was out in the main current and running. And that's the way it goes, out there in the deep water with some other power under you and driving you, keeping you whole until finally you hit the rapids and go over the falls.

That's how I come to be in on the robbery of Strother's Store over in the mining camp. There was the other boys wanted to do it, claimed old Strother kept a mint under the floor behind the cashbox and I said Well OK. When we got over there I felt no fear, I still cannot explain how I walked right up on the porch and butted my rifle right through the plate glass and opened the door and walked inside like it was my store and not Strother's, but let me tell you it inspired a measure of confidence in those boys that went inside behind me, yes indeed. And you know the strange thing is, I walked into that store holding my rifle up like I was looking to shoot something, walked in and straight back past them tables all laid up with can-goods and linens and bottled water, right back to the rear wall where Strother had all his bridles and reins hung up and I turned around to face front, leaned against the wall and just stood there. I didn't want a goddamned thing. I didn't care about money, or the things worth stealing in that store. I felt then as I did ever since. I felt mad with temper, and like I could just keep it under my skin if nobody pushed at me. And so goddamned afraid. Afraid of what I've never been truly sure, but I know if the Sheriff walked into the middle of that robbery or any other one and shot us all down I wouldn't have much cared, that's the kind of feeling I'm speaking of. And I felt that way until the day I hit Judson Church and looked back on what had gone before, and knew I had to wait in that little house of the Lord, wait there for my redemption in whatever form it was coming and at least I was in a sanctified place.

So I just stood there in Strother's Store while the boys whooped it up and made a mess of the place, and Bob Hanks come back to me, said Rocky what's the matter? And I said I'm just fine, Bob. You just go on and do what you came to do, that's all. And Bob looked at me strange a moment but went on back to work, and when the boys was still and quiet and standing in the doorway with their bags full up I walked over to where they stood and past them and out the door. I stepped down to the road and got in behind the wheel of your truck, Momma, started it up. The boys all filed down and got in, climbed onto the bed, and nobody said a word to me.

They had found old Strother's money pile and split it five ways. Three thousand dollars and change. Everything Strother had in the world and Bob Hanks come over to me with six one-hundred-dollar bills saying This here's your share Rock. And I said Thank you kindly and Bob drew on the whisky bottle he'd been carrying round and grinned at me. Well sir, he said, you're quite welcome.

And you know Momma it was all my plans after that, the branch bank over in Federalsville, the general store out to Middle River, right down to the night I shot Betty Shadwell dead on her daddy's front porch and knew I had become the man who speaks to you now in the sure voice of death, dead in the ice, you might even say in the frozen waste of time. Out here in the snow it is surely the end of the world. I could hear the sound of my breath setting up against the air like a rasp: the end of the world I swear.

Outside the church it was going to sunset, the day's light drawing down to that twilight filled with fire-color that burns on the snow before it proceeds to die right into the night. I stirred the wood on the grate and was thankful for that bit of stove-heat, wrapped my coat around me and tried to lay down on a pew and saw it wasn't going to work. So I went on and lay down on the floor up against the back wall of the church with a Philadelphia hymnal under my head and the Winchester right there in easy reach. But sleep wasn't about to come. No ma'am. I just lay there, listening to the mice scrap and itch around the floorboards, thieves like me, looking for what isn't there, for what will never be there and you know how your mind goes into a kind of trance when you're too tired to sleep, how you think crazy things, think the moon moves faster than it does? I lay there on the floor of Judson Church and lived in that half-a-dream, and I saw your face Momma, and I saw Daddy's, and I saw Rita Clair's face too, it was Rita as I saw her

the last time up on the hill over town, sitting on a blanket with
that man's workshirt on over nothing, her dress and underwear
laid to one side on the grass. We made love up there on that
hill, squatting down on that old blanket and moving together
and the bees moaning around us and crickets working, every
now and again a hot breeze come to rustle in our hair. I had
my hands up under that shirt, all over her like I wanted to be
more than just inside her, I wanted to melt into her. As if I
could just disappear and become part of that one moment,
forever, lost in it, outside of this voice that speaks to you now.
I raised my face to the sky and the sky was blue as I had never
seen and there were clouds as white and soft and eternal-
looking as you can imagine and I swear it was as if me and Rita
were being raised together into that sky, lifted up, me holding
Rita and her in my lap, the both of us panting and wheezing
and crying out. We went up in the air floating right out over
the brow of that hill, then we started to come down like we
were stones settling to the bottom of a slow river, coming down
through green light and silence, our ears filled up, our eyes
covered over and I thought then, That's right, we're just like
rocks thrown into a river. You don't know where you come
from or where you're gone, you just get picked up and thrown.
But you can have one little moment, yes sir, you can have Rita
Clair's sweet fine body on a hill in the middle of a hot summer
so as to have a glimpse of what might have been, like looking
through a little crack into the future or the past and not
knowing which way you're looking, but seeing it all filled up
with light and the smell of honey. I laid there, Momma,
remembering everything I tell you now, Daddy going the way
he did, you turning away from me in your grief, having that
little taste of Rita Clair, that little glimpse of heaven, and
knowing I wasn't fit to have no more than that, and the way I
went to stealing and could hate myself so bad and still be so
calm, standing at the window of the church and seeing the
Sheriff and his deputies out there at the treeline like I knew
they would be, just shapes out there in those long coats and big
hats and the straight black lines of their rifle barrels up against
the snow.

There was a thin light seeping into the church, that watery

first light you get on a winter dawn. I stood up and shook out of my coat and went to the window and there they were, standing out there looking at my trace across the snowfield, the way it ended right at the church steps.

I turned away from the window, sat down in a pew. They wouldn't just walk up to the door and knock. No sir. Not with a man like me inside. Sheriff'd try to get me to come out peaceable, lay down my gun, throw it out in the snow. But he'd be prepared to shoot me.

I got my rifle and went to the window on the other side of the church, unlocked it and slid it up. The stained-glass face of Jesus rose up in front of me and then I saw the snow stretching down to Rucker's Creek and I leaned out and propped my piece against the outside wall of the church, let myself out and down to the snow, waited. I heard nothing. I knew they wouldn't come across the pasture, not with the risk of me being inside the church. They'd be fanning out just inside the treeline, trying to surround me. I started for the trees thinking I could at least get into the woods myself. The snow was frozen over, a crust my boots dropped through an inch and I saw they'd track me anywhere I went but I had to go, there was nothing else to do. I was halfway to the treeline when I heard my name called out, hollow, booming around in the air. I turned and it was Stewart McCarty standing under the stained-glass window I'd left out of with his scattergun trained on me. *Mr. Lee*, he called out, *just stand where you are real still and put down your rifle*. I could see the smoke of his breath. I raised my Winchester and fired, hit Stewart somewhere above the waist and he grunted, slammed back against the church and slid a red streak down the wall, flopping around in the snow and I turned and ran for the trees.

I could hear the sound of the creek and a man I thought looked like Roy John stepped around in some birches up to my right, and then I knew it was him when he yelled to me, *Rockwell Lee, give yourself up now. No use in running no more.*

I turned to the direction of his voice. New snow started to fall. His shape moved back and forth in the trees. *Roy*, I called out. *Roy, help me. What happened, it was an accident.*

Roy John came into full view, aiming his rifle at me. I thought I saw movement behind him. Snow filled the air.

Roy, I said. *Roy, you know me. You know my momma.*

I know what you done, Rock. You're gonna have to come home with us.

The peculiar thing is that I had no intention of killing anyone at the Shadwell place, there or any other place, we just meant to get on out of there with the silver because Bob Hanks knew where the old man kept it in the house. If the old man hadn't come out of the house firing his pistol. I just meant to let go a warning shot, blow out a front window, I swear I didn't even see Betty there on the porch, what was she doing there anyway? You answer me that. I didn't even see her till she fell. Rockwell Lee Junior may have been a robber but he was no murderer. That was a pure accident. It was never meant to be. No sir. So when I lifted my rifle with the intent to throw it down and give myself up and tell my story, Roy John blew off my left shoulder.

The force of it shoved me back and I stumbled, and I had the strangest feeling of surprise but I stayed on my feet and kept hold of my gun. Blood and bone and muscle had sprayed out over the snow like a mist, I could look right down into the hole in my coat where my shoulder had been, an awful burning and the falling snow melting in the wound, steam wisping up out of the hole and my shoulder looking that way got me angry, mad with temper all over again and that terrible fear and I raised my Winchester over my head with my right arm yelling *Goddamn you, Roy, look what you done.*

The second shot was a shotgun, catching me square in the chest, I went off the ground, legs kicking and the force of that shot knocking my right boot off. Damn if I was going to let them take me laying on the ground, I got up again and don't you know I was an awful mess, I looked like the mouth of hell, blood everywhere and my coat hanging on me in rags.

I swayed there in the falling snow. My breath was hard to come by, I could hear air sucking right in through the holes in my chest and the whole lot of them come out of the trees then, the Sheriff, Roy John, the rest of the deputies just coming up around me and looking at me and I could see it was Stewart

McCarty who fired the shotgun round. He was back on his feet under that Jesus window and at first I thought I had been shot by a ghost but then I knew I had only wounded him. My eyesight began to go on me then, frayed around the edges in all that whiteness and air filled with snow like an old sheet hung out to dry and coming apart in a heavy wind. Roy John walked up to me and took off his long coat and put it around me. The Sheriff came up behind Roy to handcuff my wrists together and standing there half-dead for sure I heard the sound of bells, out in the distance of that snowy air, out in some reach of that wild snowy air there was the slow music of bells and I looked out to the hills and clouds trying to see where that music came from and why it was coming to me. Roy John looked at me and said *What is it, Rock?*

And I said *Roy, don't you hear 'em? Like church bells.* I raised the handcuffs, my hands clasped together in a fist pointed west and said *Out there.*

I turned back to Roy John and my knees went to plain water, I fell straight down in the snow on my knees, like a man about to pray, a man calling for mercy. And that is one thing I did not want to be, a man calling for mercy. I did not want to ask for anything, not food or water, no rest, not even for my own life, and I said *Roy, Help me up, now. Don't let me stay down here.* The Sheriff stood beside Roy, his shape as big as a tree, the two of them lifting me up, one on either side, and the Sheriff said *Let's go, Roy.* And they led me across that snow-covered meadow with the rest of the posse behind us, me with one boot gone and walking short-legged in a sock the same meadow I'd walked across the night before to get to Judson Church. The treeline moved up on us as if the trees were sailing in from a long way off and I could see the sleigh and the two roans snorting and blowing wet smoke in that air and I hope you're happy, Momma, because this is the first and last time you will ever hear this story, your only son shot at Rucker's Creek not five miles from his place of birth, his blood running over the ice like oil and into the water to cloud up colored like a rose and swirl away. I've always heard it said the wars of heaven are fought on righteous ground, Momma, and the godly man shall be the victor. So Roy John helped me up into that sleigh and threw a saddle blanket over me and I lay where I lay, an end to my so-called life of crime, nobody to know how lost I truly was, the man who built his own gallows in the snow, out behind the house of the Lord. I am the man who sought restitution by himself and alone in a place of his own choosing. I am the man who surrendered with one boot gone on St. Valentine's Day, the year of our Lord nineteen hundred and thirteen, with the smell of salt and woodsmoke and gunpowder in the air.

The last of this Lee family is gone now, Daddy crossed over, Rockwell Junior the robber and murderer shot down at Judson Church, and Momma you know you died with Daddy on that covered bridge and are as gone as me and him, yes you are, sad and gone, and we have suffered for what we didn't know back when and what we couldn't find, and for what we didn't even know we'd lost. And now we are gone, we are history. We are stories nobody tells, Momma, we have disappeared back down to the bottom of that river once and for all.

We are in the company of time. Ours is the testament of snow. We are alone together.

"As with many of my stories, I think of 'The Wars of Heaven' as a musical event, developing outward from impressionistic images and a few resonant phrases. The story rose in me slowly, the dream of a man who places himself in the world having dispensed with any hope of destiny. The narrative was born as I began to improvise inside the character of Rockwell Lee: his history, his predicament, his agony. I imagined him through the sound of his voice as he played out his hours in the snow, lyrical in his own devastation."

Born in West Virginia, Richard Currey has lived in New Mexico for nearly ten years. His short stories have appeared in The North American Review, *in the 1988* O. Henry Prize Stories *and in* The Best American Short Stories 1988. *His first novel,* Fatal Light, *was recently published.*

Published in High Plains Literary Review.

MARY GORDON

TEMPORARY SHELTER

He hated the way his mother piled the laundry. The way she held the clothes, as if it didn't matter. And he knew what she would say if he said anything, though he would never say it. But if he said, "Don't hold the clothes like that, it's ugly, how you hold them. See the arms of Dr. Meyers' shirt, they hang as if he had no arms, as if he'd lost them. And Maria's dress, you let it bunch like that, as if you never knew her." If he said a thing like that, which he would never do, she'd laugh and store it up to tell her friends. She'd say, "My son is crazy in love. With both of them. Even the stinking laundry he's in love with." And she would hit him on the side of the head, meaning to be kind, to joke, but she would do it wrong, the blow would be too hard. His ears would ring, and he would hate her.

Then he would hate himself, because she worked so hard, for him; he knew it was for him. Why did she make him feel so dreadful? He was thirteen, he was old enough to understand it all, where they had come from, who they were and why she did things. She wanted things for him. A good life, better than what she had. Better than Milwaukee, which they'd left for the shame of her being a woman that a man had left. It wasn't to be left by a man that she'd come to this country, that her parents brought her on the ship, just ten years old, in 1929, when they should have stayed home, if they'd had sense, that year that turned out to be so terrible for the Americans. For a few months, it was like a heaven, with her cousins in Chicago. Everybody saying: Don't worry, everyone needs shoes. Her father was a cobbler. But then the crash, and no one needed shoes, there were no jobs, her mother went out to do stran-

gers' laundry, and her father sat home, his head in his hands
before the picture of the Black Madonna and tried to imagine
some way they could go back home.

"And I was never beautiful," his mother said, and he believed that that was something he would have to make up to
her. Someday when he was a man. Yes, he would have to make
it up to her, and yet she said it proudly, as if it meant that
everything she'd got she had got straight. And he would have
to make it up to her because his father who'd lived off her
money and sat home on his behind had left them both without
a word. When he, Joseph, was six months old. And he would
have to make it up to her that she had come to work for Dr.
Meyers, really a Jew—once you were one you always were
one—though he said he was a Catholic, and the priests knelt at
his feet because he was so educated. And he would have to
make it up to her because he loved the Meyers, Doctor and
Maria. When he was with them, happiness fell on the three of
them like a white net of cloud and set them off apart from all
the others. Yes, someday he would have to make it up to her
because he loved the Meyers in the lightness of his heart,
while in his heart there was so often mockery and shame for his
mother.

He couldn't remember a time when he hadn't lived with the
Meyers in White Plains. His mother got the job when he was
two, answering an ad that Dr. Meyers had put in the *Irish
Echo*. No Irish had applied, so Dr. Meyers hired Joseph's
mother, Helen Kaszperkowski, because, he had explained with
dignity, it was important to him that the person who would be
caring for his daughter shared the Faith. Joseph was sure he
must have said "The Faith" in the way he always said it when
he talked about the Poles to Joseph and his mother. "I believe
they are, at present, martyrs to the Faith." He would speak of
Cardinal Mindszenty, imprisoned in his room, heroically defying Communism. But the way Dr. Meyers said, "The Faith"
made Joseph feel sorry for him. It was a clue, if anyone was
looking for clues, that he had not been born a Catholic, and all
those things that one breathed in at Catholic birth he'd had to
learn, as if he had been learning a new language.

But of course no one would have to search for clues, the

doctor never tried to hide that he was a Jew, or had been born a Jew, as he would say. He would tell the story of his conversion calmly, unfurling it like a bolt of cloth, evenly, allowing it to shine, allowing the onlooker to observe, without his saying anything, the pattern in the fabric. He had converted in the 1920s, when he had been studying art, in Italy, in a city called Siena. Joseph had looked up Siena in Dr. Meyers' atlas. He had been pleased when Dr. Meyers came into the library and found him there, rubbing his finger in a circle round the area that was Siena, touching the dark spot that marked it, as if he were a blind child. He was seven then, and Dr. Meyers took him on his lap. How comfortably he fit there, on Dr. Meyers' lean, dry lap, a lap of safety.

Not like his mother's lap, which he had to share with her stomach. Holding Joseph on his lap and not afraid to kiss a little boy the way all of Joseph's uncles were, Dr. Meyers showed him the pictures in the book of Cimabue and Simone Martini and explained to him the silence and the holiness, the grandeur and the secrecy. He used the pictures for his business now, his business in liturgical greeting cards, holy pictures, stationery. The business that had bought him this house and all these things. And Joseph understood why he had left his family (his family said he could never see them again) and all he had been born to. For the quiet sad-faced mothers and their dark commanding baby sons.

He understood it all; so did Maria. They had loved it all, the silence and the grandeur, since they had been small, before they went to school when Dr. Meyers took them with him to Daily Mass, the only children there, kneeling together, looking, very still as every other person rose and went up to Communion. They made up lives for all the people, and they talked about them even when they no longer went to Daily Mass; when they were older, in the parish school, they talked about those people. The woman who was always pregnant (they said expecting, thinking it more polite) and the crippled woman, and the Irish man who wore a cap, and the old, the very old Italian lady dressed entirely in black who sat at the very back of the church and said the Rosary out loud, in Italian, during the whole Mass, even during the silence of the Consecration. But

the person they thought of most and considered most theirs
was the very small woman who was extremely clean. They
imagined her in her small house alone (they were sure she
lived alone), brushing her hat, her black felt hat with the
feather band around it, brushing her purple coat with its velvet
collar and buttons of winking glass, polishing her old lady's
shoes till they looked beautiful. Then putting on her hat without looking in the mirror because if she did she would have to
see the horror that was her face. For on the side of her nose
grew a shiny hard-skinned fruit, larger than a walnut, but a
purple color. Joseph and Maria talked about it, never once
mentioning it to Dr. Meyers. They thought that the woman
must be a saint, because, despite the terrible cross God had
given her, her face was as sweet as an angel's.

Joseph thought that Maria, too, must be a saint because she
never lost her patience with his mother, although she lost
patience with everything else. His mother was terrible to Maria; every day of her life she was terrible. If he didn't know
how good a woman his mother was, and how much she loved
the Meyers and how grateful she was to them, he would think
she hated Maria. That was how she acted. It was mainly
because Maria was sloppy, she really was, his mother was
right, much as he loved her, much as he thought Maria was a
saint, he knew his mother was right. She left the caps off of pens
so that the pockets of her skirts turned black; she threw her
clothes around the room, she dropped her towels on the floor,
she scrunched up papers into a ball and threw them into the
wastebasket, and missed, and didn't bend to put them properly
into the bin; she made her bed with lumps, sometimes the
lumps were just the blankets or the sheets, sometimes they
were her socks or underwear or books she'd fallen asleep
reading. As if she didn't understand you made a bed for the
look of it, not just so that if someone (Joseph's mother) asked if
you had made your bed you would be free to answer yes.

He wondered what Maria thought about his mother. They
never spoke about her. No, once they had spoken about her,
and it would have been much better if they'd never had the
conversation. Once his mother had said such awful things,
called Maria a pig, a slut, a hussy, a disgrace, and she'd just

stood there, going white. Although she always had high color-
ing, this day she had gone dead white and made her body stiff
and clenched her fists beside her body as if she wanted, really
very badly wanted, to hit Joseph's mother and all her life was
put into her fists, keeping them clenched so they would not.
She had excused herself and left the room, walking slowly as
though she had to show them, Joseph and his mother, that she
didn't need to run. And Joseph for once had shouted at his
mother, "Why are you so horrible to her?" And his mother had
shouted, opened her lips, showed her strong yellow teeth; her
tongue spat out the words, "How dare you take her part against
me. The filthy, filthy pig. They're all alike. Fine ladies, with
someone like me to clean up their shit. And you too, don't
forget it. You're not one of them, you're *my* flesh and blood,
whether you like it or you don't. They'll leave you in the end,
don't you forget it. In the end I'll be the only thing you have."

She couldn't be right, the Meyers would not leave him. So
he left his mother sobbing in the kitchen and went upstairs to
where he knew Maria would be sitting, still and white as if she
had shed blood. He knocked on her door and then walked in.
He saw her sitting as he knew she would be, and he sat down
beside her on her bed.

"I'm sorry she's so mean. You should do something. You
should tell your father."

"No," she said. "If I say something, he might say something
to her, and she might want to leave, or he might make her
leave, and you'd leave too."

He should not have come into her room; he wished he
hadn't heard it. And wished later that he hadn't heard, been
made to hear, the conversation at the table, Dr. Meyers talking
to them both, Maria and his mother, calmly, saying that he
understood both sides and that they must be patient with each
other. Our Lord had loved both sisters, Martha and her sister
Mary, there was room for all beneath the sight of God.

What he said made nothing better. His mother said she just
did it for the girl's own good, these things were important in a
woman's life, she, Helen Kaszperkowski, knew that. And then
Maria said she would try to be better at these things. And Dr.
Meyers lifted up his knife and fork and said, "Good, good."

And Joseph knew he had no home, there was no place that was his really, as Maria's place was with her father. He was here or he was there, but it was possible, although he felt himself much happier beside the Meyers, that his mother had been right and it was beside her that he must find his place, must live.

But what was it, that happiness he felt beside the Meyers if it was not where he belonged? He thought about the things the three of them did together. The train into the city and the dressing up, the destination always one of those high, gray-stoned buildings with the ceiling beautiful enough to live on, carved or vaulted, and the always insufficient lights. The joy those buildings gave him, the dry impersonal air, the rich, hard-won minerals: the marble and the gold, where no wet breath—of doubt, of argument or of remorse—could settle or leave trace. And how the voice of Dr. Meyers came into its own; the thick dental consonants, the vowels overlong and arched, belonged there. Everybody else's speech offended in those rooms, seemed cut off, rushed, ungiving and unloved. But Dr. Meyers' voice as he described a painting or a pillar wrapped around whatever he called beautiful and made it comfortable and no longer strange. It belonged then, to Joseph and Maria; Dr. Meyers had surrounded it with their shared history and let its image float in slowly, like a large ship making its way to harbor, safely to its place inside their lives.

And then there were the treats, the lunches at the automat, the brown pots of baked beans or macaroni, the desserts at Rumpelmayers and the silly games, the game they played with cream puffs. "It is important," Dr. Meyers would say in Rumpelmayers, in the room that looked just like a doll's house, pink and white and ribboned like a doll, "it is important," he would say, making his face look pretend-serious, "to know exactly how to eat a cream puff. When I was in Paris, very great ladies would say to me, *"C'est de la plus grande importance savoir manger une creampuff comme il faut."* He would keep on his pretend-serious face and cut into one cream puff deliberately, carving up pieces with the right mix of pastry and cream, then popping them into his mouth like Charlie Chaplin.

"But, my children," he would say, "it takes a lot of practice. You must eat many cream puffs before you can truly say you know how to eat them *comme il faut*."

Then he would order one cream puff for each of them and say, "That's good, you're getting the idea, but I don't think it's quite yet *comme il faut*." So, with a pretend-serious face he would order another for them, and then another, then when he could see them stuffed with richness and with pleasure at the joke he would say, "Ah, I think you're getting there. You are learning the fine art of eating cream puffs *comme il faut*."

Then they would go to the afternoon movies, the Three Stooges, Laurel and Hardy, movie after funny movie, and Dr. Meyers laughed the hardest, laughed till he coughed and they hit him on the back, then laughed at how hard they were hitting him. And then they would walk outside. Outside, where, while they had pleased themselves in warmth and darkness, the sky had grown somber. And quickly, sharply, they left behind the silly men who fought and shouted just to make them laugh. They'd wend their way through the commuters to St. Patrick's for the five-thirty, the workers' Mass. And pray, amidst the people coming from their offices in suits, the women, some in hats, some taking kerchiefs from their handbags, all of them kneeling underneath the high dark ceiling where the birettas of dead cardinals hung rotting; always they chose a pew beside the statue of Pope Pius, waxy white, as if he were already dead. Then, blurred by the sacraments and silenced, they walked to Grand Central, boarded the train, too hot or too cold, always, and looked out the windows, pressed their cheeks against the glass and played "I Spy."

And at home Joseph's mother waited, served them dinner when they arrived, served them in anger for she knew they had left her out. Once they invited her to come with them to the Metropolitan Museum. Dr. Meyers showed her the Ming vases and her only comment was "I'd hate to have to dust all those," and Dr. Meyers laughed and said it was extraordinary how one never thought of all the maintenance these treasures took, and then his mother smiled, as if she had said the right thing. But he could see Maria look away, pretending not to be there for his sake, and his heart burned up with shame, and he was glad that Dr. Meyers never asked his mother to come along again, and he knew it was one more thing he would have to make up to her when he was grown up and a man.

What was Maria thinking when she pretended not to look and not to be there? Sometimes he couldn't keep the thought away, the thought that those two hated each other. It must not be true. His mother said she was doing things for Maria's own good, and Maria never said a thing about his mother. But could they both be lying to him? No, not lying, but the sin, as Father Riordan called it, of concealing truth. A venial sin, but did they live it? It was more likely that his mother lived in sin, in venial sin of course. God forbid that she would live in mortal sin. But was her unkindness venial sin? And the way she found wrong everything about Maria? Why did she hate Maria's hair?

As far as he could see and understand there could be nothing in Maria's thick black hair to hate. His mother acted as if Maria's hair were there to balk, to anguish, to torment her. "Nobody thinks of me," she would say after she had begun, "and that disgusting hair. Nobody thinks of what it means for me, that hair all over the place. In the shower, in those brushes. Think of it, she never cleans them out. I tell her and I tell her, and she leaves it in there, that disgusting hair until I don't know what use it is to her, a brush in that condition, and I clean it out myself. Because he likes things right, likes her to have things right, although he don't mind if somebody else does it for her. To tell the truth, that's the way he likes it best, some fat Polack cleaning up after the princess."

How could she stay with them, the Meyers, hating them so? She did it for him, so he could grow up here, in this house, with these "advantages." The large house with its high walls full of pictures. Scenes of European streets and buildings. Drawings by people hundreds of years dead. Velasquez. Goya. The house with its green lawn and dark enshadowed garden and its vivid shocks: the day lilies, orange-yellow; purple lupins; columbines with veins like blood. And the things that Dr. Meyers taught that she knew she could not teach her son: poetry and how to use a fork, the names of emperors and which tie went with which suit, and all the lessons. All the lessons that Maria got, Joseph got too: piano, French, and in the summer, tennis. "The teacher comes for one, he comes for two," said Dr. Meyers shrugging. "'Still he has to come." He said it as if it were a joke, the statement final and yet supplicating, and the lifted shoulders. Joseph knew, though no one had told him, that Dr. Meyers learned this kind of sentence, how to say it, from his grandfather the rabbi. Joseph heard the words like that, the tone of them when he and Maria sneaked into the synagogue for Yom Kippur.

It was something Maria had wanted badly. She was not like him. When something rose up before her eyes as if it were a figure on a road she was approaching, she would run to it the way she always ran, headlong and holding nothing back, the way she ran in games, and in the garden on a summer night, just for the pleasure. How beautiful she looked then after running, her hair falling out of her barrette, the sweat that beaded in the cleft above her lip like seed pearls, her white cheeks flushed as if a wing had touched them, a wing dipped in roses. Or in blood. No one could beat her when she ran; it was one reason why the other children in the neighborhood didn't want to play with her. She had to win, and she held nothing back. It didn't bother Joseph; he was glad to let her win. He understood her rages when she lost; the things she said were horrible; sometimes she hit him hard, wanting to hurt. He knew just what she felt. She felt that it was meant for her to win, so when she lost it was as if some plan had been spoiled or some promise broken. And then she was so sorry afterwards, she came to him with such important gifts, wonderful gifts, thought up in heaven. Sometimes they were too good; what she had done was not so bad that she should give them. Like the time she went into her savings to buy him a fountain pen just like her father's, from the jewelry store in town. Because when he had beaten her in tennis she'd hit him on the back so hard he'd fallen over, and his teeth had bitten through his lip. "It's too much," he said, though she knew how he loved it: the black shiny bottom and the silver top. "Real silver," she said, "here, look at the mark." And then they both got scared. "Don't use it where anyone can see it. Not your mother and not anyone at school. The nuns will ask you where you got it. Keep it someplace secret." And he had, for he was good at that, was

best at keeping secrets. No one had ever found the pen. Or
found the thing she had no right to give him: the gold necklace
with the Jewish star that was her mother's mother's.

Maria's mother had been Jewish too, but renounced it to
marry Dr. Meyers. She'd died soon after Maria was born,
puerperal fever, it was called; Joseph imagined she had turned
completely purple. He and Maria often looked at her pictures.
It was the only thing he envied that she had: pictures of the
absent parent. He had no pictures of his father; his mother
talked with happiness about the day she burnt them up. "I
held a match to them and—pfft—good-bye." One day Maria
said, "Maybe one of my mother's sisters had a baby in Milwaukee on the day that you were born. Then the hospital had a
mixup, you know you hear of these things all the time. And
that baby was you, and the baby that your mother had is living
now with my aunt." She spat on the floor. "It serves them
right." She'd never seen her aunt, her mother's favorite sister,
who had told Maria's mother that she had no sister, her sister
was dead.

Joseph had been frightened when she'd made that story up,
frightened that she really believed it. Frightened too, because
he wanted to believe it. And knew what that meant: he wished
his mother not his mother. And he wanted to run downstairs,
run down to his mother, ask was there something he could do
to help her, sit beside her, tell her about school, remind her
Dr. Meyers said he had the seeing eye, the clever hand, that
Dr. Meyers said he was training him to take over the business
one day, so the Lord would be honored with things of beauty.
See, Mother, Joseph wanted to say, I have the seeing eye, the
clever hand. You will never have to worry about money. I will
take care of you, and everything you suffer now I will make up
to you when I become a man.

But he did not do that; he sat instead beside Maria, looking
at the photographs, thinking about the dark, sad-faced woman
who had never held her child, who left her brothers and her
sisters and her parents to marry Dr. Meyers. His people, too,
had refused to speak to him, but he could bear it, Dr. Meyers
could, you could see it in his eyes that could go cold. Maria's,
too, could do that. She didn't have her mother's eyes, light

brown as if they had once been Maria's blazing color, but she had wept so for her family that they had faded.

It was after Maria had given Joseph her grandmother's necklace that she got the idea: they must go into the synagogue. He could imagine how she'd thought it up, alone, at night in bed, her eyes wide open in the dark, awake and lying on her back in the first cold of autumn. It must have been then she decided that she would ask Moe Brown. Moe Brown who owned the candy store and loved her. He always gave her an extra soda free, and he gave one to Joseph too. She'd told Moe both her parents had been born Jewish. "But they gave it up," she said, as if it were a car they had got tired of. It frightened Joseph to hear her say it like that, so lightly, when it was the most important thing Dr. Meyers had ever done, had won for himself the salvation of his soul, the fellowship of Christ, a place in heaven.

But she had been right to talk about it that light way. It made Moe feel that he could talk about it, it was not so terrible. "The way I figure, honey," Moe said, "is live and let live. But personally I don't get it. Once a Jew always a Jew. Ask the late Mr. Hitler."

"Oh, if the Germans won the war, my father and I would have been sent to concentration camps. We would have died together," Maria said, her eyes getting tearful. Which was the kind of thing that made Moe love her. And made Joseph feel if that had happened, he would go with them, Maria and her father, and would die with them, suffer their same fate. But what would happen to his mother?

Moe had no idea that when Maria asked him all those things about the temple and the services she was planning to sneak in. Joseph had no idea himself, and when she told him, he was shocked. Didn't she know that Catholics were forbidden to attend the services of other faiths? And they would be sure to be found out. Moe said that there were people in the back collecting tickets.

"Listen, dodo," she said, "we'll wait till it's started. Way started. Then we'll sneak up to that balcony Moe said there was. With the people that have no tickets. Everyone'll be paying attention to the service. It's a very sad day. The day of atonement."

"But we won't know what to wear or what to do. I don't have one of those little hats."

"A yarmulke," she said, casually, as if she'd used the word every day of her life. "It's a reform temple. You don't need one."

"It's a terrible idea," he said, stamping his foot and feeling close to tears, because he knew he couldn't stop her.

"All right, don't go. I'll go myself. It's not your heritage anyway."

He couldn't let her go. To let her go meant he was not a part of her, her life, her past, her family. And then suppose she got in trouble. He could not leave her alone.

The plan worked perfectly. They waited ten minutes after the last person had gone into the temple. Carefully, they opened up the heavy door and saw the staircase to the balcony, just as Moe had described it. No one saw them climb the stairs or sit in the last seat in the back. How happy she seemed then, her face filmed with the lightest sweat, the down above her lips just moistened, her eyes shining with the look he knew so well: her look of triumph. They watched below. The man who sang, whom Moe had called the cantor, had the most beautiful voice Joseph had ever heard. The cantor's voice made him forget Maria. He rode the music, let it carry him. The sadness and the loneliness, the darkness and the hope. The winding music, thick and secret. Like the secrets of his heart. The secrets he had had to keep from everyone, that he would have to keep forever. When he felt Maria pulling at his arm, he realized that for the first time in his life when he was with her he had forgotten she was there.

"Let's go," she whispered silently.

"Why?" he mouthed at her. He didn't want to go.

"I hate this. I'm leaving."

He knew he must leave with her. It was the reason he was here, to be with her, and to protect her if danger came. He couldn't leave her now, and she had broken it, the ladder of the music. He had lost his footing; now he must drop down.

When they got outside, she ran away from him. He ran

after, knowing he couldn't catch her, waiting for her to be out of breath. When he caught up to her, he saw that she was crying.

"I hated it. It was so dark and ugly. It was disgusting. Let's not talk about it ever again. Let's just forget we ever did it."

"Okay," he said. He let her run home by herself.

But he did not forget it, the dark secret music, like the secrets of his heart. The music that traveled to a God who listened, distant and invisible, and heard the sins of men and their atonement in the darkness and in darkness would forgive or not forgive. But would give back to men the music they sent up, a thick braid of justice and kept promises and somber hope.

He knew she didn't like it because it was nothing like the music that she loved, the nun's high voices that had changed her life, that made her know that she would never marry but would join them, singing in the convent, lifting up to God those voices which, except for these times, were silent the whole day. That day in the convent she was far away from him, and knew it, and looked down at him from the lit mountain on whose top she stood, and kept him from the women's voices, rising by themselves into the air, so weightless, neither hopeful nor unhopeful, neither sorrowing nor free from sorrow, only rising, rising without effort above everything that made up life. You never saw the faces of the women who made these sounds that rose up, hovered high above their heads and disappeared. You saw only the light that struck the floor, shot through the blue glass and the red glass of the windows, slowed down, thickened, landing finally as oblong jewels on the wooden floor. He saw Maria rise up on the breaths of the faceless nuns, rise up and leave him, leave the body that ran and knocked down, that lay on the grass. The body she loved that did always what she told it, that could dance and climb or run behind him and put cool hands over his eyes and say "Guess who?" as if it could be someone different. But in the chapel she rose up and wanted to leave the body life that she had loved. Leave him and all their life together. The men singing in the temple did not want to rise up and leave. And that was why he liked them better. And why she did not.

They heard the nuns' music the day Sister Lucy was professed. Sister Lucy who had been Louise La Marr and who had worked for Dr. Meyers. For five years she had been his secretary. "She was, of course, much more than a secretary. I deferred to her in so many questions of taste," Dr. Meyers had said. Neither Joseph nor Maria remembered her very well; they had been seven when she entered Carmel, and she'd not made much of an impression. "God, when I think she was right there, right in my father's office, and I didn't talk to her. I didn't pay attention to her. But that's the way it is with saints, from what I've read," Maria said.

Maria had begun reading all the books she could get about cloistered nuns. She would come to Joseph, holding in her hands the story of a Mexican woman, who had seen the Virgin Mary, a French woman a hundred years dead, a Spanish woman whose father had been a count, and say, "Listen to this. Do you think it sounds like me?" Of course it would sound nothing like her, but he saw how much she wanted it and he'd say, "I think so. Yes. The part when she was young, our age, sounds like you."

Then she would slap the book against the outside of her thigh, the front, the back, twisting her wrist. Then she would lie down on his bed or on the floor and put her hands behind her head and look up dreamily toward the ceiling. "I know they'll let me write to you in Carmel," she would say, "so don't worry. We'll always be best friends. Even though we'll never see each other again. Except through the grille. The last time we'll see each other without the grille will be the day of my profession." Then she would rise away from him, rise up into that world that was the breath of all those women, whose faces were never seen by men.

It was the end of everything, he understood now, her idea to join the convent. It was the first thing of hers he couldn't be a part of, the first thing that she kept back. He'd always known that there were things she hadn't told him before, things she thought about his mother, for example. But he had understood that. Always before, when they were together something pushed forward, pushed against him. She was always running toward him, running away from something else, something she didn't like, or was afraid of, or was bored by, or despised. And then, whatever she ran from became theirs: they opened it, like a surprise lunch, devoured it, took it in. Nothing was wasted; nothing could not be used. With her the hurts, the slights, the mockery of boys who found his life ridiculous, his mother's mistakes and tricks and hatreds, his sense that he was in the eyes of God unworthy, and in the eyes of man a million times inferior to the Meyers, all meant nothing when he was with Maria. Over all that she threw the rich cloak of her fantasy and all her body life.

Now she was taking back the cloak. Bit by bit she pulled it, leaving naked the poor flesh of all his doubts and failures and his fears. She began spending hours with Sister Berchmans, who had terrified them both. But now Maria said that Sister Berchmans was her spiritual adviser and a saint. Maria said that Sister had confided to her that she knew she frightened the children, but it was because she felt she must be distant to avoid establishing particular affections for her students, which would get in the way of her life with God. Maria said she wouldn't be surprised if Sister Berchmans entered Carmel, although it was nothing the nun had said, it was an idea that Maria had picked up "from certain hints which I'm not free to tell you."

For the first time, he disliked Maria, when she made her lips small and her eyes downcast and spoke of Sister Berchmans and the letters Sister Lucy had sent her "which I don't feel free to show." To punish her, he became friends with Ronald Smalley, who collected rocks and vied with Joseph for the eighth-grade mathematics prize. When he came home one day, holding a crystal of rose quartz, she mooned around him asking what he did at Ronald's house. "Nothing," he said, to taunt her.

"You're disgusting," she said, stamping her foot. "You don't even care that I had a completely disgusting time here all alone on this rotten Sunday while you were off with your stupid friend and his disgusting rocks."

But to please her he gave up Ronald. And she was pleased, and he was pleased to know that he had pleased her. For she had no friends; she could not keep a friend. When she tried to make a friend, the friendship ended sharply, and with grief.

For no one but he understood her, he felt, and for the gift of her was willing to put up with her tempers and her scenes. For he knew that to keep them together she kept silent about his mother, kept silent so he would not be sent away. So she was his. His and her father's. And now Sister Berchamans', who must keep herself for God.

But he suspected it was Sister Berchmans at the back of everything. Her white face looking out at him from her white coif. What did she see when she looked at him? And what had she told Dr. Meyers? Or did she never dare to speak to Dr. Meyers; had she spoken only in confession to Father Cunningham, who did the nun's bidding like a boy?

Joseph knew it was her fault. Because Maria told her things, and she had got things wrong. He knew the nun had spoken in confession, and then Father Cunningham had come to Dr. Meyers, and now everything was gone. He looked up at his mother, now, holding the Meyers' laundry.

"Look, it's not the end of the world. For me, it's a good thing. Listen, Butch, for both of us. A house to call our own. With my name on the deed. No one else's, only mine. And yours, someday, if you don't leave your mother in the lurch."

They were sending him away, though they were keeping on his mother. Every day his mother could come back here to their home, the white house with the green shutters, the green-striped awning in the summer and the screened-in porch that in the winter turned into a house of glass. But how could he come back? He would have no part in the house now. What had been his room would become—what? What did they need a new room for, what could they do with his when they already had so many? The library and Dr. Meyers' study, Maria's room, the playroom (now their toys were gone and workmen years ago set up a Ping-Pong table there), his mother's laundry room, her sitting room (though never once in all the years had she had a guest). Would the Meyers move from the house themselves? Would they buy some place smaller, thinking to themselves, Now Joseph and his mother are not here the house is wrong for us? No, they would never leave the library with its bookshelves specially made, the deep shadowy garden with its day lilies and columbines, the willow that grew roots into the plumbing, which Maria made her father promise never to cut down. No, they would never leave the house. It was their home.

But he had thought it was his home. What would he be allowed to take from this house with him? They had come, his mother often told him (he could not remember coming here) with nothing. And where had all the things he had lived with come from? The dresser and the bed, the Fra Angelico Madonna, the picture of the squirrel by Dürer and the horse by Stubbs, the paperweight that dropped white snow on the standing boy? He asked his mother which of all these things were theirs.

"You've got a head on your shoulders, I'll tell you that," she said. "It's good stuff, the stuff in your room. I've got an eye for things like that, and I can tell you. Ask him, when he takes you on this little trip to tell you with the priest. Ask him if you can take the stuff in your room. But don't tell him that I told you first."

Dr. Meyers had arranged for Joseph and himself to go on a weekend retreat with the Passionists in Springfield, Massachusetts. He had told Joseph's mother he would tell Joseph about his decision, his decision that they would have to leave the house. But he had asked Joseph's mother to keep quiet, to let him tell Joseph himself. But she had not kept quiet. She had told him: They are sending you away.

"I guess they want to get rid of you before the two of you get any bright ideas. Of course, she'd be the one to think it up, but you'd be the one to get the blame."

His mother was right: Maria was the one with bright ideas, ideas that rose up, silver in a dark sky, shimmered and then flew.

"It's like he just noticed what you've got between your legs. Like he just figured out she don't have the same thing between hers. Or maybe he needed the priest to tell him."

Put the clothes down, Mother, he wanted to say. You have no right to touch them. You are filthy, with your red hair that you dye one Sunday night a month, with your fat body and your ugly clothes, your red hands and your yellow teeth. And with your filthy heart. The thing he had between his legs, his shame, that did things he could not help, that left the evidence of all he wished he could not be, the body life that he, because he was her son, was doomed to. And his mother knew, she found the evidence, the sheets, showing the thing he could not help, there in the morning. It all happened while he slept, and not his fault, even the priest said not his fault. But still it happened, all because he was her son. And now they knew, and they were sending him away. Because they did not want him in the house now with Maria. But Maria had nothing to do with all that. She hovered above it, like a nun, a saint. He prayed that they would never tell her, she would never know the things they knew about him. Perhaps if he left and said nothing they would not tell.

"I guess you're okay to be her playmate, but God forbid anything else. And for a husband, let's face it, he's got something better in mind than some dumb Polack whose mother washed his shitty underwear for ten years straight."

Why wouldn't she stop talking? He wanted something terrible to happen. She wouldn't be quiet till he said something to make her.

"Maria doesn't want to get married," he said, quietly so she would not know how he hated her and how he dreaded living with her by themselves in some house that belonged to her alone. "She's going to be a nun."

Joseph's mother snorted. Her lips lifted and she showed her yellow teeth. He thought of Maria's mother in the photograph, her sad face frowning, looked at his mother, snorting, throwing laundry into the machine and wondered how it was that he could be her son.

"Wise up, buddy. There's no convent in the world that would take that one."

He was almost as tall as his mother. She could say anything about him, terrible things, he wouldn't answer back. But she could not say things about Maria.

"Sister Berchmans said they'd take her when she finished school."

"The nun tell you that?"

"No, but I know it's true."

"Yeah, and you can buy the Brooklyn Bridge for fifteen bucks. Listen, nobody tells you this, or tells them it, because they're too polite. But they don't take Jews in the convent. And she'll always be a Jew."

"You made that up. Who told you that?" he said. Now he was shouting at his mother. Now he clenched his fists. It was the first time in his life that he had clenched his fists at her. And it just made her laugh.

"Just look at them, those nuns. Just look at all their faces. Ever see a face like her? Just think about it. She'll find out and get her heart broken to boot, but it'll be too late. All his money won't be able to buy her way in. Cause they don't let them in."

She poked her finger at his chest. *They. Don't. Let. Them. In.* Each word the blow she wanted it to be. Could she be right? They wouldn't be so terrible. Was it the word of God? The God who sent unbaptized babies down to limbo? Who would separate a mother and a child because no water had been poured? He mustn't think about it. It was the sacrament of baptism he thought of. The indelible, fixed sign.

Was there a sign on them because their blood was Jewish? No, it couldn't be. He would find out from Dr. Meyers. He would ask him a clever way. This weekend at the monastery, when they were alone.

He packed his suitcase for himself. Pajamas, underwear, a shirt, his slippers. Then he packed an extra pair of pajamas. In case it happened. That thing in the night.

Maria was angry when they left. She dreaded being home for a whole weekend with Joseph's mother. But where could she go? She had no friends. She couldn't go to Sister Berchmans. For a moment Joseph was glad, then he hated the thought of her alone with his mother. He was glad when Dr. Meyers left her money for the movies and suggested she go to the library. She brightened at the thought of that. Then she would go to Moe's, she said, "And get a double black-and-white and think of you two fasting."

Her father pretended to slap her, then kissed her on both cheeks.

"What will become of you? I ask myself. I suppose you will have to live with your father forever."

Maria smiled her pious smile and looked at Joseph, as if they two knew the truth. But Joseph looked away. Over Maria's shoulder he could see his mother.

They drove four hours to the monastery, speaking easily of things, of school and politics, of Dr. Meyers' days in Europe, of his promise one day to show Joseph Chartres.

"One day you may decide that you would like to go away to school. Remember, you have only to ask. I know what it's like to be a young boy. You can always come to me, you know, with any problem."

No I cannot, he thought, you are sending me away. The home you call yours I called mine. And now I have no home.

"Thank you," he said, and looked out the window where the rain was turning the gray pavement black.

A lay brother named Brother Gerald showed them to their room. Two iron beds and on the green walls nothing but a crucifix.

"Well, no distractions. That can certainly be said. Better a bare room than an excrescent display of Hallmark piety," said Dr. Meyers, flipping the gold clips of his suitcase. He hung up his shirts and put his shaving kit out on the bed. "And now to supper, whatever that will be. Certainly not as good as what your mother cooks."

Why had his mother told him? Every second now, he had to wait for Dr. Meyers' words. Each bite of food might bring those words closer, every step around the grounds. Each time Dr. Meyers laid a hand on Joseph's shoulder, he was sure it was the time. But Saturday went by, the early Mass, the Rosary, Confessions, Vespers, dinnertime. And when it was his turn to speak to the retreat master, Joseph sat dumbly, listening to Father Mulvahy talk about bad companions and the dangers of the flesh. He knew what dangers of the flesh were. They could make you lose your home. He thought about the garden, deep in shadow. He thought about Maria and his mother's words. Perhaps he should ask Father Mulvahy if she'd told the truth. But he did not know how.

"Joseph, I have something difficult to tell you," Dr. Meyers said, Sunday after Mass, when Joseph thought the time was wrong. Fresh from Communion, polished by the glow of silence, of the Sacrament, they walked to the refectory alone.

"In some ways, Joseph, you are like my son. I've always loved you as a son. And because I love you as a son, I fear for the salvation of your soul. I pray for it, I pray for it every morning, as I do for my own daughter's."

Dr. Meyers kept his hand on Joseph's shoulder. Their feet made ugly sounds in the wet grass. He thought of Maria, of the gift of her ideas and words. He thought of the gold star, the secret gift nobody knew she gave him. Was his living in the house a danger to their souls? It could not be. Dr. Meyers must have got it wrong.

"Your nature, Joseph, is not passionate, like my Maria's. Nevertheless, you are a young man now. And to put difficulties in a young man's path is a cruelty I hope I would not be guilty of."

You are guilty of the cruelty of sending me away. Of separating me from everything I love. Of sending me to live alone, in ugliness and hatred with the mother whom I cannot love.

Joseph nodded soberly when Dr. Meyers said, "I thought it best," and ended with the news of his gift to Joseph and his mother of the house.

"But you must never be a stranger, Joseph. You are like our family. Our home is yours."

But you have sent me from your home, my home. I have no home. There is no place for me.

"Thank you, sir," he said.

"You're a good boy, Joseph," said Dr. Meyers squeezing his shoulders. "For you I have no fears. But what will happen to Maria?"

He felt his spine light up, as if a match had been struck at the base. A hot wire went up into his skull, and then back down his spine.

"I think she'll become a nun," said Joseph, looking daringly at Dr. Meyers.

Sadly, Dr. Meyers shook his head. "Think of how she is. There is no convent that would have her."

Joseph felt his throat go hot like melting glass. It could not be that what his mother said was right. It could not be that

they knew the same thing, his mother and Dr. Meyers, knew
this thing he and Maria did not know.

Why did they know and never tell their children? They were
cruel the both of them. The cruelty he thought was just his
mother's, Dr. Meyers shared. He might have thought that he
kept silent out of kindness, but it was not kindness. It was fear.

But Joseph knew what he would do. He would get Dr.
Meyers to send him away to school. He would not see Maria.
He would write to her. And his letters would make her think of
him in the right way. Make her think of him so she would love
him, want to live with him, the body life, and not the life that
rose up past the body, not the life of Sister Berchmans and the
white-faced nuns. He would make her feel that only with him
could her life be happy. He would make her want to marry him
before they went to college. He would do that so that she
would never know that they would never let her have it. He
would marry her before she could find out that because of her
blood they would keep back from her her heart's desire.

"I would like to go away to school," he said to Dr. Meyers.

"Of course, Joseph," Dr. Meyers said. "We can arrange
anything you want."

"A writer may favor one of her works for reasons that are not
entirely trustworthy. A finished work lives for a writer largely
in memory; most of us dislike rereading what we have already
published. Flannery O'Connor compared the experience with
'chewing on the carpet.' Too many things that we could have
done better jump out at us, like disappointed or rejected lovers
who would have made us happier keeping themselves from
view.

"Part of the memory of a work includes the process of its
composition. One loves something, then, because of the ease of
its birth: the rush and thunder of a rapid labor. Or one can
love it because of the final victory over the intransigent mass,
the remembrance of the phrase worked over and over until

finally, it yielded its meaning, finally the words fell next to one another sleeping peacefully like biddable good children in each other's exhausted and formerly refusing arms. Sometimes, though, one does reread and realize that something happened that one is glad of. One is tempted to say: 'That's pretty good, I wonder who wrote that?' For the reader reading is never the writer writing. One always comes to one's own work a stranger.

"My fondness for 'Temporary Shelter' is a fondness both for the memory of its creation and for what I believe I was, in some places, able to effect. The first two thirds of the story took me several months. I wrote the last third in a hotel room after a lunch with my dearest friend. At eleven o'clock that night, I looked up, finished, turned to the newspaper and discovered I could catch a twelve o'clock showing of Jules et Jim. I am proud of the story's evocation of atmosphere: the Meyers' house, the physical life of Maria, the experience in the synagogue and the cathedral. Joseph is a character who touches my heart. He is of that most vulnerable of species: the adolescent male. His collision with the heedless and lovable Maria continues to interest me so that after three years, rereading it, I am spared some of the usual horrors."

Mary Gordon's short stories have been collected in Temporary Shelter. *She is the author of three novels:* Final Payments, The Company of Women *and* Men and Angels. *She lives in upstate New York with her husband two children.*

Published in the author's collection, Temporary Shelter.

MAX APPLE

RESEARCH

In that crazy spring when the Dow broke 1800, the physics group was fully invested. It was a good time to be in Los Alamos. Henry Wu had called everyone together in November and predicted the coming bull market. He said he was not interested in averages—they were only a sidebar to his comprehensive theory of exchange.

In November not everyone believed Henry Wu, but by January we were convinced. The physics group forgot that Wu was just a computer operator who worked for Lazlo. Everyone put his savings and his grant money into the market. Every time the Dow spiked, the noise from the conference room sounded like a football cheering section. Wu had wired the Cray supercomputer to a forty-five-inch TV, the kind used to show sports in hotel lobbies. The Cray could play games around the stock market ticker tape. It added current trading on all the world's markets. It was on-line for every commodity. If you wanted to know the price of a ton of steel in Borneo, Wu had it for you in local currency in a microsecond. He flashed the moving averages every fifteen minutes. His yield curves popped like black holes.

Lazlo, our Nobel Prize winner, sat in his leather armchair with a bucket of fried chicken beside him, watching his protégé. Lazlo was the only one who stayed out of the rally. He said he had put all his Nobel money into H.J. Heinz seven years ago and never regretted it. He said Heinz owned Weight Watchers and he believed that staying slim was the only big project still available to the developed world. He said that he was too old to care about growth stocks and Third World investments.

Nobody paid any attention to Lazlo. He didn't do any research. He was at Los Alamos only because the Joint Chiefs insisted. Every year he went to Washington to testify for greater defense expenditures. His Nobel Prize had been a lucky accident, but in a way, it encouraged everyone. If he could win the Nobel Prize, we thought, anyone could do it. We were all used to Lazlo sitting in his chair, munching on chicken, while someone gave a paper. Lazlo ate fried chicken the way other people smoke cigarettes. He liked to keep a piece on a napkin and nibble during meetings. He left a trail of crumbs everywhere. Nobody else would sit in his leather chair. The maid told him she was going to stop cleaning the chair, but it didn't make any difference to Lazlo.

Yesterday, when my wife told me she was falling in love with Henry Wu, I blamed Lazlo. My first thought was not to kill Henry Wu, but to kill Lazlo. Why had he hired a computer operator when he had no work for the man to do? Why did he give a refugee a fifty-million-dollar Cray and twenty-four hours a day to play the stock market? Wu himself said only America could afford to do such a thing.

"In the Orient people would sell their blood and hair for one afternoon with the Cray. Here, I get it all the time, free."

When I knew the truth I went to Lazlo's office. But neither he nor Wu was there. Vera, the cleaning lady, said they had gone out for a drive. She laughed. As I walked down the corridor I heard two proton-beam technicians discussing July options.

By the time I got back to my office I had stopped blaming Lazlo. Anyway, Henry Wu in our midst was as much my fault as Lazlo's.

Last July I drove Lazlo to Albuquerque to pick up Wu at the airport. His plane, scheduled for nine P.M., arrived three hours late. While we waited Lazlo sat in an airport chair pumping quarters into a TV. When Wu got off the plane he kissed Lazlo's hand and called him a great man. Lazlo told Wu that now that he was in the American Southwest, he didn't have to be humble. He could forget Oriental politeness. Still, Wu tried to be polite. He took us to the airport snack bar and attempted to pay for three coffees with his American Express card.

From Lazlo's description, I thought Wu would be arriving straight from China, but it turned out he had lived in Guam for two years and then in Hawaii for four years. Although he dreamed of research, his job in Hawaii had been selling computers at Sears. Henry Wu answered Lazlo's ad in *Scientific American*. He was slender and tan, even around his eyes. It was not possible to guess his age.

When he got to the car, Lazlo asked Henry Wu if he had a valid driver's license. Wu opened his briefcase and brought out a leather-covered document. It was full of stamps, like a passport. There was no photograph, and all the writing was in Chinese.

"How do I know this is a valid license?" Lazlo said. "How do I know it's even a driver's license?"

Wu picked it up and started to translate.

"I believe you," Lazlo said, "but I advertised for a computer operator with a valid driver's license and you wrote that you had one."

"You didn't specify country," Wu said.

At that moment I chose to be decent. Had I stayed out of it, Lazlo might have bought him a ticket right there and sent him back to Hawaii. It was clear that Lazlo wanted a chauffeur, not a computer assistant.

Lazlo had probably been plotting a way to afford a chauffeur for years. Calling Wu a computer assistant was clever. I didn't think Lazlo had that much cleverness left. Lazlo owns a 1959 Buick that he starts now and then. He likes to talk about cars. In the physics lounge, Lazlo buttonholes people with questions about horsepower and torque and fuel injection, but he is afraid to drive his own car. He admits it.

"I can't relax when I drive," he said, "but if someone else is at the wheel, I can hit alpha waves faster than the car can go from zero to sixty. I am an auto enthusiast, but only as a passenger."

At quarter past midnight in the parking lot at the Albuquerque airport I looked at the Chinese document, flipped through it like a deck of cards, and then gave my keys to Henry Wu.

"It looks good to me," I said.

Lazlo and I got into the back and buckled up.

Henry Wu bowed to thank me. Then he pulled on a pair of kidskin driving gloves. Lazlo poked me in the ribs and winked. Wu started the car and stayed in first gear all along the feeder road. I didn't want to embarrass him by saying anything. I wasn't sure he even knew about gears. When he hit I-25 he went up to fifty-five and put the Honda into overdrive. Lazlo handed Wu directions and flashed a thumbs-up sign. On the highway both Lazlo and I fell asleep. For me it was unusual, but Lazlo always falls asleep. Whenever you look into his office he has his head on his desk. I was tired because I had been up for two consecutive nights, bombarding my sample with high-energy particles. I had to be there to monitor the readings, but sometimes there were three- or four-hour stretches with nothing to do. I volunteered to take Lazlo to the airport because he asked me when I knew I had a few hours to kill.

Henry Wu woke both of us by using the horn. When we opened our eyes, he demonstrated parallel parking in front of the particle accelerator building.

"Very good," Lazlo said. "I'm sure you'll be a fine assistant."

"I have high technical competence," Henry Wu said. "The Cultural Revolution ruined me. Always, I belonged at Bell Labs or at Princeton. Instead they made me a silk farmer."

That was the only time I ever heard Wu say anything about the way he had been treated or what he had done in China. He was a patriotic American, as most naturalized citizens are. He didn't mind enriching a few physicists at Los Alamos but he chose not to destroy Wall Street. If I hadn't let him drive my Honda that night, he might be in Hawaii now selling portable computers to children.

But I know the truth and the truth is, I can't blame Lazlo or myself. Emily did not have to fall in love with Wu. I still don't know how it happened. Henry Wu is half her size and has no facial hair. He smokes Virginia Slims. The long cigarettes look like dinner knives in his tiny fists.

Emily is the one who told me. She came into my office yesterday. I knew that it was serious. She never interrupts my work. She looked as sad as if the market had dropped 150 points.

"It has to do with money only indirectly," she said. "It has to do with Henry Wu."

I thought she was going to tell me that he had programmed the Cray to put everyone's money into his own Swiss bank account. I never trusted him. Even though all his stock calculations were accurate, I was still not sure he even had a valid driver's license. Emily told me straight out that she was in love with Henry Wu.

I didn't know what to say. I thought it was a joke. It was as if the Englishman, Higgins, in the office next door popped in to tell me casually that he had discovered gravity was a Newtonian error.

Emily is the only woman I have ever known intimately. She is my definition of a woman. We have been married for six years, almost ready, I thought, to start a family. A sample of her blood bombarded by neutrinos as old as the universe is the heart of my work.

"What do you mean, you love Henry Wu?"

"I mean I think about him all the time. When I'm at Safeway, when I'm reading or exercising, all the time. I keep hoping I'll hear his footsteps. I think about kissing him."

Kissing Henry Wu seemed to me like kissing a cantaloupe.

"Is it his stock market program that's made you fall in love with him?" I couldn't think of any other reason.

"Money has nothing to do with it. Henry has no personal investments. His interest is wholly theoretical. He knows he could go to Hong Kong or Singapore and sell his program for a fortune, but he doesn't want to undermine capitalism. He loves this country."

She sat in a swivel chair across from my desk. I didn't know what to do. I walked over and kissed the top of her head. She touched my hand. I have seen such moments in the movies many times, but nothing prepared me for it.

Emily offered to move out of the house.

I told her no, it would be easier for me to move into the lab. I had a couch and a small refrigerator, and there was a hot plate and a microwave in the lounge.

She said that was nice of me. She seemed surprised that I would still be decent to her.

"Why wouldn't I want to be nice to the woman I love?"

She was pale and looked ready to cry. We sat in my office for a few minutes without saying anything. Then Emily stood to leave. When she got to the door I asked her if this meant we weren't going to have a child. She cried then and walked out the door.

On my desk was a profile of a large molecule, hemoglobin, that had been cut into strands, bombarded, and then bonded to various materials. The hemoglobin was Emily's. She gave it willingly.

We were in the kitchen of our married-student housing at Yale. She was reading a recipe book. I snuck up behind her with a pin and a test tube and tried to talk like Dracula. Actually, I wanted her to stick me. She laughed and volunteered herself.

"Let my blood inspire you," she said.

In an odd way, it has. When I'm in the lab, looking at those molecules under the electron microscope, it now and then occurs to me that I am studying a fragment of my wife, that I am seeing in the most minute way, atom by atom, who she is.

Of course her molecular structure is similar to everyone else's, but not exactly. When I tell her things like this, Emily calls me a romantic, says that's why she fell in love with me. We met when she was a lab assistant and I was in graduate school. She said she liked how dreamy I looked when she was going from station to station cleaning up. I did like to look at her in a black lab apron and rubber gloves. When she was in the room, I couldn't concentrate. In the spring when she wore a light shirt, I could see the sides of her breasts.

On my way back to Lazlo's office I saw that Wu, as usual, was in the lounge beside the big screen. About a dozen scientists were sitting on folding chairs, watching the economy. As word of Wu's program spread in Los Alamos, people outside the physics group started drifting over to see what he was up to. Most of the time Wu was about as interesting as Lazlo asking about torque or engine-gunk buildup. Wu didn't talk about what people wanted to hear. After the first meeting he made no more market predictions. He didn't have to. Everything was still going as he said it would. He said he had used the Cray to establish a mathematical constant between liquidity and greed as measured by personal savings. His model went back to Europe in the fourteenth century, though a lot of the hard data was based entirely on his own estimates. Henry Wu saw me coming. I didn't say hello or ask about the market. He did not seem happy to see me.

"I've just discovered," he said, "that during the worst years of bubonic plague, when a quarter of the population of Europe died, the market system operated smoothly. My extrapolation tells me that nuclear war would not destroy the Street."

"I want to know about my wife, about what's going on with you and Emily."

Henry Wu moved behind the Cray as if he thought I was going to attack him. He looked at the scientists watching the screen. Nobody was listening to us. All their attention was on their investments. Wu and I both spoke quietly, making noises no louder than the Cray.

I repeated Emily's name. That was enough. Henry Wu knew what I meant. He changed the subject.

"I have been working night and day to glean the inevitable from the Standard and Poor's model. I have achieved a representation of economic reality." As he said that his beeper went off. He was embarrassed. "Lazlo probably needs a ride to Kentucky Fried Chicken . . . Sometimes I feel like I'm his slave, but it's only for a few hours a day, a small price to pay for the constant use of the big one."

When Wu left I went back to my lab. I looked at the fragments of my sample under the electron microscope. I could not stop thinking of Emily kissing Henry Wu. We had decided that when she was thirty, in just a few months, we would begin to have children. I had been ready for years. I was already dreaming of vacations with a couple of little ones in a cabin in the hills. We would teach them to ski. Emily and I both liked skiing. For children Los Alamos would be wonderful—desert, mountains, no traffic. Maybe I should have known something was wrong when Emily told me she wanted to wait until thirty. Maybe I should have known when she told me she missed big-city traffic. We were isolated in Los Alamos, but she wasn't leaving Los Alamos, she was leaving me.

My sample was now in the midst of bonding to polymers. The strands of hemoglobin curled like tiny hairs. At the atomic level matter either bonds or does not bond. In nature what can happen does happen.

The big molecule under my microscope was not recognizably Emily's. I had bombarded it with high energy so often that it no longer resembled the sticky substance of herself. But I still thought of it as a fragment of my wife. What's a person? In the sample, her DNA, though confused, was still intact. If I could insert the big molecule back into the rush of her bloodstream, everything that I had done to that single molecule would not even cause her an upset stomach.

I already had a change of clothes in my lab. There was no reason to go home at all. I didn't have a pet. I tried to think of the whole situation dispassionately. I told myself that humans are sexual creatures. Reason has never dominated either individual or group behavior. Henry Wu and Emily were acting out a pattern over which even they had little control. My anger, my jealousy, my desire to obstruct them, were as reasonable as their behavior. Each of us was just trying to spread our genes in the most efficient way. Wu and Emily wanted each other. At a fundamental level, it did not involve people. Their genes were overcoming mine. This dispassionate thinking made perfect sense but it did not convince me or make me feel any better. I thought of Henry Wu blowing his cigarette smoke through my house. Even at the level of genes I didn't see how she could prefer his.

Vera knocked to ask if I had any trash. I unlocked the door and gave her the slide I had been working on for six months. She threw it in her barrel.

"See you tomorrow," she said. "Have a nice evening."

I listened to her knock on all the other doors in the corridor. Vera has no security clearance, so she can't unlock anything. I heard her close the outside door. I tuned in a classical station on the radio and lay down on my couch to watch the sun set behind the administration building. Then I must have fallen asleep, because when I woke up it was very dark and I was a little hungry.

I walked to the kitchenette at the rear of the lounge and heard someone in there. It was Lazlo singing "Home on the Range" in his Hungarian accent. I didn't see him so I tiptoed back to my office.

The phone rang as soon as I got there. It was Emily calling to tell me she would leave the house the next week and I could live there. She said that she was sorry that she could not move away from Los Alamos. Henry had to stay because nowhere else in the world could he have twenty-four-hour access to the Cray. She told me that she would stay out of the way, never come to any social events, she didn't want things to be too hard for me.

I thanked her. Then I threw away all the rest of my slides. More than three hundred samples of her hemoglobin, bonded and unbonded, filled the incinerator.

I knew that by doing so I was destroying government property, but I knew that the property had no value. If I could face the truth about Emily and Wu, I could face it with my experiment as well. It was only a coincidence, but my life and my work at the moment coincided.

My work was as silly as Lazlo's Nobel Prize experiments. Fresh from Europe, before he even knew English, he had done his post-doc in background radiation. He produced a lot of insignificant calculations. As it happened, twenty years later, other cosmologists realized that Lazlo's work proved the Big Bang theory. By then Lazlo was a washed-up old man eating fried chicken and telling congressional committees to spend more on defense because fear and suspicion breed caution.

By the time he went to Sweden to pick up his prize, Lazlo was a joke in the scientific community. He hadn't published a paper in fifteen years. During conferences he never asked questions. On his notepads he doodled. Whenever someone would take him along, he liked to go to the stock-car races in Albuquerque. Or, when he would get a ride to Santa Fe, he liked to buy turquoise from the Indians as if he were a weekend tourist. He wore a gaudy turquoise ring on each hand.

I wondered if I was going to become a Lazlo. It's something

every scientist worries about. When we reach thirty, we know our best work is behind us.

At three A.M. I went back to the kitchenette for a glass of milk. Lazlo was there cooking Heinz vegetable soup. When he saw me drinking milk he asked if he could have a little for his soup. He drank the soup from a cup stained with coffee. I remembered hearing Vera say that Lazlo's office was so dirty that he would be evicted from a public housing project.

"Did you hear Henry Wu yesterday?" Lazlo asked. "He showed everyone how he adjusts the constant in his formula. He thinks he understands the movement of capital since the beginning of the fourteenth century."

"I'm not interested in what Henry Wu thinks."

At that hour Lazlo and I were alone in the three-story physics building. He seemed happy to have company. He wanted to talk.

"Since Wu started everyone in the market it's so quiet that you can hear the field mice at night. There used to be people here all the time. Computations ran through the night. I even remember seeing you here now and then."

"Do you think people are not working as hard because everyone is busy with the stock market?"

"I think," Lazlo said, "that if I didn't know the Russians so well, I'd believe they sent Henry Wu to keep us from all the Star Wars business."

"You mean you think he's a Soviet plant?"

"No, the Russians are not that clever."

"Who sent him, then?"

"The gods. They're not always malicious."

I didn't know what he meant.

Lazlo put his arm around me. For the first time I thought of him as a wise man, someone from whom I could learn. I was ashamed of myself for years of thinking that his Nobel Prize was insignificant. Right there, in the middle of the night, I admitted that I thought of him as an old fool, and I decided to apologize.

"You were not wrong," Lazlo said. "The only thing you didn't realize is that the rest of them are worse."

Together we walked toward the Cray. "I'm going to show

you what he's doing, what has turned world-class scientists into idiots."

Lazlo ran the Cray.

"Wu gives them a graphics program just like the IBM makes for kids. He shows them pictures and they think he's a genius because the market is going up thirty points a day. Physicists are as greedy as pigs."

The big screen flashed a fuzzy human image. It looked female above the waist, but the figure had long, muscular male legs and thighs. The figure was walking slowly across the pitch-black space. It carried a walking stick as if there were a place in the void to set it down.

"You should listen to Wu narrate this," Lazlo said. "He tells them this bisexual figure is humanity and the walking stick is money." Lazlo in his Hungarian accent tried to imitate Wu's high-pitched Oriental voice in characteristic inflection.

"Stick disappears, figure wobbles. Remember importance of capital. In midst of plague, market economy flourished."

Lazlo laughed at his own imitation. On the screen the figure wobbled like a dying star.

"Henry Wu's constant," Lazlo said. "They talk about it like it's a prime number, like it's something in the universe that won't decay. Because they're making money they watch his cartoons and believe his mumbo jumbo."

The old man pushed some buttons and the screen became black once more. The Cray still hummed, waiting for more instructions.

"My wife left me for Henry Wu yesterday." I told this to Lazlo as a fact, friend to friend. He said nothing.

"I've been bombarding my molecule for four years with no results to speak of. Tonight I threw it away. I was hoping that next year we would have a child."

Lazlo pushed some more buttons on the Cray. He was having fun.

"Henry Wu thinks I don't know how to use this machine. He thinks I sleep nights. How old is your wife?"

"Twenty-nine."

The screen flashed two figures. I knew that it was Henry Wu

and Emily followed by three squat Eurasian children. They were walking slowly through the emptiness of the big screen.

"Those are the children I might have had."

"No," Lazlo said, "those are only prime numbers. Wu's program makes images. Those figures are the square of your wife's age."

It was only twenty-nine squared, but the segments moving along on the big screen brought tears to my eyes.

"I'm sorry," Lazlo said. He erased the image. "Someday your work may be fruitful. If not the Nobel Prize, maybe you'll win other prizes. At least you won't be a Henry Wu, making cartoons."

I followed Lazlo back to the lounge. I noticed he was wearing slippers. He started to open another can. "Cream of tomato this time. It's very good, you'll see. I like all the cream soups."

Down the hall the Cray hummed, and through the Los Alamos darkness, the physicists, asleep, were awaiting the happiness of another opening bell on Wall Street. Henry Wu's bull roared through the universe. His Eurasian children sprang from my wife. Lazlo and I shared a cup of soup. In the morning, I told him, I'll prick myself and start again with a new molecule, this time my own.

" 'Research' is the most useful story I've ever written. It convinced me to withdraw a portion of my retirement fund from the stock market a few months before the plunge of October 1987. I also like the story because it gave me a chance to talk about matters I don't understand, science and computers, and to mingle this hardware of modernism with the old-fashioned human problems of love and ambition."

Max Apple is the author of The Oranging of America, Zip, Free Agents and The Propheteers. He is currently living in New York with his two children.

Published in Harper's.

MONA SIMPSON

LAWNS

steal. I've stolen books and money and even letters. Letters are great. I can't tell you the feeling, walking down the street with twenty dollars in my purse, stolen earrings in my pocket. I don't get caught. That's the amazing thing. You're out on the sidewalk, other people all around, shopping, walking, and you've got it. You're out of the store, you've done this thing you're not supposed to do, but no one stops you. At first it's a rush. Like you're even for everything you didn't get before. But then you're left alone, no one even notices you. Nothing changes.

I work in the mailroom of my dormitory, Saturday mornings. I sort mail, put the letters in these long narrow cubbyholes. The insides of mailboxes. It's cool there when I stick in my arm.

I've stolen cash—these crisp, crackling, brand-new twenty-dollar bills the fathers and grandmothers send, sealed up in sheets of wax paper. Once I got a fifty. I've stolen presents, too. I got a sweater and a football. I didn't want the football, but after the package was messed up on the mail table, I had no choice, I had to take the whole thing in my daypack and throw it out on the other side of campus. I found a covered garbage can. It was miles away. Brand-new football.

Mostly, what I take are cookies. No evidence. They're edible. I can spot the coffee cans of chocolate chip. You can smell it right through the wrapping. A cool smell, like the inside of a pantry. Sometimes I eat straight through a can during just my shift.

Tampering with the United States mail is a Federal Crime, I know. Listen, let me tell you, I know. I got a summons in my mailbox to go to the Employment Office next Wednesday. Sure I'm scared.

The University cops want to talk to me. Great. They think, suspect is the word they use, that one of us is throwing out mail instead of sorting it. Wonder who? Us is the others. I'm not the only sorter. I just work Saturdays, mail comes, you know, six days a week in this country. They'll never guess it's me.

They say this in the letter, they think it's out of LAZINESS. Wanting to hurry up and get it done, not spend the time. But I don't hurry. I'm really patient on Saturday mornings. I leave my dorm early, while Lauren's still asleep, I open the mailroom— it's this heavy door and I have my own key. When I get there, two bags are already on the table, sagging, waiting for me. Two old ladies. One's packages, one's mail. There's a small key opens the bank of doors, the little boxes from the inside. Through the glass part of every mail slot, I can see. The astroturf field across the street over the parking lot, it's this light green. I watch the sky go from black to gray to blue while I'm there. Some days just stay foggy. Those are the best. I bring a cup of coffee in with me from the vending machine— don't want to wake Lauren up—and I get there at like seven-thirty or eight o'clock. I don't mind it then, my whole dorm's asleep. When I walk out it's as quiet as a football game day. It's eleven or twelve when you know everyone's up and walking that it gets bad being down there. That's why I start early. But I don't rush.

Once you open a letter, you can't just put it in a mailbox. The person's gonna say something. So I stash them in my pack and throw them out. Just people I know. Susan Brown, I open, Annie Larsen, Larry Helprin. All the popular kids from my high school. These are kids who drove places together, took vacations, they all ski, they went to the prom in one big group. At morning nutrition—nutrition, it's your break at two o'clock for donuts and stuff. California state law, you have to have it.

They used to meet outside on the far end of the math patio, all in one group. Some of them smoked. I've seen them look at

each other, concerned at ten in the morning. One touched the
inside of another's wrist, like grown-ups in trouble.

And now I know. Everything I thought those three years,
worst years of my life, turns out to be true. The ones here get
letters. Keri's at Santa Cruz, Lilly's in San Diego, Kevin's at
Harvard and Beth's at Stanford. And like from families, their
letters talk about problems. They're each other's main lives.
You always knew, looking at them in high school, they weren't
just kids who had fun. They cared. They cared about things.

They're all worried about Lilly now. Larry and Annie are
flying down to talk her into staying at school.

I saw Glenn the day I came to Berkeley. I was all unpacked
and I was standing there leaning into the window of my father's
car, saying "Smile, Dad, jeez, at least try, would you?" He was
crying because he was leaving. I'm thinking oh, my god, some
of these other kids, carrying in their trunks and backpacks are
gonna see him, and then finally, he drives away and I was sad.
That was the moment I was waiting for, him gone and me alone
and there it was and I was sad. I took a walk through campus
and I'd been walking for almost an hour and then I see Glenn,
coming down on a little hill by the infirmary, riding on one of
those lawn mowers you sit on, with grass flying out of the side
and he's smiling. Not at me but just smiling. Clouds and sky
behind his hair, half of Tamalpais gone in fog. He was wearing
this bright orange vest and I thought, fall's coming.

I saw him that night again in our dorm cafeteria. This's the
first time I've been in love. I worry. I'm a bad person, but
Glenn's the perfect guy, I mean for me at least, and he thinks
he loves me and I've got to keep him from finding out about
me. I'll die before I'll tell him. Glenn, OK, Glenn. He looks
like Mick Jagger, but sweet, ten times sweeter. He looks like
he's about ten years old. His father's a doctor over at UC Med.
Gynecological surgeon.

First time we got together, a whole bunch of us were in
Glenn's room drinking beer, Glenn and his roommate collect
beer cans, they have them stacked up, we're watching TV and
finally everybody else leaves. There's nothing on but those

gray lines and Glenn turns over on his bed and asks me if I'd
rub his back.

I couldn't believe this was happening to me. In high school,
I was always ending up with the wrong guys, never the one I
wanted. But I wanted it to be Glenn and I knew it was going to
happen, I knew I didn't have to do anything. I just had to stay
there. It would happen. I was sitting on his rear end, rubbing
his back, going under his shirt with my hands. His back felt so
good, it was smooth and warm, like cement around a pool.

All of a sudden, I was worried about my breath and what I
smelled like. When I turned fourteen or fifteen, my father told
me once that I didn't smell good. I slugged him when he
said that and didn't talk to him for days, not that I cared about
what I smelled like with my father. He was happy, though,
kind of, that he could hurt me. That was the last time, though,
I'll tell you.

Glenn's face was down in the pillow. I tried to sniff myself
but I couldn't tell anything. And it went all right anyway.

I don't open Glenn's letters but I touch them. I hold them
and smell them—none of his mail has any smell.

He doesn't get many letters. His parents live across the Bay
in Marin County, they don't write. He gets letters from his
grandmother in Michigan, plain, even handwriting on regular
envelopes, a sticker with her return address printed on it,
Rural Route #3, Guns Street, see, I got it memorized.

And he gets letters from Diane, Di, they call her. High
school girlfriend. Has a pushy mother, wants her to be a
scientist, but she already got a C in Chem 1A. I got an A+,
not to brag. He never slept with her, though, she wouldn't,
she's still a virgin down in San Diego. With Lilly. Maybe they
even know each other.

Glenn and Di were popular kids in their high school. Redwood High. Now I'm one because of Glenn, popular. Because
I'm his girlfriend, I know that's why. Not 'cause of me. I just
know, OK, I'm not going to start fooling myself now. Please.

Her letters I hold up to the light, they've got fluorescent
lights in there. She's supposed to be blond, you know, and
pretty. Quiet. The soft type. And the envelopes. She writes on

these sheer cream-colored envelopes and they get transparent and I can see her writing underneath, but not enough to read what it says, it's like those hockey lines painted under layers of ice.

I run my tongue along the place where his grandmother sealed the letter. A sharp, sweet gummy taste. Once I cut my tongue. That's what keeps me going to the bottom of the bag, I'm always wondering if there'll be a letter for Glenn. He doesn't get one every week. It's like a treasure. Cracker Jack prize. But I'd never open Glenn's mail. I kiss all four corners where his fingers will touch, opening it, before I put it in his box. Sometimes I hold it up and blow on it.

I brought home cookies for Lauren and me. Just a present. We'll eat 'em or Glenn'll eat 'em. I'll throw them out for all I care. They're chocolate chip with pecans. This was one good mother. A lucky can. I brought us coffee, too. I *bought* it.

Yeah, OK, so I'm in trouble. Wednesday, at ten-thirty, I got this notice I was supposed to appear. I had a class, Chem 1C, pre-med staple. Your critical thing. I never missed it before. I told Glenn I had a doctor's appointment.

OK, so I skipped it anyway and I walk into this room and there's these two other guys, all work in the mailroom doing what I do, sorting. And we all sit there on chairs on this green carpet. I was staring at everybody's shoes. And there's a cop. University cop, I don't know what's the difference. He had this sagging, pear-shaped body. Like what my dad would have if he were fat, but he's not, he's thin. He walks slowly on the carpeting, his fingers hooked in his belt loops. I was watching his hips.

Anyway, he's accusing us all and he's trying to get one of us to admit we did it. No way.

"I hope one of you will come to me and tell the truth. Not a one of you knows anything about this? Come on, now."

I shake my head no and stare down at the three pairs of shoes. He says they're not going to do anything to the person who did it, right, wanna make a bet, they say they just want to know, but they'll take it back as soon as you tell them.

I don't care why I don't believe him. I know one thing for

sure and that's they're not going to do anything to me as long as I say, NO, I didn't do it. That's what I said, no, I didn't do it, I don't know a thing about it. I just can't imagine where those missing packages could have gone, how letters got into garbage cans. Awful. I just don't know.

The cop had a map with Xs on it every place they found mail. The garbage cans. He said there was a group of students trying to get an investigation. People's girlfriends sent cookies that never got there. Letters were missing. Money. These students put up Xeroxed posters on bulletin boards showing a garbage can stuffed with letters.

Why should I tell them, so they can throw me in jail? And kick me out of school? Four-point-oh average and I'm going to let them kick me out of school? They're sitting there telling us it's a felony. A Federal Crime. No way, I'm gonna go to medical school.

This tall, skinny guy with a blond mustache, Wallabees, looks kind of like a rabbit, he defended us. He's another sorter, works Monday/Wednesdays.

"We all do our jobs," he says. "None of us would do that." The rabbity guy looks at me and the other girl, for support. So we're going to stick together. The other girl, a dark blonde, chewing her lip, nodded. I loved that rabbity guy that second. I nodded too.

The cop looked down. Wide hips in the coffee-with-milk-colored pants. He sighed. I looked up the rabbity guy. They let us all go.

I'm just going to keep saying no, not me, didn't do and I just won't do it again. That's all. Won't do it anymore. So, this is Glenn's last chance for homemade cookies. I'm sure as hell not going to bake any.

I signed the form, said I didn't do it, I'm OK now. I'm safe. It turned out OK after all, it always does. I always think something terrible's going to happen and it doesn't. I'm lucky.

I'm afraid of cops. I was walking, just a little while ago, today, down Telegraph with Glenn, and these two policemen, not the one I'd met, other policemen, were coming in our direction. I started sweating a lot. I was sure until they passed us, I was sure it was all over, they were there for me. I always think that. But at the same time, I know it's just my imagination. I mean, I'm a four-point-oh student, I'm a nice girl just walking down the street with my boyfriend.

We were on our way to get Happy Burgers. When we turned the corner, about a block past the cops, I looked at Glenn and I was flooded with like this feeling. It was raining a little and we were by People's Park. The trees were blowing and I was looking at all those little gardens coming up, held together with stakes and white string.

I wanted to say something to Glenn, give him something. I wanted to tell him something about me.

"I'm bad in bed," that's what I said, I just blurted it out like that. He just kind of looked at me, he was nervous, he just giggled. He didn't know what to say, I guess, but he sort of slung his arm around me and I was so grateful and then we went in. He paid for my Happy Burger, I usually don't let him pay for me, but I did and it was the best goddamn hamburger I've ever eaten.

I want to tell him things.

I lie all the time, always have, but I keep track of each lie I've ever told Glenn and I'm always thinking of the things I can't tell him.

Glenn was a screwed-up kid, kind of. He used to go in his backyard, his parents were inside the house I guess, and he'd find this big stick and start twirling around with it. He'd dance, he called it dancing, until if you came up and clapped in front of him, he wouldn't see you. He'd spin around with that stick until he fell down dead on the grass, unconscious, he said he did it to see the sky break up in pieces and spin. He did it sometimes with a tire swing, too. He told me when he was spinning like that, it felt like he was just hearing the earth spinning, that it really went that fast all the time but we just don't feel it. When he was twelve years old or something, his parents took him in the city to a clinic t'see a psychologist. And then he stopped. See, maybe I should go to a psychologist. I'd get better, too. He told me about that in bed one night. The ground feels so good when you fall, he said to me. I loved him for that.

"Does anything feel that good now?" I said.

"Sex sometimes. Maybe dancing."

Know what else he told me that night? He said, right before we went to sleep, he wasn't looking at me, he said he'd been thinking what would happen if I died. He said he thought how he'd be at my funeral, all my family and my friends from high school and my little brother would all be around at the front and he'd be at the edge in the cemetery, nobody'd even know who he was.

I was in that crack, breathing the air between the bed and the wall. Cold and dusty. Yeah, we're having sex. I don't know. It's good. Sweet. He says he loves me. I have to remind myself. I talk to myself in my head while we're doing it. I have to say, it's OK, this is just Glenn, this is who I want it to be and it's just like rubbing next to someone. It's just like pushing two hands together, so there's no air in between.

I cry sometimes with Glenn, I'm so grateful.

My mother called and woke me up this morning. Ms. I'm-going-to-be-perfect. Ms. anything-wrong-is-your-own-fault. Ms. if-anything-bad-happens-you're-a-fool.

She says if she has time, she MIGHT come up and see my dorm room in the next few weeks. Help me organize my wardrobe, she says. She didn't bring me up here, my dad did. I wanted Danny to come along, I love Danny.

But my mother has NO pity. She thinks she's got the answers. She's the one who's a lawyer, she's the one who went back to law school and stayed up late nights studying while she still made our lunch boxes. With gourmet cheese. She's proud of it, she tells you. She loves my dad, I guess. She thinks we're like this great family and she sits there at the dinner table bragging about us, to us. She Xeroxed my grade card first quarter with my Chemistry A+ so she's got it in her office and she's got the copy up on the refrigerator at home. She's sitting there telling all her friends that and I'm thinking, you don't know it, but I'm not one of you.

These people across the street from us. Little girl, Sarah, eight years old. Maybe seven. Her dad, he worked for the army, some kind of researcher, he decided he wants to get a sex-change operation. And he goes and does it, over at Stanford. My mom goes out, takes the dog for a walk, right. The mother CONFIDES in her. Says the thing she regrets most is she wants to have more children. The little girl, Sarah, eight years old, looks up at my mom and says, "Daddy's going to be an aunt."

Now that's sad, I think that's really sad. My mom thinks it's a good dinner table story, proving how much better we are than them. Yeah, I remember exactly what she said that night. "That's all Sarah's mother's got to worry about now, is that she wants another child. Meanwhile, Daddy's becoming an aunt."

She should know about me.

So my dad comes to visit for the weekend. Glenn's dad came to speak at UC one night, he took Glenn out to dinner to a nice place, Glenn was glad to see him. Yeah, well. My dad. Comes to the dorm. Skulks around. This guy's a BUSINESSMAN, in a three-piece suit, and he acts inferior to the eighteen-year-old freshmen coming in the lobby. My dad. Makes me sick right now thinking of him standing there in the lobby and everybody seeing him. He was probably looking at the kids and looking jealous. Just standing there. Why? Don't ask me why, he's the one that's forty-two years old.

So he's standing there, nervous, probably sucking his hand, that's what he does when he's nervous, I'm always telling him not to. Finally, somebody takes him to my room. I'm not there, Lauren's gone, and he waits for I don't know how long.

When I come in he's standing with his back to the door looking out the window. I see him and right away I know it's him and I have this urge to tiptoe away and he'll never see me.

My pink sweater, a nice sweater, a sweater I wore a lot in high school was over my chair, hanging on the back of it and my father's got one hand on the sweater shoulder and he's like rubbing the other hand down an empty arm. He looks up at me, already scared and grateful when I walk into the room. I feel like smashing him with a baseball bat. Why can't he just stand up straight?

I drop my books on the bed and stand there while he hugs me.

"Hi, Daddy, what are you doing here?"

"I wanted to see you." He sits in my chair now, his legs crossed and big, too big for this room, and he's still fingering the arm of my pink sweater. "I missed you so I got away for the weekend," he says. "I have a room up here at the Claremont Hotel."

So he's here for the weekend. He's just sitting in my dorm room and I have to figure out what to do with him. He's not going to do anything. He'd just sit here. And Lauren's coming back soon so I've got to get him out. It's Friday afternoon and the weekend's shot. OK, so I'll go with him. I'll go with him and get it over with.

But I'm not going to miss my date with Glenn Saturday night. No way. I'd die before I'd cancel that. It's bad enough missing dinner in the cafeteria tonight. Friday's eggplant, my favorite, and Friday nights are usually easy, music on all the stereos all down the hall. We usually work, but work slow and talk and then we all meet in Glenn's room around ten.

"Come, sit on my lap, honey." My dad like pulls me down and starts bouncing me. BOUNCING ME. I stand up. "OK, we can go somewhere tonight and tomorrow morning, but I have to be back for tomorrow night. I've got plans with people. And I've got to study, too."

"You can bring your books back to the hotel," he says. "I'm supposed to be at a convention in San Francisco, but I wanted to see you. I have work, too, we can call room service and both just work."

"I still have to be back by four tomorrow."

"All right."

"OK, just give a minute." And he sat there in my chair while I called Glenn and told him I wouldn't be there for dinner. I pulled the phone out into the hall, it only stretches so far, and whispered. "Yeah, my father's here," I said, "he's got a conference in San Francisco. He just came by."

Glenn lowered his voice, sweet, and said, "Sounds fun."

My dad sat there, hunched over in my chair, while I changed my shirt and put on deodorant. I put a nightgown in my shoulder pack and my toothbrush and I took my chem book and we left. I knew I wouldn't be back for a whole day. I was trying to calm myself thinking, well, it's only one day, that's nothing in my life. The halls were empty, it was five o'clock, five-ten, everyone was down at dinner.

We walk outside and the cafeteria lights are on and I see everyone moving around with their trays. Then my dad picks up my hand.

I yank it out. "Dad," I say, really mean.

"Honey, I'm your father." His voice trails off. "Other girls hold their fathers' hands." It was dark enough for the lights to be on in the cafeteria, but it wasn't really dark out yet. The sky was blue. On the tennis courts on top of the garage, two Chinese guys were playing. I heard that thonk-pong and it sounded so carefree and I just wanted to be them. I'd have given up Glenn, Glenn-that-I-love-more-than-anything, at that second, I would have given everything up just to be someone else, someone new. I got into the car and slammed the door shut and turned up the heat.

"Should we just go to the hotel and do our work? We can get a nice dinner in the room."

"I'd rather go out," I said, looking down at my hands. He went where I told him. I said the name of the restaurant and gave directions. Chez Panisse and we ordered the most expensive stuff. Appetizers and two desserts just for me. A hundred and twenty bucks for the two of us.

OK, this hotel room.

So, my dad's got the Bridal Suite. He claimed that was all they had. Fat chance. Two-hundred-eighty-room hotel and all they've got left is this deal with the canopy bed, no way. It's in the tower, you can almost see it from the dorm. Makes me sick. From the bathroom, there's this window, shaped like an arch, and it looks over all of Berkeley. You can see the bridge lights. As soon as we got there, I locked myself in the bathroom, I was so mad about that canopy bed. I took a long bath and washed my hair. They had little soaps wrapped up there, shampoo, may as well use them, he's paying for it. It's this deep old bathtub and wind was coming in from outside and I felt like that window was just open, no glass, just a hole cut out in the stone.

I was thinking of when I was little and what they taught us in catechism. I thought a soul was inside your chest, this long horizontal triangle with rounded edges, made out of some kind of white fog, some kind of gas or vapor. I could be pregnant. I soaped myself all up and rinsed off with cold water. I'm lucky I never got pregnant, really lucky.

Other kids my age, Lauren, everybody, I know things they don't know. I know more for my age. Too much. Like I'm not a virgin. Lots of people are, you'd be surprised. I know a lot of things being wrong and unfair, all kinds of stuff. It's like seeing a UFO, if I ever saw something like that, I'd never tell, I'd wish I'd never seen it.

My dad knocks on the door.

"What do you want?"

"Let me just come in and talk to you while you're in there."

"I'm done, I'll be right out. Just a minute." I took a long time toweling. No hurry, believe me. So I got into bed, with my nightgown on and wet already from my hair. I turned away. Breathed against the wall. "Night."

My father hooks my hair over my ear and touches my shoulder. "Tired?"

I shrug.

"You really have to go back tomorrow? We could go to Marin or to the beach. Anything."

I hugged my knees up under my nightgown. "You should go to your conference, Dad."

I wake up in the middle of the night, I feel something's going on, and sure enough, my dad's down there, he's got my nightgown worked up to like a frill around my neck and my legs hooked over his shoulders.

"Dad, stop it."

"I just wanted to make you feel good," he says and looks up at me. "What's wrong? Don't you love me anymore?"

I never really told anybody. It's not exactly the kind of thing you can bring up over lunch. "So, I'm sleeping with my father. Oh, and let's split a dessert." Right.

I don't know, other people think my dad's handsome. They say he is. My mother thinks so, you should see her traipsing around the balcony when she gets in her romantic moods, which, on her professional lawyer schedule, are about once a year, thank god. It's pathetic. He thinks she's repulsive, though. I don't know that, that's what I think. But he loves me, that's for sure.

So next day, Saturday—that rabbity guy, Paul's his name, he did my shift for me—we go downtown and I got him to buy me this suit. Three hundred dollars from Saks. Oh, and I got shoes. So I stayed later with him because of the clothes, and I was a little happy because I thought at least now I'd have something good to wear with Glenn. My dad and I got brownie sundaes at Sweet Dreams and I got home by five. He was crying when he dropped me off.

"Don't cry, Dad. Please," I said. Jesus, how can you not hate someone who's always begging from you.

Lauren had Poly Styrene on the stereo and a candle lit in our room. I was never so glad to be home.

"Hey," Lauren said. She was on her bed, with her legs propped up on the wall. She'd just shaved. She was rubbing in cream.

I flopped down on my bed. "Ohhhh," I said, grabbing the sides of the mattress.

"Hey, can you keep a secret about what I did today?" Lauren said. "I went to that therapist, up at Cowell."

"You have the greatest legs," I said, quiet. "Why don't you ever wear skirts?"

She stopped what she was doing and stood up. "You think they're good? I don't like the way they look, except in jeans." She looked down at them. "They're crooked, see?" She shook her head. "I don't want to think about it."

Then she went to her dresser and started rolling a joint. "Want some?"

"A little."

She lit up, lay back on her bed and held her arm out for me to come take the joint.

"So, she was this really great woman. Warm, kind of chubby. She knew instantly what kind of man Brent was." Lauren snapped her fingers. "Like that." Brent was the pool man Lauren had an affair with, home in LA.

I'm back in the room maybe an hour, putting on mascara,

my jeans are on the bed pressed, and the phone rings and it's my dad and I say, "Listen, just leave me alone."

"You don't care about me anymore."

"I just saw you. I have nothing to say. We just saw each other."

"What are you doing tonight?"

"Going out."

"Who are you seeing?"

"Glenn."

He sighs. "So you really like him, huh?"

"Yeah, I do and you should be glad. You should be glad I have a boyfriend." I pull the cord out into the hall and sit down on the floor there. There's this long pause.

"We're not going to end up together, are we?"

I felt like all the air's knocked out of me. I looked out the window and everything looked dead and still. The parked cars. The trees with pink toilet paper strung between the branches. The church all closed up across the street.

"No, we won't, Daddy."

He was crying. "I know, I know."

I hung up the phone and went back and sat in the hall. I'm scared, too. I don't know what'll happen.

I don't know. It's been going on I guess as long as I can remember. I mean, not the sex, but my father. When I was a little kid, tiny little kid, my dad came in before bed and said his prayers with me. He kneeled down by my bed and I was on my back. PRAYERS. He'd lift up my pajama top and put his hands on my breast. Little fried eggs, he said. One time with his tongue. Then one night, he pulled down the elastic of my pajama pants. He did it for an hour and then I came. Don't believe anything they ever tell you about kids not coming. That first time was the biggest I ever had and I didn't even know what it was then. It just kept going and going as if he was breaking me through layers and layers of glass and I felt like I'd slipped and let go and I didn't have myself anymore, he had me, and once I'd slipped like that I'd never be the same again.

We had this sprinkler in our back lawn, Danny and me used to run through it in the summer and my dad'd be outside, working on the grass or the hedge or something and he'd squirt us with the hose. I used to wear a bathing suit bottom, no top—we were this modern family, our parents walked around the house naked after showers and then Danny and I ended up both being these modest kids, can't stand anyone to see us even in our underwear, I always dress facing the closet, Lauren teases me. We'd run through the sprinkler and my dad would come up and pat my bottom and the way he put his hand on my thigh, I felt like Danny could tell it was different than the way he touched him, I was like something he owned.

First time when I was nine, I remember, Dad and me were in the shower togther. My mom might have even been in the house, they did that kind of stuff, it was supposed to be OK. Anyway, we're in the shower and I remember this look my dad had. Like he was daring me, knowing he knew more than I did. We're both under the shower. The water pasted his hair down on his head and he looked younger and weird. "Touch it. Don't be afraid of it," he says. And he grabs my thighs on the outside and pulls me close to him, pulling on my fat.

He waited till I was twelve to really do it. I don't know if you can call it rape, I was a good sport. The creepy thing is I know how it felt for him, I could see it on his face when he did it. He thought he was getting away with something. We were supposed to go hiking but right away that morning when we got into the car, he knew he was going to do it. He couldn't wait to get going. I said I didn't feel good, I had a cold, I wanted to stay home, but he made me go anyway and we hiked two miles and he set up the tent. He told me to take my clothes off and I undressed just like that, standing there in the woods. He's the one who was nervous and got us into the tent. I looked old for twelve, small but old. And right there on the ground, he spread my legs open and pulled my feet up and fucked me. I bled. I couldn't even breathe the tent was so small. He could have done anything. He could have killed me, he had me alone on this mountain.

I think about that sometimes when I'm alone with Glenn in my bed. It's so easy to hurt people. They just lie there and let you have them. I could reach out and choke Glenn to death, he'd be so shocked, he wouldn't stop me. You can just take what you want.

My dad thought he was getting away with something but he didn't. He was the one that fell in love, not me. And after that day, when we were back in the car, I was the one giving orders. From then on, I got what I wanted. He spent about twice as much money on me as on Danny and everyone knew it, Danny and my mom, too. How do you think I got good clothes and a good bike and a good stereo? My dad's not rich, you know. And I'm the one who got to go away to college even though it killed him. Says it's the saddest thing that ever happened in his life, me going away and leaving him. But when I was a little kid that day, he wasn't in love with me, not like he is now.

Only thing I'm sad about isn't either of my parents, it's Danny. Leaving Danny alone there with them. He used to send Danny out of the house. My mom'd be at work on a Saturday afternoon or something or even in the morning and my dad would kick my little brother out of his own house. Go out and play, Danny. Why doncha catch some rays. And Danny just went and got his glove and baseball from the closet and he'd go and throw it against the house, against the outside wall, in the driveway. I'd be in my room, I'd be like dead, I'd be wood, telling myself this doesn't count, no one has to know, I'll say I'm still a virgin, it's not really happening to me, I'm dead, I'm blank, I'm just letting time stop and pass, and then I'd hear the sock of the ball in the mitt and the slam of the screen door and I knew it was true, it was really happening.

Glenn's the one I want to tell. I can't ever tell Glenn.

I called my mom. Pay phone, collect, hour-long call. I don't know, I got real mad last night and I just told her. I thought when I came here, it'd just go away. But it's not going away. It makes me weird with Glenn. In the morning, with Glenn, when it's time to get up, I can't get up. I cry.

I knew it'd be bad. Poor Danny. Well, my mom says she might leave our dad. She cried for an hour, no jokes, on the phone.

How could he DO this to me, she kept yelping. To her.
Everything's always to her.

But then she called an hour later, she'd talked to a psychiatrist already, she's kicked Dad out, and she arrives, just arrives
here at Berkeley. But she was good. She says she's on my side,
she'll help me, I don't know, I felt OK. She stayed in a hotel
and she wanted to know if I wanted to stay there with her but I
said no, I'd see her more in a week or something, I just wanted
to go back to my dorm. She found this group. She says, just in
San Jose, there's hundreds of families like ours, yeah, great,
that's what I said. But there's groups. She's going to a group of
other thick-o mothers like her, these wives who didn't catch
on. She wanted me to go to a group of girls, yeah, molested
girls, that's what they call them, but I said no, I have friends
here already, she can do what she wants.

I talked to my dad, too, that's the sad thing, he feels like he's
lost me and he wants to die and I don't know, he doesn't know
what he's doing. He called in the middle of the night.

"Just tell me one thing, honey. Please tell me the truth.
When did you stop?"

"Dad."

"Because I remember once you said I was the only person
who ever understood you."

"I was ten years old."

"OK, OK. I'm sorry."

He didn't want to get off the phone. "You know, I love you,
honey. I always will."

"Yeah, well."

My mom's got him lined up for a psychiatrist, too, she says
he's lucky she's not sending him to jail. I *am* a lawyer, she
keeps saying, as if we could forget. She'd pay for me to go to a
shrink now, too, but I said no, forget it.

It's over. Glenn and I are, over. I feel like my dad's lost me
everything. I sort of want to die now. I'm telling you I feel
terrible. I told Glenn and that's it, it's over. I can't believe it
either. Lauren says she's going to hit him.

I told him and we're not seeing each other anymore. Nope. He
said he wanted to just think about everything for a few days.

He said it had nothing to do with my father but he'd been feeling a little too settled lately. He said we don't have fun anymore, it's always so serious. That was Monday. So every meal after that, I sat with Lauren in the cafeteria and he's there on the other side, messing around with the guys. He sure didn't look like he was in any kind of agony. Wednesday, I saw Glenn over by the window in this food fight, slipping off his chair and I couldn't stand it, I got up and left and went to our room.

But I went and said I wanted to talk to Glenn that night, I didn't even have any dinner, and he said he wanted to be friends. He looked at me funny and I haven't heard from him. It's, I don't know, seven days, eight.

I know there are other guys. I live in a dorm full of them, or half-full of them. Half girls. But I keep thinking of Glenn 'cause of happiness, that's what makes me want to hang onto him.

There was this one morning when we woke up in his room, it was light out already, white light all over the room. We were sticky and warm, the sheet was all tangled. His roommate, this little blond boy, was still sleeping. I watched his eyes open and he smiled and then he went down the hall to take a shower. Glenn was hugging me and it was nothing unusual, nothing special. We didn't screw. We were just there. We kissed, but slow, the way it is when your mouth is still bad from sleep.

I was happy that morning. I didn't have to do anything. We got dressed, went to breakfast, I don't know. Took a walk. He had to go to work at a certain time and I had that sleepy feeling from waking up with the sun on my head and he said he didn't want to say good-bye to me. There was that pang. One of those looks like as if at that second, we both felt the same way.

I shrugged. I could afford to be casual then. We didn't say good-bye. I walked with him to the shed by the Eucalyptus Grove. That's where they keep all the gardening tools, the rakes, the hoes, the mowers, big bags of grass seed slumped against the wall. It smelled like hay in there. Glenn changed into his uniform and we went to the North Side, up in front of the Chancellor's manor, that thick perfect grass. And Glenn gave me a ride on the lawn mower, on the handlebars. It was bouncing over these little bumps in the lawn and I was hanging onto the handlebars, laughing. I couldn't see Glenn but I knew he was there behind me. I looked around at the buildings and the lawns, there's a fountain there, and one dog was drinking from it.

See, I can't help but remember things like that. Even now, I'd rather find some way, even though he's not asking for it, to forgive Glenn. I'd rather have it work out with him, because I want more days like that. I wish I could have a whole life like that. But I guess nobody does, not just me.

I saw him in the mailroom yesterday, we're both just standing there, each opening our little boxes, getting our mail— neither of us had any—I was hurt but I wanted to reach out and touch his face. He has this hard chin, it's pointy and all bone. Lauren says she wants to hit him.

I mean, I think of him spinning around in his backyard and that's why I love him and he should understand. I go over it all and think I should have just looked at him and said I can't believe you're doing this to me. Right there in the mailroom. Now when I think that, I think maybe if I'd said that, in those words, maybe it would be different.

But then I think of my father—he feels like there was a time when we had fun, when we were happy together. I mean, I can remember being in my little bed with Dad and maybe cracking jokes, maybe laughing, but he probably never heard Danny's baseball in his mitt the way I did or I don't know. I remember late in the afternoon, wearing my dad's navy blue sweatshirt with a hood and riding bikes with him and Danny down to the diamond.

But that's over. I don't know if I'm sorry it happened. I mean I am, but it happened, that's all. It's just one of the things that happened to me in my life. But I would never go back, never. And what hurts so much is that maybe that's what Glenn is thinking about me.

I told Lauren last night. I had to. She kept asking me what happened with Glenn. She was so good, you couldn't believe it, she was great. We were talking late and this morning we drove down to go to House of Pancakes for breakfast, get something good instead of watery eggs for a change. And on

the way, Lauren's driving, she just skids to a stop on this
street, in front of this elementary school. "Come on," she says.
It's early, but there's already people inside the windows.

We hooked our fingers in the metal fence. You know, one of
those aluminum fences around a playground. There were pi-
geons standing on the painted game circles. Then a bell rang
and all these kids came out, yelling, spilling into groups. This
was a poor school, mostly black kids, Mexican kids, all in bright
colors. There's a Nabisco factory nearby and the whole air
smelled like blueberry muffins.

The girls were jump roping and the boys were shoving and
running and hanging onto the monkey bars. Lauren pinched
her fingers on the back of my neck and pushed my head against
the fence.

"Eight years old. Look at them. They're eight years old. One
of their fathers is sleeping with one of those girls. Look at her.
Do you blame her? Can you blame her? Because if you can
forgive her you can forgive yourself."

"I'll kill him," I said.

"And I'll kill Glenn," Lauren says.

So we went and got pancakes. And drank coffee until it was
time for class.

I saw Glenn yesterday. It was so weird after all this time. I
just had lunch with Lauren. We picked up tickets for Talking
Heads and I wanted to get back to the lab before class and I'm
walking along and Glenn was working, you know, on the lawn
in front of the Mobi Building. He was still gorgeous. I was just
going to walk, but he yelled over at me.

"Hey, Jenny."

"Hi, Glenn."

He congratulated me, he heard about the NSF thing. We
stood there. He has another girfriend now. I don't know, when
I looked at him and stood there by the lawn mower, it's
chugging away, I felt the same as I always used to, that I loved
him and all that, but he might just be one of those things you
can't have. Like I should have been for my father and look at
him now. Oh, I think he's better, they're all better, but I'm
gone, he'll never have me again.

I'm glad they're there and I'm here, but it's strange, I feel more alone now. Glenn looked down at the little pile of grass by the lawn mower and said, "Well, kid, take care of yourself," and I said, "You too, bye," and started walking.

So, you know what's bad, though, I started taking stuff again. Little stuff from the mailroom. No packages and not people I know anymore.

But I take one letter a Saturday, I make it just one and someone I don't know. And I keep 'em and burn 'em with a match in the bathroom sink and wash the ashes down the drain. I wait until the end of the shift. I always expect it to be something exciting. The two so far were just everyday letters, just mundane, so that's all that's new, I-had-a-pork-chop-for-dinner letters.

But something happened today, I was in the middle, three quarters way down the bag, still looking, I hadn't picked my letter for the day, I'm being really stern, I really mean just one, no more, and there's this little white envelope addressed to me. I sit there, trembling with it in my hand. It's the first one I've gotten all year. It was my name and address, typed out, and I just stared at it. There's no address. I got so nervous, I thought maybe it was from Glenn, of course, I wanted it to be from Glenn so bad, but then I knew it couldn't be, he's got that new girlfriend now, so I threw it in the garbage can right there, one of those with the swinging metal door and then I finished my shift. My hands were sweating, I smudged the writing on one of the envelopes.

So all the letters are in boxes, I clean off the table, fold the bags up neat and close the door, ready to go. And then I thought, I don't have to keep looking at the garbage can, I'm allowed to take it back, that's my letter. And I fished it out, the thing practically lopped my arm off. And I had it and I held it a few minutes, wondering who it was from. Then I put it in my mailbox so I can go like everybody else and get mail.

"I wrote 'Lawns' the way I write most things, in pieces. The afternoon I began it, I felt like a criminal, reckless and alone. Mostly because I was poor. I'd gone to the bank machine and found I was overdrawn. I'd thought I had at least thirty dollars in the account but somehow I knew the machine was right and I'd subtracted wrong. I lived in New York then, I was twenty-five and wandering with no purpose in the afternoon on Columbus Avenue. I had three dollars and some change in my pocket. I walked into the Cherry Coffee Shop and ordered coffee and an enormous Jewish pastry. I was in graduate school and though it sounds exaggerated now to say it, I couldn't afford to be ordering what I was ordering in the Cherry Coffee Shop. But I sat down and started writing in the same spiral notebook I took notes in for Ed White's literature class.

" 'Lawns' went through many hands. I wrote it in a kind of desperate flash while working dead in the middle of a long novel which eventually became Anywhere But Here. *I was nowhere near finishing it or liking it. 'Lawns' came fast and with pleasure. It was a kind of breathless writing, urgent and desperate, which was how I felt. It was also a kind of release for me. Years earlier, I'd been a free-lance journalist and I'd done a long piece about incest and incest treatment. I'd worked on the piece maybe six months, driving to San Jose from my home in San Francisco every night after my regular job. I knew teen-age girls, women who'd been molested as children, mothers, sisters, fathers who had loved and molested their daughters. I was especially taken with a crayon drawing given to me by a play therapist, a woman who worked in a room full of toys with a picture of Nepal over her desk. A two-year-old molested by her grandfather had drawn herself on a tiny boat being pursued by a huge gray whale. In the course of therapy, she'd gone back to the picture. Later, she'd drawn in a weapon. She'd harpooned the whale.*

"I worked on the piece months, finally submitted it to The New York Times Magazine. *Eight months later, they got back to me, saying that incest was no longer a newsworthy topic. The* San Francisco Chronicle's Sunday Magazine *eventually (and generously) bought and ran the story, but they made*

many (necessary for their format) cuts. I felt I'd never been able to say most of what I'd learned. That was often true of journalism. You got more from the world than you could give back, in writing.

"So I wrote 'Lawns.' My friend Allan Gurganus tampered with the end. An editor named Jane Ciabattari, who had worked at the Chronicle's Sunday Magazine, *bought 'Lawns' for* Redbook, *where she worked. She left the magazine, though, and after a long lunch with an editor there who wanted to change most everything, I went home, worried, wrote a letter, tried to fight, lost and finally withdrew the story. Many magazines wrote back saying the subject matter was impossible. I felt thrilled when I opened the acceptance letter from* The Iowa Review. *I remember the day. I'd rushed into my apartment, dropping my books and backpack on the floor, ripping open the envelope. It was the second story I'd had accepted for publication. I celebrated with my friends. It's always meant a lot to me."*

Mona Simpson's short fiction has appeared in The Paris Review, Ploughshares, The Iowa Review, The North American Review *and other publications. Her stories have been selected for* Best American Short Stories, *the Pushcart Prize anthology. Her first novel was* Anywhere But Here.

Published in The Iowa Review.

LARRY BROWN
FACING THE MUSIC

For Richard Howorth

I cut my eyes sideways because I know what's coming.

"You want the light off, honey?" she says. Very quietly.

I can see as well with it as without it. It's an old movie I'm watching, Ray Milland in *The Lost Weekend*. This character he's playing, this guy will do anything to get a drink. He'd sell children, probably, to get a drink. That's the kind of character Ray's playing.

Sometimes I have trouble resting at night, so I watch the movies until I get sleepy. They show them, all-night movies, on these stations from Memphis and Tupelo. There are probably a lot of people like me, unable to sleep, lying around watching them with me. I've got remote control so I can turn it on or off and change channels. She's stirring around the bedroom, doing things, doing something—I don't know what. She has to stay busy. Our children moved away and we don't have any pets. We used to have a dog, a little brown one, but I accidentally killed it. Backed over its head with the station wagon one morning. She used to feed it in the kitchen, right after she came home from the hospital. But I told her, no more. It hurts too much to lose one.

"It doesn't matter," I say, finally, which is not what I'm thinking.

"That's Ray Milland," she says, "Wasn't he young then." Wistful like.

So he was. I was too once. So was she. So was everybody. But this movie is forty years old.

"You going to finish watching this?" she says. She sits on the bed beside me. I'm propped up on the TV pillow. It's blue corduroy and I got it for Christmas last year. She said I was spending so much time in the bed, I might as well be comfortable. She also said it could be used for other things, too. I said what things?

I don't know why I have to be such a bastard to her, like it's her fault. She asks me if I want some more ice. I'm drinking whiskey. She knows it helps me. I'm not so much of a bastard that I don't know she loves me.

Actually, it's worse than that. I don't mean anything against God by saying this, but sometimes I think she worships me.

"I'm okay," I say. Ray has his booze hanging out the window on a string—hiding it from these boozethieves he's trying to get away from—and before long he'll have to face the music. Ray can never find a good place to hide his booze. He gets so drunk he can't remember where he hid it when he sobers up. Later on, he's going to try to write a novel, pecking the title and his name out, but he's going to have a hard time. Ray is crazy about that booze, and doesn't even know how to type.

She may start rubbing on me. That's what I have to watch out for. That's what she does. She gets in bed with me when I'm watching a movie and she starts rubbing on me. I can't stand it. I especially can't stand for the light to be on when she does it. If the light's on when she does it, she winds up crying in the bathroom. That's the kind of bastard I am.

But everything's okay, so far. She's not rubbing on me yet. I go ahead and mix myself another drink. I've got a whole bottle beside the bed. We had our Christmas party at the fire station the other night and everybody got a fifth. My wife didn't attend. She said every person in there would look at her. I told her they wouldn't, but I didn't argue much. I was on duty anyway and couldn't drink anything. All I could do was eat my steak and look around, go get another cup of coffee.

"I could do something for you," she says. She's teasing but she means it. I have to smile. One of those frozen ones. I feel like shooting both of us because she's fixed her hair up nice and she's got on a new nightgown.

"I could turn the lamp off," she says.

I have to be very careful. If I say the wrong thing, she'll take it the wrong way. She'll wind up crying in the bathroom if I say the wrong thing. I don't know what to say. Ray's just met this good-looking chick—Jane Wyman—and I know he's going to steal a lady's purse later on. I don't want to miss it. I could do the things Ray Milland is doing in this movie and worse. Boy. Could I. But she's right over here beside my face wanting an answer. Now. She's smiling at me. She's licking her lips. I don't want to give in. Giving in leads to other things, other givings.

I have to say something. But I don't say anything.

She gets up and goes back over to her dressing table. She picks up her brush. I can hear her raking and tearing it through her hair. It sounds like she's ripping it out by the roots. I have to stay here and listen to it. I can understand why people jump off bridges.

"You want a drink?" I say. "I could mix you up a little something."

"I've got some Coke," she says, and she lifts her can to show me. Diet Coke. At least a six-pack a day. The refrigerator's crammed full of them. I can hardly get to my beer for them. I think they're only one calorie or something. She thinks she's fat and that's the reason I don't pay enough attention to her, but it isn't.

She's been hurt. I know she has. You can lie around the house all your life and think you're safe. But you're not. Something from outside or inside can reach out and get you. You can get sick and have to go to the hospital. Some nut could walk into the fire station one night and kill us all in our beds. You can read about things like that in the paper any morning you want to. I try not to think about it. I just do my job and then come home and try to stay in the house with her. But sometimes I can't.

Last week, I was in this bar in town. I'd gone down there with some of these boys we're breaking in, rookies. Just young boys, nineteen or twenty. They'd passed probation and wanted to celebrate, so a few of us older guys went with them. We drank a few pitchers and listened to the band. It was a pretty good band. They did a lot of Willie and Waylon stuff. I'm thinking about all this while she's getting up and moving around the room, looking out the windows.

I don't go looking for things. I don't. But later on, well, there was this woman in there. Not a young woman. Younger than me. About forty. She was sitting by herself. I was in no hurry to go home. All the boys had gone, Bradshaw, too. I was the only one of the group left. So I said what the hell. I went up to the bar and bought two drinks and carried them over to her table. I sat down with them and I smiled at her. And she smiled back. In an hour we were over at her house.

I don't know why I did it. I'd never done anything like that before. She had some money. You could tell it from her house and things. I was a little drunk, but I know that's no excuse.

She took me into her bedroom and she put a record on, some nice slow orchestra or something. I was lying on the bed the whole time, knowing my wife was at home waiting up on me. This woman stood up in the middle of the room and started turning. She had her arms over her head. She had white hair piled up high. When she took off her jacket, I could tell she was something nice underneath. She took off her shirt, and her breasts were like something you'd see in a movie, deep long things you might only glimpse in a swimming suit. Before I knew it she was on the bed with me putting one of them in my mouth.

"You sure you don't want a drink?" I say.

"I want you," she says, and I don't know what to say. She's not looking at me. She's looking out the window. Ray's coming out of the bathroom now with the woman's purse under his arm. But I know they're all going to be waiting for him, the whole club. I know what he's going to feel. Everybody's going to be looking at him.

When this woman got on top of me, the only thing I could think was: God.

"What are we going to do?" my wife says.

"Nothing," I say. But I don't know what I'm saying. I've got these big soft nipples in my mouth and I can't think of anything else. I'm trying to remember exactly how it was.

I thought I'd be different somehow, changed. I thought

she'd know what I'd done just by looking at me. But she didn't. She didn't even notice.

I look at her and her shoulders are jerking under the little green gown. I'm always making her cry and I don't mean to. Here's the kind of bastard I am: My wife's crying because she wants me, and I'm lying here watching Ray Milland, and drinking whiskey, and thinking about putting another woman's breasts in my mouth. She was on top of me and they were hanging right over my face. It was so wonderful, but now it seems so awful I can hardly stand to think about it.

"I know how you feel," she says, "but how do you think I feel?"

She's not talking to me. She's talking to the window and Ray is staggering down the street in the hot sunshine, looking for a pawnshop so he can hock the typewriter he was going to use to write his novel.

A commercial comes on, a man selling dog food. I can't just sit here and not say anything. I have to say something. But, God, it hurts to.

"I know," I say. It's almost the same as saying nothing. It doesn't mean anything.

We've been married for twenty-three years.

"You don't know," she says. "You don't know the things that go through my mind."

I know what she's going to say. I know the things going through her mind. She's seeing me on top of her with her legs locked around my back. But she won't take her gown off. She'll just push it up. She never takes her gown off anymore, doesn't want me to see. I know what will happen. I can't do anything about it. Before long she'll be over her rubbing on me and if I don't start she'll stop and wind up crying in the bathroom.

"Why don't you have a drink?" I say. I wish she'd have a drink. Or go to sleep. Or just watch the movie with me. Why can't she just watch the movie with me?

"I should have just died," she says. "Then you could have gotten you somebody else."

I guess maybe she means somebody like the friendly woman with the nice house and the nice nipples.

I don't know. I can't find a comfortable place for my neck.

"You shouldn't say that," I say.

"Well it's true. I'm not a whole woman anymore. I'm just a burden on you."

"You're not."

"Well you don't want me since the operation."

She's always saying that. She wants me to admit it. And I don't want to lie anymore, I don't want to spare her feelings anymore, I want her to know I've got feelings too and it's hurt me almost as bad as it has her.

But that's not what I say. I can't say that.

"I do want you," I say. I have to say it. She makes me say it.

"Then prove it," she says. She comes close to the bed and she leans over me. She's painted her brows with black stuff and her face is made up to where I can hardly believe it.

"You've got too much makeup on," I whisper.

She leaves. She's in the bathroom scrubbing. I can hear the water running. Ray's got the blind staggers. Everybody's hiding his whiskey from him and he can't get a drink. He's got it bad. He's on his way to the nut house.

Don't feel like a lone ranger, Ray.

The water stops running. She cuts the light off in there and then she steps out. I don't look around. I'm watching a hardware store commercial now. Hammers and Skilsaws are on the wall. They always have this pretty girl with large breasts selling their hardware. The big special this week is garden hose. You can buy a hundred feet, she says, for less than four dollars.

The TV is just a dim gray spot between my socks. She's getting on the bed, setting one knee down and pulling up the hem of her gown. She can't wait. I'm thinking of it again, how the woman's breasts looked, how she looked in her shirt before she took it off, how I could tell she had something nice underneath and how wonderful it was to be drunk in that moment when I knew what she was going to do.

It's time now. She's touching me. Her hands are moving, sliding all over me. Everywhere. Ray is typing with two fingers somewhere, just the title and his name. I can hear the pecking of his keys. That old boy, he's trying to do what he knows he should. He has responsibilities to people who love him and

need him; he can't let them down. But he's scared to death.
He doesn't know where to start.

"You going to keep watching this?" she says, but dreamylike,
kissing me, as if she doesn't care one way or the other.

I don't say anything when I cut the TV off. I can't speak. I'm
thinking of how it was on our honeymoon, in that little room at
Hattiesburg, when she bent her arms behind her back and
slumped her shoulders forward, how the cups loosened and fell
as the straps slid off her arms. I'm thinking that your first love
is your best love, that you'll never find any better. The way she
did it was like she was saying, here I am, I'm all yours, all of
me, forever. Nothing's changed. She turns the light off, and we
reach to find each other in the darkness like people who are
blind.

---

*"The evolution of a story from murky idea to typewritten page
is sometimes a long and wandering process for me, but I can
still remember where I was and what I was doing when the first
vague images of this one came into my head. I was sitting in my
truck at a red light in Oxford one night, waiting to turn onto
South Ninth. All of a sudden I had a man and a woman on a
bed, with the television playing, and something wrong with
them. And for days afterward, it wouldn't go away. Sometimes
they do, but this one didn't, so I had to write it. I already had
a pretty good idea of what was going on. By the time I rolled in
the paper and turned on the machine, I knew. And I just
carried on from there. As for explaining why that particular
picture came to me in the first place, I can't. It was just
suddenly there, a thought like the thoughts everybody has
sometimes. What If?*

*"To make my people, I have to become them for a while. (I
don't like to call them characters.) Even if they are only make-
believe and products of my imagination, I have to live in their
skins, wear their clothes. I knew what that man on that bed*

*felt. He was scared to death. All I had to do was show why,
and try to offer him a way out.*

*"The rest of it, the bits and pieces, come from anywhere,
from everywhere. Mostly they come from listening to people,
from living, from memory, and condensing it all down to
imagination. Miss Welty has said that the writer gets no points
for style, since that's born in you, and a varying number of
points for imagination, which is left up to you. I go along with
that."*

*Larry Brown was born in Oxford, Mississippi, in 1951. He
served in the United States Marine Corps from 1970 to 1972,
and has worked as a firefighter for the City of Oxford for the
last fifteen years. He runs a small country store at Tula on his
days off, and lives at Yocona. His work has appeared in*
Easyriders, The Twilight Zone, Fiction International, Mississippi Review, The Greensboro Review *and* St. Andrews Review.
His first collection of short stories is Facing the Music.

Published in The Mississippi Review.

FREDERICK BARTHELME

COOKER

I tell Lily I'm tired of complaining about things, about my job, about the people I work with, about the way things are at home with her, about the kids and the way the kids don't seem to be coming along, about the country, the things the politicians say on television, on "Nightline" and on "Crossfire" and the other news programs, tired of complaining about everybody lying all the time, or skirting the truth, staying just close enough to get by, tired of having people at the office selectively remember things, or twist things ever so slightly in agrument so that they appear to be reasonable, sensible, and thoughtful, tired of making excuses for my subordinates and supervisors alike, tired of rolling and tumbling and being in a more or less constant state of harangue about one thing or another.

Lily, who is sitting on the railing of our deck petting the stray cat that has taken up with us, nods as I talk, and when I stop to think of the next thing I'm tired of complaining about, says to me, "I'm tired, too, Roger."

Our children—Christine, who is eight, and Charles, who is eleven—are in the yard arguing about the hose. Charles has the nozzle tweaked up to maximum thrust, and he's spattering water all around Christine, making her dance to get out of the way.

"Charles," I say, waving at him to tell him to get the hose away from Christine. "Quit screwing around, O.K.?"

"Ah, Dad. I'm not hurting her. I'm just playing with her. We're just playing."

"We are not," Christine says. "I'm not, anyway. I don't want to play this way." She twists herself into a collection of crossed limbs, a posture that says "pout" in a big way.

"Why don't you water those bushes over there?" Lily says, indicating the bushes that line our back fence. "They look as if they could use the water."

I say, "The thing is, I hate all these people. There's almost nobody I don't hate. Sometimes I see something on TV and I just go into a rage, you know?"

"What things?" she says. "See what things?"

"Somebody says a self-serving thing, I don't know, some guy'll say something about preserving the best interests of something or other, doing the best job he can and all that, upholding standards, and you can look at this guy and tell that what he's thinking is how can he make this sound good, how can he sell this thing he's saying, whatever it is."

"You're talking about the preachers, right?"

"They're all preachers now. They're all holier-than-thou, self-righteous killers. I mean, everybody's a flack these days, they'll say anything just as long as they can keep on making their killings. I see this all the time at work. A guy'll come in and make a big argument for his own promotion, and when he's done I don't even recognize the world he's talking about. Remember that interne we had last fall, kid from Colorado? Then we hired him, right? You know why? Because he made friends with Lumming and what's-his-name, the other guy in production."

"Mossy—isn't that it? Mosely?"

"Something. But when the personnel committee met to talk about this job, Lumming and Mossy didn't say a word about being friendly with this kid. They said he was the greatest thing since sliced bread. It was a clear and simple lie. No question."

"You're complaining about the office," Lily says. "I thought the point of this talk was that you wanted to stop complaining."

"I do, but this stuff is driving me nuts. I don't want to be in a world where this stuff goes on."

"Go to Heaven," Lily says.

"Thanks. That's real interestingly cynical."

"Why not do a little discipline? Ease up." She spins herself off the railing and thumps as her feet hit the deck. "Besides, what would you do if you didn't complain? You wouldn't have anything to talk about."

"You're a charmer," I say. "You're a swell guy. An ace wife and companion."

"Mother of your children," she says, rolling the Weber into place.

"You cooking out here tonight?"

"You are," she says. "Therapy."

I don't mind that. In fact, I'm pleased that she's found something for me to do, something to occupy me, take my mind off the office and the things people are doing wrong. I used to be a lot more easygoing than I am now, and Lily, of course, recognizes that. Watching her mess with the grill, I wonder if she doesn't miss that more than anything else. "What am I cooking?" I ask. I should know the answer to this. I helped bring the groceries in from the car, helped her put them away. I have no idea what groceries they were.

"Lamb chops," she says.

This makes me feel better. Lamb chops, and suddenly the world is new, a place of mystery and possibility. Lily and my mother are the only two women on the planet who believe a lamb chop is a reasonable and appropriate thing to cook for dinner. That she wants them barbecued means I get to look up the recipe in the twenty-four-page no-nonsense Weber Kettle cookbook. I say, "We've got lamb chops?"

"Yep." She's redistributing the coals in the Weber, evening them. She squats beside the cooker and wiggles the bottom vent back and forth to release the ashes into the ash catcher, then dumps the ashes over the side of the deck. "I am serving corn and the lima beans, if you're interested."

"I love the lima beans," I say.

"So get cracking."

I go into the storage closet that opens onto the deck. I'm getting the barbecue tools. As I come out of there, I think: I have no desire to touch Lily. I don't know why, but that's what I think. She's not unattractive—in fact, she's quite lovely—but I don't want to touch her. It's not a desperate thing; I'm not thinking how awful it would be. But at the same time it's a clear thing. There isn't any question. She probably doesn't want to touch me, either. I wouldn't blame her. It's been a while since I've been in any kind of shape; I don't even like to touch me. I try to remember the last time we touched—apart from the usual, casual touches that happen without thinking. It's been weeks, maybe months. Not twelve months, but two, maybe.

I arrange my tools—barbecue tweezers and fork, hickory chips, Gulf lighter fluid—on the redwood table, and I think what brought this stuff about Lily to mind was a TV show I watched last night on CNN: A Los Angeles sex therapist answers all your questions after midnight. What struck me was the assumptions this woman made. She managed, without literally specifying, to predicate everything she said on a version of the ideal relationship which was a joke to me: one man and one woman having happy sex together forever. This was the implicit ideal. Now, we all know that's just plain wrong. It'll never happen. And yet here was this woman taking callers' questions, answering with the kind of dull-witted assurance and authority that characterizers these people: Here are the solutions, follow these three easy steps, put your little foot. I got angry watching this program. Somebody called in from Fairfax, Virginia, said sex wasn't interesting, and asked why this woman didn't get real.

I watched for an hour. This woman wore a lot of eye makeup. Not as much as Cleopatra, but plenty, more than enough. She was good-looking—a dark-skin, dark-hair type, with a handful of freckles—but there was something of the born-again about her, that kind of earnest matter-of-factness that makes you want to run the other way. Almost everybody's born-again these days; if you're not born-again you're out to lunch, yours is a minority view, you lose. Anyway, this woman had an easy rapport with the announcer, who was a newsman, and they traded asides, little jokes between callers' questions—he apologized a lot about his hopeless manhood.

I don't make too much of a mess with the cooking, though I'm pretty angry when I bring the chops in and drip lamb juice on the carpet in the living room. But before I have time to get worse, Lily's got the plate of chops out of my hands and is

telling me to remember three weeks ago, when I threw barbecue at the kitchen window.

"That was pork," I say. "And I don't know why you feel you
have to remind me about it all the time anyway. I cleaned it
up, didn't I?"

"Yes, Roger." She's circling the table, dropping lamb chops
on the plates. "It took you two hours, too."

"But it was real cool, Dad," Charles says, making a throwing
move. "Splat!"

I say, "No, my little porcupine, it wasn't."

"I agree," Christine says. "It was childish." She's repeating
what she heard her mother say immediately after I tossed the
pork chops.

"How old is she?" I ask Lily. I kiss the top of Christine's
head and then take my chair. "If you're real good," I say to
Christine, "we can get a dog later, O.K.?" She knows, I think,
that this is a joke.

"I think maybe you're trying too hard again, Dad," Charles
says. He's taken to adding "Dad" to every sentence. It's annoying.

"Yeah, Dad," Lily says. "Take it easy, would you?" She
pinches Charles' ear and turns him to face his dinner.

Charles squirms, trying to get away from her. "Jesus, Mom,"
he says.

"None of that, kid," I say. I wave my fork at him for empha-
sis, point it at him, wiggle it.

"Who wants a stupid dog, anyway?" Christine says. She's
using an overhand grip on her spoon, shoving the food on her
plate around to make sure that nothing touches anything else.
She's always eaten this way, ever since she was four. She'll eat
all of one vegetable, then all of the next, and so on. I've tried
to stop it, but Lily says it's O.K., so I haven't made much
progress. She says Christine will grow out of it. I say I know
that, but what will she grow into? Lily says I'm a hard-liner.

"You want a dog," I say to Christine. "What are you talking
about? All you said for the last three weeks is how much you
want a dog."

"That was before," she says.

"Before what?" Charles says. He turns to me as if we are

co-conspirators. "She wants one, Dad. I know she does. She's lying."

"Don't call your sister a liar," Lily says. "Roger, tell him."

"Your mother's right, Charles. Don't call Christy a liar, O.K.? Not nice." I'm just about finished with my first lamb chop. The mint-flavored apple jelly is glistening on my plate. I feel pretty good.

"It's true," Charles says. "What do you want me to do? Do you want me to lie, too?"

Christine is playing with her food, twirling her chop in the clear space she's left for it on her plate. "I wanted a dog," she says, "but now I don't. Can't anybody understand that?"

"I can't," Charles says.

"Eat your dinner, Charles," Lily says. "You can understand *that*, can't you?"

I know I shouldn't tease the kids the way I do—like telling them we can get a dog. It's a standing joke in our house. They knew we're not getting a dog. And they know why: Daddy's bad about dogs, about pets in general. Daddy looks at a dog and what he sees is a travel club for ticks and fleas. Try explaining that to a kid. Lily and I used to have big fights about it, but I won. I outlasted her. I'm not proud of it, but it's O.K. I don't mind winning one every now and then. She still thinks I'll come around after a while, but she's wrong about that. I've told the kids they can have fish, but they don't want fish.

So there's a history going on about this dog stuff, in the family, and I tease them about it all the time; it might sound cruel, but it seems to me they ought to understand. You can't always get with you want and all that. It's important that they know what's going on, that once they know no dog's forthcoming, then the dog is fair game. Lily says I'm crazy on this one, that kids don't work the way we do. She says I'm building a horrible distrust. She says it's not smart, that when I'm old and pathetic they'll trick me—tell me they're coming to see me and then not show, or take me out for a drive and slam me into a home or something.

"O.K.," I say. "I'm sorry I brought up the dog. The dog remark was a bad idea. No dog. Christine?"

"What?" She's petulant. "I know," she says.

"I shouldn't have said a thing about the dog, O.K.? I don't know why I did. I'm upset."

"Daddy's upset about the office, sweetheart," Lily says.

"I'm sorry," Christine says.

"He shouldn't take it out on us," Charles says. He turns to me, gives me a real adult look. "You shouldn't, Dad."

I don't think I like the way Charles is turning out. For a time, his early moves toward adulthood, the grave looks and the knowing nods, were charming, even touching. After all, he's a boy, a kid, and it's nice to see him practicing. But it gets old.

"I know that, Charles," I say. "Thank you."

"Well," he says, "I'm just trying to help."

Lily pats his arm. I don't know why mothers always pat their children's arms. It's disgusting. "Yes, Charles," she says. "But Daddy's tired. Let's just be quiet and eat, what do you say? Daddy's had a hard day."

"Another one?"

"That's enough, Charles," she says.

And it is enough. After that, we eat in silence. I watch Christine, who eats her corn first, kernel by kernel, then the beans. She doesn't even touch her lamb chop. When I finish eating, I take my plate to the kitchen, scrape the used food into the brown paper bag we keep under the sink—only now it's out on the kitchen floor in front of the cabinet—and put my plate under the faucet. I turn on the water for a few seconds to rinse, then go back through the dining area, stop behind Lily for a minute, and cross the room toward the back door. "I'm going to straighten up out here," I say. "I may water for a while."

"You're going to water?" Charles says.

"Finish eating," Lily says. "I think your father might want some individual time."

"What's individual time?" Christine says.

"Don't be dumb," Charles says to her.

What I'm thinking about, out there on the deck, is that I'm not living the way I ought to be living, not the way I thought I would be. It's all obvious stuff—women, mostly. I'm not Mr.

Imagination on the deal. A woman stands for a connection and another way of living, something like that. So I'm thinking about the woman on "West 57th," the TV show, and the dewy young girls in the movies—though you don't see them as much as you used to—and thinking of the poor approximations that throng the malls. I'm not thinking anything *about* these women, I'm only thinking *of* them.

I put the charcoal lighter back in the storage closet, finger the hickory chips, think for a minute about sitting down in there. This closet is about six feet square, lined with empty cardboard boxes that our electronics came in; we've kept computer boxes, stereo boxes, TV and VCR boxes, speaker boxes, tape-recorder boxes. Then I decide to do it, to sit down just the way I want to, and I go back to the deck and get one of the white wire chairs and put it in the storage room and sit down, my feet up on the second shelf of the bookcase that I bought from Storehouse so the junk we keep in the storage closet will be more orderly: charcoal, lighter, and chips on the bottom shelf, plant foods and insecticides on the second, plant tools on the third, also on the third electric tools (saw, drill, sander), and accessories on the top. It isn't too bad in there. From where I sit I can see out across the deck to the small lump of forest that borders one side of our lot. She always puts plants out there in the summer, and I look at those—pencil cactus, other euphorbias.

Lily comes out and walks right past the door of the storage closet out to the edge of the deck, looking around for me. "Roger?" she calls. "Roger, where are you?"

"Back here."

She turns and looks at me in the closet. "What are you doing in there, Roger?"

I say, "Thinking about my sins," which is a thing my mother always used to say when I was a kid, that she was thinking about her sins. She didn't have any sins to think about, of course, which is why it was a funny thing to say.

"Why don't you come out of there? Sit out here with me, O.K.?"

I say, "Fine," and pick up my chair and carry it back out to the spot on the deck where I got it.

She closes the storage door behind me. "Now," she says, sitting down on the deck railing. "You've got this nice family, these two kids and everything, this good job, and things are going great, right?"

"Things are O.K."

"Right. And you're complaining all the time about everything."

"Right."

"And you don't want to complain."

"Right."

"So you're like Peter Finch," she says. "In that movie, whatever it was. The one where he went out the window and said he was as mad as hell, remember?"

"Sure," I say. "What's the point?"

"Where'd it get him?" Lily says. "He's dead as a doornail. I mean, that's not *why* he's dead, but he is dead. I think there's a lesson in that."

I nod and say, "That lesson would be . . ."

"Take it easy, Greasy," Lily says.

"But everything's wrong now. People'll say anything. Everybody's transparent and nobody minds—like you, for example. Here, now. What you want is for me not to be upset. That's all. You don't care what I'm upset about, you just want me over it."

"Well?"

"In a better world we'd deal with the disease, not the symptom."

"In a better world we wouldn't have the disease," she says.

"Good point."

"Thank you."

Charles come out of the house carrying a sleeping bag, a yellow ice chest, some magazines, and the spread off his bed. "I'm camping out tonight, O.K.?" he says as he passes us.

I start to say no, but then Lily catches my eye and gives her head a little sideways shake. This means that she has already signed off on things.

"Watch out for spiders," I say.

"There aren't any spiders," Lily says, shaking her head. She smiles at Charles and holds out her arm to him, and he comes over for a kiss, trailing his equipment.

I nod. "That's right. No spiders. I just said that."

"Your daddy's having a hard time," Lily says.

Charles is hanging around in an annoying way, lingering. It's as if he doesn't really want to camp out in the back yard after all.

"I don't care about them anyway," he says. "I play with spiders at school." He waits a second, then says, "Dad, I'm making a tent. Is it O.K. if I use the boards behind the garage?"

I say sure.

It's dark, and we've got a pretty good tent in the yard. I'm in there with Charles. He's reading a car magazine and listening to a Bon Jovi tape on the portable we got him for his last birthday. I've already asked him to turn it down twice, and the second time he went inside for his earphones. It must be midnight. I'm lying on my back under the tent, my feet sticking out the back end of it, my head on one of the three pillows he brought out. The floor of our place here is cardboard, but we've got a rug over that, a four-by-seven thing that Lily and I got at Pier 1 about fifteen years ago. I got it out of the garage, where it's been a couple of years.

The bugs aren't too bad. Both of us rubbed down with Off, so there's this thin, slightly turpentine smell in the air.

I get along well enough with Charles. We're not like some "Father Knows Best" thing, but we do all right. He has his world and I have mine. Looking at him there in the tent, his head hopping with music, his eyes on the magazine, I have an idea what he's about, what it's like for him. I mean, he sees the stuff I see on TV and he believes it, or maybe he believes nothing, or maybe he recognizes that none of it makes any difference to him anyway. I guess that's it. And if that's it, he's right. Let 'em lie. We've got the yard, the bedspread tent, there are crickets around here, and pretty soon a cat will stick its head in the opening at the front of the tent, look us over, maybe even come in and curl up. What goes on out there is entertainment; I'm not saying it won't touch him, but the scale is so big that really it won't. We'll do another Grenada—what a pathetic, disgusting, hollow, ignorant joke that was—but he'll be in school, or doing desk work for some Army rocker, or waiting for his second child. He's just like me, he's out of it. He can get in if he wants to—he can be a TV guy, a reporter, a senator, a staff person. It's America. He can be anything, do anything. I'm stumped.

"What're you doing, Dad?" Charles says.

I keep looking at the top of the tent. "Thinking about you."

"Oh." He waits a minute, then he says, "Well? Is it a mystery or what?"

"It's no mystery," I say, rolling over on my side so I can look at him. He's got the earphones down around his neck. "What're you reading?"

"Bigfoot." He flashes the magazine at me. It's called *Bigfoot*. "The truck, you know?"

"Monster truck," I say.

"Right. It's a whole magazine about Bigfoot—how they got started, what happened, you know. . . ."

"You interested in trucks?" I say. What I'm thinking is, I don't like the way this sounds, this conversation. It sounds like conversations on television, fathers and sons in tortured moments. "Never mind," I say.

"Not really," he says, answering me anyway.

"I don't know why I'm out here, Charles," I say. "Am I bothering you?"

"Not really. I mean, it's strange, but it's not too bad."

"I'm just a little off track today, know what I mean? I think I'm down on my fellow-man—talking weenies everywhere, talking cheaters and liars. I mean, normally it doesn't bother me, I just play through. You do what you can. Pick up the junk and paste it back together whatever way you can."

"Dad? Are you drunk?"

"Nope," I say. "I haven't been drunk for ten years, Charles. There's nothing to drink about." I sit up, crossing my legs, facing him. "I never wanted to have a son—any child, for that matter. You and Christine are Lily's doing, what she wanted. I didn't mind, you see. It's not like I hate kids or anything, it's just that having kids wasn't the great driver for me. You're a problem, you know? Kids are. I don't want to treat you like a pet, but you're small—and, of necessity, kind of dumb. I don't mean dumb, but there's stuff you don't know, see what I mean?"

"Sure," he says.

"It's not stuff I can tell you."

"Dad," he says, "are you sure you're O.K.? You want me to get Mom?" He's up, bent over, already on his way out.

"Well . . . sure. Get Mom."

I lie down again when he's gone. I feel fine, I feel O.K. In a minute Lily's crawling into the tent. "Roger?" she says. "What's going on? Do you feel all right?"

"I'm functional."

Charles comes in long enough to get his magazine and his tape recorder. "I think I'll stay inside tonight," he says.

"I talked to him," I say to Lily.

"Uh-huh." She's got an arm across my chest and she's patting me.

"So long, Sport," I say to Charles as he backs out of the tent.

"Night, Dad," he says.

I'm left there in the tent with my wife. I say, "I'm acting up, I guess."

"A little."

"But that's acceptable, right? Now and then?"

"It's fine," she says.

"It's by way of a complaint, huh? So we're back where we started from."

"Yep."

"It's not a vague complaint in my head," I say. "It's just that it covers everything. There are too many things to list. You start listing things that are wrong and you either make them smaller and sort of less wrong, or you go on forever. You got forever?"

"Sure." She waits a few seconds after she says that; I can feel her waiting. Then she says, "But I've got to go to the mall sometime."

"All right."

She gets up on her knees and twists around so she can lie down on her back alongside me. She takes my right hand in

her left. "See there? You're not completely gone. You're O.K.
We've just got to take it one thing at a time. We've got to go
binary on this one."

———————————————————

" 'Cooker,' it turns out, is a sketch for a novel—that's the
'weird guy, plagued by the persistence of ordinary woes, goes
back-and-forth over edge' novel. Originally 'Cooker' was just a
story, with a story's limitations and half-life, then I liked it so
much, and thought it was so well focused, that I began thinking about enlarging it. This happened before, when I wrote a
story in 1982 called 'The Browns' which later became the novel
Second Marriage.

"There are two intriguing 'keys' in the story: first the way it
challenges credibility when, toward the end, the father tells the
son that he did not particularly want to have a child. This
stretches things to the breaking point—a parent wouldn't say
it—but I wanted to see if I could persuade readers that it was
not only possible for a parent to say it, but that there might
even be an argument for doing so—something about a higher
respect accorded the son by the father.

"Second, there is what makes the story expandable—the
father's discomfort in the world, his disenfranchisement, his
lack of recourse. All these touch a thread I take to be characteristic of all our lives—the sense of diminished control and the
tendency to decide that 'everything is wrong,' even if that
decision only exacerbates our undoing. The undoing—or its
avoidance—is what the story was, and the novel will be, about."

Frederick Barthelme's short stories have been collected in
Moon Deluxe and Croma. His novels include Tracer, Second
Marriage and Two Against One. He is the editor of Mississippi
Review and teaches at the University of Southern Mississippi.

Published in The New Yorker.

VERONICA GENG

A LOT IN COMMON

On January 10, 1941, at Piedmont Hospital in Atlanta, my mother wrote in the space for my first name on my birth certificate: "Annabelle." She was from Philly, but went down South with my father when the Army assigned him to Fort McPherson, and she must have gotten carried away. When she snapped out of it, she renamed me for her younger sister Vera. My baby book, bound in pink cloth, *Our Baby's First Seven Years,* was a present from Aunt Vera, and still has her congratulations card pasted in it:

May life bring *EVERY* joy to bless
  That tiny "dream of *HAPPINESS!*"

The book has a page for Baby's First Gifts, and my mother filled it in with her neat secretarial-school penmanship: "Bathinette—Granma. Toys—Granpa. Bunting—Aunt Vera. White wool shawl—Aunt Laura. Gold cross and chain—Ondine and Charlie O'Donnell. Baby hot water bottle—Mary Virginia Stealey. Gold heart necklace—Atlanta Q.M. Depot gang. Silver orange juice cup—Daddy. Sweater, cap, and booties—Mr. and Mrs. King (grocer). Piggie bank—Aunt Thelma." On the page for Favorite Toys, my mother wrote, "Horace the Horse" (a red stuffed horse with a white string mane). "At eleven months, Ronnie 'loved' it and sat on it." (I was nicknamed Ronnie so Aunt Vera wouldn't have to be Big Vera.)

•

When *Our Baby's First Seven Years* was full—when seven years' worth of physical development, food preferences, vocabulary growth, trips, and names of playmates had been duly

organized, recorded, and put away—my life was on the brink
of shapelessness, bereft of a unifying principle, vulnerable to
any dangerous pattern that might come along and attach itself
to my future in seven-year cycles of bad luck or a seventy-
seven-year evil spell. But on that very day, my seventh birthday, January 10, 1948, someone I would meet thirty-five years
later, a friend of mine named Donald, was born. This turn of
fortune took place in a postwar New Jersey suburb, or maybe it
was Brooklyn. His parents must have named him after the
Hollywood song-and-dance man Donald O'Connor, who had
been doing a series of low-budget Universal musicals as the
juvenile lead opposite such starlets as Ann Blyth and was
destined to make the Francis the Talking Mule movies.

•

Back in Philly, I celebrated many January 10ths with my
best friend, Marie, whose parents owned a greeting-card shop.
(After school, I'd help her put price tags on the cards with tiny
oval clips, making fun of the verses—"May life bring EVERY
joy to bless"—and then we'd go sit on a park bench and draw
pictures of women wearing spike heels and those seamed stockings with squared-off reinforcements up the backs of the ankles.) One birthday she gave me a record album of fairy tales
read by some actor; and whenever we listened to "Sleeping
Beauty," as the Prince approached the briar hedge that had
grown higher and higher till it covered the castle where lay the
Princess in her hundred-year sleep, Marie would stop the
record and intone, "He came to the edge of an impen—, an
impen—, an impen—, an impenetrable forest."

•

On January 10, 1949, after Donald's first birthday party, a
gathering of relatives at home, wherever that was, he fell
asleep on the sofa; and as his mother carried him to his crib,
tucked him in, and kissed his toys good night, he half woke to
the rustling of her full-skirted cocktail dress of changeable
taffeta, a popular fabric of the period, shimmering black green
black green black green black in a sensuous poetry of flux
which made a lifelong impression on him. I don't know how I
know this, but in that moment he internalized a blissful,
bamboozling mockery of his own intellectual rigor. When he

turned five—January 10, 1953—his kindergarten teacher had
him sent to a nearby college or university for I.Q. testing, a fad
of the era. Little Donnie was seated in front of a board with
different geometric-shaped holes in it, given a selection of
geometric blocks, and told to fit each block in the correct hole.
"You must be joking," he said, as with a sweep of one small
hand he sent the blocks flying.

•

Bobby Fischer used to say things like "Crash!" and "Ka-
boom!" when he captured pieces. At fourteen, he won the U.S.
Chess Championship—on January 7, 1958, just three days
before my seventeenth birthday. He was a mysterious intimate
—a peer I knew of but didn't know. A better me, out there
untouchable. Hazel-eyed Bobby, however, was not the one
whose passage would intersect with mine. He had been born
on March 9th (or, according to one source, 12th), on a life path
to Brooklyn, Cleveland, "I've Got a Secret," Mar del Plata,
Stockholm, Cuba by telex, Zagreb, Spassky, silence. Not even
close.

•

On January 10, 1963, Donald's fifteenth birthday, his parents
gave him a Raleigh English bike. He made his preferred sandwiches (peanut butter and marshmallow fluff), lashed his collection of 45s to the bike rack, and left home, cycling due west
through Pennsylvania. Near the Maumee River in northwest
Ohio, on the outskirts of Defiance, with 714 miles on the
odometer, he finally realized that being a ward of the state
wasn't all it was cracked up to be, and retraced his route. (I'm
sure this is right about the 714, because it was also Joe Friday's
badge number.)

•

That year, I was just out of the University of Pennsylvania
and living in New York for the first time. My younger brother,
Steve, was studying bad-younger-brother behavior, hanging
around the city and getting in trouble. On my birthday we
went to the Five Spot and heard Roland Kirk play weird
instruments he'd invented and named—stritch and manzello. I
don't want to name the deep trouble my brother got into
around that time; it scared me, and one night I refused to let

him stay in my apartment even though it was raining. I still think about this, although he forgave me and later a psychiatrist told me science couldn't say what I should have done.

•

Donald spent his twentieth birthday—January 10, 1968—buying a mattress for his first New York pad. He was carrying it back from Dixie Foam, balanced on his head, when he heard rolling thunder. The hard rain that had been predicted for five years began to fall, saturating the foam and turning it into a giant, burdensome, oppressive household sponge. He became a feminist.

•

I don't remember much about my birthdays through the nineteen-seventies, but probably they had something to do with sex.

•

By Donald's twenty-sixth birthday—January 10, 1974—he had wandered out to L.A. Some girlfriend called him that afternoon and asked him to meet her in fitting room No. 7 in the lingerie department at Bullock's, in Westwood. When he pulled the curtain, he found her in there wearing nothing but a lacy black garter belt, mesh stockings, spike heels, and an apron, bending over a chafing dish and a lighted can of Sterno, making his favorite dessert, crêpes with Clementine-orange sections and Cointreau *flambés:* mother, sister, hostess, lover. . . . Bullock's pressed charges. Neither Donald nor the girlfriend served any time, but the store's inhospitality so aroused his antibureaucratic temperament that he stopped feeling guilty about frittering away his life at the track.

At Santa Anita, where he went most mornings, the trainers and stablehands welcomed his presence around the stalls, for he had a way with the horses. His magic was to call them by names he made up instead of the monikers laid on them by the owners. One day, after Donald had made his usual pre-race visit to the paddock, a magnificent chestnut stallion who had not lived up to his potential (neither would I if I were on the books as Can't Get Arrested), having heard for the first time what he must have felt all along was his true name, went out smoking, sprinted clear along the inside, was in full flight at midstretch, and crossed the wire with something left—winner by six lengths in the Nature vs. Nurture Futurity. This, of course, was the famed champion henceforth known unofficially as Impenetrable.

Once a few stories like that got around, Donald's services were widely sought for consultations and christenings. Among his successes over the next decade were High I.Q., the semiretired fourteen-year-old he nicknamed High Heels to inspire her stunning comeback in the 1975 Bobby Fischer Memorial Sweepstakes; 1976's Dixie Derby sensation, Marie, a big bay mare who had suffered from an aging crisis until Donald tactfully called her Philly; Changeable Taffeta (the first thoroughbred yearling he was hired to name), who in 1977 swept the Cross and Chain Handicap and the Silver Orange Juice Cup; Booties, who won in a waltz after crashing the 1979 Dragnet Invitational; Stritch and Manzello, the siblings who took win and place for a combined purse of $850,000 in the 1981 Sterno Hospitality Classic;' and the 40–1 long shot who captured the 1982 Piggie Bank Stakes, the amazing Just a Coincidence.

On Donald's thirty-fifth birthday—January 10, 1983—his secretary made a list, for thank-you notes, of the presents he got (and I believe these touched his heart more than the huge fees he commanded): white cashmere saddle blanket—Calumet Farm; gold I.D. bracelet—Mom and Dad; silk-covered hot-water bottle in black and green stripes, racing colors of Grimm Stables—Grimm brothers; silver horse-insignia roach clip—Chet (groom, Pimlico); greeting card with verse ("May life bring EVERY joy to bless/Ese pequeñito sueño de FELICIDAD!")—Angel Cordero.

•

January 10, 1988, was my forty-seventh birthday, Donald's fortieth. Some years ago he had wandered back East, to New York, and made his home here, and we'd met through my boyfriend, Jimmy, a photographer who had taken his picture. When we first found out we had the same birthday, we didn't make a big deal out of it, but as we became friends it seemed more and more significant. This year, we discussed offering ourselves for a new kind of study by those people in Minnesota who studied twins. Our hypothesis was that the many similarities in our lives formed a pattern; that discovering the pattern made us feel happy; and that our case might provide valuable data for investigating the phenomenon of friends reared apart. But we were afraid of being rebuffed as astrology cranks, or as frauds who had subjectively distorted the truth out of pure longing to have a lot in common. So, with a sweep of his hand and mine, we sent the scientific method flying, and threw a party.

"This was done as a birthday present for a friend who really is named Donald, really does have the same birthday as mine, and really was throwing a party with me. I had always written satires and parodies, which, even at their most cheerful, were based on criticism or self-criticism; but here, for the first time, there were no negative impulses whatsoever. I just wanted to express my affection in the form of a unique, prettily made object. Something heartfelt but also careful and technically polished—nothing sloppy. Since I intended to publish the story, I didn't want to embarrass or exploit this person, so I made a rule that all the parts about my life would be true but all the parts about his life would be invented. This gave me a sense of structure, and responsibility, within which I felt permitted to write about myself and my family more directly than I ever had, and to let loose a lot of free associations, trusting that a pattern would develop. Some magic was operating. I was in a state of joyfully controlled abandon. This is my ideal of what every writing experience should be. I love remembering it. I hope to find it again.

"Looking at the story from a distance, I like the way it distinguishes between fact and fiction. And between history and wishful thinking. Also, I'm happy that its extreme particularities and coincidences don't seem to make other people feel excluded. Maybe it touches a chord about the fortunes of friendship."

Veronica Geng has been a regular contributor to The New Yorker *for about ten years. Harper & Row has published two collections of her comic fiction:* Partners *and* Love Trouble Is My Business.

Published in The New Yorker.

ISABEL HUGGAN

ORPHA KNITTING

Orpha thought she knew why she had suddenly, for the first time in her life, started to knit. The reason was it looked good. It made her look good and might even have the additional benefit of making her good, just the way she'd been told it would when she was a child. *The devil finds work for idle hands* and *Busy fingers do the Lord's work*. She had elected to be stubborn and lazy, had refused to learn, had deliberately dropped the needles and tangled the yarn in clumsy fits of temper. But now? Now she looked good and industrious and pure of heart. Who had ever thought ill of a woman knitting? Madame Defarge and the French Revolution aside, what woman knitting had ever thought ill? Ah, that was really it then, wasn't it? Knitting could make you good from the inside out. Women who knit are God-fearing, family-loving caretakers of society, keeping the feet of Our Boys warm in the trenches, fashioning baby cardigans in pale pastels, belief in the future manifest in every stitch. Women who knit make the world good.

I must be a good woman, Orpha would think, smiling. How could I be otherwise and be knitting? Impossible. Think a harlot would knit? A shoplifter, childbeater, cheater at cards or stealer of other wives' husbands? Never. Those women are the sort who never lift a finger in their lives, unless to paint their nails. *Those* women just don't care.

What I am doing, Orpha decided, is making something of myself, just the way my mother wanted me to. I must exist if I knit—isn't that Descartes? *Je tricote, donc je suis*. I am pulling myself together in the careful twist of wool around needle, in the looping and twisting and never letting go. There is a virtue here, yes, I am saving myself by this good deed. *Woman Saves Self with Knitting Needle*. No more woolly thoughts, not while knitting knots. All for naught? Oh, surely not, thought Orpha. Surely not.

Orpha and her husband and her children live in a red brick house on a street where all the houses are red brick. Under a canopy of old maples (once there were elms but, of course, they are dead and gone), this street is in a part of town much sought after because it is well settled and established. Even the houses have settled in, sagging comfortably in the earth. Surprising, Orpha thinks, that something made of brick should sag, and realizes how deep is her childhood belief that the little pig's house was safe from the wolf because it was brick. "You're a real brick, Orph," her friends would say because she was steadfast, never let them down, never sagged. And yet here is the brick house she lives in, with gaps and cracks in the mortar, with an enormous split in the wall of the basement where water drips in every spring. When they moved in—was that nine years ago or ten?—she and Russell had had to wedge pieces of carpet under the stove and fridge; the kitchen slanted from east to west and if you set an egg on the counter near the toaster it would roll right along to the sink. But the house *looks* substantial. You can't tell from the outside.

Last year on one of those educational specials on television, there'd been a program on continental drift, with computerized diagrams of what the shifting plates must look like. They'd all been watching—Orpha, Russell, Stuart and Jenny—since these science shows were one of the few things Orpha allowed; most of the stuff on the box, she said, was a sham and a waste of time. Even the news was unreliable, really, slanted and cut and arranged for sensational value. That night none of them had said a word until it was over, had sat in rapt fascination watching great swatches of land unlock and collide, millions of years pressed into their shining tube. Time and the shape of things, the mysterious energy at the earth's core, reduced to moving dots of color on the screen. Recent film footage gave visual proof of new chasms appearing along the San Andreas Fault—made more dramatic by a clutch of wide-eyed zealots predicting the world's end would begin in California. Earnest scientists in book-lined labs pointed at maps, documented their theories, gave support to their hypotheses, tied the whole thing up. No question, by the end of the program this business of shift and drift was something you could believe in.

"Maybe there'll soon be a new religion to sign up for," said Orpha, as she flicked off the set. She had risen quickly at the commercial, knowing that the program following was one her children would watch if she didn't prevent them. "Something vaguely Heraclitean, I'd imagine, celebrating flux and flow." Orpha had done her graduate work in pre-Socratic philosophy, and it was an old joke between her and Russell that she could find a place for Heraclitus in any conversation. Occasionally, after a little too much wine with dinner, say, or if she was feeling dissatisfied about some aspect of her life, Orpha would speak the name with bitterness, aware that those years of study had come only to this, a clever irrelevant remark now and again.

"Flux would certainly account for why the drains in the basement don't work," Russell said, stretching his arms above his head, laughing. Always ready to find the humor, ready to lean back and let life happen. Not uptight like me, Orpha decided.

"But things aren't moving *here*, Dad," said Stuart, his thin face so like his father's, except for the intensity of his small, narrow nose and his slightly crossed hazel eyes. He was at an age—had always been, perhaps—when he could not bear being left out of adult banter. He would pop up, butt in, wanting to connect and be part of it all. Was it possible to be so irritated by your own child and still be a good mother? There was one to knit about, thought Orpha.

"What I mean is, we're on the Shield here," said Stuart, responding to his mother's sudden turn of the head with an urgent rise in the pitch of his voice. "*It* isn't moving. Everything is solid where *we* are."

Stuart had done a school project on mining—when was that, grade six?—and all the information he had gathered had clung like lichen to a rock ever since. He had loved the Canadian Shield for some reason and had made that the heart of his project. Maybe it was simply the heraldic connotations of the word, the chivalrous sound of that pre-Cambrian base that so appealed to him; he was, ordinarily, a child whose interests were literary rather than scientific. On the map he drew and colored that year, there was a wonderful sweeping strength in the way the Shield fanned out from Hudson Bay, dipping down to where they sat in a red brick house on the tree-lined street. Ah, what Blake could have done with that, had he lived here instead of in England's green and pleasant land. *Bring me my arrows of desire, Bring me my shield of igneous rock.*

"Nothing is solid anywhere, inland or not," Orpha said sharply, wanting in some deep, peevish part of herself to put him down, to quiet that shrill, insistent, thirteen-year-old voice. There was something about Stuart these days that reduced her to an adolescent level of response—she knew it and couldn't stop it, kept trying to disguise these feelings from him and herself. Unsuccessfully. "You've studied the atom this fall, Stuart, you know that everything's always in motion. Besides, nothing is certain, nothing is stable, nothing is sure. Your father is right. We have flux in the basement of our lives." She was smiling, this was meant after all to be a joke, but her voice felt harsh and wicked in her throat.

Sure enough, Jenny began to cry. "That's *horrible*, Mom. You're saying we can't be sure of anything, like we could have an earthquake right here, aren't you? I'm going to have nightmares now and it'll be your fault."

Ever searching for the dramatic moment, ten-year-old Jenny put her head in her hands and wept. There had been a heavy, melancholic cast to her chubby features since birth, something sweetly brooding in her expression even as she slept. "She enjoys crying, I swear she does," Orpha would say after one or another of their tearful arguments—they'd been meeting head-on since Jenny was two. She'd laugh and shrug to show Russell she was just kidding, didn't for a moment believe what she was saying.

Now what she did was to reach down to the floor beside the couch and pick up her knitting. It was her new gesture. "If you say you're going to have nightmares, then you'll have nightmares," she said to Jenny in the calm and reasonable tone she'd been adopting lately. "It all depends on what you want. Don't exaggerate everything."

"Well, *you* did," said Jenny, lip thrust out, defiant, ready for a quarrel about something, anything, nonexistent earthquakes. A curve of dark hair fell forward on her cheek in exactly the same way as her mother's, and she brushed it back with an angry hand.

"You did, actually," said Russell, smiling, taking the edge off, the peaceable peacemaker at work. "I think it may be a family failing." He looked over at Orpha and winked, indicating he was on her side, at the same time as he reached towards Jenny and pushed her shoulder in a mocking, comradely sort of way. It was odd, when you thought of it, that Russell's field was conflict—he taught history at the university, where he had made his reputation with a course on revolution—and what he sought in his own life was to avoid disagreement of even the mildest kind.

Orpha began to knit without even looking at the pattern book. She didn't care if she had to rip it out later, she had to do something now to keep from lashing out, slapping that sulky face of Jenny's. Her only female child, flesh of her flesh, and she wanted to hit her more often than not. She never had, aside from a few flash-temper spankings during the tantrum years, but her restraint was due more to Russell's benign interventions than her own inclinations. When she considered the way he interfered with her responses, always smoothing things over, always rearranging and tamping down, she could get so angry. And yet, without him, what then? What would she do without him at this moment, for example?

She looked over at her son, sitting there with his damn glasses sliding down his nose again, intense and thin, endlessly holding forth about how much he knew. She wanted, desperately, for him to be silent, but she did not have the same urge to slap him as she did Jenny. Something more awful and sinister, like stuffing his socks in his mouth and hissing at him, "Shut up, Stuart." And then she'd push his glasses up his nose and fasten them to his forehead with tape so they sat properly on his face for once. Oh, imagine! Honestly! Where did these

thoughts come from? I'm barely forty, it can't be the meno-
pause yet, she thought, knitting.

Knitting, knitting, Orpha knows there is blackness in her
heart and is frightened because there is no reason for it. No
reason at all. It is just there. She hopes that as long as she is
knitting no one will know what she is thinking. She hopes she
will stop thinking if she can only knit hard enough.

Another call from Brenda. It comes, as do must of Brenda's
calls, well after midnight, after the bottle of vodka is gone.
Without the solace of drink, the phone offers itself to Brenda as
an alternative to suffering alone. The call means the following
scene takes place: Russell turning over in bed, slowly putting
the pillow over his head, never worrying that the ringing
means death or disaster, always assuming it will be Brenda
again. Russell hunching the duvet up around his shoulders as
Orpha is saying, "Hang on, Bren, I'll go downstairs. Wait till I
pick up the phone there, okay now? Don't hang up, now . . ."
Finding her dressing gown on the hook behind the door,
feeling her way out of the dark into the carpeted hallway where
a nightlight makes eerie shadows float along the walls as she
hurries down the stairs. In the kitchen, plugging in the kettle
even before picking up the phone, knowing she will need a cup
of tea while she sits there, wishing she still smoked, wishing
there were a packet of cigarettes in the house for such emer-
gencies. Listening to Brenda's raspy breathing, somehow able
to smell the smoke through the receiver and wanting to feel
the bite of that smoke at the back of her throat. Saying loudly,
"Hang up now, Russ," and knowing he would; eavesdropping
would be the last thing he'd do in the middle of the night. He
hates knowing how unhappy people are, he never wants details
of Brenda's troubles after one of these calls even if Orpha offers
them in marital fellowship. "It's a shame, a rotten bloody shame,"
is all he ever says, cutting her off, preventing her from telling.
This is not history, it is present, immediate pain, and he wants
no part of it.

The reason for the calls is the same every time—the breaking up of Brenda and Nick's marriage, going on now for four,
five years. Some marriages end wham, bang, lipstick on the

collar and by god, into the courts and out again, free and ready to roll. Others take a very long time, splitting, mending, breaking, fixing—no one ever seems to know the right thing to do. Trial separations, trial reunions, sweet reconciliations and sad, sad leavings. Marriage in remission, shifting affections, deep hostilities, incompatible love.

No wonder Brenda drank.

Brenda and Orpha had been friends since they were Jenny's age—all those years collected and stored between them, shared responsibility for an enormous amount of knowledge. What this meant to Orpha was you had to take the bad with the good, you had to answer the phone when it rang, had to listen to the hysteria and anger and not respond in kind.

(But oh, how to respond kindly on these nights when Brenda's slurred voice would slug its way through the air looking for someone to hurt, and find her, Orpha, in the dark. Drunk and malicious, the voice would mutter and croon, abusive and hurtful. "Did I wake your hubby up? Hmmm? Did you have your man all warm and cosy there beside you, and did I wake him up and make him mad? Oh, but your Russie never *gets* mad, does he, Orph? Don't you wish he would? Just once? Get really *mad?*" And Orpha would sit and listen, thinking that maybe someday she could collect this debt, but for now she would dwell on the years they had shared, waiting until Brenda blew herself out like a storm. After all, if she were Brenda, she might feel this bad. Wondering if Brenda would sit in the dark and listen to her.)

Remembering twenty years ago, Brenda's wedding—the first of them all—and her not being the maid of honor as she'd expected. Brenda saying, "Oh jeez, Orphie, don't take this wrong but see my mother picked these dresses and I never thought, and jeez, you can see how terrible you'd look in these crinolines and all this tulle. It's not even your color, Orph, it doesn't suit you. Look. I'm sorry, I never thought it meant so much to you. Don't be mad, okay? Okay?"

Looking at herself in the mirror and knowing Brenda was right, Orpha smiled at her best friend who was going off and getting married and not finishing university. Brenda was so

smart—she had even had the wit to quote Pascal to her parents
when they tried to dissuade her from marrying Nick—and she
always won. "Sure, okay, you're right, I'm far too plump to
wear this stuff," Orpha said, hating herself for being both
overweight and vain. "But I want so much to be a part of your
day, Bren. Let me sing, how about that? I could wear something else if I sing."

And so another girl wore the dress and Orpha sang, standing
in the choir loft of the small Presbyterian church, with bright
spring light shining in the window and falling on her opened
music as if on cue. Handel, chosen by Brenda's mother. *Father
in Heaven abiding, Who hears our prayers at all times, Grant
us . . .* Grant us what? Happiness forever? That's all we were
asking for with our weddings, with our white dresses and
bridesmaids and trailing bouquets. That's all. Orpha tries now
to remember the rest of the line, with Brenda's voice raging
hot in her ear, tries to find the melody, finds it, hums it in her
head . . . no, the words have all melted back into time. Gone.
To the music of Handel and Bach, to the strains of Mendels-
sohn and Brahms, they'd had it wrong. Now Brenda weeps on
the phone bitter and blaming, and Orpha sits in the dark,
waiting and fearful. Grant us what? Grant us anything, Lord, it
doesn't matter what. Nothing lasts forever. Nothing lasts.

Since she began knitting last year, Orpha has made the following items: A curling sweater for Russell with sleeves that are
too long but which he cheerfully rolls up. A yellow cardigan for
Jenny who says it doesn't *go* with anything, and a pullover for
Stuart who complains it is itchy at the neck. Two pairs of
bedsocks for her mother who is in a chronic-care home and
whose feet are always cold. (Her mother always has the socks
on when Orpha visits every Tuesday. She wants to encourage
her daughter in this late-blooming proficiency which she re-
gards as a good omen. Orpha has taken a long time to settle,
she thinks.) Four scarves in varying shades of blue for the
family to wear in the annual Christmas photograph. Three
sweaters and bonnets for newborns. (You never know nowadays who's going to have a baby next; some friends are having
late ones, others have teen-age daughters starting early.) A

variety of Barbie doll outfits for Jenny and her friends, and
several pairs of mitts. Twenty-seven squares for an afghan; this
was how she began the knitting and she still hasn't finished it.
Nine dishcloths out of string to use at the summer cottage.

Stuart is bright enough to do well at school in everything but
math. This year, in grade eight, he is having a real struggle
with algebra, to the point where his teacher suggested during
parents' night interview that Russell and Orpha arrange for
private tutoring. "I can't give extra attention to every student
who needs it," the teacher had said, managing to shed responsibility and pass it on. Annoyed, but seeing he had no choice,
Russell put up notices for a tutor on bulletin boards around the
university. Orpha put an ad in the community paper, stuck
more notices on the board at the health food store and in the
window of the bookshop where she works part-time. Within a
week there were several applicants, eventually whittled down
to three likely prospects among whom Stuart was told to choose,
since it was important, Orpha said, that he feel *involved*. He
picked the one she liked least, an engineering student named
Mike.

"I don't dislike him," she said to Russell. "I just have reser-
vations. He seems, I don't know, kind of thuggish."

"You have a noticeable bias against engineers," said Russell
with a laugh, picking up an armload of books to take back to
the library. "You always did prefer us bookish types."

"We all have our weaknesses," Orpha said. "Well, anyway,
maybe I meant sluggish rather than thuggish, come to think of
it. As long as he engineers some algebra into Stuart's head, the
rest doesn't matter."

Mike's own head sat squarely on a short, thick neck which
seemed barely to rise from his shoulders, giving him a heavy-
jawed appearance strangely at variance with a soft, barely
audible voice. He had his pale blond hair cut very short so that
in an odd way his head seemed hairless, a protuberance of
muscle and bone, an extra limb stuck on his solid, stocky body.
He wore sweatshirts with the university crest on the chest, a
mode of dressing that struck Orpha as particularly unimagina-
tive. "Typical engineer's approach to fashion," she said at sup-

per that night, describing Mike's wardrobe to Russell. "Needs the shirt to remind him where to go every day."

Stuart got up suddenly from the table, his thin face flaming with indignation. "You think you're so smart," he said to his mother. "Well, *he* can do algebra and *he* can help me get good marks. And you can't. And I wish you'd shut up." And before he could be told to go to his room to cool off, he ran up the stairs.

"He's right, you know," said Russell. "We do go on."

Orpha considered flinging her plate of chicken and peas to the floor and storming out, considered making a speech about the tyranny of the bland, considered busting into tears and throwing her arms around Jenny, who was sitting there watching with wide eyes, waiting to see what would happen next. "Ah will try to mend mah ways," she said, in a mocking imitation of a Southern accent, chastened slave implicit in her bent head and apologetic tone. "Ah does have a wicked tongue in my head, an' ah truly repents."

Laughter, supper goes on, the end.

But not the end, because Orpha knew Stuart's anger was deep and had to be acknowledged by her in some other real way. When Mike arrived for his next session, there were cups of hot chocolate and muffins set out on the table, and she said, carefully so that Stuart would hear, "We really do appreciate what you're doing, Mike. Neither of us have a head for math at all. Have you always been good at it?"

Little conversations then, Mike mumbling in his soft voice and looking at the floor while he'd answer her questions. Over the winter weeks, the habit of a few moments spent chatting either before or after the tutoring—Orpha realized it had become part of her expectations. Sometimes, baleful sideways glances from Stuart to indicate that his mother was monopolizing Mike and embarrassing him, and sometimes, painful silences when no one could think of anything to say. Then Mike would eat and drink with gusto, making appreciative noises as he swallowed, and Orpha would stand by the stove wiping the countertops, or chopping up vegetables for supper. "There is a rustic quality to our relationship, such as it is," she said to Russell one night after the children had gone to bed and they could talk freely. "Maybe it comes from his being a country boy, but I feel like a farm wife when he's in the kitchen. Or else something lurking and barely verbal in a Bergman film."

March, and for Stuart the Easter exams coming, for Mike the end of term. Intense work and increased supplies of food and drink from Orpha, urging Mike to have a second bagel, another glass of milk, an apple to take in his pocket.

"You have to keep your strength up," she'd say, patting Stuart's thin, bony shoulder. "Both of you."

One afternoon Stuart announced he had to leave early, he was doing his friend Andy's paper route that week. "Andy's got mono," he said. "And there are two other kids in our class who might have it too. It'd be a neat way to get out of exams."

Stuart out the door quickly with that last remark, Mike gets ready to pull his books and papers together and leave too, but Orpha stops him with the offer of more hot chocolate. "There's only a little left in the pan, Mike, you might as well finish it up," she says.

He sits at the table in the family room looking at the floor, his back to Orpha, waiting for the second cup he doesn't really want, while she stirs the milk and wonders what to say. Looks at the top of his head where the fair hair swirls out from a central point—a small, flat whirlpool of wispy hair that shows the scalp beneath. And as she stares at this place, she is struck by the babyish quality of the pale skin under the hair. He really isn't very old, she thinks, remembering her babies and the vulnerable softness right at the top of their heads, and her fear of washing their hair for those first few months. A deliberate strategy, it seemed, to keep new mothers anxious and sleepless, that business of the soft spot. Dreaming at night that she, forgetful, had carelessly brushed the baby's hair with her own stiff brush and managed to mash its brains. Waking from these dreams (with both children, the same dream) and patting the forehead of the sleeping infant, touching where it was safe to touch, feeling such tenderness and apprehension.

And out of somewhere comes the memory of her father's bald spot, how there had been a joke when she was a child that he had lost his hair through Orpha and her mother kissing the top of his head, day after day. The little round hairless patch

grew larger with each passing year until finally there was a
shiny, hard leathery dome fringed with gray. "Your mother
won't let me alone, just look at this," he'd say to Orpha when
she was home on weekends once she'd gone away to university, was out working, married, away. "Oh Daddy," she'd say,
bending over the chair to kiss his bald head, "I think you've
had a secret harem for years. Mom and I couldn't have done all
this ourselves!"

And then, soon after that, looking at him in his coffin, his face
untroubled and dreaming, his skin powdered carefully by the
undertaker so that there was no shine. Subdued by death, the
matte finish on his scalp was ludicrous on the white satin
pillow. Wanting to laugh, or shout, or to kiss him one last
time—but holding back, of course, not doing it. Why had she
not made that one last gesture? How long ago had it been, yes,
five years this spring. Had she really been so fearful of his
lifeless form, her father no longer her father?

Still looking at the top of Mike's head, walking over to where
he sits, seeing that exposed place of male vanity, thinking of
her father, her babies, unraveling old thoughts, she bends and
kisses his bald spot. Startled, Mike turns, reaching up to swat
whatever had—a fly? a kiss? this woman?—and looks at her
with clear and curious eyes. He sees a woman still bending,
her dark hair falling on either side of her pensive face, still
dreaming. And as she is beginning to straighten, he rises,
catches her hand and moves toward her. And both of them,
daring, eye-to-eye, kiss.

A passionate kiss that has nothing to do with anything but
itself. Unexpected, inarticulate, inevitable, intrinsic. His soft
young mouth so unlike Russell's, nearly like a girl's, nearly like
kissing her own fearful self, Orpha thinks. Opening her lips
and kissing, loving the taste of hot chocolate and toast in his
mouth. Opening her eyes fully now, seeing the table, the
room, Mike's face, pulling apart, oh! what if Jenny . . . Stuart
. . . Russell . . .

"And do you know what he *did?*" she said next to Brenda,
telling all this on the phone late at night, whispering even
though she was sure Russell wasn't listening, was sprawled
deep in sleep on her side of the bed, keeping it warm for her

return. "D'you know? He took his pulse! He did! He looked at me with great amazement and put his two fingers on his wrist. It was the most moving gesture, somehow. Oh, I don't know, as if his heart was racing and he feared for his life. Maybe he has a heart condition, who knows?" (Laughter, great hiccups of laughter.) "Or well, maybe he was testing the effects of the kiss, what kind of rush it gave him. Maybe there's a drug equivalent to the middle-age kiss."

More laughter, hers and Brenda's, sitting in their dark kitchens after midnight pretending their sadnesses can be dispelled by laughter, by sharing, by analysis. Women find such peculiar ways of getting through, Orpha thinks, and that makes her laugh even harder.

Stuart did just fine without a tutor, as it turned out. It was near the time when Mike would have been quitting anyway, so nothing much was said when he phoned to say he couldn't come back. No one mentioned him much. He had never been part of their lives in any real way, and Stuart said now he thought he was kind of boring. Russell had only met him twice. "Nice boy, wasn't he? Turned out to be the right medicine, didn't he?"

Sometimes Orpha would find herself weeping when she was alone, especially in the kitchen, where she would imagine him sitting, surprised by her again and again. She would touch her mouth with her hand and imagine the softness of his lips and the swirl her tongue made in his mouth before they drew apart. Who had been more surprised, she wondered, Mike or herself? When had she ever done anything so wildly out of place, so absurdly satisfying?

A funny story for Brenda, that's all it was now, nothing to feel sad about, but still she wept, and took to keeping paper towels in her pocket just in case. "Imagine!" she said to Brenda weeks later, although Brenda was drunk and not listening. "I still do think about him, you know. About the kissing. Everything. Do you suppose I might turn into one of those women who go around picking up teen-age boys? Do you think my moral fiber is disintegrating? Is this how it starts?"

* * *

One night in June the children and Orpha are having supper in front of the television set because Jenny has a school assignment to watch the news. Russell is off at the Learned Society meetings in Vancouver, and Orpha is at loose ends, and enjoying it. She pours herself a glass of wine to drink with the hot dogs, and flips through a magazine as her children check off the day's litany of horrors. War and famine, starvation and mutilation, hijackings and crashes, slickly and quickly into their heads and out again. Barely observed. Orpha is preparing one of her speeches about televised news when her attention is caught by a woman on the screen with a long sad face. She has those mournful pouches under the eyes that give an impression of great fatigue and resignation. She is sitting in a green living room talking to an off-screen reporter about her husband, recently ousted as leader of a political party. She is being asked to comment on his downfall, and the interviewer is using phrases such as "just unceremoniously dumped." She is being baited; the network wants temper, reaction, *color*.

Orpha is struck by two things. The furnishings in the room are tasteful and forgettable except for a lampshade, directly to the left of the woman's shoulder, which has been set askew. In that orderly room the shade becomes a comic turn, the apparent flaw begging forgiveness for everything else. The other thing she notices is that the politician's wife is knitting. Her hands, which move industriously with a life of their own during the entire interview, are broad-knuckled and scarlet-nailed. "So much for my theory about women with painted nails," Orpha says aloud, and the children make shushing noises.

Even when the woman stops to collect her thoughts, her hands are working. She seems to be making one of those Arran sweaters—there is a large heap of beige wool on her lap. She eventually speaks with candor, telling how upset she is at the press's treatment of her husband. "Oh, if you only *knew* him," she says, "the way we in the family do. Why he phones home every day, no matter where he is. Always has done. We've always been a close-knit family." The needles click and loop and whirr—the fingers and the wool change places so swiftly it seems like a magic art, a sleight of hand. Of course, thinks

Orpha, it is all trickery and subterfuge. The woman is clearly lying. An expert liar and knitter. An expert wife.

It is late summer and the family is at the cottage on a pretty stretch of river not far from where they live. The cottage is a small, dun-colored prefab set on cement blocks on the sandy banks. It slipped badly during the spring thaw so that now it lists badly, rather like a stranded ship. Russell explains to Jenny that it has nothing to do with shifting plates and tries to enlist her aid as he lies down in the shallow space under the cottage with a jack and pieces of wood, trying to prop up the tilting side. He discusses water tables and the properties of sand, but Jenny is not convinced and will not come under to help him, in case the cottage may collapse. She stays at the edge, watching.

The mosquitoes are so bad this season everyone smells of bug spray, and there is an odor of lemon oil and tar and sweat that is sharp and pleasant, in contrast to the darker smells of the riverbank—fish and mud and rotting wood. Orpha is sitting out on the end of their small dock, and beside her Stuart is casting a line into the water, catching catfish and letting them go. He pulls up his hook now and again, and there is always a fish, wriggling and ugly, caught through its mouth. "Ugly as sin," Orpha says, and Stuart says, "It can't help it, Mom, it's only a catfish." She does not like to see her son engaged in this cold-hearted play, but what is there to say? They *are* only catfish, after all, and he does throw them back.

She is knitting a very difficult, intricate pattern, a lacy dress with a drawstring waist, the first thing she has made for herself. As she knits she thinks about writing a letter to Brenda; their last call ended with Orpha slamming the receiver down in anger. "I've had enough, Bren," she had said, in what seemed to her at the time a cold and final voice. "You sicken me with your self-pity and the way you try to make me feel as bad as you do. I hate these drunk calls. Don't phone again unless you're sober." That had been two months ago and there'd been no word from Brenda. Orpha is thinking now maybe she should get in touch, and wonders what made her so angry that night. Why is she fed up? Is she really frightened by Brenda?

She realizes, as she sits in the sunlight knitting, that even the most complicated pattern she can find is not enough to still her mind. She cannot keep the darkness out, even with this. How utterly laughable anyway, thinks Orpha, that a woman like me would knit to keep herself together. She looks over at her husband's pale legs sticking out from under the cottage, and sees Jenny crouched nearby, holding her father's bottle of beer and talking to him. Connected, but still careful. She looks at her son's skinny frame and the ridge of spine down his back as he leans away from her on the other side of the dock, watching for the slightest movement in the amber water. She looks at her own brown skin, only a few mauve veins showing through here and there, and thinks how beautiful she is at this age. Thinks of Brenda, who will never be happy, ever.

She does not really plan to do what she does, but she is aware that she is doing it and that it is the only thing to do. She stands up suddenly, so that the knitting falls from her lap into the water. It seems like an accident. She makes no sound but stands there watching the swift current take it away, the needles floating up like slender masts from the bulky bundle of yarn. Slowly it submerges as it disappears around a clump of speedwell and loosestrife at the bend in the river.

"Perhaps I feel so fondly about this story because it is the first one published since The Elizabeth Stories. *Here, instead of telling a story from a child's point of view, I'm on the edge of an adult woman's consciousness, which requires another kind of writing entirely. Although Elizabeth's growth was described in terms of fragments, those 'moments' were building her character 'like coral atolls in the Pacific . . . moment upon moment'; here, however, the fragments suggest the increasing disintegration Orpha feels in her life, against which she so feebly fights back with her knitting. Here, I wanted to portray someone who is undergoing the terror I believe comes to all of us as we realize 'there is flux in the basement of our lives,' and in spite of ourselves we are, in Paul Simon's words, 'slip-sliding*

away.' This story is about the slow progression of awareness, nothing like the brilliant epiphanies of childhood.

"I like this story too because of how it came to me, very differently from the way most of my stories have—usually they've been constructed organically over a period of time by carefully juxtaposing various feelings, memories, images. But this one came slamming in from outer space, wham-bang. Suddenly there was a line in my head: Orpha knew exactly why she had begun to knit. *I knew no one of this name, nor do I knit . . . but it seemed such a compelling line, I felt obligated to do something with it, to try to discover who Orpha was, and what the knitting might mean. This took me a very long time, off and on for months, wondering about this mysterious woman. It wasn't until I began to see Orpha's hairstyle that she herself, and her life, began to come clear. I saw her daughter's hair then, so much like her mother's, and I saw the way Orpha's hair swung forward as she kissed the top of the boy's head, and then I knew she had kissed her father that way, and that she was honeycombed with hollow regrets—the way we all are. As my sympathy for her grew, scene after scene materialized, and all I had to do was choose among them. Heraclitus was part of the story from very early on, as a counterbalance to this need of Orpha's to knit everything together into a meaningful pattern. I've been sitting happily on a Heraclitean riverbank for years, and it was lovely having an opportunity to use that in a story."*

Isabel Huggan's short fiction has been collected in The Elizabeth Stories. *She currently lives in Nairobi, Kenya, with her husband and daughter.*

Published in Western Living.

ROBERT COOVER

THE PHANTOM OF THE MOVIE PALACE

We are doomed, Professor! The planet is rushing madly toward Earth and no human power can stop it!" "Why are you telling me this?" asks the professor petulantly and sniffs his armpits. "Hmm. Excuse me, gentlemen," he adds, switching off his scientific instruments and, to their evident chagrin, turning away, "I must take my bath." But there is already an evil emperor from outer space in his bathtub. Even here then! He sits on the stool and chews his beard despondently, rubbing his fingers between his old white toes. The alien emperor, whose head looks like an overturned mop bucket, splashes water on the professor with his iron claw and emits a squeaky yet sinister cackle. "You're going to rust in there," grumbles the professor in his mounting exasperation.

The squat gangster in his derby and three-piece suit with boutonniere and pointed pocket handkerchief waddles impassively through a roomful of hard-boiled wisecracking bottle-blond floozies, dropping ashes on them from his enormous stogie and gazing from time to time at the plump bubble of fob watch in his hand. He wears a quizzical self-absorbed expression on his face, as though to say: Ah, the miracle of it all! the mystery! the eternal illusion! And yet . . . It's understood he's a dead man, so the girls forgive him his nasty habits, blowing at their décolletages and making such vulgar remarks and noises as befit their frolicsome lot. They are less patient with the little bugger's longing for the ineffable, however, and are likely, before he's rubbed out (will he even make it across the room? no one expects this), to break into a few old party songs just to clear the air. "How about 'The Sterilized Heiress'?" someone whispers even now. "Or, 'The Angle of the Dangle!' " " 'Roll Your Buns Over!' " "Girls, girls . . . !" sighs the gangster indulgently, his stogie bobbing. " 'Blow the Candle Out!' "

The husband and wife, in response to some powerful code from the dreamtime of the race, crawl into separate beds, their only visible concession to marital passion being a tender exchange of pajamas from behind a folding screen. Beneath the snow-white sheets and chenille spreads, they stroke their strange pajamas and sing each other to sleep with songs of faith and expediency and victory in war. "My cup," the wife gasps in her chirrupy soprano as the camera closes in on her trembling lips, the luminescent gleam in her eye, "runneth over!" and her husband, eyelids fluttering as though in prayer, or perhaps the onset of sleep, replies: "Your precious voice, my love, here and yet not here, evokes for me the diaphanous adjacency of presence—" (here, his voice breaks, his cheeks puff out) "—and loss!"

The handsome young priest with the boyish smile kneels against the partition and croons a song of a different sort to the nun sitting on the toilet in the next stall. A low unpleasant sound is heard; it could be anything really, even prayer. The hidden agenda here is not so much religious expression as the filmic manipulation of ingenues: the nun's only line is not one, strictly speaking, and even her faint smile seems to do her violence.

The man with the axe in his forehead steps into the flickering light. His eyes, pooled in blood, cross as though trying to see what it is that is cleaving his brain in two. His chest is pierced with a spear, his groin with a sword. He stumbles, falls into a soft plash of laughter and applause. His audience, still laughing and applauding as the light in the film flows from viewer to viewer, rises now and turns toward the exits. Which are locked. Panic ensues. Perhaps there's a fire. Upon the rippling velour, the man with the split skill is staggering and falling, staggering and falling. *"Oh my god! Get that axe!"* someone screams, clawing at the door, and another replies: *"It's no use! It's only a rhetorical figure!"* *"What—?!"* This is worse than anyone thought. *"I only came for the selected short subjects!"* someone cries irrationally. They press their tear-streaked faces against the intractable doors, listening in horror to their own laughter and applause, rising now to fill the majestic old movie palace until their chests ache with it, their hands burn.

Ah, well, those were the days, the projectionist thinks, changing reels in his empty palace. The age of gold, to phrase a coin. Now the doors are always open and no one enters. His films play to a silence so profound it is not even ghostly. He still sweeps out the vast auditorium, the grand foyer and the mezzanine with their plaster statues and refreshment stands, the marble staircase, the terraced swoop of balcony, even the orchestra pit, library, rest rooms, and phone booths, but all he's ever turned up is the odd candy wrapper or popcorn tub he's dropped himself. The projectionist does this intentionally, hoping one day to forget and so surprise himself with the illusion of company, but so far his memory has been discouragingly precise. All that human garbage—the chocolate mashed into the thick carpets, the kiddy-pee on the front-row seats and the gum stuck under them, sticky condoms in the balcony, the used tissues and crushed cups and toothless combs, sprung hairpins, stools clogged with sanitary napkins and water fountains with chewing gun and spittle and soggy butts—used to enrage him, but now he longs for the least sign of another's presence. Even excrement in the Bridal Fountain or black hair grease on the plush upholstery. He feels like one of those visitors to an alien planet, stumbling through endless wastelands in the vain search for life's telltale scum. A cast-out orphan in pursuit of a lost inheritance. A detective without a clue, unable even to find a crime.

Or, apropos, there's that dying hero in the old foreign legion movie (and where is that masterpiece? he should look for it, run it again some lonely night for consolation) crawling inch by inch through the infinite emptiness of the desert, turning the sand over in his fingers in the desperate hope of sifting out something—a dead weed perhaps, a mollusk shell, even a bottle cap—that might reassure him that relief, if not near at hand, at least once existed. Suddenly, off on the horizon, he sees, or seems to see, a huge luxury liner parked among the rolling dunes. He crawls aboard and finds his way to the first-class lounge, where tuxedoed gentlemen clink frosted glasses and mill about with ladies dressed in evening gowns and glittering jewels. "Water——!" he gasps hoarsely from the floor, which unexpectedly makes everyone laugh. "All right, whiskey then!" he wheezes, but the men are busy gallantly helping the ladies into lifeboats. The liner, it seems, is sinking. The men gather on the deck and sing lusty folk ballads about psychologically disturbed bandits. As the ship goes down, the foreign legionnaire, even while drowning, dies at last of thirst, a fool of sorts, a butt of his own forlorn hopes, thereby illustrating his commanding officer's earlier directive back at the post on the life of the mercenary soldier: "One must not confuse honor, gentlemen, with bloody paradox!"

The mischievous children on the screen now, utterly free of such confusions, have stolen a cooling pie, glued their teacher to her seat, burned a cat, and let an old bull loose in church. Now they are up in a barn loft, hiding from the law and plotting their next great adventure. "Why don't we set the school on fire?" suggests one of them, grinning his little freckle face gap-toothed grin. "Or else the truant officer?" "Or stick a hornets' nest in his helmet?" "Or in his *pants!*" They all giggle and snicker at this. "That's great! But who'll get us the hornets' nest?" They turn, smiling, toward the little one, squatting in the corner, smeared ear to ear with hot pie. "Kith my ath," she says around the thumb in her mouth. The gap-toothed kid clasps one hand to his forehead in mock shock, rolls his eyes, and falls backwards out the loft door.

Meanwhile, or perhaps in another film, the little orphan girl, who loves them all dearly, is crawling up into the hayloft on the rickety wooden ladder. No doubt some cruel fate awaits her. This is suggested by the position of the camera, which is following close behind her, as though examining the holes in her underwear. Or perhaps those are just water spots—it's an old film. He reverses it, bringing the orphan girl's behind back down the ladder for a closer look. But it's no good. It's forever blurred, forever enigmatic. There's always this unbridgeable distance between the eye and its object. Even on the big screen.

Well, and if I *were* to bridge it, the projectionist thinks, what then? It would probably be about as definitive an experience as hugging a black hole—like all those old detective movies in which the private eye, peering ever closer, only discovers, greatly magnified, his own cankerous guilt. No, no, be happy with your foggy takes, your painted backdrops and bobbing ship models, your dying heroes spitting blood capsules, your faded ingenues in nunnery loos or up loft ladders. Or wherever she might be. In a plane crash or a chorus line or a mob at the movies, or carried off by giant apes or ants, or nuzzled by grizzlies in the white wastes of the Klondike. The miracle of artifice is miracle enough. Here she is, for example, tied to the railroad tracks, her mouth gagged, her bosom heaving as the huge engine bears down upon her. Her muffled scream blends with the train's shrieking whistle, as sound effects, lighting, motion, acting, and even set decor—the gleaming ribbons of steel rails paralleling the wet gag in her mouth, her billowing skirts echoing the distant hills—come together for a moment in one conceptual and aesthetic whole. It takes one's breath away, just as men's glimpses of the alleged divine once did, projections much less convincing than these, less inspiring of true awe and trembling.

Sometimes these flickerings on his big screen, these Purviews of Cunning Abstractions, as he likes to bill them, actually set his teeth to chattering. Maybe it's just all this lonely space with its sepulchral room presence more dreadful than mere silence, but as the footage rolls by, music swelling, guns blazing, and reels rattling, he seems to see angels up there, or something like angels, bandannas on their faces and bustles in their skirts, aglow with an eery light not of this world. Or of any other, for that matter—no, it's scarier than that. It's as though their bones (as if they had bones!) were burning from within. They seem then, no matter how randomly he's thrown the clips together, to be caught up in some terrible enchantment of continuity, as though meaning itself were pursuing them (and him! and him!), lunging and snorting at the edge of the frame, fangs bared and dripping gore.

At such times, his own projections and the monumental emptiness of the auditorium spooking him, he switches everything off, throws all the houselights on, and wanders the abandoned movie palace, investing its ornate and gilded spaces with signs of life, even if only his own. He sets the ventilators and generators humming, works the grinding lift mechanisms, opens all the fountain cocks, stirs the wisps of clouds on the dome, and turns on the stars. What there are left of them. To chase the shadows, he sends the heavy ornamented curtains with their tassels and fringes and all the accompanying travelers swooping and sliding, pops on the floods and footlights, flies the screen and drops the scrim, rings the tower chimes up in the proscenium, toots the ancient ushers' bugle. There's enough power in this place to light up a small town and he uses it all, bouncing it through the palace as though blowing up a balloon. Just puzzling out the vast switchboard helps dispel those troublesome apparitions; as they fade away, his mind spreading out over the board as if being rewired—s-*pop!* flash! *whirr!*—it feels to the back of his neck like the release of an iron claw. He goes then to the mezzanine and sets the popcorn machine thupping, the cash register ringing, the ornamental fountain gurgling. He throws the big double doors open. He lets down the velvet ropes. He leans on the showtime buzzer.

There are secret rooms, too, walled off or buried under concrete during the palace's periodic transformations, and sometimes, fleeing the grander spaces, he ducks down through the low-ceilinged maze of subterranean tunnels, snapping green and purple sugar wafers between his teeth, the crisp translucent wrapper crackling in his fist like the sound of fire on radio, to visit them: old dressing rooms, kennels and stables, billiard parlors, shower rooms, clinics, gymnasiums, hairdressing salons, garages and practice rooms, scene shops and prop rooms, all long disused, mirrors cracked and walls crumbling, and littered with torn posters, the nibbled tatters of old theatrical costumes, mildewed movie magazines. A ghost town within a ghost town. He raids it for souvenirs to decorate his lonely projection booth: an usherette's brass button, some child star's paperdolls, old programs and ticket rolls and colored gelatin slides, gigantic letters for the outdoor marquee. A STORY OF PASSION BLOODSHED DESIRE & DEATH! was the last appeal he posted out there. Years ago. THE STRANGEST LOVE A MAN HAS EVER KNOWN! DON'T GIVE AWAY THE ENDING! The only reason he

remembers is because he ran out of D's and had to change
BLOODSHED to BLOOSHED. Maybe that's why nobody came.

He doesn't stay down here long. It's said that, beneath this
labyrinth from the remote past, there are even deeper levels,
stair-stepped linkages to all the underground burrowings of the
city, but if so, he's never found them, nor tried to. It's a kind of
Last Frontier he chooses not to explore, in spite of his compul-
sive romanticism, and, sooner or later, the dark anxiety which
this reluctance gives rise to drives him back up into the well-lit
rooms above. Red lines, painted in bygone times on the tunnel
floors and still visible, point the way back, and as he goes, nose
down and mufflered in clinging shadows, he finds himself
longing once more for the homey comforts of his little projection booth. His cot and coffeepot and the friendly pinned-up
stills. His stuffed peacock from some demolished Rivoli or
Tivoli and his favorite gold ticket chopper with the silver
filigree. His bags of hard-boiled eggs and nuts. The wonderful
old slides for projecting blizzards and sandstorms, or descend-
ing clouds for imaginary ascensions (those were the days!), or
falling roses, rising bubbles or flying fairies, and the one that
says simply (he always shouts it aloud in the echoey auditorium): "PLEASE READ THE TITLES TO YOURSELF. LOUD READING
ANNOYS YOUR NEIGHBORS." Also his stacked collections of gossip
columns and animation cels and Mighty Wurlitzer scores. His
tattered old poster for *Hearts and Pearls: or, The Lounge-
Lizard's Lost Love*, with its immemorial tag line: "The picture
that could change your life!" (And it has! It has!) And all his
spools and tins and bins and snippets and reels of film. Film!

Oh yes! *Adventure!* he thinks, taking the last of the stairs up
to the elevator lobby two at a time and—*kfthwump!*—into the
bright lights. *Comedy!* He is running through the grand foyer
now, switching things off as he goes, dragging the darkness
along behind him like a fluttering cape. Is everything still
there? How could he have left it all behind? He clambers
breathlessly up the marble staircase, his heels clocking hollowly as though chasing him, and on into the projection room
tunnel, terror and excitement unfolding in his chest like a
crescendo of luminous titles, rolling credits—*Romance!*

"Excuse me," the cat woman moans huskily, peering at him

over her shoulder as she unzippers her skin, "while I slip into something more comfortable . . ." The superhero, his underwear bagging at the seat and knees, is just a country boy at heart, tutored to perceive all human action as good or bad, orderly or dynamic, and so doesn't know whether to shit or fly. What good is his famous X-ray vision *now?* "But—but all self-gratification only leads to tragedy!" he gasps as she presses her hot organs up against him. "Yeah? Well, hell," she whispers, blowing in his ear, "what doesn't?" Jumpin' gee-whillikers! Why does he suddenly feel like crying?

"Love!" sings the ingenue. It's her only line. She sings it again: "Love!" The film is packed edge to edge with matings or implied matings, it's hard to find her in the crowd. "Love!" There is a battle cry, a war, perhaps an invasion. Sudden explosions. Ricocheting bullets. Mob panic. "Love!" She's like a stuck record. "Love!" "*Stop!*" Bodies are tumbling off of ramparts, horses are galloping through the gates. "Love!" "*Everything's different now!*" someone screams, maybe he does. "Love!" She's incorrigible. "*Stop her, for god's sake!*" They're all shouting and shooting at *her* now with whatever they've got: arrows, cannons, death rays, blowguns, torpedoes—"Love . . . !"

The apeman, waking from a wet dream about a spider monkey and an anteater, finds himself in a strange place, protected only by a sticky breechcloth the size of a luncheon napkin, and confronted with a beautiful High Priestess, who lights up two cigarettes at once, hands him one, and murmurs: "Tell me, lard-ass, did you ever have the feeling that you wanted to go, and still have the feeling that you wanted to stay?" He is at a loss for words, having few to start with, so he steps out on the balcony to eat his cigarette. He seems to have been transported to a vast city. The little lights far below (he thinks, touching his burned tongue gingerly: Holy ancestors! The stars have fallen!) tremble as though menaced by the darkness that encases them. The High Priestess steps up behind him and runs her hand under his breechcloth. "Feeling moody, jungle boy?" World attachment, he knows, is the fruit of the tree of passion, which is the provoker of wrath as well as of desire, but he doesn't really know what to do with his knowledge, not with the exploitative hand of civilization abusing his noble innocence like this. Except maybe to yell for the elephants.

"Get away from that lever!" screams the scientist, rushing into his laboratory. But there's no one in there, he's all alone. He and all these bits and pieces of human flesh he's been stitching together over the years. There's not even a lever. That, like everything else in his mad, misguided life, is just wishful thinking. He's a complete failure and a presumptuous ass to boot. Who's he to be creating life when he can't even remember to brush his own teeth? This thing he's made is a mess. It doesn't even smell good. Probably it's all the innovations that have done him in. All these sex organs! Well, they were easier to find than brains, it's not entirely his fault, and no one can deny he did it for love. He remembers a film (or seems to: there is a montage effect) in which the mad scientist, succeeding where he in his depressing sanity has failed, lectures his creation on the facts of life, starting with the shinbone. "The way I see it, kid, it's forget the honors, and go for the bucks." "Alas, I perceive now that the world has no meaning for those who are obliged to pass through it," replies the monster melancholically, tearing off the shinbone and crushing his creator's skull with it, "but one must act as though it might."

Perhaps it's this, he thinks, stringing up a pair of projectors at the same time, that accounts for his own stubborn romanticism —not a search for meaning, just a wistful toying with the idea of it, because: what else are you going to do with that damned bone in your hand? Sometimes, when one picture does not seem enough, he projects two, three, even several at a time, creating his own split-screen effects, montages, superimpositions. Or he uses multiple projectors to produce a flow of improbable dissolves, startling sequences of abrupt cuts and freeze frames like the stopping of a heart, disturbing juxtapositions of slow and fast speeds, fades in and out like labored breathing. Sometimes he builds thick collages of crashing vehicles or mating lovers or gun-toting soldiers, cowboys, and gangsters all banging away in unison, until the effect is like time-lapse photography of passing clouds, waves washing the shore. He'll run a hero through all the episodes of a serial at once, letting him be burned, blasted, buried, drowned, shot, run down, hung up, splashed with acid, or sliced in two, all at the same time, or he'll select a favorite ingenue and assault her with a thick impasto of pirates, sailors, bandits, gypsies, mummies, Nazis, vampires, Martians, and college boys until the terrified expressions on their faces pale to a kind of blurred, mystical affirmation of the universe. Which, not unexpectedly, looks a lot like stupidity. And sometimes he leaves the projector lamps off altogether, just listens in the dark to the sounds of blobs and ghouls, robots, galloping hooves and screeching tires, creaking doors, screams, gasps of pleasure and fear, hoots and snarls and blown noses, fists hitting faces and bodies pavements, arrows targets, rockets moons.

Some of these stratagems are his own inventions, others come to him through accident—a blown fuse, the keystoning rake of a tipped projector, a mislabeled film, a fly on the lens. One night he's playing with a collage of stacked-up disaster movies, for example, when the layering gets so dense the images get stuck together. When he's finally able to peel one of them loose, he finds it stripped of its cracking dam, but littered with airliner debris, molten lava, tumbling masonry, ice chunks, bowing palm trees, and a whey-faced captain from other clips. This leads him to the idea ("What seems to be the trouble, Captain?" someone was asking, her voice hushed with dread and earnestness, as the frames slipped apart, and maybe he should have considered this question before rushing on) of sliding two or more projected images across each other like brushstrokes, painting each with the other, so to speak, such that a galloping cowboy gets in the way of some slapstick comedians and, as the films separate out, arrives at the shootout with custard on his face; or the dying heroine, emerging from montage with a circus feature, finds herself swinging by her stricken limbs from a trapeze, the arms of her weeping lover in the other frame now hugging an elephant's leg; or the young soldier, leaping bravely from his foxhole, is creamed by a college football team, while the cheerleaders, caught out in no-man's land, get their pom-poms shot away.

He too feels suddenly like he's caught out in no-man's-land on a high trapeze with pie on his face, but he can't stop. It's too much fun. Or something like fun. He drives stampedes through upper-story hotel rooms and out the windows, moves a monster's hideous scar to a dinner plate and breaks it, beards a breast, clothes a hurricane in a tutu. He knows there's something corrupt, maybe even dangerous, about this collapsing of boundaries, but it's also liberating, augmenting his film library exponentially. And it's also necessary. The projectionist understands perfectly well that when the cocky test pilot, stunt-flying a biplane, leans out to wave to his girlfriend and discovers himself unexpectedly a mile underwater in the clutches of a giant squid, the crew from the submarine meanwhile frantically treading air a mile up the other way, the crisis they suffer— *must* suffer—is merely the elemental crisis in his own heart. It's this or nothing, guys: sink or fly!

So it is with a certain rueful yet giddy fatalism that he sweeps a cops-and-robbers film across a domestic comedy in which the goofy rattle-brained housewife is yattering away in the kitchen while serving her family breakfast. As the frames congeal, the baby gets blown right out of its highchair, the police chief, ducking a flipped pancake, gets his hand stuck in the garbage disposal, and the housewife, leaning forward to kiss her husband while telling him about her uncle's amazing cure for potato warts, drops through an open manhole. She can be heard still, carrying on her sad screwball monologue down in the city sewers somewhere, when the two films separate, the gangster, left behind in the kitchen, receiving now the husband's sleepy good-bye kiss on his way out the door to work. The hood, disgusted, whips out his gat to drill the mug (where the hell is Lefty? what happened to that goddamn bank?), but all he comes out with is a dripping eggbeater.

Lefty (if it is Lefty) is making his getaway in a hot-wired Daimler, chased through the streets of the crowded metropolis by screaming police cars, guns blazing in all directions, citizens flopping and tumbling as though the pavement were being jerked out from under them. Adjacently, cast adrift in an open boat, the glassy-eyed heroine is about to surrender her tattered virtue to the last of her fellow castaways, a bald-headed sailor with an eyepatch and a peg leg. The others watch from outside the frame, seeing what the camera sees, as the sailor leans forward to take possession of her. "Calamity is the normal circumstance of the universe," he whispers tenderly, licking the salt from her ear, as the boat bobs sensuously, "so you can't blame these poor jackshites for having a reassuring peep at the old run-in." As her lips part in anguished submission, filling the screen, the other camera pulls back for a dramatic overview of the squealing car chase through the congested city streets: he merges the frames, sending Lefty crashing violently into the beautiful cave of her mouth, knocking out a molar and setting her gums on fire, while the sailor suddenly finds himself tonguing the side of a skyscraper, with his social finger up the city storm drains. "Shiver me timbers and strike me blind!" he cries, jerking his finger out, and the lifeboat sinks.

He recognizes in all these dislocations, of course, his lonely quest for the impossible mating, the crazy embrace of polarities, as though the distance between the terror and the comedy of the void were somehow erotic—it's a kind of pornography. No wonder the sailor asked that his eyes be plucked out! He overlays frenzy with freeze frames, the flight of rockets with the staking of the vampire's heart, Death's face with thrusting buttocks, cheesecake with chaingangs, and all just to prove to himself over and over again that nothing and everything is true. Slapstick *is* romance, heroism a dance number. Kisses kill. Back projections are the last adequate measure of freedom and great stars are clocks: no time like the presence. Nothing, like a nun with a switchblade, is happening faster and faster, and cause (that indefinable something) is a happy ending. Or maybe not.

And then . . .

THE NEXT DAY

. . . as the old titles would say, back when time wore a white hat, galloping along heroically from horizon to horizon, it happens. The realization of his worst desires. Probably he shouldn't have turned the Western on its side. A reckless practice at best, for though these creatures of the light may be free from gravity, his projectors are not: bits and pieces rattle out every time he tries it, and often as not, he ends up with a roomful of unspooled film, looping around his ears like killer ivy. But he's just begun sliding a Broadway girlie show through a barroom brawl (ah, love, he's musing, that thing of anxious fear, as the great demonic wasteland of masculine space receives the idealized thrust of feminine time), when it occurs to him in a whimsical moment to try to merge the choreography of fist and foot against face and floor by tipping the saloon scene over.

Whereupon the chorus-line ingenue, going on for the ailing star, dances out into the spotlight, all aglow with the first sweet flush of imminent stardom, only to find herself dropping goggle-eyed through a bottomless tumult of knuckles, chairs, and flying bottles, sliding—*whoosh!*—down the wet bar, and disappearing feet-first through a pair of swinging doors at the bottom of the frame. Wonderful! laughs the projectionist. Worth it after all! The grizzled old prospector who's started the brawl in the first place, then passed out drunk, wakes up onstage now as the frames begin to separate in the ingenue's glossy briefs and pink ankle-strap shoes, struggling with the peculiar sensation that gravity might not know which way it wants him to fall. Thus, his knees buckle, suggesting a curtsy, even as his testicles, dangling out of the legbands of the showgirl's briefs like empty saddlebags, seem to float upward toward his ears. He opens his mouth, perhaps to sing, or else to yelp or cadge a drink, and his dentures float out like ballooned speech. "Thith ith dithgratheful!" he squawks, snatching at air as he falls in two directions at once to a standing ovation. *"Damn your eyeth!"*

Over in the saloon, meanwhile, the brawl seems to have died down. All eyes not closed by fist or drink are on the swinging doors. He rights the projector to relieve the crick in his neck from trying to watch the film sideways, noting gloomily the clunk and tinkle of tumbling parts within, wishing he might see once more that goofy bug-eyed look on the startled ingenue's face as the floor dropped out from under her. There is a brief clawed snaggle as the film rips erratically through the gate, but an expert touch of his finger on a sprocket soon restores time's main illusion. Of which there is little. The swinging doors hang motionless. Jaws gape. Eyes stare. Not much moves at all except the grinding projector reels behind him. Then slowly the camera tracks forward, the doors parting before it. The eye is met by a barren expanse of foreground mud and distant dunes, undisturbed and utterly lifeless. The ingenue is gone.

He twists the knob to reverse, but something inside the machine is jammed. The image turns dark. Hastily, his hands trembling, he switches off, slaps the reels onto a spare projector, then reverses both films, sweeps them back across each other. Already changes seem to have been setting in: someone thrown out of the saloon window has been thrown back in, mouth crammed with an extra set of teeth, the stage is listing in the musical. Has he lost too much time? When the frames have separated, the old prospector has ended up back in the town saloon all right, though still in the ingenue's costume and with egg on his face, but the ingenue herself is nowhere to be seen. The ailing star, in fact, is no longer ailing, but is back in the spotlight again, belting out an old cowboy song about the saddleback image of now: *"Phantom Ri-i-i-ider!"* she bawls, switching her hips as though flicking away flies. "When stars are *bright* on a frothy *night*—"

He shuts both films down, strings up the mean gang movie with the little orphan girl in it: the water spots are there, but the loft ladder is empty! She's not in the nunnery either, the priest croons to an empty stall, as though confessing to the enthroned void—nor is she in the plummeting plane or the panicking mob or the arms, so to speak, of the blob! The train runs over a ribbon tied in a bow! The vampire sucks wind!

He turns off the projectors, listens intently. Silence, except for the faint crackle of cooling film, his heart thumping in his ears. He is afraid at first to leave his booth. What's happening out there? He heats up cold coffee on his hot plate, studies his pinned-up publicity stills. He can't find her, but maybe she was never in any of them in the first place. He's not even sure he would recognize her, a mere ingenue, if she were there— her legs maybe, but not her face. But in this cannibal picture, for example, wasn't there a girl being turned on the spit? He can't remember. And whose ripped-off heat shield is that winged intergalactic emperor, his eyes glazed with lust and perplexity, clutching in his taloned fist? The coffee is boiling over, sizzling and popping on the burners like snapped fingers. He jerks the plug and rushes out, caroming clumsily off the doorjamb, feeling as dizzy and unhinged as that old prospector in the tights and pink pumps, not knowing which way to fall.

The cavernous auditorium, awhisper with its own echoey room presence, seems to have shrunk and expanded at the same time: the pocked dome presses down on him with its terrible finitude, even as the aisles appear to stretch away, pushing the screen toward which he stumbles further and further into the distance. "Wait!" he cries, and the stage rushes forward and slams him in the chest, knocking him back into the first row of seats. He lies there for a moment, staring up into what would be, if he could reach the switchboard, a starlit sky, recalling an old Bible epic in which the elders of a city condemned by the archangels were pleading with their unruly citizens to curb their iniquity (which looked something like a street fair with dancing girls) before it was too late. "Can't you just be friends?" they'd cried, and he wonders now: Why not? Is it possible? He's been so lonely . . .

He struggles to his feet, this archaic wish glimmering in the dark pit of his mind like a candle in an old magic lantern, and makes his way foggily up the backstage steps, doom hanging heavy over his head like the little orphan girl's water-spotted behind. He pokes around in the wings with a kind of lustful terror, hoping to find what he fears most to find. He kicks at the tassels and furbelows of the grand drapery, flounces the house curtains and travelers, examines the screen: is there a hole in it? No, it's a bit discolored here and there, threadbare in places, but just as it's always been. As are the switchboard, the banks of lights, the borders, drops, swags and tracks above. Everything seems completely normal, which the projectionist knows from his years in the trade is just about the worst situation he could be in. He tests out the house phone, pokes his nose in the empty trash barrels, braves the dusky alleyway behind the screen. And now our story takes us down this shadowed path, he murmurs to himself, feeling like a rookie cop, walking his first beat and trying to keep his chin up, danger at every strangely familiar turn, were there any in this narrow canyon. Old lines return to him like recalled catechism:

She was the sort of girl who . . . Little did he know what fate
. . . A few of the characters are still alive . . . He's aware of
silhouettes flickering ominously just above his head—clutching
hands, hatted villains, spread legs—but when he looks, they
are not there. It's all in your mind, he whispers, and laughs
crazily to himself. This seems to loosen him up. He relaxes. He
commences to whistle a little tune.

And then he sees it. Right at nose level in the middle of his
precious screen: a mad vicious scatter of little holes! His untuned
whistle escapes his puckered lips like air from a punctured tire.
He shrinks back. Bullet holes—?! No, not so clean as that, and
the wall behind it is unmarked. It's more like someone has
been standing on the other side just now, kicking at it with
stiletto heels. He's almost unable to breathe. He staggers around
to the front, afraid of what he'll find or see. But the stage is
bare. Or maybe that *is* what he was afraid of. Uneasily, watched
by all the empty seats, he approaches the holes punched out in
the screen. They form crude block letters, not unlike those
used on theater marquees, and what they spell out is: BEWARE
THE MIDNIGHT MAN!

He gasps, and his gasp echoes whisperingly throughout the
auditorium, as though the palace itself were shuddering. Its
irreplaceable picture sheet is ruined. His projections will always bear this terrible signature, as though time itself were
branded. He steps back, repelled—just as the huge asbestos
fire curtain comes crashing down. *Wha—?!* He ducks, falls into
the path of the travelers sweeping across him like silken whips.
The lights are flaring and vanishing, flaring again, colors changing kaleidoscopically. He seems to see rivers ascending, clouds
dropping like leaded weights. He fights his way through the
swoop and swat of rippling curtains toward the switchboard,
but when he arrives there's no one there. The fire curtain has
been flown, the travelers are tucked decorously back in the
wings like gowns in a closet. The dream cloth with its frayed
metallic threads has been dropped before the screen. The
house curtains are parting, the lights have dimmed. Oh no . . . !

Even as he leaps down into the auditorium and charges up
the aisle, the music has begun. If it is music. It seems to be
running backwards, and there are screams and honkings and

wild laughter mixed in. He struggles against a rising tide of garish light, bearing down upon him from the projection booth, alive with flickering shades, beating against his body like gamma rays. "I don't need that spear, it's only a young lion!" someone rumbles through the dome, a bomb whistles, and there's a crash behind him like a huge mirror falling. "Look out! It's— *aaarrghh!*" "Sorry, ma'am!" "Great Scott, whaddaya call *that?!*" "Romance aflame through dangerous days and—" "You don't mean—?!" The uproar intensified—"*What* awful truth?"—and his movements thicken as in a dream. He knows if he can reach the overhanging balcony lip, he can escape the projector's rake, but even as he leans against this storm of light—"I'm afraid you made one fatal mistake!"—he can feel his body, as though penetrated by an alien being from outer space, lose its will to resist. "No! No!" he cries, marveling at his own performance, and presses on through, falling momentarily blinded, into the musky shelter of the back rows.

He sprawls there in the dark, gripping a cold bolted foot, as the tempest rages on behind him, wondering: *now* what? Which calls to mind an old war film in which the two surviving crew members of a downed plane, finding themselves in enemy territory, disguise themselves as the front and back end of a cow to make their escape. They get caught by an enemy farmer and locked in a barn with the village bull, the old farmer muttering, "Calves or steaks! Calves or steaks!" "*Now* what?" the airman in the back cries as the bull mounts them, and the one up front, sniffing the fodder, says: "Well, old buddy, I reckon that depends on whether or not you get pregnant." Such, roughly, are his own options: he can't leave, and staying may mean more than he can take. Already the thundering light is licking at his heels like an oncoming train, and he feels much like she must have felt, gagged and tied to the humming track: "Not all of us are going to come back alive, men, and before we go out there, I—" "Oh, John! Don't!" "Mad? I, who have solved the secret of life, you call me mad?" *WheeeeeooOOOOooooo!* "Please! Is *nothing* sacred?" He drags himself up the aisle, clawing desperately—"Catch me if you can, coppers!"—at the carpet, and then, driven by something like the downed airmen's craving for friendly pastures, clambers—"We accept him,

one of us, one of us . . ."—to his feet. If I can just secure the
projection booth, he thinks, lumbering forward like a second-
string heavy, maybe . . .

But he's too late. It's a disaster area. He can't even get in the
door, his way blocked by gleaming thickets of tangled film
spooling out at him like some monstrous birth. He hacks his
way through to cut off the projectors, but they're not even
there anymore, nothing left but the odd takeup reel, a Maltese
cross or two like dropped coins, a lens blotted with a lipsticked
kiss. His stuffed peacock, he sees through the rustling under-
brush of film, has been plucked. Gelatin slides are cooking in
his coffeepot. He stares dumbly at all this wreckage, unable to
move. It's as though his mind has got outside itself somehow,
leaving his skull full of empty room presence. Ripped-up
publicity stills and organ scores, film tins, shattered glass slides,
rolls of punched tickets lie strewn about like colossal endings.
All over his pinned-up poster for *Hearts and Pearls*, she has
scribbled: FIRST THE HUNT, THEN THE REVELS! The only publicity photo still up on the wall is the one of the cannibals, only
now someone *is* on the spit. *He* is. This spit begins to turn. He
flees, one hand clapped over his burning eyes, the other clawing through the chattery tentacles of film that now seem to be
trying to strangle him.

He staggers into the mezzanine, stripping scraps of clinging
celluloid from his throat, his mind locked into the simplistic
essentials of movement and murder. He throws the light switch.
Nothing happens. The alcove lights are also dead, the newel
post lamps on the marble staircase, the chandeliers in the
grand foyer. Darkness envelops him like swirling fog, teeming
with menace. Turning to run, he slaps up against a tall column.
At least, he thinks, hanging on, it didn't fall over. The marble
feels warm to his touch and he hugs it to him as the ingenue's
insane giggle rattles hollowly through the darkened palace,
sweeping high over his head like a passing wind or a plague of
twittering locusts. The column seems almost to be moving, as
though the whole room, like a cyclorama, were slowly pivoting.
He recalls an old movie in which the killer finds himself
trapped on a merry-go-round spinning out of control, sparking
and shrieking and hurling wooden horses into the gaping crowd

like terrorists on suicide missions. The killer, too: he lets go, understanding at last as he slides helplessly across the polished terrazzo floor the eloquent implications of pratfalls. What he slams into, however, is not a gaping crowd, but the drinking fountain near the elevator lobby, its sleek ceramic skin as cold to the touch as synthetic flesh. He can hear the cavernous gurgle and splatter of water as though the fountains throughout the movie palace might be overflowing. Yes, his pants are wet and his toes feel squishy inside their shoes.

He's not far, he realizes, from the stairwell down to the rooms below, and it occurs to him, splashing over on his hands and knees (perhaps he's thinking of the bomb shelters in war movies or the motherly belly of the whale), that he might be able to hide out down there for a while. Think things out. But at the head of the stairs he feels a cold draft: he leans over and sweeps the space with his hand: The stairs are gone, he would have plummeted directly into the unchartered regions below! It's not completely dark down there, for he seems to see a dim roiling mass of ballroom dancers, drill sergeants, cartoon cats, and restless natives, like projections on smoke, vanishing even as they billow silently up toward him. Is that the ingenue among them? The one in the grass skirt, her eyes starting from their sockets? Too late. Gone, as though sucked away into the impossible chasms below.

He blinks and backs away. The room has come to a stop, a hush has descended. The water fountains are silent. The floor is dry, his pants, his shoes. Is it over? Is she gone? He finds a twist of licorice in his pocket and, without thinking, slips it between his chattering teeth. Whereupon, with a creaking noise like the opening of a closet door, a plaster statue leans out of its niche and, as he throws himself back against the wall, smashes at his feet. The licorice has disappeared. Perhaps he swallowed it whole. Perhaps it was never there. He's reminded of a film he once saw about an alien conspiracy which held its nefarious meetings in an old carnival fun house, long disused and rigged now ("now" in the film) for much nastier surprises than rolling floors and booing ghosts. The hero, trying simply to save the world, enters the fun house, only to be subjected to everything from death rays and falling masonry to iron maidens, time traps, and diabolical life-restoring machines, as though to problematize his very identity through what the chortling funhouse operators call in their otherworldly tongue "the stylistics of absence." In such a maze of probable improbability, the hero can be sure of nothing except his own inconsolable desires and his mad faith, as firm as it is burlesque, in the prevalence of secret passages. There is always, somewhere, another door. Thus, he is not surprised when, hip-deep in killer lizards and blue Mercurians, he spies dimly, far across the columned and chandeliered pit into which he's been thrown, what appears to be a rustic wooden ladder, leaning radiantly against a shadowed wall. Only the vicious gnawing at his ankles surprises him as he struggles toward it, the Mercurians' mildewed breath, the glimpse of water-spotted underwear on the ladder above him as he starts to climb. Or are those holes? He clambers upward, reaching for them, developed as always to his passionate seizure of reality, only to have them vanish in his grasp, the ladder as well: he discovers he's about thirty feet up the grand foyer wall, holding nothing but a torn ticket stub. It's a long way back down, but he gets there right away.

He lies there on the hard terrazzo floor, crumpled up like a lounge-lizard in a gilded cage (are his legs broken? his head? *something* hurts), listening to the whisperings and twitterings high above him in the coffered ceiling, the phantasmal tinkling of the chandelier crystals, knowing that to look up there is to be lost. It's like the dockside detective put it in that misty old film about the notorious Iron Claw and the sentimental configurations of mass murder: "What's frightening is not so much being able to see only what you want to see, see, but discovering that what you think you see only because *you want to see it* . . . sees you . . ." As he stands there on the damp shabby waterfront in the shadow of a silent boom, watching the night fog coil in around the tugboats and barges like erotic ribbons of dream, the detective seems to see or want to see tall ghostly galleons drift in, with one-eyed pirates hanging motionless from the yardarms like pale Christmas tree decorations, and he is stabbed by a longing for danger and adventure—another door, as it were, a different dome—even as he is overswept by a paralyzing fear of the unknown. "I am menaced," he whispers, glancing up at the swaying streetlamp (but hasn't he just warned himself?), "by a darkness beyond darkness . . ." The pirates, cutlasses in hand and knives between their teeth, drop from the rigging as though to startle the indifferent barges, but even as they fall they curl into wispy shapes of dead cops and skulking pickpockets, derelicts and streetwalkers. One of them looks familiar somehow, something about the way her cigarette dances between spectral lips like a firefly (or perhaps that *is* a firefly, the lips his perverse dream of lips) or the way her nun's habit is pasted wetly against her thighs as she fades away down a dark alley, so he follows her. She leads him, as he knew she would, into a smoky dive filled with slumming debutantes and sailors in striped shirts, where he's stopped at the door by a scarred and brooding Moroccan. "The Claw . . . ?" he murmurs gruffly into his cupped hands, lighting up. The Moroccan nods him toward the bar, a gesture not unlike that of absolution, and he drifts over, feeling a bit airy as he floats through the weary revelers, as though he might have left part of himself lying back on the docks, curled up under the swaying lamp like a piece of unspooled trailer. When he sets his revolver on the bar, he notices he can see right through it. "If it's the Claw you're after," mutters the bartender, wiping a glass nervously with a dirty rag, then falls across the bar, a knife in his back. He notices he can also see through the bartender. The barroom is empty. He's dropped his smoke somewhere. Maybe the bartender fell on it. The lights are brightening. There's a cold metallic hand in his pants. He screams. Then he realizes it's his own.

He's lying, curled up still, under the chandelier. But not in the grand foyer of his movie palace as he might have hoped. It seems to be some sort of eighteenth-century French ballroom. People in gaiters, frocks, and periwigs are dancing minuets around him, as oblivious to his presence as to the distant thup and pop of musket fire in the street. He glances up past the chandelier at the mirrored ceiling and is surprised to see, not himself, but the ingenue smiling down at him with softly parted lips, an eery light glinting magically off her snow-white teeth and glowing in the corners of her eyes like small coals, smoldering there with the fire of strange yearnings. "She is the thoroughly modern type of girl," he seems to hear someone say, "equally at home with tennis and tango, table talk and tea. Her pearly teeth, when she smiles, are marvelous. And she smiles often, for life to her seems a continuous film of enjoyment." Her smile widens even as her eyes glaze over, the glow in them burning now like twin projectors. "Wait!" he cries, but the room tips and, to the clunk and tinkle of tumbling parts, all the people in the ballroom slide out into the public square, where the Terror nets them like flopping fish.

Nor are aristocrats and mad projectionists their only catch. Other milieus slide by like dream cloths, dropping swashbucklers, cowboys, little tramps, singing families, train conductors and comedy teams, a paperboy on a bicycle, gypsies, mummies, leather-hatted pilots and wonder dogs, neglected wives, Roman soldiers in gleaming breastplates, bandits and gold diggers, and a talking jackass, all falling, together with soggy cigarette butts, publicity stills, and flattened popcorn tubs, into a soft plash of laughter and applause that he seems to have heard before. "Another fine mess!" the jackass can be heard to bray mournfully, as the mobs, jammed up behind police barricades in the dark but festive Opera House square, cry out for blood and brains. "The public is never wrong!" they scream. "Let the revels begin!"

Arc lights sweep the sky and somewhere, distantly, an ancient bugle blows, a buzzer sounds. He is pulled to his feet and prodded into line between a drunken countess and an animated pig, marching along to the thunderous piping of an unseen organ. The aisle to the guillotine, thickly carpeted, is lined with red velvet ropes and leads to a marble staircase where, on a raised platform high as a marquee, a hooded executioner awaits like a patient usher beside his gigantic ticket chopper. A voice on the public address system is recounting, above the booming organ and electrical chimes, their crimes (hauteur is mentioned, glamour, dash and daring), describing them all as "creatures of the night, a collection of the world's most astounding horrors, these abominable parvenus of iconic transactions, the shame of a nation, three centuries in the making, brought to you now in the mightiest dramatic spectacle of all the ages!" He can hear the guillotine blade rising and dropping, rising and dropping, like a link-and-claw mechanism in slow motion, the screams and cheers of the spectators cresting with each closing of the gate. "There's been some mistake!" he whimpers. If he could just reach the switchboard! Where's the EXIT sign? Isn't there always . . . ? "I don't belong here!" "Ja, zo, it iss der vages off cinema," mutters the drunken countess behind him, peeling off a garter to throw to the crowd. Spots appear on his clothing, then get left behind as he's shoved along, as though the air itself might be threadbare and discolored, and there are blinding flashes at his feet like punctures where bright light is leaking through.

"It's all in your mind," he seems to hear the usherette at the foot of the stairs whisper, as she points him up the stairs with her little flashlight, "so we're cutting it off."

"What—?!" he cries, but she is gone, a bit player to the end. The animated pig has made his stuttering farewell and the executioner is holding his head aloft like a winning lottery ticket or a bingo ball. The projectionist climbs the high marble stairs, searching for his own closing lines, but he doesn't seem to have a speaking part. "You're leaving too soon," remarks the hooded executioner without a trace of irony, as he kicks his legs out from under him. "You're going to miss the main feature." "I thought I was it," he mumbles, but the executioner, pitilessly, chooses not to hear him. He leans forward, all hopes dashed, to grip the cold bolted foot of the guillotine, and as he does so, he notices the gum stuck under it, the dropped candy wrapper, the aroma of fresh pee in plush upholstery. Company at last! he remarks wryly to himself as the blade drops, surrendering himself finally (it's a last-minute rescue of sorts) to that great stream of image-activity that characterizes the mortal condition, recalling for some reason a film he once saw (*The Revenge of Something-or-Other*, or *The Return of*, *The Curse of* . . .), in which—

Robert Coover's first novel, The Origin of the Brunists, *was the winner of the 1966 William Faulkner Award. His other works include* The Universal Baseball Association, J. Henry Waugh, Prop.; Pricksongs and Descants: A Theological Position; The Public Burning; A Political Fable; Spanking the Maid; Gerald's Party; Whatever Happened to Gloomy Gus of the Chicago Bears; *and* A Night at the Movies. *He is a member of the American Academy of Arts and Letters.*

Published in Coover's collection, A Night at the Movies.

SUE MILLER

TRAVEL

The room at the tourist hotel was small, with casement windows that opened out over the kitchen annex. Starting at about seven in the morning, the happy incomprehensible banter of the kitchen staff, the crash and clatter of garbage cans and dishes, would rise into Oley and Rob's room. Oley lay in bed and listened. From the bathroom floated in the smell of fermenting strawberries. Oley and Rob had bought them at the market on their first day in Trujillo. An impassive Indian woman had sat next to an enormous basket of the fruit, a deep basket at least four feet in diameter. It seemed romantic, the luxuriance of so many strawberries gleaming uniformly fat and red, so unlike the parsimony of pint boxes in the supermarket at home, boxes in which only the top layer of fruit was red; the buyer knew that distributed underneath were the ones with hard white patches or soft sides. Oley and Rob bought a large bag of the fruit from the Indian woman, and a bottle of wine. On their first night in the hotel they'd played gin rummy in their room, eating and drinking. Then, drunk, full, they'd made love, smelling the strawberries in each other's mouths, and then on each other's skin, everywhere.

Rob was gone from the bed already. Probably out taking pictures. He was doing a travel article. It had been gray and overcast since they'd arrived in Trujillo, so he didn't want to do the ruins yet, or the plaza. He got up early to do interiors—churches, museums—before they were crowded with people, whose appeal or lack of it to potential tourists he couldn't control. Once she would have gone with him, held the cameras and lenses he wasn't using. But there was some silent agreement they'd reached about this now and he let her sleep on alone.

She got up and went into the bathroom. The smell of fermenting strawberries was much stronger, almost sickening, in here. The plastic bag rested on the windowsill, and she could see that the strawberries had exuded a little pool of pinkish liquid, in which they sat. She picked up the bag and dropped it into the wastebasket. A little of it had oozed out onto the sill.

As she hunched over on the toilet, the complicated, funky smell of their lovemaking the night before rose to her nostrils too. She reached over to the sink and filled the water glass. She lowered it between her legs and splashed herself with little handfuls of the warm water four or five times. She stood up and dabbed at herself with a towel. Bright laughter floated up from the kitchen. She pushed the heavy nickel handle and the toilet flushed violently.

Rob came back full of energy, with presents for Oley. He dumped them on her naked thighs as she lay stretched out on the bed, and then sat in the room's only chair, the desk chair, to watch her open them. There was a little white box that held silver earrings and a necklace nested in slightly soiled cotton; a tiny, brightly colored basket in a brown paper bag; and a greenish fruit he couldn't remember the name of. She thanked him over and over. She put on the jewelry and looked at herself in the hand mirror he gave her. The dangling earrings brushed against the sides of her neck.

"And pictures?" she asked. She was trying to be generous too. "Did you get any good pictures?"

He raised the camera, as though to fiddle with it. Then it was in front of his face. It clicked. "One, anyway," he said, and smiled at her.

Olympia had flown to Lima with money that Rob had mailed to her. He'd called her long-distance three times from Peru before she'd agreed to join him. She had at first been determined not to. Rob had decided only two months earlier that he couldn't marry her. They'd been living together for more than a year. She had asked him to move out.

He wanted her to join him, he said on the phone, because he was lonely, because they'd always traveled so well together. Why couldn't they still be loving friends, especially in a far-away place? She ought to see Peru at least this once. He'd be more than happy to pay all her expenses.

Oley had missed Rob, the excitement he brought into her life. She'd grown up in a safe, small town and was a little afraid of anything new or random. In New Haven she was a teacher; her work was regular and held no surprises for her. When Rob had lived with her, was her lover, she liked the feeling of involvement with passing events he introduced her to, the way life seemed to reach in and touch him. His voice on the telephone seemed like that exciting, random touch. She decided to go.

After she'd made the decision, when she began to think about seeing Rob again, Oley felt, in spite of herself, a return of the hope that had fueled her during their year together: the hope that given enough time, she could will Rob into the kind of love that would make him want to stay. She had to consciously remind herself that she was going only to have a good time, only to travel.

And at first it had seemed as though it might work on that basis. In the airport, watching him walk toward her, tanned, his hair longer than when she'd last seen him, she felt a rush of intense passion that made her throat hurt. They'd had the night with the strawberries and for a few days after that they'd been happy. Rob made little ceremonies of every meal, every gift he gave her. She spoke no Spanish and so he had to act as her interpreter to the world. She felt sheltered and protected, cared for in a way that hadn't been possible for a long time at home. There her toughness, her competence, had been things she felt she needed to stress as it became clearer and clearer to her that he was choosing not to marry her.

But as the slow days passed in Trujillo, Oley came to resent the very gifts, the courtliness that had at first charmed her. She was sometimes unpleasant to Rob, petulant. She didn't like herself then, but she wasn't able to stop. Everything he gave her, everything he did for her, reminded her only of what he wouldn't give, wouldn't do.

As they crossed the plaza on their way to the bakery, three little boys with shoeshine kits followed them, their clothes

ragged, their faces dirty. They were always on the plaza, noisy
and cheerful. The first day, Rob and Oley had decided to have
a shoeshine, and had hired the two thinnest, smallest boys. A
group of ten or so, all with their wooden kits, assembled to
watch the process, chatting and commenting while the chosen
boys stylishly and elaborately polished and buffed. On the final
buffing, their cloths took on a life of their own, cracking and
whipping through the air.

The second day, in their eagerness for business, the boys
had followed Rob and Oley without noticing that they were
both wearing sandals. Rob had stopped finally and pointed this
out. He'd asked them what color they would polish his bare
feet, and they'd laughed at this joke, at themselves. Now they
always trailed behind Rob and Oley, laughing, calling out.
They seemed to like Rob. He told Oley that they'd become
very familiar, were sometimes quite insulting in their comments on the condition of his Frye boots, of Oley's shoes.

Today Rob delivered a long dramatic monologue to the boys
as they crossed the plaza, his face and voice mournful. The
boys laughed and danced around him, egging him on. Oley felt
edged out, ignored.

They crossed to a side street, leaving the ragged group
behind, and Oley asked him what he'd been saying.

"Long sad story," said Rob. He lifted an imaginary violin and
began to play. "I'm so poor I can't afford even a shoeshine. And
if I had the money I ought to take it home to my even poorer
mother, who sits alone with fourteen babies, trying to make
supper from a cup of meal and one starving guinea pig. In
fact, if I had the money, I ought to take it home to the guinea
pig of my mother, who hasn't had anything to eat since . . ."
He stopped abruptly, looking at Oley.

"Not funny, O?" He bent to look at her face. "You no like?"

She shook her head. They walked a block in silence. The
dark men turned to stare at Oley, who was tall and fair, with
straight blond hair hanging down her back and over her
shoulders.

"Well, I'd hate to ask you *why*," Rob said finally, with
hostility in his voice. "I'd be so fucking scared you'd tell me."

She pressed her lips together, and then spoke. She'd never

felt more like a schoolteacher. "It seems unkind," she said, "when by their standards we're so rich, for you to make fun of their poverty."

He shrugged. "Therein, of course, lies the joke," he said. They turned into the bakery, pushing aside the beaded curtain. Everyone looked up at them for a moment, at the tall, long-haired man dressed a little like a cowboy in his jeans and work shirt, and his blond companion. "Clearly they thought it was funny," he said, behind her. "If they can laugh at it, then there must be some level on which it *is* funny."

There were empty tables in the back, and they walked toward them through the groups of Peruvians nearer the front. There were mostly men in the bakery, except for the women who worked behind the counter.

"The trouble with you, Oley, is that you always imagine everyone else has exactly your sensibility." As he said this, Rob was pulling the chair out for Oley. She sat down. "And they don't. They don't. By and large, the human race is tougher and has a better sense of humor than you do, O."

He sat down opposite her and Oley looked at him. She would never, she felt, not find him attractive.

"That's just how *you* imagine them," she said. "And that's just because you think everyone is like *you*. So you see, we're not really so different after all."

Oley had met Rob when he came to take photographs of the preschool kids she taught. Oley, who was often somber and shy when she met new people, whose high school yearbook photo had "Still Waters Run Deep" under it, was animated and energetic around the children. Rob took as many pictures of her as he did of the kids.

She was aware of using her playfulness with the children to charm him, and felt, a few times during the day, guilty enough about this element of duplicity to draw back suddenly into a shy stiffness. But the children insisted on the Oley they knew. "Not *that* way, Oley," they'd say. "Do it the *other* way, the *silly* way."

He took her out for dinner that night. The combination of his own almost childish energy and his having seen her earlier so full of life made it easier for her to continue what she couldn't help thinking of as a charade during the meal. Even as they made love back in her apartment, she wanted to tell him he'd made a mistake, that she wasn't who he thought she was.

As the week in Trujillo went by, Oley and Rob spent more and more time after dinner in the hotel bar. They played gin rummy, keeping a running score, and drank foaming, lemony Pisco sours. The bar was as old as the rest of the hotel, paneled in mahogany and mirrored on one side. Louvered doors opened into the dining room and the lobby. A large fan with wooden blades twirled slowly overhead. The bartender, a short, plump Indian man with liquid black eyes, stared at Oley almost constantly; at her size, they speculated, at her blondness, her freckles.

"And my boobs," Oley said. She was drunk. "Boobs'll do it every time, the world over. It's amazing how predictable it all is."

"I'll drink to that. I'll drink to predictability," he said, spreading his cards on the table, "and I'll go down with three."

"Bastard," she said.

They still made love every night, always with the same skillful familiarity with each other's bodies, but they postponed until later and later the time when they'd leave the warm light of the bar and climb the wide wooden staircase together. Each night, undressing, getting ready for sure pleasure, Oley felt increasingly that it was a capitulation that shamed her somehow. More than once they were the last people to leave the bar, but the solemn, handsome bartender never complained, never rushed them, never stopped staring and blushing.

"He loves you, O," Rob said. He lay naked on the bed, watching Oley undress.

"I know," Oley said sadly. She carefully folded her jeans and shirt, then came to sit on the edge of the bed.

"You know how I know?" Rob asked.

"No."

" 'Cause he doesn't charge us for about half of what we drink. Your half, I figure." He had moved over to accommodate her. Now he began to stroke her back and arms.

Oley looked at him. "Is that true?"

"As sure as I'm about to screw you madly."

"No, wait. Tell me the truth." She put her hands on his, to still them. "He's been giving us free drinks?"

"You. *You*, anyway. I asked that Chilean guy, you know, the one with the fat wife and all the kids?" Oley nodded. "I asked him if he was getting free drinks and he said not. Said it must be because the guy's so smitten with you. *Everybody* knows it, Oley. My big, blond Oley."

She turned from him. "Oh, that's so sad."

"Why? What's so sad about it?"

"I don't know. Everything. That he's a grown man; and his world is so small that he sees me as some kind of *princess*. And all he has to offer me is Pisco sours. And I'm up here fucking you, who couldn't care less at some level. And he ends up, really, giving *you* the drinks. It just all seems so . . . misplaced and pathetic."

Rob was silent a moment. Then he began stroking her arm again. His hand touched lightly the side of Oley's breast and she felt the dropping sensation inside that was, for her, the beginning of desire. "Well, he can't give you the drinks without treating me too. That's just how it is."

"I know. That's what I mean."

They sat in silence. Then Rob said, "I *do* care, O. I can't do it your way, but I do care."

"I know," she said. And then, because she was very drunk, she said again, "That's what I mean."

Oley had thought she wouldn't hear from Rob again after their first night together. She had gotten used to this in New Haven; though it was something she'd been unprepared for when she first arrived—that men could sleep with you and then simply never call you, never try to see you again. She had had one lover all through college, actually someone she'd known a little in high school too, so her experience was limited. And such a thing would have been in some sense impossible in the town where she'd grown up, if only because she would have known the man, or at least who he was, before she slept with him, and would have continued to see him at least

occasionally afterward. In New Haven, men could just disappear, and did; although she would occasionally glimpse someone she'd slept with going into a bookstore or crossing a street.
A few times she'd waved or said hello, but she realized by their
lack of response that she wasn't supposed to do that. She wasn't
supposed to exist anymore; she was just a place they'd been, a
town they'd passed through and chosen not to visit again.

After the painful shock of the first few times, that was all
right with Oley. It gave her a kind of freedom she hadn't
imagined possible, and she discovered a side to herself sexually
that was different and wilder than any of the parts of herself
that lived responsibly day by day in New Haven.

Besides, she had come to understand that the men who
would call her back were people she thought of as thick, dull;
people who saw only the good, steady side of herself. The men
she liked, the men who let her imagine herself as other than
the way she was, were not men who wanted to spend much
time with quiet young Head Start teachers.

And so, when Rob called back, she was surprised and even a
little disturbed. There was a part of her that didn't want to
have to cope with him as a real possibility, as a real disappointment. But she told him she'd meet him for a drink Friday
evening to look at the proofs of the pictures he'd taken; and
when she saw them, she saw suddenly who she could be, how
she could be, with him. Off and on during the difficult year
he'd lived with her, Oley would look at the pictures he'd taken
of her before he knew who she was, in order to remind herself
of what she could be to someone else.

Rob left Oley alone in the hotel for two days. A reporter
they'd met who was covering the revolutionary movement for a
British paper had told him that the rebels were planning to
take over the train from Cuzco to Machu Picchu. Rob thought
he should fly in right away and get his pictures. He didn't think
it was a good idea for Oley to come along. It was as he stood
peeling bills from a roll of money he carried with him that Oley
understood how completely dependent on him she'd let herself
become in this world. She was actually frightened to be alone.

The first day she didn't deviate from the routines they had

set up together. Wherever she went, she smiled and nodded at the people who spoke to her. Laboriously she counted out money when she made a purchase, and occasionally she murmured the Spanish Rob had taught her for "I don't understand" when someone seemed to expect her to respond. Otherwise she was silent and alone all day. In the evening she ate in the hotel dining room and went to bed early, without stopping in the bar.

But the next morning the sun was shining for the first time since Oley had arrived in Peru, and after breakfast she went to the desk in the hotel lobby and asked the clerk about transportation to the ruins.

"Ah, the Professor!" the clerk said, and made a quick phone call. Then she explained to Oley that there was a local expert on the ruins who would take her on a guided tour for free, a kind of promotional deal he offered. He would come for her in his car later in the afternoon.

He showed up at about three-thirty. Oley was surprised at his appearance. He looked like a Latin crooner, a slicked-back Andy Williams. He wore pale clothes and a golfer's sweater, buttoned casually at the waist. His mustache was thin, his hair a preposterously brilliant black, and he spoke careful, formal English. He smiled at Oley and revealed elaborate structures of gold where most of his teeth should have been.

When Oley went outside with him, she discovered that his car was an ornately finned American model from the fifties, badly repainted a bilious green. There were several other passengers in it, other distinguished visitors to Peru, the Professor told Oley. The car had been fitted with a broken plastic cap on its roof which now read TAX. Oley hesitated a moment, then inquired whether she could not pay the Professor something for the privilege of taking the tour with him. The Professor assured her that it was his privilege, he was pleased to do it *gratis,* in order to let people know about his shop, a shop specializing in reproductions of the ruins' artifacts.

As Oley got in, the Professor introduced the other tourists. The Indian man behind the wheel revved the car noisily, and they sped away from the tourist hotel, leaving a trail of rubber and exhaust to delight the shoeshine boys gathered on the plaza.

The car had no shocks at all, and on every bump and curve Oley and the other passengers were thrown and swung from side to side in the back seat. The Professor sat in front with a massive Dutch woman, who had, like him, a small mustache. He rested his arm along the back of the seat, and with his face turned to his group, he made conversation in his stilted English about the ruins, about their countries of origin, about Peru.

Oley, glad to have an opportunity to speak English at last, grew expansive. She chatted with the massive Dutch woman and her shy female companion, and with the skinny and uncommunicative German student who completed their group.

It took about fifteen minutes to get to the ruins. They loomed ugly and unpromising in the flat terrain, so many dirt piles. Up close, more of what they might once have been was visible, and there were groups of archaeology students working to restore them; but Oley was disappointed. She was in the process of deciding that she preferred the living, slightly decrepit town to the parched desolation of the ruins, when they came to the section where intact samples of the relief work remained in the sand. Abruptly her disappointment vanished. The artwork here was both stylized and sexual, and Oley found herself moved by it. But the Professor's explanations of the meaning of the figures irritated her. He kept talking about things like the symbolic fusion of the spirit and the will as the stood in front of the intertwined tongues and bodies. The Dutch woman, her friend and the German student stood, listened, nodded. But Oley began to lag behind the group. The Professor frowned at her, calling out from time to time that she was missing the discussion of the detail. Momentarily she would rejoin them; but then she would again find his monologue maddening, and drop back. She felt as though she were a naughty American child among adults.

On their way back to town, the driver pulled off the highway into what looked like an abandoned gas station. It was the Professor's gallery. The group of gringos clambered obediently out of the car, which rose several inches with each one's departure. The shop was sweltering. It was full of black-and-white prints, scrolls and little clay sculptures. The Professor swung into a sales pitch. He had a way of unrolling the prints that reminded Oley of the shoeshine boys, their elaborate display with their cloths.

The Dutch woman seemed interested. After looking at what seemed to Oley an endless number of samples, she bought two prints. Oley had moved nearer to the door, waiting for the transactions to be over. The reproductions in the shop were stark, precise, Egyptian. They had none of the sensuality of the actual reliefs, and they seemed expensive to Oley. And even though there were a few less expensive, less unattractive pieces of sculpture, Oley didn't want anything. The moment the Professor had gone into his pitch, she felt angry at him for trapping her here, for his false generosity. She was determined to buy nothing.

The German student liked one of the prints, but said that the price was too high. Oley moved into the doorway to try to catch a breeze as she watched the Professor at work. He came down a bit; the student, more animated than he'd been all day, pushed for an even lower price. Slowly they narrowed in on the range they could agree on, and the purchase was made. Then the little group was left standing in the shop, waiting for a signal from the Professor that they could leave, that his driver would take them back. But it became clear that he, in turn, was waiting for Oley to buy something. Everyone else had paid the price for the tour. It was her turn. The group looked expectantly at her.

The Professor walked over closer to her and picked up one of the clay figures. "You have, perhaps, found something you would like, Miss Erickson?" he asked.

"No. Nothing," Oley answered. She could hear the defiance in her own voice.

The Professor paused for only a moment. "Ah, well, then," he said. "Perhaps I can point out to you some things which you may not have noticed." He gestured to where the scrolls lay rolled up like tubes of wallpaper on the shelf.

There was another moment of silence. Then Oley, still standing in the doorway, said, "I'm not going to buy anything,

Professor. I'm sorry, I misunderstood your meaning, and really thought the tour was free." Oley thought she could feel the group recoil from her slightly in the shop. "Besides," she said, "I really can't afford it."

She turned and walked outside, let herself into the car. The driver, leaning against the auto in the hot sun, looked confused. Slowly the little group of tourists meandered out too. Last came the Professor, looking seedy and defeated. Oley felt sorry for him, actually. The driver took his silent lurching load back to town.

When Oley got back to the tourist hotel, she went up to her room. She ran herself a deep tub and lay in it for a long while, occasionally twisting the old-fashioned nickel-plated knob with her toes to let more hot water in. Her breasts floated above the water. The nipples tightened in the cool air. Oley dipped a washcloth into the steaming tub and laid it across his chest.

She lay in the tub until the sky outside turned purple; then black. When she got out, her fingers and toes were wrinkled into what she and her mother had called "raisin skin" when she was small. She noticed, on the windowsill, a little red stain the maid had missed when she cleaned, the hardened juice of the strawberries.

She dressed and went to the bar. She sat at one of the wooden tables by herself and ordered a Pisco sour. The table was next to the louvered windows which opened out onto the plaza. Through the slats she could see, in the glare of the fluorescent streetlamps, the shoeshine boys, their workday over, huddled in a tiny group around one bench. She watched them.

From time to time during the evening, one of the other guests with whom she was familiar—the fat wife of the Chilean, the British reporter—came and talked to Oley for a while. But for the most part she sat alone. The bartender brought over a fresh drink or bowl of peanuts as soon as she'd finished the one before. Slowly the boys on the plaza drifted away. When the last two lay down on one of the benches, Oley got up. She bumped into a chair on her way to the bar, and its legs scraped noisily on the bare floor.

She asked the bartender how much everything was. He looked at her, his eyes blazing with devotion, and shook his

head. "Please," she said in Spanish, "how much?" Again he
shook his head. Oley felt her eyes fill with tears. "You are very
generous," she said in English. "Too generous." He smiled
shyly, partly, Oley saw, because he was missing several teeth.
"Thank you," he said in slow English. She reached over and
touched the immaculate sleeve of his white coat. "No," she
said. "Thank *you*. Gracias. Thank you." She patted his arm
gently; then turned and carefully walked out of the bar.

Rob came back early the next morning. Oley was still in bed,
a little hung over. Rob was excited. He had met a man on the
plane from Cuzco who wanted to buy American dollars and
would meet him on the plaza in half an hour. Oley got out of
bed and dressed slowly. Rob paced the room impatiently,
leaned out the casement window into the kitchen noise. Oley
knew it wasn't just the illegal exchange rate that excited him,
but the idea of the black market, of doing something illicit. She
was familiar with this impulse of his. He'd once, for the same
reason, bought a gun from a black guy they'd met in a bar in
New Haven. He didn't want it for anything. He had kept it for
months in the bureau drawer in her apartment.

He and Oley had made a special trip to Block Island by ferry
in order to get rid of it, finally. They hadn't even stayed
overnight. They just took the ferry over, dropping the gun in
the water on the way, and returned that evening.

As they stepped out of the hotel lobby, Oley looked over
toward the plaza. The sky was white again today, with high
clouds. The flat gray stones in the plaza still gleamed darkly
from their daily early-morning washing. The shoeshine boys,
six or seven of them today, stood near the fountain at the
plaza's center, talking and gesturing. Two of the cement benches
that studded the radiating pathways of the plaza were occupied, one by an itinerant secretary, the typewriter on his knees
clattering faintly in the morning air as the old man next to him
dictated, the other by a man in a sports jacket and sunglasses,
holding a briefcase on his lap.

"Is that the guy?" Olympia asked.

"The very one," Rob said. He patted his shirt pocket. Before
they'd left their room, he'd put eight hundred-dollar bills into

it, folded in half. Oley had protested that it seemed too much, but he'd said they would need it in Arequipa, the next city on their itinerary.

The shoeshine boys spotted Rob and approached, waving and calling out. Even though Rob barely nodded to them, they followed him and Oley over to the man. But when Rob and Oley sat down and began talking, they fell back slightly. A few of them set their kits down and sat on them at a little distance, watching the trio on the bench.

The man chatted politely with Oley and Rob for a while, at first about how they liked traveling in Peru. Their enthusiasm seemed to amuse him. He was slim and good-looking. His face was slightly pockmarked. He began to talk about himself. He seemed anxious to explain himself to Oley in particular. He spoke fluent English, with only a slight accent. He'd gone to school in America, UCLA, he told Oley, and majored in engineering. He wanted to leave Peru, where his opportunities were so limited, to move to the United States; but the government wouldn't let him take Peruvian money out of the country. "They would strip me of my birthright, as it were," he said. "My parents are not wealthy, but they have worked hard all of their lives for me, for their only son. But the government would have me leave the country a pauper. You, a rich North American, must understand that I cannot go to the United States a pauper."

"I'm not rich," said Oley.

"Of course you are," said the man politely.

"No." Oley shook her head. "Really. I'm a schoolteacher. Schoolteachers aren't rich."

"Schoolteachers in America are rich," the man announced in his gentle, apologetic voice. "They own houses, cars, land."

Oley thought of her tiny apartment on the fringe of the ghetto in New Haven. She felt, suddenly, a pang of homesickness for its bare familiarity. She wanted to describe it to the man, but she knew there was no point.

"And here I find you traveling in my country," he persisted intently. "Such travel is expensive, is it not?"

Rob was watching Oley with interest. Oley saw that he expected her to say that the money was his, to separate herself from him, repudiate him, as she'd done in one way or another, she realized, all week. She felt suddenly as though she should apologize to him.

"Yes, you're right," she said to the man. Her voice was soft and regretful, as though she were acknowledging something shameful about herself. "It is terribly expensive."

She felt Rob's eyes on her.

"Well, then," the man said. "You understand my circumstance entirely, then. Americans don't like poor foreigners, so that I must be certain, before I leave, to amass enough money to fit easily and smoothly into your world."

He turned to Rob and they proceeded to the details of their exchange. Oley watched them. Rob's face was animated, lively, full of the energy that had always attracted her, that she had always wanted to have herself, but didn't. He and the man laughed about something. Oley looked over at the shoeshine boys. She felt like them, shut out, an onlooker.

The man opened the briefcase on his knees. He left the lid up to shield the interior from view, but the shoeshine boys had caught a glimpse of its contents. They seemed in unison, audibly, to draw their breath in. They approached slightly nearer and made a silent semicircle around the three adults on the bench. In the briefcase, neatly banded, were stacks of Peruvian currency, perhaps more than most of the shoeshine boys would earn in a lifetime. They watched with rapt attention, whispering a little among themselves, as Rob and the man exchanged dollars for soles. Oley noted that when she and Rob got up and walked away, the shoeshine boys for the first time didn't follow or call to them. Unmolested, she and Rob walked back into the cool, dim lobby of the tourist hotel.

When they got up to their room, Rob began pulling the money from his pockets and throwing it on the bed. "We're rich, Oley! Rich! Rich!" he cried. Oley sat in the chair and watched him. When he'd emptied his pockets and turned to her, grinning, she said softly, "I've got to go home, Rob." He looked at her for a moment, the smile fading, and then he sat down on the bed without pushing the money out of the way.

"Oley," he said. He shook his head. "Olympia. How come I knew you were going to say that?"

*   *   *

In late August, Oley found a manila envelope leaning against the door to her apartment. It was postmarked New York and stamped PHOTOGRAPH. DO NOT BEND. Because it was very hot outside and she'd been at a faculty meeting all day, she went around the apartment throwing open the windows and then she fixed herself a glass of iced tea before she opened it. Inside was a blowup of the picture Rob had taken of her in the tourist hotel in Trujillo. Oley felt in the corners of the envelope for a written message, but there was none. Just the picture. She looked at it carefully.

Wearing the delicate necklace and earrings that she still had in the dresser in her bedroom, the Oley in the picture stretched out naked on the bed and looked directly into the camera. Rob had lightened her body and darkened the background, so she seemed almost to float toward the camera, her gaze blankened and bold.

Oley looked at the picture a long time, trying to recognize herself in it. Then she picked up her iced tea and carried it into the bedroom. The cubes clinked gently together as she walked. She set the glass down on top of the bureau, opened the top drawer, and took out the necklace and earrings. Standing in front of her full-length mirror, she took off all her clothes and put on the jewelry. She looked at her familiar reflection—the solid wide hips, the large breasts, the pubic hair dark in spite of her blondness. She stood in her bedroom and looked at herself. On the breeze that stirred through the apartment and lightly touched her body floated the sound of someone's transistor radio, the rhythm of teen-aged voices in conversation. She closed her eyes and tried to imagine herself making love with Rob, the familiar sequence of sensations she had thought of as shapes they made together. She couldn't. That possibility seemed remote, as far away as the small town she'd grown up in, as far away as the Olympia Rob had created in the photograph.

" 'Travel' is a fictional stew that simmered for a long time in my subconscious or preconscious mind—or wherever it is that ideas for stories take shape.

"Some ingredients I can trace the source of. An undergraduate writing student of mine named a character in one of her stories Olympia (Oley). Before we parted ways, I asked her permission to use the name someday, thinking already that it would be pleasurable to play with it and the image of a naked courtesan it would call up for those who remembered Manet. (Thank you, Kathy Brewer.)

"A trip to Peru and an experience there with a seedy 'Professor' like the one in the story seemed to cry out to be used fictionally. I consciously stored those memories.

"And the notion of travel itself as a metaphor, as a way people have of distancing themselves from what's predictable and familiar in their lives, lives they finally do have to return to—this was, I think, the ingredient that made the others work together.

"But once I began to write, it was my concern for, my belief in Oley that propelled me. Simply, I wanted to tell her story, to make the reader feel for her."

Sue Miller *is the author of* The Good Mother *and of a collection of short fiction,* Inventing the Abbots and Other Stories. *Her fiction has appeared in* The Best American Short Stories. *She lives in Cambridge, Massachusetts, with her husband and son.*

Published in the author's collection, Inventing the Abbots and Other Stories.

ANDRE DUBUS
THE CURSE

itchell Hayes was forty-nine years old, but when the cops
left him in the bar with Bob, the manager, he felt much
older. He did not know what it was like to be very old, a
shrunken and wrinkled man, but he assumed it was like this:
fatigue beyond relieving by rest, by sleep. He also was not a
small man: his weight moved up and down in the hundred and
seventies and he was five feet and ten inches tall. But now his
body seemed short and thin. Bob stood at one end of the bar;
he was a large black-haired man, and there was nothing in front
of him but an ashtray he was using. He looked at Mitchell at
the cash register and said: "Forget it. You heard what Smitty
said."

Mitchell looked away, at the front door. He had put the
chairs upside down on the tables. He looked from the door,
past Bob to the empty space of floor at the rear; sometimes
people danced there, to the jukebox. Opposite Bob, on the
wall behind the bar, was a telephone; Mitchell looked at it. He
had told Smitty there were five guys and when he moved to
the phone one of them stepped around the corner of the bar
and shoved him: one hand against Mitchell's chest, and it
pushed him backward; he nearly fell. That was when they were
getting rough with her at the bar. When they took her to the
floor Mitchell looked once at her sounds, then looked down at
the duckboard he stood on, or at the belly or chest of a young
man in front of him.

He knew they were not drunk. They had been drinking
before they came to his place, a loud popping of motorcycles
outside, then walking into the empty bar, young and sunburned and carrying helmets and wearing thick leather jackets

in August. They stood in front of Mitchell and drank drafts. When he took their first order he thought they were on drugs and later, watching them, he was certain. They were not relaxed, in the way of most drinkers near closing time. Their eyes were quick, alert as wary animals, and they spoke loudly, with passion, but their passion was strange and disturbing, because they were only chatting, bantering. Mitchell knew nothing of the effects of drugs, so could not guess what was in their blood. He feared and hated drugs because of his work and because he was the stepfather of teen-agers: a boy and a girl. He gave last call and served them and leaned against the counter behind him.

Then the door opened and the girl walked in from the night, a girl he had never seen, and she crossed the floor toward Mitchell. He stepped forward to tell her she had missed last call, but before he spoke she asked for change for the cigarette machine. She was young, he guessed nineteen to twenty-one, and deeply tanned and had dark hair. She was sober and wore jeans and a dark blue T-shirt. He gave her the quarters but she was standing between two of the men and she did not get to the machine.

When it was over and she lay crying on the cleared circle of floor, he left the bar and picked up the jeans and T-shirt beside her and crouched and handed them to her. She did not look at him. She lay the clothes across her breasts and what Mitchell thought of now as her wound. He left her and dialed 911, then Bob's number. He woke up Bob. Then he picked up her sneakers from the floor and placed them beside her and squatted near her face, her crying. He wanted to speak to her and touch her, hold a hand or press her brow, but he could not.

The cruiser was there quickly, the siren coming east from town, then slowing and deepening as the car stopped outside. He was glad Smitty was one of them; he had gone to high school with Smitty. The other was Dave, and Mitchell knew him because it was a small town. When they saw the girl Dave went out to the cruiser to call for an ambulance, and when he came back he said two other cruisers had those scumbags and were taking them in. The girl was still crying and could not talk to Smitty and Dave. She was crying when a man and woman lifted her onto a stretcher and rolled her out the door and she vanished forever in a siren.

Bob came in while Smitty and Dave were sitting at the bar drinking coffee and Smitty was writing his report: Mitchell stood behind the bar. Bob sat next to Dave as Mitchell said: "I could have stopped them, Smitty."

"That's our job," Smitty said. "You want to be in the hospital now?"

Mitchell did not answer. When Smitty and Dave left, he got a glass of Coke from the cobra and had a cigarette with Bob. They did not talk. Then Mitchell washed his glass and Bob's cup and they left, turning off the lights. Outside Mitchell locked the front door, feeling the sudden night air after almost ten hours of air conditioning. When he had come to work the day had been very hot, and now he thought it would not have happened in winter. They had stopped for a beer on their way somewhere from the beach; he had heard them say that. But the beach was not the reason. He did not know the reason, but he knew it would not have happened in winter. The night was cool and now he could smell trees. He turned and looked at the road in front of the bar. Bob stood beside him on the small porch.

"If the regulars had been here," Bob said.

He turned and with his hand resting on the wooden rail he walked down the ramp to the ground. At his car he stopped and looked over its roof at Mitchell.

"You take it easy," he said.

Mitchell nodded. When Bob got in his car and left, he went down the ramp and drove home to his house on a street that he thought was neither good nor bad. The houses were small and there were old large houses used now as apartments for families. Most of the people had work, most of the mothers cared for their children, and most of the children were clean and looked like they lived in homes, not caves like some he saw in town. He worried about the older kids, one group of them anyway. They were idle. When he was a boy in a town farther up the Merrimack River, he and his friends committed every mischievous act he could recall on afternoons and nights when they were idle. His stepchildren were not part of that group.

They had friends from the high school. The front porch light was on for him and one in the kitchen at the rear of the house. He went in the front door and switched off the porch light and walked through the living and dining rooms to the kitchen. He got a can of beer from the refrigerator, turned out the light, and sat at the table. When he could see, he took a cigarette from Susan's pack in front of him.

Down the hall he heard Susan move on the bed then get up and he hoped it wasn't for the bathroom but for him. He had met her eight years ago when he had given up on ever marrying and having kids, then one night she came into the bar with two of her girl friends from work. She made six dollars an hour going to homes of invalids, mostly what she called her little old ladies, and bathing them. She got the house from her marriage, and child support the guy paid for a few months till he left town and went south. She came barefoot down the hall and stood in the kitchen doorway and said: "Are you all right?"

"No."

She sat across from him and he told her. Very soon she held his hand. She was good. He knew if he had fought all five of them and was lying in pieces in a hospital bed she would tell him he had done the right thing, as she was telling him now. He liked her strong hand on his. It was a professional hand and he wanted from her something he had never wanted before: to lie in bed while she bathed him. When they went to bed he did not think he would be able to sleep, but she kneeled beside him and massaged his shoulders and rubbed his temples and pressed her hands on his forehead. He woke to the voices of Marty and Joyce in the kitchen. They had summer jobs, and always when they woke him he went back to sleep till noon, but now he got up and dressed and went to the kitchen door. Susan was at the stove, her back to him, and Marty and Joyce were talking and smoking. He said good morning, and stepped into the room.

"What are you doing up?" Joyce said.

She was a pretty girl with her mother's wide cheekbones and Marty was a tall good-looking boy, and Mitchell felt as old as he had before he slept. Susan was watching him. Then she poured him a cup of coffee and put it at his place and he sat. Marty said: "You getting up for the day?"

"Something happened last night. At the bar." They tried to conceal their excitement, but he saw it in their eyes. "I should have stopped it. I think I *could* have stopped it. That's the point. There were five guys. They were on motorcycles but they weren't bikers. Just punks. They came in late, when everybody else had gone home. It was a slow night anyway. Everybody was at the beach."

"They rob you?" Marty said.

"No. A girl came in. Young. Nice-looking. You know: just a girl, minding her business."

They nodded, and their eyes were apprehensive.

"She wanted cigarette change, that's all. Those guys were on dope. Coke or something. You know: they were flying in place."

"Did they rape her?" Joyce said.

"Yes, honey."

"The *fuck*ers."

Susan opened her mouth then closed it and Joyce reached quickly for Susan's pack of cigarettes. Mitchell held his lighter for her and said: "When they started getting rough with her at the bar I went for the phone. One of them stopped me. He shoved me, that's all. I should have hit him with a bottle."

Marty reached over the table with his big hand and held Mitchell's shoulder.

"No, Mitch. Five guys that mean. And coked up or whatever. No way. You wouldn't be here this morning."

"I don't know. There was always a guy with me. But just one guy, taking turns."

"Great," Joyce said. Marty's hand was on Mitchell's left shoulder; she put hers on his right hand.

"They took her to the hospital," he said. "The guys are in jail."

"They are?" Joyce said.

"I called the cops. When they left."

"You'll be a good witness," Joyce said.

He looked at her proud face.

"At the trial," she said.

*   *   *

The day was hot but that night most of the regulars came to the bar. Some of the younger ones came on motorcycles. They were a good crowd: they all worked, except the retired ones, and no one ever bothered the women, not even the young ones with their summer tans. Everyone talked about it: some had read the newspaper story, some had heard the story in town, and they wanted to hear it from Mitchell. He told it as often as they asked but he did not finish it because he was working hard and could not stay with any group of customers long enough.

He watched their faces. Not one of them, even the women, looked at him as if he had not cared enough for the girl, or was a coward. Many of them even appeared sympathetic, making him feel for moments that he was a survivor of something horrible, and when that feeling left him he was ashamed. He felt tired and old, making drinks and change, moving and talking up and down the bar. At the stool at the far end Bob drank coffee and whenever Mitchell looked at him he smiled or nodded and once raised his right fist, with the thumb up.

Reggie was drinking too much. He did that two or three times a month and Mitchell had to shut him off and Reggie always took it humbly. He was a big gentle man with a long brown beard. But tonight shutting off Reggie demanded from Mitchell an act of will, and when the eleven o'clock news came on the television and Reggie ordered another shot and a draft, Mitchell pretended not to hear him. He served the customers at the other end of the bar, where Bob was. He could hear Reggie calling: Hey Mitch; shot and a draft, Mitch. Mitchell was close to Bob now. Bob said softly: "He's had enough."

Mitchell nodded and went to Reggie, leaned closer to him so he could speak quietly, and said: "Sorry, Reggie. Time for coffee. I don't want you dead out there."

Reggie blinked at him.

"Okay, Mitch." He pulled some bills from his pocket and put them on the bar. Mitchell glanced at them and saw at least a ten-dollar tip. When he rang up Reggie's tab the change was sixteen dollars and fifty cents, and he dropped the coins and shoved the bills into the beer mug beside the cash register. The mug was full of bills, as it was on most nights, and he kept his hand in there, pressing Reggie's into the others, and saw the sunburned young men holding her down on the floor and one kneeling between her legs, spread and held, and he heard their cheering voices and her screaming and groaning and finally weeping and weeping and weeping, until she was the siren crying then fading into the night. From the floor behind him, far across the room, he felt her pain and terror and grief, then her curse upon him. The curse moved into his back and spread down and up his spine, into his stomach and legs and arms and shoulders until he quivered with it. He wished he were alone so he could kneel to receive it.

Andre Dubus selected this story, the first he completed after a serious accident, and wrote the editor about his choice:

"I'm sending you a story I wrote in bed at home in January 1987. I choose it because even physically it was difficult to write. I'd had eleven operations and my right leg was in a cast. I finished the story on a Saturday, and my daughter Cadence, four then, was playing there, standing beside the bed. When I wrote the last word I began to weep. She looked at me. I told her I was crying because I was happy, because I had written a story and she said: 'This is the greatest day of my life. Daddy wrote a story.' "

Andre Dubus is the author of The Times Are Never So Bad, Finding a Girl in America, Adultery and Other Choices, Separate Flights, We Don't Live Here Anymore: The Novellas of Andre Dubus *and* Voices from the Moon. *He has served in the Marine Corps and was a Guggenheim Fellow and a member of the Writer's Workshop at the University of Iowa. His stories have appeared numerous times in* The Best Short Stories *and the* O. Henry Prize Collection. *He lives with his family in Haverhill, Massachusetts.*

Published in Playboy.

PETER TAYLOR

THE GIFT OF THE PRODIGAL

There's Ricky down in the washed river gravel of my drive-way. I had my yardman out raking it before seven A.M.—the driveway. It looks nearly perfect. Ricky also looks nearly perfect down there. He looks extremely got up and cleaned up, as though he had been carefully raked over and smoothed out. He is wearing a three-piece linen suit, which my other son, you may be sure, wouldn't be seen wearing on any occasion. And he has on an expensive striped shirt, open at the collar. No tie, of course. His thick head of hair, parted and slicked down, is just the same tan color as the gravel. Hair and gravel seem equally clean and in order. The fact is, Ricky looks this morning as though he belongs nowhere else in the world but out there in that smooth spread of washed river gravel (which will be mussed up again before noon, of course—I'm resigned to it), looks as though he feels perfectly at home in that driveway of mine that was so expensive to install and that requires so much upkeep.

Since one can't see his freckles from where I stand at this second-story window, his skin looks very fair—almost transpar-ent. (Ricky just misses being a real redhead, and so never lets himself get suntanned. Bright sunlight tends to give him skin cancers.) From the window directly above him, I am able to get the full effect of his outfit. He looks very masculine stand-ing down there, which is no doubt the impression his formfit-ting clothes are meant to give. And Ricky *is* very masculine, no matter what else he is or isn't. Peering down from up here, I mark particularly that where his collar stands open, and with several shirt buttons left carelessly or carefully undone, you can see a triangle of darker hair glistening on his chest. It isn't hard to imagine just how recently he has stepped out of the shower. In a word, he is looking what he considers his very best. And this says to me that Ricky is coming to me *for* something, or *because of* something.

His little sports car is parked in the turnaround behind this house, which I've built since he and the other children grew up and since their mother died. I know of course that, for them, coming here to see me can never really be like coming home. For Rick it must be like going to see any other old fellow who might happen to be his boss and who is ailing and is staying away from the office for a few days. As soon as I saw him down there, though, I knew something was really seriously wrong. From here I could easily recognize the expression on his face. He has a way, when he is concerned about something, of knitting his eyebrows and at the same time opening his eyes very wide, as though his eyes are about to pop out of his head and his eyebrows are trying to hold them in. It's a look that used to give him away even as a child when he was in trouble at school. If his mother and I saw that expression on his face, we would know that we were apt to be rung up by one of his teachers in a day or so or maybe have a house call from one of them.

Momentarily Ricky massages his face with his big right hand, as if to wipe away the expression. And clearly now he is headed for the side door that opens on the driveway. But before actually coming over to the door he has stopped in one spot and keeps shuffling his suede shoes about, roughing up the smooth gravel, like a young bull in a pen. I almost call out to him not to *do* that, not to muss up my gravel, which even his car wheels haven't disturbed—or not so much as he is doing with his suede shoes. I *almost* call out to him. But of course I don't really. For Ricky is a man twenty-nine years old, with two divorces already and no doubt another coming up soon. He's been through all that, besides a series of live-ins between marriages that I don't generally speak of, even.

For some time before coming on into the house, Ricky remains there in that spot in the driveway. While he stands there, it occurs to me that he may actually be looking the place over, as though he'd never noticed what this house is like until now. The old place on Wertland Street, where he and the other children grew up, didn't have half the style and convenience of this one. It had more room, but the room was mostly in pantries and hallways, with front stairs and back stairs and third-floor servants' quarters in an age when no servant would be caught dead living up there in the attic—or staying anywhere else on the place, for that matter. I am not unaware, of course, how much better that old house on Wertland was than this one. You couldn't have replaced it for twice what I've poured into this compact and well-appointed habitation out here in Farmington. But its neighborhood had gone bad. Nearly all of Charlottesville proper has, as a matter of fact, either gone commercial or been absorbed by the university. You can no longer live within the shadow of Mr. Jefferson's Academical Village. And our old Wertland Street house is now a funeral parlor. Which is what it ought to have been five years before I left it. From the day my wife, Cary, died, the place seemed like a tomb. I wandered up and down the stairs and all around, from room to room, sometimes greeting myself in one of Cary's looking glasses, doing so out of loneliness or out of thinking *that* couldn't be *me* still in my dressing gown and slippers at midday, or fully dressed—necktie and all—at three A.M. I knew well enough it was time to sell. And, besides, I wanted to have the experience at last of making something new. You see, we never built a house of our own, Cary and I. We always bought instead of building, wishing to be in an established neighborhood, you know, where there were good day schools for the girls (it was before St. Anne's moved to the suburbs), where there were streetcars and buses for the servants, or, better still, an easy walk for them to Ridge Street.

My scheme for building a new house after Cary died seemed a harebrained idea to my three older children. They tried to talk me out of it. They said I was only doing it out of idleness. They'd laugh and say I'd chosen a rather expensive form of entertainment for myself in my old age. That's what they *said*. That wasn't all they *thought*, however. But I never held against them what they thought. All motherless children—regardless of age—have such thoughts. They had in mind that I'd got notions of marrying again. Me! Why, I've never looked at another woman since the day I married. Not to this very hour. At any rate, one night when we were having dinner and they were telling me how they worried about me, and making it plainer than usual what they thought my plans for the future were or might be, Ricky spoke up—Ricky who never gave a thought in his life to what happened to anybody except himself—and he came out with just what was on the others' minds. "What if you should take a notion to marry again?" he asked. And I began shaking my head before the words were out of his mouth, as did all the others. It was an unthinkable thought for them as well as for me. "Why not?" Ricky persisted, happy of course that he was making everybody uncomfortable. "Worse things have happened, you know. And I nominate the handsome Mrs. Capers as a likely candidate for bride."

I *think* he was referring to a certain low sort of woman who had recently moved into the old neighborhood. You could depend upon Rick to know about her and know her name. As he spoke he winked at me. Presently he crammed his wide mouth full of food, and as he chewed he made a point of drawing back his lips and showing his somewhat overlarge and overly white front teeth. He continued to look straight at me as he chewed, but looking with only one eye, keeping the eye he'd winked at me squinched up tight. He looked for all the world like some old tomcat who's found a nasty morsel he likes the taste of and is not going to let go of. I willingly would have knocked him out of his chair for what he'd said, even more for that common look he was giving me. I knew he knew as well as the others that I'd never looked at any woman besides his mother.

Yet I laughed with the others as soon as I realized they were laughing. You don't let a fellow like Ricky know he's got your goat—especially when he's your own son, and has been in one bad scrape after another ever since he's been grown, and seems always just waiting for a chance to get back at you for something censorious you may have said to him while trying to help him out of one of his escapades. Since Cary died, I've tried mostly just to keep lines of communication open with him. I think that's the thing she would have wanted of me— that is, not to shut Rick out, to keep him talking. Cary used to

say to me, "You may be the only person he can talk to about
the women he gets involved with. He can't talk to me about
such things." Cary always thought it was the women he had
most on his mind and who got him into scrapes. I never used
to think so. Anyway, I believe that Cary would have wished
above all else for me to keep lines open with Rick, would have
wanted it even more than she would have wanted me to go
ahead in whatever way I chose with schemes for a new house
for my old age.

The house was *our* plan originally, you see, hers and mine.
It was something we never told the children about. There
seemed no reason why we should. Not talking about it except
between ourselves was part of the pleasure of it, somehow.
And that night when Ricky came out with the speculation
about my possibly marrying again, I didn't tell him or the
others that actually I had already sold the Wertland Street
house and already had blueprints for the new house here in
Farmington locked away in my desk drawer, and even a contractor all set to break ground.

Well, my new house was finished the following spring. By
that time all the children, excepting Rick, had developed a real
enthusiasm for it. (Rick didn't give a damn one way or the
other, of course.) They helped me dispose of all the superflu-
ous furniture in the old house. The girls even saw to the details
of moving and saw to it that I got comfortably settled in. They
wanted me to be happy out here. And soon enough they saw I
was. There was no more they could do for me now than there
had been in recent years. They had their good marriages to
look after (that's what Cary would have wished for them), and
they saw to it that I wasn't left out of whatever of their
activities I wanted to be in on. In a word, they went on with
their busy lives, and my own life seemed busy enough for any
man my age.

What has vexed the other children, though, during the five
years since I built my house, is their brother Ricky's continuing
to come to me at almost regular intervals with new ordeals of
one kind or another that he's been going through. They have
thought he ought not to burden me with his outrageous and

sometimes sordid affairs. I think they have especially resented
his troubling me here at home. I still go to the office, you see,
two or three days a week—just whenever I feel like it or when
I'm not playing golf or bridge or am not off on a little trip to
Sarasota (I stay at the same inn Cary and I used to go to). And
so I've always seen Ricky quite regularly at the office. He's had
every chance to talk to me there. But the fact is Rick was never
one for bringing his personal problems to the office. He has
always brought them home.

Even since I've moved, he has always come *here*, to the
house, when he's really wanted to talk to me about something. I
don't know whether it's the two servants I still keep or some of
the young neighbors hereabouts who tell them, but somehow
the other children always know when Ricky has been here.
And they of course can put two and two together. It will come
out over Sunday dinner at one of their houses or at the Club—in
one of those little private dining rooms. It is all right if we eat
in the big dining room, where everybody else is. I know I'm
safe there. But as soon as I see they've reserved a private room
I know they want to talk about Ricky's latest escapade. They
will begin by making veiled references to it among themselves.
But at last it is I who am certain to let the cat out of the bag.
For I can't resist joining in when they get onto Rick, as they all
know very well I won't be able to. You see, often they will
have the details wrong—maybe they get them wrong on
purpose—and I feel obliged to straighten them out. Then one
of them will run to me, pretending shocked surprise: "How
ever did you know about it? Has *he* been bringing his troubles
to *you* again? At his age you'd think he'd be ashamed to!
Someone ought to remind him he's a grown man now!" At that
point one of the girls is apt to rest her hand on mine. As they
go on, I can hear the love for me in their voices and see it in
their eyes. I know then what a lucky man I am. I want to say
to them that their affection makes up for all the unhappiness
Ricky causes me. But I have never been one to make speeches
like that. Whenever I have managed to say such things, I have
somehow always felt like a hypocrite afterward. Anyway, the
talk will go on for a while till I remember a bridge game I have
an appointment for in the Club lounge, at two o'clock. Or I

recall that my golf foursome is waiting for me in the locker room.

I've never tried to defend Rick from the others. The things he does are really quite indefensible. Sometimes I've even found myself giving details about some escapade of his that the others didn't already know and are genuinely shocked to hear—especially coming from me. He was in a shooting once that everybody in Farmington and in the whole county set knew about—or knew about, that is, in a general way, though without knowing the very thing that would finally make it a public scandal. It's an ugly story, I warn you, as, indeed, nearly all of Ricky's stories are.

He had caught another fellow in bed with a young married woman with whom he himself was running around. Of course it was a scandalous business, all of it. But the girl, as Rick described her to me afterward, was a real beauty of a certain type and, according to Rick, as smart as a whip. Rick even showed me her picture, though I hadn't asked to see it, naturally. She had a tight little mouth, and eyes that—even in that wallet-sized picture—burned themselves into your memory. She was the sort of intense and reckless-looking girl that Ricky has always gone for. I've sometimes looked at pictures of his other girls, too, when he wanted to show them to me. And of course I know what his wives have looked like. All three of his wives have been from good families. For, bad as he is, Ricky is not the sort of fellow who would embarrass the rest of us by *marrying* some slut. Yet even his wives have tended to dress themselves in a way that my own daughters wouldn't. They have dressed, that is to say, in clothes that seemed designed to call attention to their female forms and not, as with my daughters, to call attention to the station and the affluence of their husbands. Being the timid sort of man I am, I used to find myself whenever I talked with his wife—whichever one—carefully looking out the window or looking across the room, away from her, at some inanimate object or other over there or out there. My wife, Cary, used to say that Ricky had bad luck in his wives, that each of them turned out to have just as roving an eye as Ricky himself. I can't say for certain whether this was true for each of them in the beginning or whether it was something Ricky managed to teach them all.

Anyway, the case of the young married woman in whose bed—or apartment—Ricky found that other fellow came near to causing Ricky more trouble than any of his other escapades. The fellow ran out of the apartment, with Rick chasing him into the corridor and down the corridor to a door of an outside stairway. It was not here in Farmington, you see, but out on Barracks Road, where so many of Rick's friends are—in a development that's been put up on the very edge of where the horse farms begin. The fellow scurried down the outside stairs and across a parking lot toward some pastureland beyond. And Rick, as he said, couldn't resist taking a shot at him from that upstairs stoop where he had abandoned the chase. He took aim just when the fellow reached the first pasture fence and was about to climb over. Afterward, Rick said that it was simply too good to miss. But Rick rarely misses a target when he takes aim. He hit the fellow with a load of rat shot right in the seat of the pants.

I'll never know how Rick happened to have the gun with him. He told me that he was deeply in love with the young woman and would have married her if her husband had been willing to give her a divorce. The other children maintain to this day that it was the husband Rick meant to threaten with the gun, but the husband was out of town and Rick lost his head when he found that other fellow there in his place. Anyhow, the story got all over town. I suppose Ricky himself helped to spread it. He thought it all awfully funny at first. But before it was over, the matter came near to getting into the courts and into the paper. And that was because there was something else involved, which the other children and the people in the Barracks Road set didn't know about and I did. In fact, it was something that I worried about from the beginning. You see, Rick naturally took that fellow he'd blasted with the rat shot to a doctor—a young doctor friend of theirs—who removed the shot. But, being a friend, the doctor didn't report the incident. A certain member of our judiciary heard the details and thought perhaps the matter needed looking into. We were months getting it straightened out. Ricky went out of town for a while, and the young doctor ended by having to move away permanently—to Richmond or Norfolk, I think. I only give this incident in such detail in order to show the sort of low company Ricky has always kept, even when he seemed to be among our own sort.

His troubles haven't all involved women, though. Or not primarily. And that's what I used to tell Cary. Like so many people in Charlottesville, Rick has always had a weakness for horses. For a while he fancied himself a polo player. He bought a polo pony and got cheated on it. He bought it at a stable where he kept another horse he owned—bought it from the man who ran the stable. After a day or so, he found that the animal was a worthless, worn-out nag. It couldn't even last through the first chukker, which was humiliating of course for Ricky. He daren't try to take it onto the field again. It had been all doped up when he bought it. Ricky was outraged. Instead of simply trying to get his money back, he wanted to have his revenge upon the man and make an even bigger fool of *him*. He persuaded a friend to dress himself up in a turtleneck sweater and a pair of yellow jodhpurs and pretend just to be passing by the stall in the same stable where the polo pony was still kept. His friend played the role, you see, of someone only just taking up the game and who thought he *had* to have that particular pony. He asked the man whose animal it was, and before he could get an answer he offered more than twice the price that Rick had paid. He even put the offer into writing— using an assumed name, of course. He said he was from up in Maryland and would return in two days' time. Naturally, the stableman telephoned Ricky as soon as the stranger in jodhpurs had left the stable. He said he had discovered, to his chagrin, that the pony was not in as good condition as he had thought it was. And he said that in order that there be no bad feeling between them he was willing to buy it back for the price Ricky had paid.

Ricky went over that night and collected his money. But when the stranger didn't reappear and couldn't be traced, the stableman of course knew what had happened. Rick didn't return to the stable during the following several days. I suppose, being Ricky, he was busy spreading the story all over

town. His brother and sisters got wind of it. And I did soon
enough. On Sunday night, two thugs and some woman Ricky
knew but would never identify—not even to me—came to his
house and persuaded him to go out and sit in their car with
them in front of his house. And there they beat him brutally.
He had to be in the hospital for five or six days. They broke his
right arm, and one of them—maybe it was the woman—was
trying to bite off the lobe of his left ear when Ricky's current
wife, who had been out to some party without the favor of his
company, pulled into the driveway beside the house. The
assailants shoved poor Ricky, bruised and bleeding and with
his arm broken, out onto the sidewalk. And then of course they
sped away down the street in their rented car. Ricky's wife and
the male friend who was with her got the license number, but
the car had been rented under an assumed name—the same
name, actually, as some kind of joke, I suppose, that Ricky's
friend in jodhpurs had used with the stablekeeper.

Since Ricky insisted that he could not possibly recognize his
two male assailants in a lineup, and since he refused to identify
the woman, there was little that could be done about his actual
beating. I don't know that he ever confessed to anyone but me
that he knew the woman. It was easy enough for me to imagine
what *she* looked like. Though I would not have admitted it to
Ricky or to anyone else, I would now and then during the
following weeks see a woman of a certain type on the streets
downtown—with one of those tight little mouths and with
burning eyes—and imagine that she might be the very one. All
we were ever able to do about the miserable fracas was to see
to it finally that that stable was put out of business and that the
man himself had to go elsewhere (he went down into North
Carolina) to ply his trade.

There is one other scrape of Ricky's that I must mention,
because it remains particularly vivid for me. The nature and
the paraphernalia of this one will seem even more old-fashioned
than those of the other incidents. Maybe that's why it sticks in
my mind so. It's something that might have happened to any
number of rough fellows I knew when I was coming along.

Ricky, not surprising to say, likes to gamble. From the time

he was a young boy he would often try to inveigle one of the
other children into making wagers with him on how overdone
his steak was at dinner. He always liked it very rare and when
his serving came he would hold up a bite on his fork and, for a
decision on the bet, would ask everyone what shade of brown
the meat was. He made all the suggestions of color himself.
And one night his suggestions got so coarse and vile his mother
had to send him from the dining room and not let him have a
bite of supper. Sometimes he would try to get the other
children to bet with him on the exact number of minutes the
parson's sermon would last on Sunday or how many times the
preacher would use the word *Hell* or *damnation* or *adultery*.
Since he has got grown, it's the races, of course, he likes—
horse races, it goes without saying, but also such low-life affairs
as dog races and auto races. What catches his fancy above all
else, though, are the chicken fights we have always had in our
part of the country. And a few years ago he bought himself a
little farm a dozen miles or so south of town where he could
raise his own game chickens. I saw nothing wrong with that at
the time. Then he built an octagonal barn down there, with a
pit in it where he could hold the fights. I worried a little when
he did that. But we've always had cockfights hereabouts. The
birds are beautiful creatures, really, though they have no brains,
of course. The fight itself is a real spectacle and no worse than
some other things people enjoy. At Ricky's urging, I even went
down to two or three fights at his place. I didn't bet, because I
knew the stakes were very high. (Besides, it's the betting that's
illegal.) And I didn't tell the other children about my going.
But this was after Cary was dead, you see, and I thought
maybe she would have liked my going for Ricky's sake, though
she would never have acknowledged it. Pretty soon, sizable
crowds began attending the fights on weekend nights. Cars
would be parked all over Ricky's front pasture and all around
the yard of the tenant house. He might as well have put up a
sign down at the gate where his farm road came off the highway.

The point is, everyone knew that the cockfights were on.
And one of his most regular customers and biggest bettors was
one of the county sheriff's right-hand men. I'm afraid Rick must
have bragged about that in advertising his fights to friends—

friends who would otherwise have been a little timid about coming. And during the fights he would move about among the crowd, winking at people and saying to them under his breath, "The deputy's here tonight." I suppose it was his way of reassuring them that everything was all right. I don't know whether or not his spreading the word so widely had anything to do with the raid, but nevertheless the deputy was present the night the federal officers came stealing up the farm road, with their car lights off and with search warrants in their pockets. And it was the deputy who first got wind of the federal officers' approach. He had one of his sidekicks posted outside the barn. Maybe he had somebody watching out there every night that he came. Maybe all along he had had a plan for his escape in such an emergency. Rick thought so afterward. Anyhow, the deputy's man outside knew at once what those cars moving up the lane with their lights off meant. The deputy got the word before anyone else, but, depend upon Ricky, he saw the first move the deputy made to leave. And he was not going to have it. He took out after him.

The deputy's watchman was prepared to stay on and take his chances. (He wasn't even a patrolman. He probably only worked in the office.) I imagine he was prepared to spend a night in jail if necessary, and pay whatever fine there might be, because his presence could explain one of the sheriff's cars being parked in the pasture. But the deputy himself took off through the back-woods on Ricky's property and toward a county road on the back of the place. Ricky, as I've said, was not going to have that. Since the cockfight was on his farm, he knew there was no way out of trouble for himself. But he thought it couldn't, at least, do him any harm to have the deputy caught along with everybody else. Moreover, the deputy had lost considerable amounts of money there at the pit in recent weeks and had insinuated to Ricky that he suspected some of the cocks had been tampered with. (I, personally, don't believe Ricky would stand for that.) Ricky couldn't be sure there wasn't some collusion between the deputy and the feds. He saw the deputy's man catch the deputy's eye from the barn doorway and observed the deputy's departure. He was right after him. He overtook him just before he reached the woods. Fortunately, the deputy wasn't armed. (Ricky allowed no one to bring a gun inside the barn.) And fortunately Ricky wasn't armed, either, that night. They scuffled a little near the gate to the woods lot. The deputy, being a man twice Rick's age, was no match for him and was soon overpowered. Ricky dragged him back to the barn, himself resisting—as he later testified—all efforts at bribery on the deputy's part, and turned in both himself and his captive to the federal officers.

Extricating Ricky from that affair and setting matters aright was a long and complicated undertaking. The worst of it really began for Ricky after the court proceedings were finished and all fines were paid (there were no jail terms for anyone), because from his last appearance in the federal courthouse Ricky could drive his car scarcely one block through that suburb where he lives without receiving a traffic ticket of some kind. There may not have been anything crooked about it, for Ricky is a wild sort of driver at best. But, anyhow, within a short time his driving license was revoked for the period of a year. Giving up driving was a great inconvenience for him and a humiliation. All we could do about the deputy, who, Ricky felt sure, had connived with the federal officers, was to get him out of his job after the next election.

The outcome of the court proceedings was that Rick's fines were very heavy. Moreover, efforts were made to confiscate all the livestock on his farm, as well as the farm machinery. But he was saved from the confiscation by a special circumstance, which, however, turned out to produce for him only a sort of Pyrrhic victory. It turned out, you see, that the farm was not in Ricky's name but in that of his young tenant farmer's wife. I never saw her, or didn't know it if I did. Afterward, I used to try to recall if I hadn't seen some such young woman when I was down watching the cockfights—one who would have fitted the picture in my mind. My imagination played tricks on me, though. I would think I remembered the face or figure of some young girl I'd seen there who could conceivably be the one. But then suddenly I'd recall another and think possibly it might be she who had the title to Ricky's farm. I never could be sure.

*   *   *

When Ricky appeared outside my window just now, I'd
already had a very bad morning. The bursitis in my right
shoulder had waked me before dawn. At last I got up and
dressed, which was an ordeal in itself. (My right hip was
hurting somewhat, too.) When finally the cook came in, she
wanted to give me a massage before she began fixing breakfast
even. Cary would never have allowed her to make that mistake. A massage, you see, is the worst thing you can do for my
sort of bursitis. What I wanted was some breakfast. And I knew
it would take Meg three quarters of an hour to put breakfast on
the table. And so I managed to get out of my clothes again and
ease myself into a hot bath, groaning so loud all the while that
Meg came up to the door twice and asked if I was all right. I
told her just to go and get my breakfast ready. After breakfast,
I waited till a decent hour and then telephoned one of my golf
foursome to tell him I couldn't play today. It's this damp fall
weather that does us in worst. All you can do is sit and think
how you've got the whole winter before you and wonder if
you'll be able to get yourself off to someplace like Sarasota.

While I sat at a front window, waiting for the postman (he
never brings anything but circulars and catalogs on Saturday;
besides, all my serious mail goes to the office and is opened by
someone else), I found myself thinking of all the things I
couldn't do and all the people who are dead and that I mustn't
think about. I tried to do a little better—that is, to think of
something cheerful. There was lots I *could* be cheerful about,
wasn't there? At least three of my children were certain to
telephone today—all but Ricky, and it was sure to be bad news
if he did. And a couple of the grandchildren would likely call,
too. Then tomorrow I'd be going to lunch with some of them if
I felt up to it. Suddenly I thought of the pills I was supposed to
have taken before breakfast and had forgotten to: the Inderal
and the potassium and the hydrochlorothiazide. I began to get
up from my chair and then I settled down again. It didn't really
matter. There was no ailment I had that could really be counted
on to be fatal if I missed one day's dosage. And then I
wholeheartedly embraced the old subject, the old speculation:
How many days like this one, how many years like this one lay
ahead for me? And finally, irresistibly, I descended to lower

depths still, thinking of past times not with any relish but remembering how in past times I had always *told* myself I'd someday look back with pleasure on what would seem good old days, which was an indication itself that they hadn't somehow been good enough—not good enough, that is, to stand on their own as an end in themselves. If the old days were so damned good, why had I had to think always how good they would someday seem in retrospect? I had just reached the part where I think there was nothing *wrong* with them and that I ought to be satisfied, had just reached that point at which I recall that I loved and was loved by my wife, that I love and am loved by my children, that it's not them or my life but *me* there's something wrong with!—had just reached that inevitable syllogism that I always come to, when I was distracted by the arrival of Saturday morning's late mail delivery. It was brought in, it was handed to me by a pair of black hands, and of course it had nothing in it. But I took it upstairs to my sitting room. (So that even the servant wouldn't see there was nothing worth having in it.) I had just closed my door and got out my pills when I heard Ricky's car turn into the gravel driveway.

He was driving so slowly that his car wheels hardly disturbed the gravel. That in itself was an ominous phenomenon. He was approaching slowly and quietly. He didn't want me to know ahead of time what there was in store for me. My first impulse was to lock my door and refuse to admit him. I simply did not feel up to Rick this morning! But I said to myself, "That's something I've never done, though maybe ought to have done years ago no matter what Cary said. He's sure to send my blood pressure soaring." I thought of picking up the telephone and phoning one of the other children to come and protect me from this monster of a son and from whatever sort of trouble he was now in.

But it was just then that I caught my first glimpse of him down in the driveway. I had the illusion that he was admiring the place. And then of course I was at once disillusioned. He was only hesitating down there because he dreaded seeing me. But he was telling himself he *had* to see me. There would be no other solution to his problem but to see his old man. I knew what he was thinking by the gesture he was making with his left hand. It's strange how you get the notion that your children are like you just because they have the same facial features and the same gestures when talking to themselves. None of it means a thing! It's only an illusion. Even now I find myself making gestures with my hands when I'm talking to myself that I used to notice my own father making sometimes when we were out walking together and neither of us had spoken a word for half an hour or so. It used to get on my nerves when I saw Father do it, throwing out his hand almost imperceptibly, with his long fingers spread apart. I don't know why it got on my nerves so. But, anyhow, I never dreamed that I could inherit such a gesture—or much less that one of my sons would. And yet there Ricky is, down in the driveway, making the same gesture precisely. And there never were three men with more different characters than my father and me and my youngest child. I watch Ricky make the gesture several times while standing in the driveway. And now suddenly he turns as if to go back to his car. I step away from the window, hoping he hasn't seen me and will go on off. But, having once seen him down there, I can't, of course, do that. I have to receive him and hear him out. I open the sash and call down to him, "Come on up, Ricky."

He looks up at me, smiles guiltily, and shrugs. Then he comes on in the side entrance. As he moves through the house and up the stairs, I try to calm myself. I gaze down at the roughed-up gravel where his suede shoes did their damage and tell myself it isn't so bad and even manage to smile at my own old-maidishness. Presently, he comes into the sitting room. We greet each other with the usual handshake. I can smell his shaving lotion. Or maybe it is something he puts on his hair. We go over and sit down by the fireplace, where there is a fire laid but not lit in this season, of course. He begins by talking about everything under the sun except what is on his mind. This is standard procedure in our talks at such times. Finally, he begins looking into the fireplace as though the fire were lit and as though he were watching low-burning flames. I barely keep myself from smiling when he says, "I've got a little problem—not so damned little, in fact. It's a matter that's got out of hand."

And then I say, "I supposed as much."

You can't give Ricky an inch at these times, you see. Else he'll take advantage of you. Pretty soon he'll have shifted the whole burden of how he's to be extricated onto your shoulders. I wait for him to continue, and he is about to, I think. But before he can get started he turns his eyes away from the dry logs and the unlit kindling and begins looking about the room, just as he looked about the premises outside. It occurs to me again that he seems to be observing my place for the very first time. But I don't suppose he really is. His mind is, as usual, on himself. Then all at once his eyes do obviously come to focus on something over my shoulder. He runs his tongue up under his upper lip and then under his lower lip, as though he were cleaning his teeth. I, involuntarily almost, look over my shoulder. There on the library table behind me, on what I call my desk, are my cut-glass tumbler and three bottles of pills—my hydrochlorothiazide, my Inderal, and my potassium. Somehow I failed to put them back in my desk drawer earlier. I was so distracted by my morbid thoughts when I came upstairs that I forgot to stick them away in the place where I keep them out of sight from everybody. (I don't even like for the servants to see what and how much medicine I take.) Without a word passing between us, and despite the pains in my shoulder and hip, I push myself up out of my chair and sweep the bottles, and the tumbler, too, into the desk drawer. I keep my back to Ricky for a minute or so till I can overcome the grimacing I never can repress when these pains strike. Suddenly, though, I do turn back to him and find he has come to his feet. I pay no special attention to that. I ease myself back into my chair saying, "Yes, Ricky." Making my voice rather hard, I say, "You've got a problem?" He looks at me coldly, without a trace of the sympathy any one of the other children would have shown—knowing, that is, as he surely does, that I am having pains of some description. And he speaks to me as though I were a total stranger toward whom he feels nothing but is just barely human enough to wish not to torture. "Man," he says—the idea of his addressing *me* that way!—"Man, you've got problems enough of your own. Even the world's greatest snotface can see that. One thing sure, you don't need to hear *my* crap."

I am on my feet so quick you wouldn't think I have a pain in my body. "Don't you use that gutter language with me, Ricky!" I say. "You weren't brought up in some slum over beyond Vinegar Hill!" He only turns and looks into the fireplace again. If there were a fire going I reckon he would have spat in it at this point. Then he looks back at me, running his tongue over his teeth again. And then, without any apology or so much as a by-your-leave, he heads for the door. "Come back here, Ricky!" I command. "Don't you dare leave the room!" Still moving toward the closed door, he glances back over his shoulder at me, with a wide, hard grin on his face, showing his mouthful of white teeth, as though my command were the funniest thing he has ever heard. At the door, he puts his big right hand on the glass knob, covering it entirely. Then he twists his upper body, his torso, around—seemingly just from the hips—to face me. And simultaneously he brings up his left hand and scratches that triangle of dark hair where his shirt is open. It is like some kind of dirty gesture he is making. I say to myself, "He really is like something not quite human. For all the jams and scrapes he's been in, he's never suffered any second thoughts or known the meaning of remorse. I ought to have let him hang," I say to myself, "by his own beautiful locks."

But almost simultaneously what I hear myself saying aloud is "Please don't go, Rick. Don't go yet, son." Yes, I am pleading with him, and I mean what I say with my whole heart. He still has his right hand on the doorknob and has given it a full turn. Our eyes meet across the room, directly, as they never have before in the whole of Ricky's life or mine. I think neither of us could tell anyone what it is he sees in the other's eyes, unless it is a need beyond any description either of us is capable of.

Presently Rick says, "You don't need to hear my crap."

And I hear my bewildered voice saying, "I do . . . I do." And "Don't go, Rick, my boy." My eyes have even misted over. But I still meet his eyes across the now too silent room. He looks at me in the most compassionate way imaginable. I don't think any child of mine has ever looked at me so before. Or perhaps it isn't really with compassion he is viewing me but with the sudden, gratifying knowledge that it is not, after all, such a one-sided business, the business between us. He keeps his right hand on the doorknob a few seconds longer. Then I hear the latch click and know he has let go. Meanwhile, I observe his left hand making that familiar gesture, his fingers splayed, his hand tilting back and forth. I am out of my chair by now. I go to the desk and bring out two Danlys cigars from another desk drawer, which I keep locked. He is there ready to receive my offering when I turn around. He accepts the cigar without smiling, and I give it without smiling, too. Seated opposite each other again, each of us lights his own.

And then Ricky begins. What will it be this time, I think. I am wild with anticipation. Whatever it will be, I know it is all anyone in the world can give me now—perhaps the most anyone has ever been able to give a man like me. As Ricky begins, I try to think of all the good things the other children have done for me through the years and of their affection, and of my wife's. But it seems this was all there ever was. I forget my pains and my pills, and the canceled golf game, and the meaningless mail that morning. I find I can scarcely sit still in my chair for wanting Ricky to get on with it. Has he been brandishing his pistol again? Or dragging the sheriff's deputy across a field at midnight? And does he have in his wallet perhaps a picture of some other girl with a tight little mouth, and eyes that burn? Will his outrageous story include her? And perhaps explain it, leaving her a blessed mystery? As Ricky begins, I find myself listening not merely with fixed attention but with my whole being. . . . I hear him beginning. I am listening. I am listening gratefully to all he will tell me about himself, about any life that is not my own.

Peter Taylor is the author of seven collections of short stories, several plays and the novel A Summons to Memphis. *He is a member of the National Academy of Arts and Letters, from whom he received the Gold Medal for Fiction. He lives in Charlottesville, Virginia.*

Published in The New Yorker.

XAM WILSON CARTIER

BE-BOP, RE-BOP &
ALL THOSE OBLIGATOS

The liquor was flowing, everyone had a plate, folks had visited all the way back to the kitchen. . . . We were just settling into the spirit of Double's funeral wake when Vole took it in mind to drive all the guests from the house.

For some reason of crisis insanity and because my first reaction to mayhem is to staple down the madness to some detail of order, I've begun to take stock of the folks in the room, to estimate the number of floating mourners who've made their way past the living room rut to the recondite sanctum in the rear of the house. There are twenty-four people poised at candid angles as far back through the room as the eye can see, including five men: two family friends and three co-workers of Double's whom I've seen two or three times. The women, role models around me, are fine-feathered birds flown from flighty Saks and Montaldos, the *haute couture* rooms. We're all, all of us are musing over inscrutable chalices of highballs, including me in spasmodic sweet-sixteenhood, thanks to the blessing of mother-gone-from-the-room, but now Vole's back, so here's my solo, about to be crimped. . . .

Vole had been resting in the bedroom away from it all when Mona threw out, "Some folks might've called him irresponsible and impulsive, but one thing about Double is, he might have been practically back down to where he started when he died, but now there was a man who could keep going when the chips were down no matter *what* it took. If it took a Tom, he'd be one, and he has his own good reasons too, he must have, considering what he stooped to just to hold on to that trifling job in parcel post. It was the best thing he'd ever lucked up on."

She sucked her teeth and shook her head.

"Truth is the light," somebody said.

"Let it shine," somebody else said.

"Now *some* folks might have said Double was a dreamer with no firm sense of direction," Mona went on, "they'd have said he was good for nothing but dead-end dreams . . . but I know better! though Double *had* him some dreams, at least til Vole started to stay on his back—she rode him all the time you know, though let it be said, Double needed some get-up and go. Don't talk about the dead, but youall know what I mean, you can't live a man's life for him; you've got to let him breathe. Vole knows that—maybe she's got another opinion—but well, you all know the story: You don't miss your water til your well runs dry!"

She raised her glass to the tune of the assents around her.

"Well, well, well." Vole appeared in the doorway looking store-rack crisp in her undefiled black dress, faille skirt riding impossible curves of her paragon legs. She raised that tight tan face, angled those highcarved cheekbones, fast-focused those radar eyes from their dusty socket-shadows. Her fingers draped the knob of the door like a mannequin's hand but for the fingernails, which she trimmed stoically in ruthless crescents. We're all looking over at her, ruffled in our own different ways, with reactions ranging from bitterness to outrage. Where are Vole's tears anyway? I'm thinking—and where's the crash of her gloom? There she stands, intact and unacceptable as usual. Her sometime pal Mona is one juror in particular who gives Vole the eye: Mona's response to Vole at the moment is disappointment that the convicted widow's alive and well.

"Having fun?" Vole flings at Mona over undermusical silence and rustling nudges, just as Mona's in process of leaning her emerald suede vested chest toward the woman beside her, in bracing gesture of *uh-oh*. . . .

"Now Vole, just calm down, honey," Mona dodges, the defense is pushed out of her instantly and she rolls on automatically: "Death is always hard, we know that, and it's hardest on the widow, yes, it always is, it's the shock, and—"

"What do you know?" Vole cut her off at the pass of her sass. "Just what in the *hell* do you know?" And I tense, since I feel

Vole building to an open storm of her closet feelings; already she's lapsed into what she calls *vulgar language in public*, brazenly defying the Salt Away Box (this being a cylindrical empty salt box that we keep family fines in; whoever cursed had to pay). "I'm tired, but I ain't crazy," Vole goes on with further indication of no-hold-barredness, her lapse into "slang" as she calls it. "I'm tired but I ain't crazy enough to think you actually give a damn about anybody's grief, least of all mine, or do I *look* like a fool? Tell me anything!" Vole's leaning forward now with arms crossed across her chest, a hanging judge, waiting. . . .

"Uh—" starts Mona. . . .

"Yeah, 'uh,'" says Vole relentlessly, leaning further toward defendant—"Come on, tell me anything, just front me right off. I'm supposed to be under the influence of widowhood, so you can't go wrong. Come on, don't let me stop your show since you know so much. Knock yourself out, come on; make like I'm not here.

"Look at you," Vole sneers on, "in your weep motif. You never did a damn thing for Double while he was alive, or for any of the rest of us" (here she gestures maternally toward me), "and you know it. But you take plenty time to rake us through with your mouth, mouth almighty, fatmouth queen, brilliantine—"

("*Goddamn*" goes someone's hushed catharris; all of us onlookers had been swept into the spirit of Vole's testimony)—

"Well surprise, fools"— Vole turns to the room at large—"I can read you like a book. But don't let that throw you—" With this last you can hear a crew of voices arming with mumbles for self-defense just in case, be prepared, but look! There's Vole, on everyone's case already . . . here she comes, snatching plates of food and drinks from visitors ("Here, I'll take that"), rushing out of the room mechanically, then back again now with armloads of hats and coats which she flings in a heap on the couch and returns for the rest.

"*If it took a Tom, he'd be one*. . . ." It's this I consider during the following frantic interval; I try not to, but can't help but think it, this peanut butter thought that sticks to the roof of my immature mind. . . . I think of the time only last week, when Double had lost his post office gig and Vole and I had passed him talking on the wallphone in the hall. . . .

"Well, do you take colored?" Double had mouthed this then in mealy manner, or so it seemed to the both of us. Vole headed one way and I another, so that *What?* we stop and stare at each other, then both jump in at once—

"Do they do what?" Vole challenges Double and then walks away with no further display, a mystery to teen-age me at the time, and I stay on to follow her words with a cop-bust frown of disgust aimed at Double, this at know-all black-and-white stage of analysis development, righteous adolescence. To tom or not to tom—seemed perfectly clear to me. . . .

Aw Double, I thought at the wake then that day, there it is, so my hump of shock and let-down can sink to its rest in the pit of my stomach—Was our case really so critical then that we were all the way down to our tommery? I asked myself again and again all through that week, near the time of your seemed-to-be sin when I thought I knew the answer, one answer: *Hell no! You can be down to death, and not down to tom!* Yet—this I know now—what could you do, standing limp with livelihood soon to be lost, as you knew, to the rake of unfeeling circumstance? What's more I'm human too and've whipped out my own slave-kerchief in time of distress, "It's reflex survival," I fibbed to myself until then when that day at your wake all your contrivance (just venial connivance, not mortal!)—all your contrivance comes floodingly clear and wet comprehension, it courses a trail through the heat of my face.

Militant memories: For months, years after his passing Double would appear through my sleep to bump a lesser dream, still bopping with the armed resistance of his dedication to "jazz"—which he said was "two, say three broad crooked jumps off to the side of the mainstream straight and narrow, out to where sound becomes sight, as it should be!"

When I think of Double that day at his wake, I see him standing beside the radio with his forefinger crooking for me to run over and check out his riff or those taps or that vamp or these changes. This I'd casually stroll up to do with cool beyond my childish years; my thumbs would be tucked in pinafore straps under fat kinky braids that laid on my chest.

"*And how's Daddy's masterpiece coming along?*"

"*Aw, I can't kick.*"

"*Well say hey, whatcha know?*"

"*Aw, you got to go!*"

"*So tell me, what's to it?*"

"*Nothin to it but to do it!*"

"*Mean to say YOU can do the do?*"

"*Can Ella Fitz cut a scat? . . . Then, don't hand me that!*"

"*Can Eisenhower dance? Say HEY—not a chance!*"

"*Hey now. And how!*"

My smallfry face at Double's knee. Abracadabra afternoons! And every day, on the way home from kindergarten at BookerTWashington School, there's hopeful harmony of Double and me, two hipsters vocaleesing to wide-angel sound up front in the Studebaker.

"*Oop bop shabam, buh do be do,*
We like to boogie, woogie, re-bop and be-bop it too!"

Yet Double has died. But why call it *death*, when in the scheme of simple reality, I should be and am convinced by the age of sixteen (time of no questions) that his passing, like his music, is more process than product by nature—that Double's demise has the matrix-free flow of an on-the-spot bop change. So since I know he's still bopping nearby in time to the tune of temporality, while Vole's handing out the coats and hats at his wake, I shake the scheme of my dream and seize the opportunity to come up with a note of relevant reality for the mourn-watchers.

"A side of Fats, anyone?" I call out, surrounded by scotchsippers' eyebrows jumping like spastic grasshoppers. "Ain't Misbehavin" has popped into mind like the miracle of the gramophone. So *apropos*! Talk about chromatic consciousness—why it's the final flipside! Besides, it was Double's favorite jam, so I put it on the hi-fi and turn it to crescendo. Then's when Vole turns to face me so suddenly that distress bends distended in our corner of the cosmos—rapport needs no words in light of the sight of Vole rushing toward me with her hand upraised, the hand which she uses to spin me in place for a heartfelt lindy hop, steps of which I fall into by rote due to Double's diligent teaching—and Vole and I, hey, well we dance past all woe for a whirlaround while!

"Be-Bop, Re-Bop, *my first novel, is about a young girl who's boosted beyond the crags of her childhood by her father's faith in upbeat black culture, especially its waypaving jazz. It's her father's cultural legacy that buoys her through anxious adolescence and into adulthood in vivid San Fran. While it celebrates the impact of jazz,* Be-Bop, Re-Bop *itself was written as jazz.*

"*I began the novel and its research in 1979—and there followed three full years of survival straits that I had to navigate each day before I dealt with my work.*

"*It was during the summer of 1982 that I was able, for the first time, to write* Be-Bop *full steam ahead, with no distractions. The Millay Colony invited me for a month, and when I reached Millay, I felt as if I'd washed up on shore. After eight years of single-parenting in an onrushing current of cashlessness, I was going through a grueling divorce mediation that already had siphoned my funds and attention for the better part of a year. Perhaps most frustratingly of all, during this period I was unable to write. It was writing that I turned to for solace and clarification; my writing empowered me.*

"*Set in rolling hills of floral glory, the Colony could have been in the heart of barren wasteland for all I cared. As for backdrop, I felt an artist's delight with conducive aesthetics . . . but I'd come to the Colony to work. And work I did, at midnight, dawn, dusk and during most of the time in between. At the end of my stay, two wealthier artists told me that I'd helped to set the tone for their own productivity. From my manic work habits they'd learned to seize the helm of their own inspiration and to steer it at their behest.*

"*It struck me that because of our limited means of financial survival, we low-income women and people of color are artists of lifetide fluidity. We learn to swim life as it ebbs and it flows, and to focus on faint distant rainbows—one was my stay at Millay—as a matter of artistic course."*

Xam Wilson Cartiér has received a number of literary awards, including an NEA Creative Writing Fellowship and a California Arts Council Grant. Her novel Be-Bop, Re-Bop *was published in 1987. Born in St. Louis, she lives in San Francisco with her daughter. Ms. Cartiér is writer-in-residence at the Western Addition Cultural Center.*

Published in Be-Bop, Re-Bop.

RICK BASS

WEJUMPKA

When Wejumpka was eleven, and Vern was forty-eight, and I was thirty, Vern made me be Wejumpka's godfather. We were drinking, playing cards, and Vern's health had been going down fast, all that fall. We were playing that ridiculous game of Liar's Poker, and got down to where the bet was that I had to be Wejumpka's godfather if I called and lost; but if Vern was bluffing—he said I had *eight* ones— then he had to marry the girl he was seeing. She was twenty, plump, with a pear-shaped face and orange hair; she had a nice laugh and two children, already, but no husband. The reason I made that bet was hoping she could do something with him; straighten him up, as I knew women could sometimes do.

Her father was thirty-five, he'd been in my high school (failed two years), a senior when I was a freshman; we'd played football together one year, and he was, or had been, a wiry little halfback who'd gotten even wirier since, working on cars in his garage out near the Pearl River. His name was Zachary and he would collect insurance money each spring when the rains brought the river right into his garage, and on up into his house. Sometimes he didn't even move out, when it flooded—just waded around, doing his chores, making sure all the circuit breakers were off: waiting for the water to go back down.

When the rains began, each March, he would sit up on the roof of his garage and listen to the weather station, praying for more and more rain: each foot of water in his shop was worth about ten thousand dollars. It's cruel, but I don't even know what his daughter's name is; and just as cruelly, I don't even think Dale did, either. We called her Zachary's girl. It was a

315

serious hand of poker. It was only about midnight, but we'd
started drinking at four in the afternoon.

Vern wasn't bluffing, it turned out, and, I suspected later,
wasn't even drunk. It was a setup. It was sort of like I'd killed
him, as in one of those hunting accidents where a best buddy
trips and pulls the trigger, shooting his partner; by winning, by
assuming responsibility for Wejumpka, I'd given Vern the last
go-ahead he needed to let go of everything, and let his spiral
have its way with him, the shortened wick of his life.

I'd really hoped to win the bet, and at least hope for Zachary's
girl to take a strong hand with him, if indeed she had said yes.
Vern wasn't the same anymore, wasn't really fun to be around—I
was playing cards with him more out of a sense of duty than
anything, and that was probably why I got so drunk, and won
Wejumpka—because I'd had duty before, and had not done so
well—in fact, I'd fucking struck out—and later that year, when
Vern got the old stop-drinking-or-you-only-have-one-year-to-live
speech from his doctor, and when he did not stop drinking, not
much, anyway—that was when I felt young and stupid for
having called an older man's bluff.

I'm a bit in the middle, now, and think I have it figured, too
late of course, that the young may bluff *or* charge, and that the
guys in the middle, like me—guys just for the first time beginning to lose things—we're the bluffers—but that the ancients,
like Vern and beyond, never bluff.

Like I said, too late.

About the boy I have won: Wejumpka. His Christian name is
Montrose, but when he was six he went on one of those father
and son campouts with the Scouts, with Vern, and they roasted
marshmallows, had canoe races, sang songs around the camp-
fire, farted chili farts, and gave each other Indian names,
drawn from a wooden box, very serious, very immortal.

The moon, high and silver over the lake. Bullfrogs drummed;
bats chittered and swooped over the lake. There was the sweet
sounds of a whipporwhill, back in the bushes, down in the
reeds by the lake. Vern was still married then.

Everyone else forgot their name, or was less than flattered
by it, and threw it in the fire.

Wejumpka remembered his; he embraced it.

About the boy I have inherited, or almost inherited: he is a hugger.

He's wild about puppies. Cats, parrots, guinea pigs—he loves all animals, even other children—even the mean ones who pushed him down and ran away when he tried to embrace them.

He's always been that way—always holding on. Perhaps even when he was in Ann's womb—and I do not mean to speak so personally, but now that she is Vern's ex-wife, instead of wife, I can say that word—perhaps even then, with some prenatal sonar, casting out into the future, he could see and feel the dark shape of that future, of what would come when he was seven, the divorce—not anything specific, not knowing anything, but just feeling a certain end to things, or rather, the absence of the thing—maybe like Zachary on his roof, watching the storms come in off the Gulf, laughing in the rain, getting filthy rich, cackling and listening to his radio with lightning popping all around him, lightning bouncing off of the trees in his front yard—maybe even then Wejumpka could tell that very soon, not long at all after he was born, there would be a jumping-off spot.

Maybe Vern said unkind words to Ann, while Wejumpka was forming in her womb.

Maybe Ann had unkind thoughts about Vern; or maybe she, too, a woman—even more so than a child—could see into the future, could feel the absence of a thing; perhaps she held on to Vern more tightly than ever, then, being wise and clairvoyant and scared in her pregnancy; and perhaps thusly she secreted an excess number of holding-on hormones, of frantic hormones, as would any sane person, and they affected the unborn child, made him be the same way.

Perhaps.

Wejumpka is a hugger.

When he was six, the year before the divorce, he dressed as Porky Pig for Halloween. The other children were dressed as devils, witches, Green Berets with rubber knives clenched in their teeth, scars tattooed on their arms, their faces; but Wejumpka was Porky Pig, and went around hugging people, when they answered the door: not asking for candy, not quite understanding that part of it, but instead just running into these strange people's houses and latching on to their legs, giving them a tight thigh hug. Vern and Ann were having some sort of dinner party, one of the famous ones in which they would end up insulting each other in front of all the guests, maybe even throwing things, and it was my job to baby-sit Wejumpka, to take him around to all the houses and bring him safely back home.

Vern and Ann had been drinking a little, when we got back, but had not started their fight yet. It's possible that they were even still a little in love, or thought that they were; when they answered the door, and saw Porky Pig, their own little Porky Pig, standing in front of them, they smiled, and felt all those feelings.

"Trick or treat!" Wejumpka shouted through his plastic mask, hopping up and down. I had explained to him how it worked; that sometimes it was best not to hug. He had to be overjoyed, in all the running chaos of the night, all the hurried darkness, at having found his way back home, at seeing his mother and father standing there in the doorway, with all the bright good light of the party behind them, all the safe noise.

"Trick or treat!" he shouted again, jumping up and down once more, and Ann frowned and took a step back.

"Why, you're *scary*," she said, and Wejumpka stopped hopping, and looked at me.

"Whose little boy are *you*?" Vern asked, bending down and peering into the mask. "I don't believe I *know* any little Porky Pig boys," he said, shaking his head, and then—I know they had been drinking—they closed the door!

"It's me!" Wejumpka screamed, struggling to get out of the hot costume and the elastic-string mask. "It's me!" he screamed. "It's your little *boy!*"

They opened the door, then, and everyone was gathered around it, all the guests were laughing too, and Wejumpka, in tears, flew into Ann's arms, crying, and she patted him on the back, did all the right things . . .

So Vern has won this bet. His little sports car has broken down, hasn't run in over a year, and sits idle in the small

woodshed-garage behind his apartment. Mice have built their
nests in and around the engine, have nibbled the insulation off
of the electrical wiring. There are birds living in the rafters of
the little shed, nesting there, and they have dappled the car
with what seems to be a hearty enthusiasm. Vern walks to
work, on the days he goes now; a blueprint for destruction!
There he goes! The town drunk! Drunk in the morning!

Sometimes Zachary's girl comes by and picks him up in her
red '69 Chevy Imperial: bald tires, no muffler, dice, all of it.
Vern slumps down in the seat and drinks rum from the bottle,
still wearing his suit, still reporting to and from work.

Ann wants the BMW, it's one of two or three things she
didn't get in the divorce, and I think that's why he refuses to
fix it—I think. I hope that's the reason. He says it's gone too far
to be fixed; that's what he tells me. He sounds sad about it,
and we both know he's right, but still, I have to say all the
right things, have to protest . . . Aww, hayull, Vern, just throw
some money at it, they can fix it . . .

Sometimes I drive Vern over to Zachary's, and they invite
me in. Zachary and his daughter and Dale and I play cards at a
little linoleum table that rocks whenever you lean your elbows
on it. Zachary's girl and Vern drink from the same bottle, but
Zach and I drink from jelly glasses. Zachary buries the insurance money.

"Lot of bad shit goin' around," Zach says, shaking his head,
studying his hand as if it is the first game of cards he has ever
played in his life; as if not knowing quite what to do, not
wanting to, or unsure of, making the first move—and Zach's
girl and Vern start to giggle, looking at each other's hands, and
Zach and I start to talk about football, about how it was—
talking as if it's going to happen again, for Chrissakes, talking,
in our rum, with hope; hope and idiocy—and Zach's girl and
Vern are sliding to the floor, sort of becoming rum themselves,
spilling, tangled, twined; and Zach sighs and looks out the
window, thinking about how Vern has money too, a little
anyway, now that the divorce is almost paid off, and thinking
too, perhaps, about Vern's rotting sports car, which Zach would
dearly love to get his hands on—he could fix it, he thinks, or at

least by damn get it out of that dark garage and out into the daylight, maybe weld it to the top of a tower, run some eight-and-five-eights-inch drill pipe into the sky out in the front yard and weld rungs to the pipe so that it was a sort of a ladder; and he could climb up into it each day after work, sit behind the steering wheel like a sailor in a crow's nest, look out over the swamp and maybe have a few drinks, lean the front seat back and turn the radio on, maybe listen to some football games in the fall . . .

When Wejumpka entered junior high school, he finally stopped hugging people. The authorities simply made him stop: they told Ann that he couldn't come to school anymore, otherwise. He was hugging the teachers, other students, the custodians and maids; it was getting to be a discipline problem.

Also, we changed his name then. He was getting too old for Wejumpka—though it's what Vern and I still call him—but God knows, Montrose was certainly nothing to fall back on. In the end he decided upon Vern Jr. I gave him a wooden bowl with a lot of names mixed up in it, and that was the one he pulled out. Fate; a lucky boy.

He is luckier than Zach's girl, for sure; luckier even than Zach, who has some malaise in his blood, some stun-slugging chemical that makes him have to lie down and rest, every time the wind changes direction; luckier than his mother, Ann, who has also laid down and quite early, gained forty pounds in a year, instead of losing the twenty she needed to; luckier than me, too, me not knowing when to bluff and when to charge, when to commit and when not to—all this bad shit going on!—and feeling, as I watch it all go by, that even though I am away from it, several steps back, I'm still moving along with it all, too, being drawn along, as is everything, everyone . . . Wejumpka, Vern Jr., knows none of this, has never had this feeling yet. That is how he is lucky.

He knows when and when not to hug. He knows that he has gone through a dark spot, gone into an absent place, and has come out on the other side; and he knows that he can do it again, then, next time, when it comes, again and again; already, he knows that: to just close his eyes, and hold on, and he'll come on through.

For his eleventh birthday, I took him and his brother, Austin, who was sixteen, water skiing for the first time. I rented a little boat with a pretty good engine, and some skis, and we went out on the reservoir in it. Neither of the boys had skiied before, and for a long time we just sat out there, feeling the warmth of the sun, looking at how far away the shore was. Zachary had come and towed the BMW away, had indeed welded it to the top of a tower, and we were so far away from the shore that we had to use binoculars to even see the white speck of it, rising out of the swamp.

We took turns looking at it through the binoculars.

"I pissed in that car the day they got the divorce," Austin bragged, proud and tough, wearing his gold earring in one ear, a dirty blue-jean jacket, though it was 100°. He smelled like a nightclub, like the boy's rest room at school, soggy sour pee-stained cigarette butts, and I wanted him to ski first, so that he would have to get cleaned off.

"I pooted in it," Wejumpka admitted in a small voice, meekly, and the two brothers looked at each other, as far away as planets, and then broke up laughing, and I laughed too, laughed at old Zachary sitting up there in the sky that had years-old poot and other in it, but I didn't laugh as much as Wejumpka and Austin; and I was thinking about how good it would be to start the boat up, to push the throttle all the way in and feel the power of it, all the roar, right there in the back of the boat, beneath me, driving me forward, raising the boat's nose into the air, it would be such a powerful thrust.

Wejumpka, in an odd gesture of bravery, wanted to ski first. It's possible that he was just showing off for Austin; or maybe he thought his father had not yet abandoned him, that he was being given one last chance, and that even as he was climbing down into the lake, buoyed by his life vest, slipping his feet into the oversized skis—even then in his staggered, hugging-poet's imagination, his father was climbing up into the car with Zachary, watching him through binoculars, giving him a final chance, maybe even elbowing Zachary and pointing to him and saying, "That's my little boy. That's my Wejumpka."

I started the motor and jockeyed the boat from side to side, getting the tow rope lined up, making sure Wejumpka had his skis ready.

He's stout; he's a strong little ruffian, something of a muscleman these days. He popped right up, a surprised look on his face that was half joy, and half anger.

I glanced back over my shoulder once and could see that he was not watching the boat, but the shore: the tops of the trees, as if waiting for something to appear—squinting, and I guessed he was trying to make out the BMW.

"He says he wants to go faster!" Austin shouted, amazed, with his long hair blowing in the wind, and he was excited for his little brother, and I felt badly for having thought of him as being a street punk, and hoped it was only a phase.

"He's pointing his thumb up, he wants to go faster!"

I looked back again and it was so, Wejumpka was leaning back like a pro, he was a natural, and already he was relaxed, had sort of a cocky but determined smirk on his face, and he was jabbing his thumb at the sky, as if trying to poke out the bottom of something, skiing with just one hand, and I eased the throttle in.

The boat raised its nose, surged forward, a lion, trying to escape, but Wejumpka was the pursuer, and would not easily be lost. I looked back once more, and he was a little pale, we had the throttle all the way in—he was crouched down again, bucking the wake, no longer showboating, but just trying to hang on—and the wall of blue trees seemed closer, then, and almost without realizing it, I noticed that we could see now the far-off white dot of the car, sitting on top of the trees, looking like the most natural thing in the world.

We skimmed over the chop of summer-wind waves. The wind was blowing my hair, too, and it felt great. The sun was beginning to burn my cheeks and shoulders. I felt like I was sixteen, like I could go through anything, and come out the other side, too.

The white dot was getting larger in the trees; we could tell now that it was a car, could even see that it was a sports car; that's how close we were.

When I looked back, Wejumpka was gone. Austin was staring openmouthed at the lake behind us.

Then we saw that he was still on the end of the rope, his skis knocked off by the fall, but that he was still holding on: submarining, like some kind of crazy, diving fishing lure— holding on, though, occasionally raising his head above the mysterious roostertail of water, his mouth a tiny, frightened "Oh," to gulp some air.

The force had to be tremendous.

"Let go!" I shouted, easing back on the throttle. "Wejumpka, LET GO!"

But he couldn't hear me, underwater. I could feel the strain on the boat—it was like pulling an anchor around the lake. But he wouldn't let go, he stayed with it, and I had to shut the engine off and coast to a stop, before he understood that it was over.

"I have no idea where the name or the character of Wejumpka came from. I've since found out that there is a Wetumpka, Alabama, but this discovery came after the story was written. I'd also sworn never to write a divorce story, and went for a long time without doing it, until a friend I worked with divorced, and we discussed it every day at lunch—rather, he'd discuss it, and I'd listen, fascinated—I'd never seen the actual process in motion, and it seemed barbaric, unbelievably brutal, better and worse than anything I could ever have imagined— and at the same time I had a friend whose health was not doing so well, and another whose health had never been better, and I was to be the godfather of the healthy friend's child: in short, for once, there was a lot going on in my life, some good, some bad, and like a typical cowardly artist, I suppose, I might have used the child Wejumpka to face up to these changes in my life rather than deal with them squarely myself.

"*Other bits and pieces came from things I saw as I was working on the story; the car being welded came from a photo my agent showed me of a place he'd seen on a trip through the South—an old race car out in the woods, welded, mysteriously, to the top of a tower out in the middle of the woods—no place of proprietorship nearby, no home, no nothing—just this car atop the tower. 'Maybe you can use this in a story,' said Tim, handing me the photo.*

"*It was just a typical scavenger-hunt sort of story, after that, using bits and pieces of whatever was available, whatever was going on at the time. As a child, I had gone water skiing and had not known better than to hold on, once I spilled, and had been dragged submarinelike, a good ways across the lake, embarrassing my father greatly, I think—not that I fell, but that I was so abnormally strange and perhaps masochistic to be able to hold on—his friend howled, I remember—and I knew later that someday I would like to end a story with that scene. I'd been holding that scene in a long time, and finally just wanted to get rid of it. While writing the story it was hard to pretend not to know that this was the story where I was finally going to use that ending.*"

Rick Bass is the author of Oil Notes, *a memoir of his time as a geologist in Mississippi, and of* The Watch, *a short-story collection, as well as* The Deer Pasture *and* Wild to the Heart, *a collection of essays. His stories have been selected for the* General Electric Younger Writers Award, Best American Short Stories, *the* Pushcart Prize anthology, New Stories from the South 1988 *and* The Paris Review Anthology of Fiction. *He divides his time between Montana and Mississippi, and is completing a novel about the Mississippi River.*

Published in The Chariton Review.

BOBBIE ANN MASON

MEMPHIS

On Friday, after Beverly dropped the children off at her former husband's place for the weekend, she went dancing at the Paradise Club in Paducah with a man she had met at the nature extravaganza at Land Between the Lakes. Since her divorce she had not been out much, but she enjoyed dancing, and her date was a good dancer. She hadn't expected that, because he was shy and seemed more at home with his hogs than with people.

Emerging from the rest room, Beverly suddenly ran into her ex-husband, Joe. For a confused moment she almost didn't recognize him, out of context. He was with a tall, skinny woman in jeans and a fringed cowboy shirt. Joe looked sexy, in a black T-shirt with the sleeves ripped out to show his muscles, but the woman wasn't pretty. She looked bossy and hard.

"Where are the kids?" Beverly shouted at Joe above the music.

"At Mama's. They're all right. Hey, Beverly, this is Janet."

"I'm going over there and get them right now," Beverly said, ignoring Janet.

"Don't be silly, Bev. They're having a good time. Mama fixed up a playroom for them."

"Maybe next week I'll just take them straight to her house. We'll bypass you altogether. Eliminate the middleman." Beverly was a little drunk.

"For Christ's sake."

"This goes on your record," she warned him. "I'm keeping a list."

Janet was touching his elbow possessively, and then the man

Beverly had come with showed up with beer mugs in his fists.
"Is there something I should know?" he said.

Beverly and Joe had separated the year before, just after
Easter, and over the summer they tried unsuccessfully to get
back together for the sake of the children. A few times after the
divorce became final, Beverly spent the night with Joe, but
each time she felt it was a mistake. It felt adulterous. A little
thing, a quirky habit—like the way he kept the glass coffeepot
simmering on the stove—could make her realize they shouldn't
see each other. Coffee turned bitter when it was left simmering
like that.

Joe never wanted to probe anything very deeply. He accepted things, even her request for a divorce, without asking
questions. Beverly could never tell if that meant he was calm
and steady or dangerously lacking in curiosity. In the last
months they lived together, she had begun to feel that her
mind was crammed with useless information, like a landfill,
and there wasn't space deep down in her to move around in, to
explore what was there. She didn't trust her intelligence anymore. She couldn't repeat the simplest thing she heard on the
news and have it make sense to anyone. She would read a
column in the newspaper—about something important, like
taxes or the death penalty—but be unable to remember what
she had read. She felt she had strong ideas and meaningful
thoughts, but often when she tried to reach for one she couldn't
find it. It was terrifying.

Whenever she tried to explain this feeling to Joe, he just said
she expected too much of herself. He didn't expect enough of
himself, though, and now she felt that the divorce hadn't
affected him deeply enough to change him at all. She was
disappointed. He should have gone through a major new phase,
especially after what had happened to his friend Chubby Jones,
one of his fishing buddies. Chubby burned to death in his
pickup truck. One night soon after the divorce became final,
Joe woke Beverly up with his pounding on the kitchen door.
Frightened, and still not used to being alone with the children,
she cracked the venetian blind, one hand on the telephone.
Then she recognized the silhouette of Joe's truck in the driveway.

"I didn't want to scare you by using the key," he said when she opened the door. She was furious: he might have woken up the children.

It hadn't occurred to her that he still had a key. Joe was shaking, and when he came inside he flopped down at the kitchen table, automatically choosing his usual place facing the door. In the eerie glow from the fluorescent light above the kitchen sink, he told her about Chubby. Nervously spinning the lazy Susan, Joe groped for words, mostly repeating in disbelief the awful facts. Beverly had never seen him in such a state of shock. His news seemed to cancel out their divorce, as though it were only a trivial fit they had had.

"We were at the Blue Horse Tavern," he said. "Chubby was going on about some shit at work and he had it in his head he was going to quit and go off and live like a hermit and let Donna and the kids do without. You couldn't argue with him when he got like that—a little too friendly with Jack Daniel's. When he went out to his truck we followed him. We were going to follow him home to see he didn't have a wreck, but then he passed out right there in his truck and so we left him there in the parking lot to sleep it off." Joe buried his head in his hands and started to cry. "We thought we were doing the best thing," he said.

Beverly stood behind him and draped her arms over his shoulders, holding him while he cried.

Chubby's cigarette must have dropped on the floor, Joe explained as she rubbed his neck and shoulders. The truck had caught fire some time after the bar closed. A passing driver reported the fire, but the rescue squad arrived too late.

"I went over there," Joe said. "That's where I just came from. It was all dark, and the parking lot was empty, except for his truck, right where we left it. It was all black and hollow. It looked like something from Northern Ireland."

He kept twirling the lazy Susan, watching the grape jelly, the sugar bowl, the honey bear, the salt and pepper shakers go by.

"Come on," Beverly said after a while. She led him to the bedroom. "You need some sleep."

*   *   *

After that, Joe didn't say much about his friend. He seemed to get over Chubby's death, as a child would forget some disappointment. It was sad, he said. Beverly felt so many people were like Joe—half conscious, being pulled along by thoughtless impulses and notions, as if their lives were no more than a load of freight hurtling along on the interstate. Even her mother was like that. After Beverly's father died, her mother became devoted to "The PTL Club" on television. Beverly knew her father would have argued her out of such an obsession when he was alive. Her mother had two loves now: "The PTL Club" and Kenny Rogers. She kept a scrapbook on Kenny Rogers and she owned all his albums, including the ones that had come out on CD. She still believed fervently in Jim and Tammy Bakker, even after all the fuss. They reminded her of Christmas elves, she told Beverly recently.

"Christmas elves!" Beverly repeated in disgust. "They're the biggest phonies I ever saw."

"Do you think you're better than everybody else, Beverly?" her mother said, offended. "That's what ruined your marriage. I can't get over how you've mistreated poor Joe. You're always judging everybody."

That hurt, but there was some truth in it. She was like her father, who had been a plainspoken man. He didn't like for the facts to be dressed up. He could spot fakes as easily as he noticed jimsonweed in the cornfield. Her mother's remark made her start thinking about her father in a new way. He died ten years ago, when Beverly was pregnant with Shayla, her oldest child. She remembered his unvarying routines. He got up at sunup, ate the same breakfast day in and day out, never went anywhere. In the spring, he set out tobacco plants, and as they matured he suckered them, then stripped them, cured them, and hauled them to auction. She remembered him burning the tobacco beds—the pungent smell, the threat of wind. She used to think his life was dull, but now she had started thinking about those routines as beliefs. She compared them to the routines in her life with Joe: her CNN news fix, telephoning customers at work and entering orders on the computer, the couple of six-packs she and Joe used to drink every evening, Shayla's tap lessons, Joe's basketball night, family night at the sports club. Then she remembered her father running the combine over his wheat fields, wheeling that giant machine around expertly, much the same way Joe handled a motorcycle.

When Tammy, the youngest, was born, Joe was not around. He had gone out to Pennyrile Forest with Jimmy Stone to play war games. Two teams of guys spent three days stalking each other with pretend bullets, trying to make believe they were in the jungle. In rush-hour traffic, Beverly drove herself to the hospital, and the pains caused her to pull over onto the shoulder several times. Joe had taken the childbirth lessons with her and was supposed to be there, participating, helping her with the breathing rhythms. A man would find it easier to go to war than to be around a woman in labor, she told her roommate in the hospital. When Tammy was finally born, Beverly felt that anger had propelled the baby out of her.

But when Joe showed up at the hospital, grinning a moon-pie grin, he gazed into her eyes, running one of her curls through his fingers. "I want to check out that maternal glow of yours," he said, and she felt trapped by desire, even in her condition. For her birthday once, he had given her a satin teddy and "fantasy slippers"' with pink marabou feathers, whatever those were. He told the children that the feathers came from the marabou bird, a cross between a caribou and a marigold.

On Friday afternoon after work the week following the Paradise Club incident, Beverly picked up Shayla from her tap lesson and Kerry and Tammy from day-care. She drove them to Joe's house, eight blocks from where she lived.

From the back seat Shayla said, "I don't want to go to the dentist tomorrow. When Daddy has to wait for me, he disappears for about *two hours*. He can't stand to wait."

Glancing in the rearview mirror at Shayla, Beverly said, "You tell your daddy to set himself down and read a magazine if he knows what's good for him."

"Daddy said you were trying to get rid of us," Kerry said.

"That's not true! Don't you let him talk mean about me. He can't get away with that."

"He said he'd take us to the lake," Kerry said. Kerry was six, and snaggletoothed. His teeth were coming in crooked—more good news for the dentist.

Joe's motorcycle and three-wheeler were hogging the driveway, so Beverly pulled up to the curb. His house was nice—a brick ranch he rented from his parents, who lived across town. The kids liked having two houses—they had more rooms, more toys.

"Give me some sugar," Beverly said to Tammy, as she unbuckled the child's seat belt. Tammy smeared her moist little face against Beverly's. "Y'all be good now," Beverly said. She hated leaving them.

The kids raced up the sidewalk, their backpacks bobbing against their legs. She saw Joe open the door and greet them. Then he waved at her to come inside. "Come on in and have a beer!" he called loudly. He held his beer can up like the Statue of Liberty's torch. He had on a cowboy hat with a large feather plastered on the side of the crown. His tan had deepened. She felt her stomach do a flip and her mind fuzz over like mold on fruit. I'm an idiot, she told herself.

She shut off the engine and pocketed the keys. Joe's fat black cat accompanied her up the sidewalk. "You need to put that cat on a diet," Beverly said to Joe when he opened the door for her. "He looks like a little hippo in black pajamas."

"He goes to the no-frills mouse market and loads up," Joe said, grinning. "I can't stop him."

The kids were already in the kitchen, investigating the refrigerator—one of those with beverage dispensers on the outside. Joe kept the dispensers filled with surprises—chocolate milk or Juicy Juice.

"Daddy, can I microwave a burrito?" asked Shayla.

"No, not now. We'll go to the mall after-while, so you don't want to ruin your supper now."

"Oh, boy. That means Chi-Chi's."

The kids disappeared into the family room in the basement, carrying Cokes and bags of cookies and potato chips. Joe opened a beer for Beverly. She was sitting on the couch smoking a cigarette and staring blankly at his pocket-knife collection in a case on the coffee table when Joe came forward and stood over her. Something was wrong.

"I'm being transferred," he said, handing her the beer. "I'm moving to Columbia, South Carolina."

She sat very still, her cigarette poised in midair like a freeze-frame scene on the VCR. A purple stain shaped like a flower was on the arm of the couch. His rug was the nubby kind made of tiny loops, and one patch had unraveled. She could hear the blip-blip-crash of video games downstairs.

"What?" she said.

"I'm being transferred."

"I heard you. I'm just having trouble getting it from my ears to my mind." She was stunned. She had never imagined Joe anywhere except right here in town.

"The plant's got an opening there, and I'll make a whole lot more."

"But you don't have to go. They can't make you go."

"It's an opportunity. I can't turn it down."

"But it's too far away."

He rested his hand lightly on her shoulder. "I'll want to have the kids on vacations—and all summer."

"Well, tough! You expect me to send them on an airplane all that way?"

"You'll have to make some adjustments," he said calmly, taking his hand away and sitting down beside her on the couch.

"I couldn't stay away from them that long," she said. "And Columbia, South Carolina? It's not interesting. They'll hate it. Nothing's there."

"You don't know that."

"What would you do with them? You can never think of what to do with them when you've got them, so you stuff them with junk or dump them at your mothers's." Beverly felt confused, unable to call upon the right argument. Her words came out wrong, more accusing than she meant.

He was saying, "Why don't you move there, too? What would keep you here?"

"Don't make me laugh." Her beer can was sweating, making cold circles on her bare leg.

He scrunched his empty can into a wad, as if he had made a decision. "We could buy a house and get back together," he said. "I didn't like seeing you on that dance floor the other night with that guy. I didn't like you seeing me with Janet. I didn't like being there with Janet. I suddenly wondered why we had to be there in those circumstances, when we could have been home with the kids."

"It would be the same old thing," Beverly said impatiently. "My God, Joe, think of what you'd do with three kids for three whole months."

"I think I know how to handle them. It's you I never could handle." He threw the can across the room straight into the kitchen wastebasket. "We've got a history together," he said. "That's the positive way to look at it." Playfully he cocked his hat and gave her a wacky, ironic look—his imitation of Jim-Boy McCoy, a used-furniture dealer in a local commercial.

"You take the cake," she said, with a little burst of laughter. But she couldn't see herself moving to Columbia, South Carolina, of all places. It would be too hot, and the people would talk in drippy, soft drawls. The kids would hate it.

After she left Joe's, she went to Tan Your Hide, the tanning salon and fitness shop that Jolene Walker managed. She worked late on Fridays. Beverly and Jolene had been friends since junior high, when they entered calves in the fair together.

"I need a quick hit before I go home," Beverly said to Jolene.

"Use Number Two—Number One's acting funny and I'm scared to use it. I think the light's about to blow."

In the changing room, Jolene listened sympathetically to Beverly's news about Joe. "Columbia, South Carolina!" Jolene cried. "What will I do with myself if you go off?"

"A few years ago I'd have jumped at the chance to move someplace like South Carolina, but it wouldn't be right to go now unless I love him," Beverly said. As she pulled on her bathing suit, she said, "Damn! I couldn't bear to be away from the kids for a whole summer!"

"Maybe he can't, either," said Jolene, skating the dressing-room curtain along its track. "Listen, do you want to ride to Memphis with me tomorrow? I've got to pick up some merchandise coming in from California—a new line of sweatsuits. It's cheaper to go pick it up at the airport than have it flown up here by commuter."

"Yeah, sure. I don't know what else to do with my week-ends. Without the kids, my weekends are like black holes." She laughed. "Big empty places you get sucked into." She made a comic sucking noise that made Jolene smile.

"We could go hear some of that good Memphis blues on Beale Street," Jolene suggested.

"Let me think about it while I work on my tan. I want to get in here and do some meditating."

"Are you still into that? That reminds me of my ex-husband and that born-again shit he used to throw at me."

"It's not the same thing," Beverly said, getting into the sunshine coffin, as she called it. "Beam me up," she said. She liked to meditate while she tanned. It was private, and she felt she was accomplishing something at the same time. In medita-tion, the jumbled thoughts in her mind were supposed to settle down, like the drifting snowflakes in a paperweight.

Jolene adjusted the machine and clicked the dial. "Ready for takeoff?"

"As ready as I'll ever be," said Beverly, her eyes hidden under big cotton pads. She was ruining her eyes at work, staring at a video display terminal all day. Under the sunlamp, she imagined her skin broiling as she slowly moved through space like that spaceship in *2001* that revolved like a rotisserie.

Scenes floated before her eyes. Helping shell purple-hull peas one hot afternoon when she was about seventeen; her mother shelling peas methodically, with the sound of Beverly's father in the bedroom coughing and spitting into a newspaper-lined cigar box. Her stomach swelled out with Kerry, and a night then when Joe didn't come back from a motorcycle trip and she was so scared she could feel the fear deep inside, right into the baby's heartbeat. Her father riding a horse along a fencerow. In the future, she thought, people would get in a contraption something like the sunshine coffin and go time-traveling, unbounded by time and space or custody arrangements.

One winter afternoon two years ago: a time with Joe and the kids. Tammy was still nursing and Kerry had just lost a tooth. Shayla was reading a Nancy Drew paperback, which was ad-vanced for her age, but Shayla was smart. They were on the living-room floor together, on a quilt, having a picnic and watching *Chitty Chitty Bang Bang*. Beverly felt happy. That day, Kerry learned a new word—*soldier*. She teased him. "You're my little soldier," she said. Sometimes she thought she could make moments like that happen again, but when she tried it felt forced. They would be at the supper table and she'd give the children hot dogs or tacos—something they liked—and she would say, "This is such fun!" and they would look at her funny.

Joe used to say to anyone new they met, "I've got a blue collar and a red neck and a white ass. I'm the most patriotic son of a bitch on two legs!" She and Joe were happy when they started out together. After work, the would sit on the patio with the stereo turned up loud and drink beer and pitch horseshoes while the steak grilled. On weekends, they used to take an ice chest over to the lake and have cookouts with friends and go fishing. When Joe got a motorcycle, they rode together every weekend. She loved the feeling, her feet clenching the foot pegs and her hands gripping the seat strap for dear life. She loved the wind burning her face, her hair flying out from under the helmet, her chin boring into Joe's back as he tore around curves. Their friends all worked at the new plants, making more money than they ever had before. Everyone they knew had a yard strewn with vehicles: motorcycles, three-wheelers, sporty cars, pickups. One year, people started buying horses. It was just a thing people were into suddenly, so that they could ride in the annual harvest parade in Fenway. Joe and Beverly never got around to having a horse, though. It seemed too much trouble after the kids came along. Most of the couples they knew then drank a lot and argued and had fights, but they had a good time. Now marriages were splitting up. Beverly could name five divorces or separations in her crowd. It seemed no one knew why this was happening. Everybody blamed it on statistics: half of all marriages nowadays ended in divorce. It was a fact, like traffic jams—just one of those things you had to put up with in modern life. But Beverly thought money was to blame: greed made people purely stupid. She admired Jolene for the simple, clear way she divorced Steve and made her own way without his help. Steve had gone on a motorcycle trip alone and when he came back he was a changed man. He had joined a bunch of born-again bikers he met at a campground in Wyoming, and afterward he tried to convert everybody he knew. Jolene refused to take the Lord as her personal saviour. "It's amazing how much spite Steve has in him," Jolene told Beverly after she moved out. "I don't even care anymore."

It made Beverly angry not to know why she didn't want Joe to go to South Carolina. Did he just want her to come to South Carolina for convenience, for the sake of the children? Sometimes she felt they were both stalled at a crossroads, each thinking the other had the right-of-way. But now his foot was on the gas.

Jolene was saying, "Get out of there before you cook!"

Beverly removed the cotton pads from her eyes and squinted at the bright light.

Jolene said, "Look at this place on my arm. It looks just like one of those skin cancers in my medical guide." She pointed to an almost invisible spot in the crook of her arm. Jolene owned a photographer's magnifying glass a former boyfriend had given her, and she often looked at her moles with it. Under the glass, tiny moles looked hideous and black, with red edges.

Beverly, who was impatient with Jolene's hypochondria, said, "I wouldn't worry abut it unless I could see it with my bare naked eyes."

"I think I should stop tanning," Jolene said.

The sky along the western horizon was a flat yellow ribbon with the tree line pasted against it. After the farmland ran out, Beverly and Jolene passed small white houses in disrepair, junky little clusters of businesses, a K mart, then a Wal-Mart. As Jolene drove along, Beverly thought about Joe's vehicles. It had never occurred to her before that he had all those wheels and hardly went anywhere except places around home. But now he was actually leaving.

She was full of nervous energy. She kept twisting the radio dial, trying to find a good driving song. She wished the radio would play "Radar Love," a great driving song. All she could get was country stations and gospel stations. After a commercial for a gigantic flea market, with dealers coming from thirty

states, the announcer said, "Elvis would be there—if he could."
Jolene hit the horn. "Elvis, we're on our way, baby!"

"There's this record store I want to go to if we have time,"
said Jolene. "It's got all these old rock songs—everything you
could name, going way back to the very beginning."

"Would they have 'Your Feet's Too Big,' by Fats Waller?
Joe used to sing that."

"Honey, they've got *everything*. Why, I bet they've got a
tape of Fats Waller humming to himself in the outhouse." They
laughed, and Jolene said, "You're still stuck on Joe."

"I can't let all three kids go to South Carolina on one airplane! If it crashed, I'd lose all three of them at once."

"Oh, don't think that way!"

Beverly sighed. "I can't get used to not having a child
pulling on my leg every minute. But I guess I should get out
and have a good time."

"Now you're talking."

"Maybe if he moves to South Carolina, we can make a clean
break. Besides, I better not fight him, or he might kidnap
them."

"Do you really think that?" said Jolene, astonished.

"I don't know. You hear about cases like that." Beverly
changed the radio station again.

"I can't stand to see you tear yourself up this way," said
Jolene, giving Beverly's arm an affectionate pat.

Beverly laughed. "Hey, look at that bumper sticker—'A
WOMAN'S PLACE IS IN THE MALL.' "

"All *right*!" said Jolene.

They drove into Memphis on Route 51, past self-service gas
stations in corrugated-tin buildings with country hams hanging
in the windows. Beverly noticed a memorial garden between
two cornfields, with an immense white statue of Jesus rising up
from the center like the Great White Shark surfacing. They
passed a display of black-velvet paintings beside a van, a ceramic-
glassware place, a fireworks stand, motels, package stores, auto
body shops, car dealers that sold trampolines and satellite
dishes. A stretch of faded old wooden buildings—grim and gray
and ramshackle—followed, then factories, scrap-metal places,
junk yards, ancient grills and poolrooms, small houses so old

the wood looked rotten. Then came the housing projects. It
was all so familiar. Beverly remembered countless trips to
Memphis when her father was in the hospital here, dying of
cancer. The Memphis specialists prolonged his misery, and
Beverly's mother said afterward, "We should have set him out
in the corncrib and let him go naturally, the way he wanted to
go."

Beverly and Jolene ate at a Cajun restaurant that night, and
later they walked down Beale Street, which had been spruced
up and wasn't as scary as it used to be, Beverly thought. The
sidewalks were crowded with tourists and policemen. At a
blues club, she and Jolene giggled like young girls out looking
for love. Beverly had been afraid Memphis would make her
sad, but after three strawberry Daiquiris she was feeling good.
Jolene had a headache and was drinking ginger ale, which
turned out to be Sprite with a splash of Coke—what bartenders
do when they're out of ginger ale, Beverly told her. She didn't
know how she knew that. Probably Joe had told her once. He
used to tend bar. Forget Joe, she thought. She needed to
loosen up a little. The kids had been saying she was like either
Kate or Allie on that TV show—whichever was the uptight
one, she couldn't remember.

The band was great—two white guys and two black guys.
Between numbers, they joked with the waitress, a middle-aged
woman with spiked red hair, and shoulder pads that fit cock-
eyed. The white lead singer clowned around with a cardboard
standup figure of Marilyn Monroe in her white dress from *The
Seven Year Itch*. He spun her about the dance floor, sneaking
his hand onto Marilyn's crotch where her dress had flown up.
He played her like a guitar. A pretty black woman in a dark
leather skirt and polka-dotted jacket danced with a slim young
black guy with a brush haircut. Beverly wondered how he got
his hair to stick up like that. Earlier, when she and Jolene
stopped at a Walgreen's for shampoo, Beverly had noticed a
whole department of hair-care products for blacks. There was a
row of large jugs of hair conditioner, like the jugs motor oil and
bleach came in.

Jolene switched from fake ginger ale to Fuzzy Navels,
which she had been drinking earlier at the Cajun restaurant.

She blamed her headache on Cajun frog legs but said she felt better now. "I'm having a blast," she said, drumming her slender fingers on the table in time with the band.

"I'm having a blast, too," Beverly said, just as an enormous man with tattoos of outer-space monsters on his arms asked Jolene to dance.

"No way!" Jolene said, cringing. On his forearm was an astounding picture of a creature that reminded Beverly of one of Kerry's dinosaur toys.

"That guy's really off the moon," Jolene said as the man left.

During the break, the waitress passed by with a plastic bucket, collecting tips for the band. Beverly thought of an old song, "Bucket's Got a Hole in It." Her grandmother's kitchen slop bucket with its step pedal. Going to hell in a bucket. Kick the bucket. She felt giddy.

"That boy's here every night," the waitress said, with a turn of her head toward the tattooed guy, who had approached another pair of women. "I feel so sorry for him. His brother killed himself and his mother's in jail for drugs. He never could hold a job. He's trouble waiting for a ride."

"Does the band know 'Your Feet's Too Big'?" Beverly asked the waitress, who was stuffing requests into her pocket.

"Is that a song, or are you talking about my big hoofs?" the woman said, with a wide, teasing grin.

On the way back to their motel on Elvis Presley Boulevard, Jolene got on a one-way street and ended up in downtown Memphis, where the tall buildings were. Beverly would hate to work so high up in the air. Her cousin had a job down here in life insurance and said she never knew what the weather was. Beverly wondered if South Carolina had any skyscrapers.

"There's the famous Peabody Hotel," Jolene was saying. "The hotel with the ducks."

"Ducks?"

"At that hotel it's ducks galore," explained Jolene. "The towels and stationery and stuff. I know a girl who stayed there, and she said a bunch of ducks come down every morning on the elevator and go splash in the fountain. It's a tourist attraction."

"The kids would like that. That's what I should be doing down here—taking the kids someplace, not getting smashed like this." Beverly felt disembodied, her voice coming from the glove compartment.

"Everything is *should* with you, Beverly!" Jolene said, making a right on red.

Jolene didn't mean to sound preachy, Beverly thought. Fuzzy Navels did that to her. If Beverly mentioned what she was feeling about Joe, Jolene would probably say that Joe just looked good right now compared to some of the weirdos you meet out in the world.

Down the boulevard, the lights spread out extravagantly. As Beverly watched, a green neon light winked off, and the whole scene seemed to shift slightly. It was like making a correction on the VDT at work—the way the screen readjusted all the lines and spacing to accommodate the change. Far away, a red light was inching across the black sky. She thought about riding behind Joe on his Harley, flashing through the dark on a summer night, cool in the wind, with sparkling, mysterious lights flickering off the lake.

The music from the night before was still playing in Beverly's head when she got home Sunday afternoon. It was exhilarating, like something she knew well but hadn't thought of in years. It came soaring up through her with a luxurious clarity. She could still hear the henna-haired waitress saying, "Are you talking about my big hoofs?" Beverly's dad used to say, "Oh, my aching dogs!" She clicked "Radar Love" into the cassette player and turned the volume up loud. She couldn't help dancing to its hard frenzy. "Radar Love" made her think of Joe's Fuzzbuster, which he bought after he got two speeding tickets in one month. One time he told the children his razor was a Fuzzbuster. Speeding, she whirled joyfully through the hall.

The song was only halfway through when Joe arrived with the kids—unexpectedly early. Kerry ejected the tape. Sports voices hollered out from the TV. Whenever the kids returned from their weekends, they plowed through the place, unloading their belongings and taking inventory of what they had left behind. Tammy immediately flung all her toys out of her toybox, looking for a rag doll she had been worried about. Joe said she had cried about it yesterday.

"How was the dentist?" Beverly asked Shayla.

"I don't want to talk about it," said Shayla, who was dumping dirty clothes on top of the washing machine.

"Forty bucks for one stupid filling," Joe said.

Joe had such a loud voice that he always came on too strong. Beverly remembered with embarrassment the time he called up Sears and terrorized the poor clerk over a flaw in a sump pump, when it wasn't the woman's fault. But now he lowered his voice to a quiet, confidential tone and said to Beverly in the kitchen, "Yesterday at the lake Shayla said she wished you were there with us, and I tried to explain to her how you had to have some time for yourself, how you said you had to have your own space and find yourself—you know, all that crap on TV. She seemed to get a little depressed, and I thought maybe I'd said the wrong thing, but a little later she said she'd been thinking and she knew what you meant."

"She's smart," Beverly said. Her cheeks were burning. She popped ice cubes out of a tray and began pouring Coke into a glass of ice.

"She gets it honest—she's got smart parents," he said with a grin.

Beverly drank the Coke while it was still foaming. Bubbles burst on her nose. "It's not crap on TV," she said angrily. "How can you say that?"

He looked hurt. She observed the dimple on his chin, the corresponding kink of his hairline above his ear, the way his hat shaded his eyes and deepened their fire. Even if he lived to be a hundred, Joe would still have those seductive eyes. Kerry wandered into the kitchen, dragging a green dinosaur by a hind foot. "We didn't have any corny cakes," he whined. He meant cornflakes.

"Why didn't Daddy get you some?"

After Kerry drifted away, Joe said, "I'm going to South Carolina in a couple of weeks. Check it out and try to find a place to live."

Beverly opened the freezer and took chicken thighs out to thaw, then began clearing dishes to keep from bursting into tears.

"Columbia's real progressive," he said. "Lots of businesses are relocating there. It's a place on the way up."

The foam had settled on her Coke, and she poured some more. She began loading the dishwasher. One of her nonstick pans already had a scratch.

"How was Memphis?" Joe asked, his hand on the kitchen doorknob.

"Fine," she said. "Jolene had too many Fuzzy Navels."

"That figures."

Shayla rushed in then and said, "Daddy, you got to fix that thing in my closest. The door won't close."

"That track at the top? Not again! I don't have time to work on it right now."

"He doesn't live here," Beverly said to Shayla.

"Well, my closet's broke and who's going to fix it?" Shayla threw up her hands and stomped out of the kitchen.

Joe said, "You know, in the future, if we're going to keep this up, we're going to have to learn to carry on a better conversation, because this stinks." He adjusted his hat, setting it firmly on his head. "You're so full of wants you don't know what you want," he said.

Through the glass section of the door she could see him walking to his truck with his hands in his pockets. She had seen him march out the door exactly that way so many times before—whenever he didn't want to hear what was coming next, or when he thought he had had the last word. She hurried out to speak to him, but he was already pulling away, gunning his engine loudly. She watched him disappear, his tail-lights winking briefly at a stop sign. She felt ashamed.

Beverly paused beside the young pin-oak tree at the corner of the driveway. When Joe planted it, there were hardly any trees in the subdivision. All the houses were built within the last ten years and the trees were still spindly. The house just to her left was Mrs. Grim's. She was a widow and kept cats. On the other side, a German police dog in a back-yard pen spent his time barking across Beverly's yard at Mrs. Grim's cats. The man who owned the dog operated a video store, and his wife mysteriously spent several weeks a year out of town. When she was away her husband stayed up all night watching TV, like a child freed from rules. Beverly could see his light on when she got up in the night with the kids. She had never really noticed that the bricks of all three houses were a mottled red and gray, like uniformly splattered paint. There was a row of vertical bricks supporting each window. She stood at the foot of the driveway feeling slightly amazed that she should be stopped in her tracks at this particular time and place.

It ought to be so easy to work out what she really wanted. Beverly's parents had stayed married like two dogs locked together in passion, except it wasn't passion. But she and Joe didn't have to do that. Times had changed. Joe could up and move to South Carolina. Beverly and Jolene could hop down to Memphis just for a fun weekend. Who knew what might happen or what anybody would decide to do on any given weekend or at any stage of life?

She brought in yesterday's mail—a car magazine for Joe, a credit-card bill he was supposed to pay, some junk mail. She laid the items for Joe on a kitchen shelf next to the videotape she had borrowed from him and forgotten to return.

"I'm partial to 'Memphis' because I'm aware of the blind alleys I went down in search of this story's final form, or the story itself. It seemed that I had a large territory for this family that was splitting apart—ranging from western Kentucky where their home was, to South Carolina, to Memphis. In an early version, I took Beverly, the central character, to Memphis and left her there—in a great deal of trouble. It didn't occur to me that this ending made it seem as though she was being punished for leaving her husband, which wasn't my intention. When that was pointed out, I knew I had to have her deal with her marriage in a more straightforward way. So I brought her back home for another scene with her ex-husband. That simple scene was so much more convincing than the bizarre scene I had originally concocted with a pervert in a bar. As I searched around for this story's true direction, the characters and the

*scenes grew more and more real, and that has become a test
for me—of how close I am to achieving the truth I'm after. In
this story, I felt I was finally seeing these people clear and
true. That's when I love them the most—when they have
emerged at last full-blown, in their own story. But I went down
one more blind alley. After bringing her back home from
Memphis, I then left Beverly inside one of those 'literary'
endings that English classes thrive on. (Beverly was gazing at
tantalizing layers of ambiguity in the reflections of the sky in
the picture window.) It took me a while to realize that passage
was meaningless and to see that what Beverly would really do
is bring in the mail and put the magazine for Joe beside the
videotape she forgot to return. Some things are just so plain
you don't see them at first."*

Bobbie Ann Mason's short stories have been collected in
Shiloh and Other Stories. *Her novels include* In Country *and*
Spence + Lila. *She was born in Kentucky and lives in Pennsylva-
nia with her husband.*

Published in The New Yorker.

RUSSELL BANKS

QUEEN FOR A DAY

The elder of the two boys, Earl, turns from the dimly lit worktable, a door on sawhorses, where he is writing. He pauses a second and says to his brother, "Cut that out, willya? Getcha feet off the walls."

The other boy says, "Don't tell me what to do. You're not the boss of this family, you know." He is dark-haired with large brown eyes, a moody ten-year-old lying bored on his cot with sneakered feet slapped against the faded green floral print wallpaper.

Earl crosses his arms over his bony chest and stares down at his brother from a considerable height. The room is cluttered with model airplanes, schoolbooks, papers, clothing, hockey sticks and skates, a set of barbells. Earl says, "We're supposed to be doing homework, you know. If she hears you tramping your feet on the walls, she'll come in here screaming. So get your damned feet off the wall. I ain't kidding."

"She can't hear me. Besides, you ain't doing homework. And *I'm* reading," he says, waves a geography book at him.

The older boy sucks his breath through his front teeth and glares. "You really piss me off, George. Just put your goddamned feet down, will you? I can't concentrate with you doing that, rubbing your feet all over the wallpaper like you're doing. It makes me all distracted." He turns back to his writing, scribbling with a ballpoint pen on lined paper in a schoolboy's three-ring binder. Earl has sandy blonde hair and pale blue eyes that turn downward at the corners and a full red mouth. He's more scrawny than skinny, hard and flat-muscled, and suddenly tall for his age, making him a head taller than his brother, taller even than their mother now, too, and able to pat their sister's head as if he were a full-grown adult already.

He turned twelve eight months ago, in March, and in May their father left. Their father is a union carpenter who works on projects in distant corners of the state—schools, hospitals, post offices—and for a whole year the man came home only on weekends. Then, for a while, every other weekend. Finally, he was gone for a month, and when he came home the last time, it was to say good-bye to Earl, George, and their sister Louise, and to their mother, too, of course, she who had been saying (for what seemed to the children years) that she never wanted to see the man again anyhow, ever, under any circumstances, because he just causes trouble when he's home and more trouble when he doesn't come home, so he might as well stay away for good. They can all get along better without him, she insisted, which was true, Earl was sure, but that was before the man left for good and stopped sending them money, so that now, six months later, Earl is not so sure anymore that they can get along better without their father than with him.

It happened on a Sunday morning, a day washed with new sunshine and dry air, with the whole family standing somberly in the kitchen, summoned there from their rooms by their mother's taut, high-pitched voice, a voice that had an awful point to prove. "Come out here! Your father has something important to say to you!"

They obeyed, one by one, and gathered in a line before their father, who, dressed in pressed khakis and shined work shoes and cap, sat at the kitchen table, a pair of suitcases beside him, and in front of him a cup of coffee, which he stirred slowly with a spoon. His eyes were red and filled with dense water, the way they almost always were on Sunday mornings, from his drinking the night before, the children knew, and he had trouble looking them in the face, because of the sorts of things he and their mother were heard saying to one another when they were at home together late Saturday nights. On this Sunday morning it was only a little worse than usual—his hands shook some, and he could barely hold his cigarette; he let it smolder in the ashtray and kept on stirring his coffee while he talked. "Your mother and me," he said in his low, roughened voice, "we've decided on some things you kids should know about." He cleared his throat. "Your mother, she thinks you oughta hear it from me, though I don't quite know so much about that as she does, since it isn't completely my idea alone." He studied his coffee cup for a few seconds.

"They should hear it from you because it's what you *want!*" their mother finally said. She stood by the sink, her hands wringing each other dry, and stared over at the man. Her face was swollen and red from crying, which, for the children, was not an unusual thing to see on a Sunday morning when their father was home. They still did not know what was coming.

"Adele, it's *not* what I want," he said. "It's what's got to be, that's all. Kids," he said. "I got to leave you folks for a while. A long while. And I won't be comin' back, I guess." He grabbed his cigarette with thumb and forefinger and inhaled the smoke fiercely, then placed the butt back into the ashtray and went on talking, as if to the table: "I don't want to do this, I hate it, but I got to. It's too hard to explain, and I'm hoping that someday you'll understand it all, but I just . . . I just got to live some- wheres else now."

Louise, the little girl, barely six years old, was the only one of the three children who could speak. She said, "Where are you going, Daddy?"

"Upstate," he said. "Back up to Holderness, where I been all along. I got me an apartment up there, small place."

"That's not all he's got up there!" their mother said.

"Adele, I can walk outa here right this second," he said smoothly. "I don't hafta explain a damned thing, if you keep that kinda stuff up. We had an agreement."

"Yup, yup. Sorry," she said, pursing her lips, locking them with an invisible key, throwing the key away.

Finally, Earl could speak. "Will . . . will you come and see us, or can we come visit you, on weekends and like that?" he asked his father.

"Sure, son, you can visit me, anytime you want. It'll take a while for me to get the place set up right, but soon's I get it all set up for kids, I'll call you, and we'll work out some nice visits. I shouldn't come here, though, not for a while. You understand."

Earl shook his head somberly up and down, as if his one anxiety concerning this event had been put satisfactorily to rest.

George had turned his back on his father, however, and now he was taking tiny, mincing half-steps across the linoleum-covered kitchen floor toward the outside door. Then he stopped a second, opened the door and stood on the landing at the top of the stairs, and no one tried to stop him, because he was doing what they wanted to do themselves, and then they heard him running pell-mell, as if falling, down the darkened stairs, two flights, to the front door of the building, heard it slam behind him, and knew he was gone, up Perley Street, between parked cars, down alleys, to a hiding place where they knew he'd stop, sit, and bawl, knew it because it was what they wanted to do themselves, especially Earl, who was too old, too scared, too confused, and too angry. Instead of running away and bawling, Earl said, "I hope everyone can be more happy now."

His father smiled and looked at him for the first time and clapped him on the shoulder. "Hey, son," he said, "you, you're the man of the house now. I know you can do it. You're a good kid, and listen, I'm proud of you. Your mother, your brother and sister, they're all going to need you a hell of a lot more than they have before, but I know you're up to it, son. I'm countin' on ya," he said, and he stood up and rubbed out his cigarette. Then he reached beyond Earl with both hands and hugged Earl's little sister, lifted her off her feet and squeezed her tight, and when the man set her down, he wiped tears away from his eyes. "Tell Georgie . . . well, maybe I'll see him downstairs or something. He's upset, I guess. . . ." He shook Earl's hand, drew him close, quickly hugged him, and let go and stepped away. Grabbing up his suitcase, in silence, without looking over once at his wife or back at his children, he left the apartment.

For good. "And good riddance, too," as their mother immediately started saying to anyone who would listen. Louise said she missed her daddy, but she seemed to be quickly forgetting that, since for most of her life he had worked away from home, and George, who stayed mad, went deep inside himself and said nothing about it at all, and Earl—who did not know how he felt about their father's abandoning them, for he knew that in many ways it was the best their father could do for them and in many other ways it was the worst—spoke of the man as if he had died in an accident, as if their mother were a widow and they half orphaned. This freed him, though he did not know it then, to concentrate on survival, survival for them all, which he now understood to be his personal responsibility, for his mother seemed utterly incapable of guaranteeing it and his brother and sister, of course, were still practically babies. Often, late at night, lying in his squeaky, narrow cot next to his brother's, Earl would say to himself, "I'm the man of the house now," and somehow just saying it, over and over, "I'm the man of the house now," like a prayer, made his terror ease back away from his face, and he could finally slip into sleep.

Now, with his father gone six months and their mother still fragile, still denouncing the man to everyone who listens, and even to those who don't listen but merely show her their faces for a moment or two, it's as if the man were still coming home weekends drunk and raging against her and the world, were still betraying her, were telling all her secrets to another woman in a motel room in the northern part of the state. It's as if he were daily abandoning her and their three children over and over again, agreeing to send money and then sending nothing, promising to call and write letters and then going silent on them, planning visits and trips together on weekends and holidays and then leaving them with not even a forwarding address, forbidding them, almost, from adjusting to a new life, a life in which their father and her husband does not betray them anymore.

Earl decides to solve their problems himself. He hatches and implements, as best he can, plans, schemes, designs, all intended to find a substitute for the lost father. He introduces his mother to his hockey coach, who turns out to be married and a new father; and he invites in for breakfast and to meet his ma the cigar-smoking vet with the metal plate in his skull who drops off the newspapers at dawn for Earl to deliver before school, but the man turns out to dislike women actively enough to tell Earl so, right to his face: "No offense, kid, I'm sure your ma's a nice lady, but I got no use for 'em is why I'm single, not 'cause I ain't met the right one yet or something"; and to the guy who comes to read the electric meter one afternoon when Earl's home from school with the flu and his mother's at work down at the tannery, where they've taken her on as an assistant bookkeeper, Earl says that he can't let the man into the basement because it's locked and he'll have to come back later when his mom's home, so she can let him in herself, and the man says, "Hey, no problem, I can use last month's reading and make the correction next month," and waves cheerfully good-bye, leaving Earl suddenly, utterly, shockingly aware of his foolishness, his pathetic, helpless longing for a man of the house.

For a moment, he blames his mother for his longing and hates her for his fantasies. But then quickly he forgives her and blames himself and commences to concoct what he thinks of as more realistic, more dignified plans, schemes, designs: sweepstakes tickets, lotteries, raffles—Earl buys tickets on the sly with his paper route money. And he enters contests, essay contests for junior high school students that provide the winner with a week-long trip for him and a parent to Washington, D.C., and the National Spelling Bee, which takes Earl only to the county level before he fails to spell *alligator* correctly. A prize, any kind of award from the world outside their tiny, besieged family, Earl believes, will make their mother happy at last. He believes that a prize will validate their new life somehow and will thus separate it, once and for all, from their father. It will be as if their father never existed.

"So what are you writing now?" George demands from the bed. He walks his feet up the wall as high as he can reach, then retreats. "I know it ain't homework, you don't write that fast when you're doing homework. What is it, a *love* letter?" He leers.

"No, asshole. Just take your damned feet off the wall, will you? Ma's gonna be in here in a minute screaming at both of us." Earl closes the notebook and pushes it away from him carefully, as if it is the Bible and he has just finished reading aloud from it.

"I wanna see what you wrote," George says, flipping around and setting his feet, at last, onto the floor. He reaches toward the notebook. "Lemme see it."

"C'mon, willya? Cut the shit."

"Naw, lemme see it." He stands up and swipes the notebook from the table as Earl moves to protect it.

"You little sonofabitch!" Earl says, and he clamps onto the notebook with both hands and yanks, pulling George off his feet and forward onto Earl's lap, and they both tumble to the floor, where they begin to fight, swing fists and knees, roll and grab, bumping against furniture in the tiny, crowded room, until a lamp falls over, books tumble to the floor, model airplanes crash. In seconds, George is getting the worst of it and scrambles across the floor to the door, with Earl crawling along behind, yanking his brother's shirt with one hand and pounding at his head and back with the other, when suddenly the bedroom door swings open, and their mother stands over them. Grabbing both boys by their collars, she shrieks, "What's the matter with you! What're you doing! What're you doing!" They stop and collapse into a bundle of legs and arms, but she goes on shrieking at them. "I can't *stand* it when you fight! Don't you know that? I can't *stand* it!"

George cries, "I didn't do anything! I just wanted to see his homework!"

"Yeah, sure," Earl says. "Sure. Innocent as a baby."

"Shut up! Both of you!" their mother screams. She is wild-eyed, glaring down at them, and, as he has done so many times, Earl looks at her face as if he's outside his body, and he sees that she's not angry at them at all, she's frightened and in pain, as if her sons are little animals, rats or ferrets, with tiny, razor-sharp teeth biting at her ankles and feet.

Quickly, Earl gets to his feet and says, "I'm sorry, Ma. I guess I'm just a little tired or something lately." He pats his mother on her shoulder and offers a small smile. George crawls on hands and knees back to his bed and lies on it, while Earl gently turns their mother around and steers her back out the door to the living room, where the television set drones on, Les Paul and Mary Ford, playing their guitars and singing bland harmonies. "We'll be out in a few minutes for 'Dobie Gillis,' Ma. Don't worry," Earl says.

"Jeez," George says. "How can she stand that Les Paul and Mary Ford stuff? Yuck. Even Louise goes to bed when it comes on, and it's only what, six-thirty?"

"Yeah. Shut up."

"Up yours."

Earl leans down and scoops up the fallen dictionary, pens, airplanes, and lamp and places them back on the worktable. The black binder he opens squarely in front of him, and he says to his brother, "Here, you wanta see what I was writing? Go ahead and read it. I don't care."

"I don't care, either. Unless it's a *love* letter!"

"No, it's not a *love* letter."

"What is it, then?"

"Nothing," Earl says, closing the notebook. "Homework."

"Oh," George says, and he starts marching his feet up the wall and back again.

Nov. 7, 1953

Dear Jack Bailey,

I think my mother should be queen for a day because she has suffered a lot more than most mothers in this life and she has come out of it very cheerful and loving. The most important fact is that my father left her alone with three children, myself (age 12½), my brother George (age 10), and my sister Louise (age 6). He left her for another woman though that's not the important thing, because my mother has risen above all that. But he refuses to send her any child support money. He's been gone over six months and we still haven't seen one cent. My mother went to a lawyer but the lawyer wants $50 in advance to help her take my father to court. She has a job as assistant book-keeper down at Belvedere's Tannery downtown and the pay is bad, barely enough for our rent and food costs in fact, so where is she going to get $50 for a lawyer?

Also my father was a very cruel man who drinks too much and many times when he was living with us when he came home from work he was drunk and he would beat her. This has caused her and us kids a lot of nervous suffering and now she sometimes has spells which the doctor says are serious, though he doesn't know exactly what they are.

We used to have a car and my father left it with us when

he left (a big favor) because he had a pickup truck. But he owed over $450 on the car to the bank so the bank came and repossessed the car. Now my mother has to walk everywhere she goes which is hard and causes her varicose veins and takes a lot of valuable time from her day.

My sister Louise needs glasses the school nurse said but "Who can pay for them?" my mother says. My paper route gets a little money but it's barely enough for school lunches for the three of us kids which is what we use it for.

My mother's two sisters and her brother haven't been too helpful because they are Catholic, as she is and the rest of us, and they don't believe in divorce and think that she should not have let my father leave her anyhow. She needs to get a divorce but no one except me and my brother George think it is a good idea. Therefore my mother cries a lot at night because she feels so abandoned in this time of her greatest need.

The rest of the time though she is cheerful and loving in spite of her troubles and nervousness. That is why I believe that this courageous long-suffering woman, my mother, should be Queen for a Day.

Sincerely yours,
Earl Painter

Several weeks slide by, November gets cold and gray, and a New Hampshire winter starts to feel inevitable again, and Earl does not receive the letter he expects. He has told no one, especially his mother, that he has written to Jack Bailey, the smiling, mustachioed host of the "Queen for a Day" television show, which Earl happened to see that time he was home for several days with the flu, bored and watching television all afternoon. Afterwards, delivering papers in the predawn gloom, in school all day, at the hockey rink, doing homework at night, he could not forget about the television show, the sad stories told by the contestants about their illness, poverty, neglect, victimization and always, their bad luck, luck so bad that you feel it's somehow deserved. The studio audience seemed genuinely saddened, moved to tears, even, by Jack Bailey's recitation of these narratives, and then elated afterwards, when the

winning victims, all of them middle-aged women, were rewarded with refrigerators, living room suites, vacation trips,
washing machines, china, fur coats and, if they needed them,
wheelchairs, prosthetic limbs, twenty-four-hour nursing care.
As these women wept for joy, the audience applauded, and
Earl almost applauded too, alone there in the dim living room
of the small, cold, and threadbare apartment in a mill town in
central New Hampshire.

Earl knows that those women's lives surely aren't much
different from his mother's life, and in fact, if he has told it
right, if somehow he has got into the letter what he has
intuited is basically wrong with his mother's life, it will be
obvious to everyone in the audience that his mother's life is
actually much worse than that of many or perhaps even most of
the women who win the prizes. Earl knows that though his
mother enjoys good health (except for "spells") and holds down
a job and is able to feed, house, and clothe her children, there
is still a deep, essential sadness in her life that, in his eyes,
none of the contestants on "Queen for a Day" has. He believes
that if he can just get his description of her life right, other
people—Jack Bailey, the studio audience, millions of people
all over America watching it on television—*everyone* will share
in her sadness, so that when she is rewarded with appliances,
furniture, and clothing, maybe even a trip to Las Vegas, then
everyone will share in her elation, too. Even he will share in it.

Earl knows that it is not easy to become a contestant on
"Queen for a Day." Somehow your letter describing the candidate has first to move Jack Bailey, and then your candidate has
to be able to communicate her sufferings over television in a
clear and dramatic way. Earl noticed that some of the contestants, to their own apparent disadvantage, downplayed the
effect on them of certain tragedies—a child with a birth defect,
say, or an embarrassing kind of operation or a humiliating
dismissal by an employer—while playing up other, seemingly
less disastrous events, such as being cheated out of a small
inheritance by a phony siding contractor or having to drop out
of hairdressing school because of a parent's illness, and when
the studio audience was asked to show the extent and depth of
its compassion by having its applause measured on a meter, it

was always the woman who managed to present the most convincing mixture of courage and complaint who won.

Earl supposes that what happens is that Jack Bailey writes or maybe telephones the writer of the letter nominating a particular woman for "Queen for a Day" and offers him and his nominee the opportunity to come to New York City's Radio City Music Hall to tell her story in person, and then, based on how she does in the audition, Jack Bailey chooses her and two other nominees for a particular show, maybe next week, when they all come back to New York City to tell their stories live on television. Thus, daily, when Earl arrives home, he asks Louise and George, who normally get home from school an hour or so earlier than he, if there's any mail for him, any letter. You're sure? Nothing? No phone calls either?

"Who're you expectin' to hear from, lover boy, your *girl*friend?" George grins, teeth spotted with peanut butter and gobs of white bread.

"Up yours," Earl says, and heads into his bedroom, where he dumps his coat, books, hockey gear. It's becoming clear to him that if there's such a thing as a success, he's evidently a failure. If there's such a thing as a winner, he's a loser. I oughta go on that goddamned show myself, he thinks. Flopping onto his bed face-first, he wishes he could keep on falling, as if down a bottomless well or mine shaft, into darkness and warmth, lost and finally blameless, gone, gone, gone. And soon he is asleep, dreaming of a hockey game, and he's carrying the puck, dragging it all the way up along the right, digging in close to the boards, skate blades flashing as he cuts around behind the net, ice chips spraying in white fantails, and when he comes out on the other side, he looks down in front of him and can't find the puck, it's gone, dropped off behind him, lost in his sweeping turn, the spray, the slash of the skates and the long sweeping arc of the stick in front of him. He brakes, turns, and heads back, searching for the small black disk.

At the sound of the front door closing, a quick click, as if someone is deliberately trying to enter the apartment silently, Earl wakes from his dream, and he hears voices from the kitchen, George and Louise and his mother:

"Hi, Mom. We're just makin' a snack, peanut butter sandwiches."

"Mommy, George won't give me—"

"Don't eat it directly off the knife like that!"

"Sorry, I was jus'—"

"You heard me, mister, don't answer back!"

"Jeez, I was jus'—"

"I don't *care* what you were doing!" Her voice is trembling and quickly rising in pitch and timbre, and Earl moves off his bed and comes into the kitchen, smiling, drawing everyone's attention to him, the largest person in the room, the only one with a smile on his face, a relaxed, easy, sociable face and manner, normalcy itself, as he gives his brother's shoulder a fraternal squeeze, tousles his sister's brown hair, nods hello to his mother and says, "Hey, you're home early, Ma. What happened, they give you guys the rest of the day off?"

Then he sees her face, white, tight, drawn back in a cadaverous grimace, her pale blue eyes wild, unfocused, rolling back, and he says, "Jeez, Ma, what's the matter, you okay?"

Her face breaks into pieces, goes from dry to wet, white to red, and she is weeping loudly, blubbering, wringing her hands in front of her like a maddened knitter. "Aw-w-w-w!" she wails, and Louise and George, too, start to cry. They run to her and wrap her in their arms, crying and begging her not to cry, as Earl, aghast, sits back on his chair and watches the three of them wind around each other like snakes moving in and out of one another's coils.

"Stop!" he screams at last. "Stop it! All of you!" He pounds his fists on the table. "Stop crying, all of you!"

And they obey him, George first, then their mother, then Louise, who goes on staring into her mother's face. George looks at his feet, ashamed, and their mother looks pleadingly into Earl's face, expectant, hopeful, as if knowing that he will organize everything.

In a calm voice, Earl says, "Ma, tell me what happened. Just say it slowly, you know, and it'll come out okay, and then we can all talk about it, okay?"

She nods, and slowly George unravels his arms from around her neck and steps away from her, moving to the far wall of the room, where he stands and looks out the window and down to the bare yard below. Louise snuggles her face in close to her mother and sniffles quietly.

"I . . . I lost my job. I got fired today," their mother says. "And it wasn't my fault," she says, starting to weep again, and Louise joins her, bawling now, and George at the window starts to sob, his small shoulders heaving.

Earl shouts, "Wait! Wait a minute, Ma, just *tell* me about it. Don't cry!" he commands her, and she shudders, draws herself together again, and continues.

"I . . . I had some problems this morning, a bunch of files I was supposed to put away last week sometime got lost. And everybody was running around like crazy looking for them, 'cause they had all these figures from last year's sales in 'em or something. I don't know. Anyhow, they were important, and I was the one who was accused of losing them. Which I didn't! But no one could find them, until finally they turned up on Robbie's desk, down in shipping, which I couldna done since I never go to shipping anyhow. But just the same, Rose blamed me, because she's the head bookkeeper and she was the last person to use the files, and she was getting it because they needed them upstairs, and . . . well, you know, I was just getting yelled at and yelled at, and it went on after lunch . . . and, I don't know, I just started feeling dizzy and all, you know, like I was going to black out again? And I guess I got scared and started talking real fast, so Rose took me down to the nurse, and I did black out then. Only for a few seconds, though, and when I felt a little better, Rose said maybe I should go home for the rest of the day, which is what I wanted to do anyhow. But when I went back upstairs to get my pocketbook and coat and my lunch, because I hadn't been able to eat my sandwich, even, I was so nervous and all, and then Mr. Shandy called me into his office. . . ." She makes a twisted little smile, helpless and confused, and quickly continues. "Mr. Shandy said I should maybe take a lot of time off. Two weeks sick leave with pay, he said, even though I was only working there six months. He said that would give me time to look for another job, one that wouldn't cause me so much worry, he said. So I said, 'Are you firing me?' and he said, 'Yes,

I am,' just like that. 'But it would be better for you all around,' he said, 'if you left for medical reasons or something.' "

Earl slowly exhales. He's been holding his breath throughout, though from her very first sentence he has known what the outcome would be. Reaching forward, he takes his mother's hands in his, stroking them as if they were an injured bird. He doesn't know what will happen now, but somehow he is not afraid. Not really. Yet he knows that he should be terrified, and when he says this to himself, *I should be terrified*, he answers by observing simply that this is not the worst thing. The worst thing that can happen to them is that one or all of them will die. And because he is still a child, or at least enough of a child not to believe in death, he knows that no one in his family is going to die. He cannot share this secret comfort with anyone in the family, however. His brother and sister, children completely, cannot yet know that death is the worst thing that can happen to them; they think this is, that their mother has been fired from her job, which is why they are crying. And his mother, no longer a child at all, cannot believe with Earl that the worst thing will not happen, for this is too much like death and may somehow lead directly to it, which is why she is crying. Only Earl can refuse to cry. Which he does.

Later, in the room she shares with her daughter, their mother lies fully clothed on the double bed and sleeps, and it grows dark, and while George and Louise watch television in the gloom of the living room, Earl writes:

Nov. 21, 1953

Dear Jack Bailey,

Maybe my first letter to you about why my mother should be queen for a day did not reach you or else I just didn't write it good enough for you to want her on your show. But I thought I would write again anyhow, if that's okay, and mention to you a few things that I left out of that first letter and also mention again some of the things in that letter, in case you did not get it at all for some reason (you know the Post Office). I also want to mention a few new developments that have made things even worse for my poor mother than they already were.

First, even though it's only a few days until Thanksgiving my father who left us last May, as you know, has not contacted us about the holidays or offered to help in any way. This makes us mad though we don't talk about it much since the little kids tend to cry about it a lot when they think about it, and me and my mother think it's best not to think about it. We don't even know how to write a letter to my father, though we know the name of the company that he works for up in Holderness (a town in New Hampshire pretty far from here) and his sisters could tell us his address if we asked, but we won't. A person has to have some pride, as my mother says. Which she has a lot of.

We will get through Thanksgiving all right because of St. Joseph's Church, which is where we go sometimes and where I was confirmed and my brother George (age 10) took his first communion last year and where my sister Louise (age 6) goes to catechism class. St. Joe's (as we call it) has turkeys and other kinds of food for people who can't afford to buy one so we'll do okay if my mother goes down there and says she can't afford to buy a turkey for her family on Thanksgiving. This brings me to the new developments.

My mother just got fired from her job as assistant bookkeeper at the tannery. It wasn't her fault or anything she did. They just fired her because she has these nervous spells sometimes when there's a lot of pressure on her, which is something that happens a lot these days because of my father and all and us kids and the rest of it. She got two weeks of pay but that's the only money we have until she gets another job. Tomorrow she plans to go downtown to all the stores and try to get a job as a saleslady now that Christmas is coming and the stores hire a lot of extras. But right now we don't have any money for anything like Thanksgiving turkey or pies, and we can't go down to Massachusetts to my mother's family, Aunt Dot's and Aunt Leona's and Uncle Jerry's house, like we used to because

(as you know) the bank repossessed the car. And my
father's sisters and all who used to have Thanksgiving with
us, sometimes, have taken our father's side in this because
of his lies about us and now they won't talk to us anymore.

I know that lots and lots of people are poor as us and
many of them are sick too, or crippled from polio and
other bad diseases. But I still think my mother should be
Queen for a Day because of other things.

Because even though she's poor and got fired and has
dizzy spells and sometimes blacks out, she's a proud woman.
And even though my father walked off and left all his
responsibilities behind, she stayed here with us. And in
spite of all her troubles and worries, she really does take
good care of his children. One look in her eyes and you
know it.

Thank you very much for listening to me and considering my mother for the Queen for a Day television show.

Sincerely,
Earl Painter

The day before Thanksgiving their mother is hired to start
work the day after Thanksgiving, in gift wrapping at Grover
Cronin's on Moody Street, and consequently she does not feel
ashamed for accepting a turkey and a bag of groceries from St.
Joe's. "Since I'm working, I don't think of it as charity. I think
of it as a kind of loan," she explains to Earl as they walk the
four blocks to the church.

It's dark, though still late afternoon, and cold, almost cold
enough to snow, Earl thinks, which makes him think of Christmas, which in turn makes him cringe and tremble inside and
turn quickly back to now, to this very moment, to walking with
his tiny, brittle-bodied mother down the quiet street, past
houses like their own—triple-decker wood-frame tenements,
each with a wide front porch like a bosom facing the narrow
street below, lights on in kitchens in back, where mothers
make boiled supper for kids cross-legged on the living room
floor watching "Kukla, Fran and Ollie," while dads trudge up
from the mills by the river or drive in from one of the plants on
the Heights or maybe walk home from one of the stores down-

town, the A&P, J.C. Penney's, Sears—the homes of ordinary families, people exactly like them. But with one crucial difference, for a piece is missing from the Painter family, a keystone, making all other families, in Earl's eyes, wholly different from his, and for an anxious moment he envies them. He wants to turn up a walkway to a strange house, step up to the door, open it and walk down the long, dark, sweet-smelling hallway to the kitchen in back, say hi and toss his coat over a chair and sit down for supper, have his father growl at him to hang his coat up and wash his hands first, have his mother ask about school today, how did hockey practice go, have his sister interrupt to show her broken dolly to their father, beg him to fix it, which he does at the table next to his son, waiting for supper to be put on the table, all of them relaxed, happy, relieved that tomorrow is a holiday, a day at home with the family, no work, no school, no hockey practice. Tomorrow, he and his father and his brother will go the high school football game at noon and will be home by two to help set the table.

Earl's mother says, "That job down at Grover Cronin's? It's only, it's a temporary job, you know." She says it as if uttering a slightly shameful secret. "After Christmas I get let go."

Earl jams his hands deeper into his jacket pockets and draws his chin down inside his collar. "Yeah, I figured."

"And the money, well, the money's not much. It's almost nothing. I added it up, for a week and for a month, and it comes out to quite a lot less than what you and me figured out in that budget, for the rent and food and all. What we need. It's less than what we need. Never mind Christmas, even. Just regular."

They stop a second at a curb, wait for a car to pass, then cross the street and turn right. Elm trees loom in black columns overhead; leafless branches spread out in high arcs and cast intricate shadows on the sidewalk below. Earl can hear footsteps click against the pavement, his own off-beat, long stride and her short, quick one combining in a stuttered rhythm. He says, "You gotta take the job, though, doncha? I mean, there isn't anything else, is there? Not now, anyhow. Maybe soon, though, Ma, in a few days, maybe, if something at the store opens up in one of the other departments, dresses or something. Bookkeeping, maybe. You never know, Ma."

"No, you're right. Things surprise you. Still . . ." She sighs, pushing a cloud of breath out in front of her. "But I am glad for the turkey and the groceries. We'll have a nice Thanksgiving, anyhow," she chirps.

"Yeah."

They are silent for a few seconds, still walking, and then she says, "I been talking to Father LaCoy, Earl. You know, about . . . about our problems. I been asking his advice. He's a nice man, not just a priest, you know, but a kind man too. He knows your father, he knew him years and years ago, when they were in high school together. He said he was a terrible drinker even then. And he said . . . other things, he said some things the other morning that I been thinking about."

"What morning?"

"Day before yesterday. Early. When you were doing your papers. I felt I just had to talk to someone, I was all nervous and worried, and I needed to talk to someone here at St. Joe's anyhow, 'cause I wanted to know about how to get the turkey and all, so I came over, and he was saying the early mass, so I stayed and talked with him a while afterwards. He's a nice priest, I like him. I always liked Father LaCoy."

"Yeah. What'd he say?" Earl knows already what the priest said, and he pulls himself further down inside his jacket, where his insides seem to have hardened like an ingot, cold and dense, at the exact center of his body.

Up ahead, at the end of the block, is St. Joseph's, a large, squat parish church with a short, broad steeple, built late in the last century of pale yellow stone cut from a quarry up on the Heights and hauled across the river in winter on sledges. "Father LaCoy says that your father and me, we should try to get back together. That we should start over, so to speak."

"And you think he's right," Earl adds.

"Well, not exactly. Not just like that. I mean, he knows what happened. He knows all about your father and all, I told him, but he knew anyhow. I told him how it was, but he told me that it's not right for us to be going on like this, without a father and all. So he said, he told me, he'd like to arrange to have a meeting in his office at the church, a meeting between me and your father, so we could maybe talk some of our problems out. And make some compromises, he said."

Earl is nearly a full head taller than his mother, but suddenly, for the first time since before his father left, he feels small, a child again, helpless, dependent, pulled this mysterious way or that by the obscure needs and desires of adults. "Yeah, but how come . . . how come Father LaCoy thinks Daddy'll even listen? He doesn't *want* us!"

"I know, I know," his mother murmurs. "But what can I do? What else can I do?"

Earl has stopped walking and shouts at his mother, like a dog barking at the end of a leash: "He can't even get in touch with Daddy! He doesn't even know where Daddy is!"

She stops and speaks in a steady voice. "Yes, he can find him all right. I told him where Daddy was working and gave him the name of McGrath and Company and also Aunt Ellie's number too. So he can get in touch with him, if he wants to. He's a priest."

"A priest can get in touch with him but his own wife and kids can't!"

His mother has pulled up now and looks at her son with a hardness in her face that he can't remember having seen before. She tells him, "You don't understand. I know how hard it's been for you, Earl, all this year, from way back, even, with all the fighting, and then when your father went away. But you got to understand a little bit how it's been for me, too. I can't . . . I can't do this all alone like this."

"Do you love Daddy?" he demands. "*Do* you? After . . . after everything he's done? After hitting you like he did all those times, and the yelling and all, and the drinking, and then, then the worst, after leaving us like he did! Leaving us and running off with that *girl*friend or whatever of his! And not sending any money! Making you hafta go to work, with us kids coming home after school and nobody at home. Ma, he *left* us! Don't you know that? He *left* us!" Earl is weeping now. His skinny arms wrapped around his own chest, tears streaming over his cheeks, the boy stands straight-legged and stiff on the sidewalk in the golden glow of the streetlight, his wet face crossed with spidery shadows from the elm trees, and he shouts, "I *hate* him! I hate him, and I never want him to come back again! If you let him come back, I swear it, I'm gonna run away! I'll leave!"

His mother says, "Oh, no, Earl, you don't mean that," and she reaches forward to hold him, but he backs fiercely away.

"No! I do mean it! If you let him back into our house, I'm leaving."

"Earl. Where will you go? You're just a boy."

"Ma, so help me, don't treat me like this. I can go lotsa places, don't worry. I can go to Boston, I can go to Florida, I can go to lotsa places. All I got to do is hitchhike. I'm not a little kid anymore," he says, and he draws himself up and looks down at her.

"You *don't* hate your father."

"Yes, Ma. Yes, I do. And you should hate him too. After all he did to you."

They are silent for a moment, facing each other, looking into each other's pale blue eyes. He is her son, his face is her face, not his father's. Earl and his mother have the same sad, downward-turning eyes, like teardrops, the same full red mouth, the same clear voice, and now, at this moment, they share the same agony, a life-bleeding pain that can be stanched only with a lie, a denial.

She says, "All right, then. I'll tell Father LaCoy. I'll tell him that I don't want to talk to your father, it's gone too far now. I'll tell him that I'm going to get a divorce." She opens her arms, and her son steps into them. Above her head, his eyes jammed shut, he holds on to his tiny mother and sobs, as if he's learned that his father has died.

His mother says, "I don't know when I'll get the divorce, Earl, but I'll do it. Things'll work out. They have to. Right?" she asks, as if asking a baby who can't understand her words.

He nods. "Yeah . . . yeah, things'll work out," he says.

They let go of one another and walk slowly on toward the church.

Dec. 12, 1953

Dear Jack Bailey,

Yes, it's me again and this is my third letter asking you to make my mother Adele Painter into queen for a day. Things are much worse now than last time I wrote to you. I had to quit the hockey team so I could take an extra paper route in the afternoons because my mother's job at Grover Cronin's is minimum wage and can't pay our bills. But that's okay, it's only junior high so it doesn't matter like if I was in high school as I will be next year. So I don't really mind.

My mother hasn't had any of her spells lately, but she's still really nervous and cries a lot and yells a lot at the kids over little things because she's so worried about money and everything. We had to get winter coats and boots this year used from the church, St. Joe's, and my mom cried a lot about that. Now that Christmas is so close everything reminds her of how poor we are now, even her job which is wrapping gifts. She has to stand on her feet six days and three nights a week so her varicose veins are a lot worse than before, so when she comes home she usually has to go right to bed.

My brother George comes home now after school and takes care of Louise until I get through delivering papers and can come home and make supper for us, because my mother's usually at work then. We don't feel too sad because we've got each other and we all love each other but it is hard to feel happy a lot of the time, especially at Christmas.

My mother paid out over half of one week's pay as a down payment to get a lawyer to help her get a divorce from my father and get the court to make him pay her some child support, but the lawyer said it might take two months for any money to come and the divorce can't be done until next June. The lawyer also wrote a letter to my father to try and scare him into paying us some money but so far it hasn't worked. So it seems like she spent that money on the lawyer for nothing. Everything seems to be getting worse. If my father came back the money problems would be over.

Well, I should close now. This being the third time I wrote in to nominate my mother for Queen for a Day and so far not getting any answer, I guess it's safe to say you don't think her story is sad enough to let her go on your show. That's okay because there are hundreds of women in America whose stories are much sadder than my mom's and they deserve the chance to win some prizes on your show and be named queen for a day. But my mom deserves that chance too, just as much as that lady with the amputated legs I saw and the lady whose daughter had that rare blood disease and her husband died last year. My mom needs recognition just as much as those other ladies need what they need. That's why I keep writing to you like this. I think this will be my last letter though. I get the picture, as they say.

Sincerely,
Earl Painter

The Friday before Christmas, Earl, George, Louise, and their mother are sitting in the darkened living room, George sprawled on the floor, the others on the sofa, all of them eating popcorn from a bowl held in Louise's lap and watching "The Jackie Gleason Show," when the phone rings.

"You get it, George," Earl says.

Reggie Van Gleason III swirls his cape and cane across the tiny screen in front of them, and the phone goes on ringing. "Get it yourself," says George. "I always get it and it's never for me."

"Answer the phone, Louise," their mother says, and she suddenly laughs at one of Gleason's moves, a characteristic high-pitched peal that cuts off abruptly, half a cackle that causes her sons, as usual, to look at each other and roll their eyes in shared embarrassment. She's wearing her flannel bathrobe and slippers, smoking a cigarette, and drinking from a glass of beer poured from a quart bottle on the floor beside her.

Crossing in front of them, Louise cuts to the corner table by the window and picks up the phone. Her face, serious most of the time anyhow, suddenly goes dark, then brightens, wide-eyed. Earl watches her, and he knows who she is listening to. She nods, as if the person on the other end can see her, and then she says, "Yes, yes," but no one, except Earl, pays any attention to her.

After a moment, the child puts the receiver down gently and returns to the sofa. "It's Daddy," she announces. "He says he wants to talk to the boys."

"I don't want to talk to him," George blurts, and stares straight ahead at the television.

Their mother blinks, opens and closes her mouth, looks from George to Louise to Earl and back to Louise again. "It's Daddy?" she says. "On the telephone?"

"Uh-huh. He says he wants to talk to the boys."

Earl crosses his arms over his chest and shoves his body back into the sofa. Jackie Gleason dances delicately across the stage, a graceful fat man with a grin.

"Earl?" his mother asks, eyebrows raised.

"Nope."

The woman stands up slowly and walks to the phone. Their mother speaks to their father; all three children watch carefully. She says, "Nelson?" and nods, listening, now and then opening her mouth to say something, closing it when she's interrupted. "Yes, yes," she says, and "yes, they're both here." She listens again, then says, "Yes, I know, but I should tell you, Nelson, the children . . . the boys, they feel funny about talking to you. Maybe . . . maybe you could write a letter first or something. It's sort of . . . hard for them. They feel very upset, you see, especially now, with the holidays and all. We're all very upset and worried. And with me losing my job and having to work down at Grover Cronin's and all. . . ." She nods, listens, her face expressionless. "Well, Lord knows, that would be very nice. It would have been very nice a long time ago, but no matter. We surely need it, Nelson." She listens again, longer this time, her face gaining energy and focus as she listens. "Yes, yes, I know. Well, I'll see, I'll ask them again. Wait a minute," she says, and puts her hand over the receiver and says, "Earl, your father wants to talk to you. He really does." She smiles wanly.

Earl squirms in his seat, crosses and uncrosses his legs, looks away from his mother to the wall opposite. "I got nothin' to say to him."

"Yes, but . . . I think he wants to say some things to you, though. Can't hurt to let him say them."

Silently, the boy gets up from the couch and crosses the room to the phone. As she hands him the receiver, his mother smiles with a satisfaction that bewilders and instantly angers him.

"H'lo," he says.

"H'lo, son. How're ya doin', boy?"

"Okay."

"Attaboy. Been a while, eh?"

"Yeah. A while."

"Well, I sure am sorry for that, you know, that it's been such a while and all, but I been going through some hard times myself. Got laid off, didn't work for most of the summer because of that damned strike. You read about that in the papers?"

"No."

"How's the paper route?"

"Okay."

"Hey, son, look, I know it's been tough for a while, believe me, I know. It's been tough for us all, for everyone. So I know whatcha been going through. No kidding. But it's gonna get better, things're gonna be better now. And I want to try and make it up to you guys a little, what you hadda go through this last six months or so. I want to make it up to you guys a little, you and Georgie and Louise. Your ma too. If you'll let me. Whaddaya say?"

"What?"

"Whaddaya say you let me try to make it up a little to you?"

"Sure. Why not? Try."

"Hey, listen, Earl, that's quite a attitude you got there. We got to do something about that, eh? Some kind of attitude, son. I guess things've done a little changing around there since the old man left, eh? Eh?"

"Sure they have. What'd you expect? Everything'd stay the same?" Earl hears his voice rising and breaking into a yodel, and his eyes fill with tears.

"No, of course not. I understand, son. I understand. I know I've made some big mistakes this year, lately. Especially with you kids, in dealing with you kids. I didn't do it right, the leaving and all. It's hard, Earl, to do things like that right. I've learned a lot. But hey, listen, everybody deserves a second chance. Right? Right? Even your old man?"

"I guess so. Yeah."

"Sure. Damn right," he says, and then he adds that he'd like to come by tomorrow afternoon and see them, all of them, and leave off some Christmas presents. "You guys got your tree yet?"

Earl can manage only a tiny, cracked voice: "No, not yet."

"Well, that's good, real good. 'Cause I already got one in the back of the truck, a eight-footer I cut this afternoon myself. There's lotsa trees out in the woods here in Holderness. Not many people and lotsa trees. Anyhow, I got me a eight-footer, Scotch pine. Them are the best. Whaddaya think?"

"Yeah. Sounds good."

His father rattles on, while Earl feels his chest tighten into a knot, and tears spill over his cheeks. The man repeats several times that he's really sorry about the way he's handled things these last few months, but it's been hard for him, too, and it's hard for him even to say this, he's never been much of a talker, but he knows he's not been much of a father lately, either. That's all over now, though, over and done with, he assures Earl; it's all a part of the past. He's going to be a different man now, a new man. He's turned over a new leaf, he says. And Christmas seems like the perfect time for a new beginning, which is why he called them tonight and why he wants to come by tomorrow afternoon with presents and a tree and help set up and decorate the tree with them, just like in the old days. "Would you go for that? How'd that be, son?"

"Daddy?"

"Yeah, sure, son. What?"

"Daddy, are you gonna try to get back together with Mom?" Earl looks straight at his mother as he says this, and though she pretends to be watching Jackie Gleason, she is listening to his every word, he knows. As is George, and probably even Louise.

"Am I gonna try to get back together with your mom, eh?"

"Yeah."

"Well . . . that's a hard one, boy. You asked me a hard one." He is silent for a few seconds, and Earl can hear him sipping from a glass and then taking a deep draw from his cigarette. "I'll tell ya, boy. The truth is, she don't want me back. You oughta know that by now. I left because *she* wanted me to leave, son. I did some wrong things, sure, lots of 'em, but I did not want to leave you guys. No, right from the beginning, this thing's been your mom's show, not mine."

"Daddy, that's a lie."

"No, son. No. We fought a lot, your mom and me, like married people always do. But I didn't want to leave her and you kids. She told me to. And now, look at this—*she's* the one bringing these divorce charges and all, not me. You oughta see the things she's charging me with."

"What about . . . what about her having to protect herself? You know what I mean. I don't want to go into any details, but you know what I mean. And what about your *girl*friend?" he sneers.

His father is silent for a moment. Then he says, "You sure have got yourself an attitude since I been gone. Listen, kid, there's lots you don't know anything about, that nobody knows anything about, and there's lots more that you *shouldn't* know anything about. You might not believe this, Earl, but you're still a kid. You're a long ways from being a man. So don't go butting into where you're not wanted and getting into things between your mom and me that you can't understand anyhow. Just butt out. You hear me?"

"Yeah. I hear you."

"Lemme speak to your brother."

"He doesn't want to talk to you," Earl says, and he looks away from George's face and down at his own feet.

"Put your mother on, Earl."

"None of us wants to talk to you."

"Earl!" his mother cries. "Let me have the phone," she says, and she rises from the couch, her hand reaching toward him.

Earl places the receiver in its cradle. Then he stands there, looking into his mother's blue eyes, and she looks into his.

She says, "He won't call back."

Earl says, "I know."

"*I think a writer loves best those stories that permit him or her entry to an obsession or release from it. 'Queen for a Day' released me from the obsessive theme of the oldest son in a broken family replacing—or, rather, trying and failing to replace—the absent father. It goes back to earlier stories, all the way to 'Searching for Survivors' in my first collection, written in the late 1960s. Back then, I thought the theme concerned abandonment and wrote it that way, numerous times over the years. It was only with 'Queen for a Day' that I realized the deeper psychological implications of the theme, realized, for instance, that there was an important psychological dimension to the story, and was able to dramatize that dimension through the boy's writing to the 'Queen for a Day' television show, his manipulation of his mother's decision not to return to his father, and his final rejection of his father. Having chased the obsession all the way home, as it were, to the taboo that gave it force in the first place, I was able to be freed of it. One says, 'Well, I finally got it right,' because it feels that way; the subject is simply no longer very interesting. One moves on, then, and one is always particularly fond of the story that frees its writer to move on.*"

Russell Banks is the author of nine books of fiction, most recently Continental Drift *and* Success Stories. *He is the winner of numerous prizes and awards, among them The O. Henry Short Story, Best American Short Story, Fels and Pushcart prizes; Guggenheim, Merrill and NEA Fellowships; the Before Columbus American Book Award, John Dos Passos Prize, American Academy and Institute of Arts and Letters Award. He divides his time between upstate New York and Princeton, New Jersey, where he teaches in the Writing Program at Princeton University.*

Published in Banks's short-story collection, Success Stories.